Dear Reader,

Welcome to another month of Duets! And allow me to introduce myself as the new editor for the line. I'm committed to bringing you the funniest, most romantic books each month from all your favorite authors. I also love to hear from you—our readers—so please drop me a line at the address below.

We have a very special treat for you in Duets #23, as Lori Foster has penned a sexy, funny story about a hero who is holding out for marriage in *Say Yes*. Then Cathy Yardley launches the first of our MAKEOVER MADNESS books with *The Cinderella Solution*. Haven't we all flipped through the pages of our favorite magazine studying makeovers and wondered what would happen to our life if we took on a completely new image?

Then men and women unexpectedly forced to live together is our theme in Duets #24. Diane Pershing traps her hero and heroine together in their job and house. Lois Greiman puts hero and heroine into the same living space and adds a healthy dose of animals. Laughs and romance fill both homes.

Enjoy our romantic comedies!

Birgit Davis-Todd
Senior Editor, Harlequin Duets

Harlequin Books
225 Duncan Mill Rd.
Don Mills, Ontario
M3B 3K9 Canada

"What are you working on?"

"I'm trying to come up with a caption," Rachel said.

Sam could have left then, probably should have left then—but he couldn't. Besides, he was the editor and needed to know everything he could about the paper, he told himself. So he walked over to her.

It was a mistake. He couldn't take his eyes off those lips. That quickening in his bloodstream started up again, as did the need to feel her skin against his own. He was having trouble breathing.

How long the moment lasted, Sam couldn't tell. But it was long enough to leave him confused. A minute earlier, he'd decided against intimacy with Rachel. Now he couldn't think about anything else....

For more, turn to page 9

From Caviar to Chaos

"So what's wrong with the cow?"

Sitting in the passenger seat in the pitch-dark, Daniel hunched his shoulders. This damned place was freezing. He wished he'd grabbed a jacket. Wished he'd never come here. Wished Jessie didn't look so damn chipper.

He hated chipper.

"You don't want to know," she answered, fiddling with the heater.

"Afraid I'd faint?" he asked.

"You might."

He snorted. "Then why'd you proposition me?"

"What?" She snapped her gaze to his.

He felt immediately better for her wide-eyed stare. "Why'd you propose that I work for you?"

"Oh." She shifted her gaze restlessly back to the road. "I felt sorry for you."

"Sorry. For me." He forced a laugh. "Well, you're entertaining, Sorenson. I'll say that for you."

"Yeah, well..." She turned the pickup into a driveway. "You ain't seen nothin' yet."

For more, turn to page 197

HARLEQUIN DUETS

ISBN 0-373-44090-1

HOT COPY
Copyright © 2000 by Diane Pershing

FROM CAVIAR TO CHAOS
Copyright © 2000 by Lois Greiman

Visit us at www.romance.net

Printed in U.S.A.

DIANE PERSHING

Hot Copy

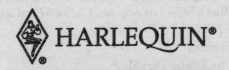

HARLEQUIN®

TORONTO • NEW YORK • LONDON
AMSTERDAM • PARIS • SYDNEY • HAMBURG
STOCKHOLM • ATHENS • TOKYO • MILAN • MADRID
PRAGUE • WARSAW • BUDAPEST • AUCKLAND

Dear Reader,

What if? are the two most utilized words in a writer's imagination. I used them a while back when I was bedridden for a couple of days and bored to distraction. What if, I asked myself, I was lying here—helpless, alone, unable to move—and I heard a stranger's footsteps slowly walking toward my bedroom? What if, furthermore, I was clothing-less under the covers, had no weapon and the phone was on the other side of the room?

As I suffer from a vivid imagination, my immediate response to my question was an adrenaline rush of terror. What else? Then the writer kicked in. Great opening for a book! And not one of those scary women-in-jeopardy things, but a comedy! Thus *Hot Copy* was born.

I adore Rachel, my heroine. She's warm, funny, super-responsible and mothers everyone around her, but forgets that she, too, has needs. That is until Sam, a sexy, been-there-done-that foreign correspondent, walks into her life. Into her house, actually. While she's in bed with a back spasm and with no clothes on... I think you get the picture.

I had so much fun writing this book, which centers around a fictional small-town newspaper in the very real town of Ojai, California, one of my favorite places to hang out and get inspired. Please write me at P.O. Box 67424, Los Angeles, CA 90067 and let me know if you had fun reading it.

Diane Pershing

Books by Diane Pershing

SILHOUETTE YOURS TRULY
FIRST DATE: HONEYMOON
THIRD DATE'S THE CHARM

Thanks to all the nice, helpful folks at
The Malibu Times, the Ojai Valley Inn,
Bart's Books and the Ojai Chamber of Commerce—
they allowed me to pester them for information.
An especially big hug to Arnold York,
newspaperman extraordinaire, and to my dear friend
Karen Portugal York, for all the Monday morning
bagels, coffee and talk.

1

THUD, THUD, THUD.

She awoke with a start and, not moving, listened for several moments. Something had woken her up, she was sure of it. But what? She strained her ears for the answer.

The house seemed quiet. A couple of bees on the other side of the screen hummed happily, and a soft spring breeze rustled the leaves of the huge oak tree outside her bedroom window. Normal neighborhood sounds, that was all. Nothing unusual.

Had she heard a dog barking just before she'd woken up? Had it been Philomena? If so, Phil wasn't barking now, which meant there were no strangers nearby.

"Whew," Rachel said out loud as her heartbeat resumed its normal rate. The noise had sounded like footsteps, but she was now certain the footsteps had been in her imagination. That steady *thud, thud, thud* she'd awoken to had undoubtedly been sound effects in her dream, maybe caused by the workmen hammering away on the Hathaways' roof on the next block.

Sure. It had been her imagination, that was all.

And good thing, Rachel decided, chuckling to herself. Here she was, lying in bed, *naked* for heaven's sake, unable to move. Defenseless. Alone. One of those worst-case scenarios from the woman-in-jeopardy movies she so loved to watch on TV.

Craning her neck to the right, she gazed at the clock by her bedside: 11:00 a.m. She attempted to shift onto her side, but the pain that shot up from her lower right hip reminded her that such a move wasn't a smart thing to make. That that very pain was, in fact, the reason she was still in bed at eleven o'clock on a Wednesday morning and not at work.

Darn back. She was healthy as a horse. Usually. Except for when her back went out every couple of years or so. Earlier that morning she'd been in her bathroom, bending to pick up the toothpaste cap that had dropped to the floor, when she felt the sudden, sharp wrenching, followed by a spasm that rendered her unable to stand. She'd fallen to her knees and, after catching her breath, had managed to gulp down a couple of ibuprofen tablets and crawl into bed.

Darn back, she thought again. It would mean two or three days out of commission while the muscles unclenched. Rachel *hated* being out of commission, *hated* when her usually reliable body failed her. And she had so much to do! The list of what she had planned for today flashed across her mind's eye like the words across a computer screen upon boot-up.

At the newspaper: approve the ad layout for the Second Time Around Spring Sale, rewrite the interview with the high school valedictorian, welcome the new editor, and work out the paycheck hassle so that the IRS stopped sending ominous letters that reduced the book-keeper to tears. In Rachel's own life: bake pecan crisps for Friday night's party at the paper, feed and water the roses, adjust a leaky faucet, go to the dry cleaner, do the food shopping, take the dog to the vet, and on and on, ad infinitum.

Thud, thud, thud, thud.

In the middle of her list-making, Rachel froze, terrified. There it was again, that sound. Definitely footsteps.

Heavy footsteps.

Masculine footsteps.

Inside her house.

And nothing had changed. She was *still* alone, *still* nude, *still* practically paralyzed. The thuds came from the back of the house, near the kitchen. Why wasn't Phil barking now? Oh, no, had the poor dog been given poison meat or something equally awful?

The footsteps stopped. The intruder must have left the wooden floors for the carpeted living room, so she couldn't hear him now. Casing the joint, checking for valuables.

Frantic, Rachel looked around for the phone, but it wasn't on her bedside table. Of course not. It was on her dressing table on the other side of the room. Darn portable phones. They might make it easier to talk while you walked around, but they were never near you when you needed them.

When you couldn't get up and get them.

Thud, thud, thud...

A weapon, she thought through the haze of terror

overtaking her. She needed something with which she could defend herself. On her bedside table were the clock, a glass of water and a book. Period. Quickly she reached for the glass, ignoring the twinge of discomfort, and held it in her hand under the blanket.

He was coming nearer. Rachel was absolutely helpless. Her bedroom backed up to the Wincellers' house, and both Edith and Ned Winceller were deaf. Everyone else in the neighborhood was at work. No one would hear her if she screamed. No one would come to her aid. They would find her here, murdered probably, blood all over the place, both Phil and her, when—and if—they found her.

Thud, thud, thud, thud, thud. He was practically here. She gripped the glass hard, wondering briefly if the lump under the blanket would even begin to fool anyone. But it was all she had, and Rachel had no intention of going down without a fight. She tensed for the confrontation.

When the man appeared in the doorway, he froze in midstride. With a shocked look on his face, he stared at her for a few heartbeats, then jerked back, saying, "Oh. I'm sorry."

He was sorry? Sorry? For what? For intending to kill her?

"I have a gun." She made her tone as threatening as she could. "Come any closer and I'll use it."

He stayed where he was for a long moment, continuing to stare at her. Then the expression on his face changed; his eyes narrowed as he assessed her. After another couple of beats, he visibly relaxed and leaned on the door frame, arms draped across his chest. One side of his mouth quirked up into a very small smile. "No need," he said, appearing completely unthreatened. "I'm not armed."

"Well, I am."

It was a lie, of course, but what was she supposed to say?—*I'm holding a glass, and it's pointed at you?*

"My dog was trained by experts to kill," she added for good measure.

He gazed at her for another few seconds, then shrugged. "If you mean that mutt who attacked me in the backyard, you wasted your money. Unless you count licking someone to death." He held up his hands in a mock surrender. "Really, you can relax. I was told the house was empty."

Rachel's eyes narrowed suspiciously. "Who told you that?"

"Mrs. Katz. The real estate agent."

"Mrs. Katz? Oh."

It dawned on her, then, just what this man was doing here. She felt the adrenaline rush of fear slip away like water down a drain, leaving her momentarily weakened, almost giddy. She removed her hand from under the covers, keeping the blanket tucked up over her chest, and showed him the glass. "My gun," she said, biting back a nervous giggle. "You're here about the house."

"It's for lease, isn't it?"

"It is."

Now that she could actually pay attention to him, she observed that he had one of those worn, cynical, extremely attractive faces with interesting creases. A man who'd been there, done that and hadn't many illusions left. His hair was thick and brown, as was his mustache and beard, all of it shot through with silver. She estimated his height at less than six feet; his body was broadly built without an ounce of fat. He was dressed in a pair of well-worn jeans with a long-sleeved blue shirt, open at the neck, its cuffs rolled up. Late thirties, early forties, she figured.

And all of him was really, she thought, quite... attractive.

As the last of her fear drained from her body, Rachel felt a shift to a whole other reaction—a mild tingle of awareness. She bit back a smile. If she could gaze admiringly at a man who'd just scared the bejesus out of her, the threat of danger was now history.

However, she remembered suddenly, she was still nude under the covers. That thought made her feel vulnerable again, although less in danger.

"Yes, it's for lease," she repeated, pulling the blanket up even higher, to just under her neck. "I'm Rachel Murray."

"Sam Kovacs." He took a step into the room, then paused. "May I?"

"Come on in." She grinned. "I figure if Connie Katz trusts you enough to let you into my house without her, you're probably not a serial killer."

"Not in this incarnation," he said wryly, striding easily over to the maple four-poster where Rachel resided.

"Forgive me for not getting up," she said with equal

wryness, shaking the hand he offered. "It's my back. I put it out this morning, and I can't move."

He stood over her now. Up close she could see his eyes. They were a piercing blue, with lots of laugh lines radiating out from the sides. No, not laugh lines, she amended silently. He wasn't the jolly type. Squint lines was more like it. Living lines.

"That's a tough one," he said, referring to her back. "I'm sorry."

She waved it away. "Don't be. A visit to the chiropractor and a couple of days on ice, and I'll be as good as new." She sounded cheerier than she felt, but other people's compassion always made her uncomfortable.

"I take it this has happened before," Sam said.

She nodded. "It's a stress thing—I hate that word, don't you? I mean, everything is stress. Anyhow, I'm fine, really, just under a lot of pressure lately. I'm kind of looking forward to a couple of days in bed," she lied.

"Well—"

A silence fell between them. He gazed around the room. He seemed awkward now, as though unused to dealing with women lying in bed for strictly medical reasons. Most men, Rachel had observed, were not at home in sickrooms.

"Can I get you anything?" he said. "I mean, do anything for you?"

She was about to ask him to get her robe from the bathroom, but immediately thought better of it. Then he'd know what she had on under the covers, which was nothing. That realization made her want to giggle, but, by nature, Rachel was really not a giggler. Belly laughs, yes. Giggles, no.

"You can get me the phone—over there." She pointed to the dressing table, mentally wincing at the mess—tissues, perfume bottles, open lipsticks all over the place. She'd meant to straighten up before leaving for work this morning.

He fetched the phone and set it on her night table. "Anything else?"

"You can lease the house," she said with another grin. "Short of that, why don't you take a look around. Come back in about ten minutes if you have any questions. Okay?" Really, it was no longer possible to conduct this conversation without clothes on. It put her at too much of a disadvantage.

"If you're sure—"

"Positive."

"All right, then."

He left, thoughtfully closing the door behind him, and she allowed herself a relieved sigh. She lay still for a moment, garnering her limited resources. She had to get her robe. Telling her sore back that a little discomfort was good for the soul, she worked her feet around until her legs dangled over the side of the bed. Oh, boy, did that hurt! But it had to be done.

Taking a deep breath, Rachel wriggled and pushed herself until she slid down onto the floor. She lay on her back for a bit, then managed to turn over onto her side, all the while muttering some G-rated curses. Why hadn't she kept up at the gym, so she had *some* muscle tone?

Heaving herself onto all fours, she slowly crawled to her bathroom, giving silent thanks that her prospective tenant couldn't see her now with her generous, quite naked butt sticking up in the air.

Once in the bathroom, she hauled herself up to the sink and, groaning with pain, took some more pills, splashed some water on her face, and yanked down the ratty chenille robe that hung on the back of the door. Her much more attractive flowered caftan hung in her closet, but the challenge of getting to it was out of the question.

In the full-length mirror next to the sink she took note of her appearance and was not thrilled. Her shoulder-length curly hair was a complete mess. And, as for the face, well, short of a full makeup job, nothing would make her look any better than her natural pleasant-looking self. She made one halfhearted attempt to finger-rake her hair into some kind of order, gave up on even trying to reach her brush, and prepared to crawl back into the bedroom.

SAM ENTERED a small, square room that contained a bed, a student's desk, and a rocking chair. As he opened and shut the closet door, he found himself wondering just what he was supposed to be looking for. He'd never leased an actual house before; he'd lived in apartments, hotels or rented rooms his entire life. There were probably things he should be noticing, but he had no idea what they were.

As he gazed out the window onto a view of the quiet

tree-lined street, he found himself thinking more about Rachel Murray than about her house. She'd been in pain, more pain than she'd wanted to admit. Sam knew all about stiff-upper-lipping it.

For fifteen years he'd been on the journalistic front lines, ducking rifle shots and homemade bombs, avoiding outbreaks of cholera, going without sleep, showers, or decent food while covering riots and floods and famines. Yeah, he knew all about ignoring the body's needs and just getting through. Still, he felt badly for her.

He'd learned to trust his first impressions, and he was pretty sure he knew a lot about this lady already. Good sense of humor, in spite of the pain. And good eyes. Large and brown, full of laughter, even with her present discomfort. A nice person, he decided.

And soft. He wasn't used to soft women. How old was she? he wondered. In her thirties, he guessed, with pleasantly round arms. From what he could tell, the rest of her was pleasantly round, too. Ate well, enjoyed herself. None of that anorexic, close-to-starving look of most of the women he'd met in his years of traveling; the chic and the worldly, the kind who knew the score, who'd lost whatever illusions they'd had years before.

No, this Rachel Murray was nothing like that. Old-fashioned but not particularly prudish. Round arms, round body, a round, pretty face, a warm, open smile. The sort of person who was without secrets.

Sure, Kovacs, he thought sardonically. Tell me another one. Everyone had secrets, private, painful areas they kept from the light of day. Rachel Murray hid hers well, that was all.

Whatever. He mentally shrugged, abandoning his train of thought. Look at the house, he admonished himself. He was supposed to knock on pipes or something, wasn't he? Check for peeling plaster?

Sam glanced at his watch. She'd asked for ten minutes, he'd given her fifteen. He opened the back door and the same ugly brown mutt that had greeted him earlier, barked joyously and leaped at him. With paws on his chest, the animal opened its jaws in a wide doggy grin, a long tongue flopping out one side of its mouth.

"Hello again, dog," Sam said, scratching behind the creature's ears. "Let's go see your mommy."

RACHEL HAD JUST maneuvered herself back into bed when a knock came on her door. "Ms. Murray?"

"Rachel," she called, panting with exertion. "Come on in."

The moment the door opened, Phil ran into the room and jumped up on the bed, trying to lick her face. "Yikes!" Rachel shrieked, pushing the dog away. The sudden movement of the mattress made her back protest. "Get off, Phil, it hurts."

With three long strides, Sam Kovacs was at the side of the bed. "Come on, boy," he ordered. "Off."

The animal obeyed, sprawling onto the floor and wagging its tail. "Girl," Rachel said, her eyes closed as she waited for the spasm to pass.

"Excuse me?"

"Phil's short for Philomena. The dog is a she, or used to be. Still is, I guess." Opening her eyes, she glared at the animal. "Traitor. You're supposed to bark. Why didn't she bark?" she asked Sam.

"When I came in? She started to, but I have a way with dogs," he said. As Phil rolled onto her back, he scratched her tummy. "Although I'm not sure why. Haven't had a lot of experience with pets."

"Oh." Rachel tried to reach behind her to adjust the pillows, but her body rebelled and she groaned. "Darn."

Looking up, Sam said, "Here. Let me do that."

He gently lifted her head, removed the pillows, then lowered her head to the mattress again. His hands were strong and competent, and it felt good to rest in them for that brief moment.

While he fluffed the pillows, he said, "Shouldn't you be in a hospital?"

"God forbid. No, really, I'm fine."

He replaced the pillows, and she sank back onto them gratefully. "There," he said, obviously pleased with being able to do something—anything—for her. "That ought to do it."

"Thanks," she said, thoroughly out of breath and feeling as though she'd just run the Iditarod and come in second.

Sam frowned. "Have you eaten? I mean, I don't cook or anything, but I can—"

"You're being very nice, but please, don't bother yourself. I'll call Wanda, my chiropractor friend, and she'll come right by with food, then she'll adjust me, and I'll be as good as new.''

He frowned again, in doubt. "Well, if you say so.''

As he gazed at her, Rachel again wished she were wearing a different robe than this one, which looked as though it belonged in the reject pile at Goodwill. It might have been fun to appear tantalizing, even glamorous, while bedridden. Something silky. Alluring. But no. She was sturdy, sensible Rachel Murray, and looked it.

A sigh escaped even as she tried to keep it back. The pain was easing now, but her little clothes-hunting excursion had cost her. She managed a tired smile. "Take a load off." She indicated the flower-patterned easy chair near the closet. "You can drag that old thing over so I don't have to turn my head too much."

He did so, and sat, splayed his hands on his knees and studied her in that observing way he had.

Rachel patted her hair self-consciously. "I don't look so hot, huh? I wasn't expecting visitors."

"You look fine."

"Not really, but—"

"Really. You have...good color."

Super. What every woman wanted to hear an attractive man say to her. Good color.

"It's called rosy cheeks," she said, "a family trait despite the dark hair. I blush easily and have to slather on sunscreen. It's a curse if you're trying to look mysterious."

That small half smile quirked up again. "Are you trying to look mysterious?"

"I gave it up years ago. What you see is all there is. So, how do you like the house?"

"I like it." He gazed around the room as he spoke. "It's so warm, so...lived in."

She chuckled. "So rundown. It needs some work, but with one thing and the other, money mostly, I haven't gotten to it. It needs paint, plus there's a couple of plumbing problems, although nothing major—we had copper pipes put in three years ago. And the electricity, if ancient, is fine. The kitchen is functional."

"I'm not much of a cook. I've always moved around too much to learn how."

Rachel's natural curiosity made her want to ask him why he moved around so much, what he did for a living, and if he was married, but she figured it would sound nosy. "I love to cook. I'd offer you a snack if I weren't immobilized. So, does the house have what you need?"

He nodded. "Three bedrooms, furnished, on a side street. Trees. And a nice feeling as you walk through. It looks—" he shrugged "—loved."

"It has been," Rachel said with a fond smile. "My sister and I have lived here forever."

"Your sister? Shouldn't she be taking care of you?"

"Leah's away at school. I hope. Though with Leah, you never know. She's thirteen years younger than I am and does a lot of college hopping, I'm afraid. But listen—"

The sudden sharp sound of a honking horn made Philomena bark excitedly as she scrambled up and dashed out of the bedroom. Sam looked at his watch. "That must be Mrs. Katz. She said she'd meet me here at eleven-thirty.''

Sam was strangely reluctant to leave Rachel Murray alone in her large four-poster and in pain. "Before I leave, are you sure I can't do anything for you?"

"No, really. I've been getting by on my own most of my life, and I'm pretty good at it now. You run along and look at houses.'' She picked up the phone and put it to her ear. "I'm going to call work and explain my absence. 'Bye, Sam Kovacs,'' she said with a warm smile. "Maybe I'll see you around.''

Again, Sam felt oddly unwilling to say goodbye. Not that he was some sort of bleeding heart do-gooder by nature, nothing of the sort. But the poor woman was in pain, and there was no one taking care of her. And that wasn't right.

Still, she seemed pretty adamant about wanting him to go, so he supposed he'd better. "Well, okay, then. Hope you get well soon.''

While hurrying out to the front of the house, he couldn't get the picture of Rachel, lying in bed, out of his mind.

Rachel. Lying in bed.

There, at the end, he'd had the oddest urge to jump into that very bed with her and check out that round body.

Stopping in his tracks, he frowned. What was that all about? Terrific, Kovacs, he chided himself. Hop right in next to her. Best thing for her back, he thought sardonically. Hell, she wasn't even the type that usually turned him on. Too domesticated.

It had been a stupid thought, he reassured himself as he closed the front door. It was probably the simple fact that the woman was prone that had turned him on for that brief instant. It had been a while for him, too long a while. He'd been too busy lately, too much on the run, taking a leave of absence from his job with the *Herald,* tying up his affairs, and traveling all the way from Eastern Europe to California, to pay much attention to his lustier side. Obviously the sight of an attractive female lying in a bed had been too much for his deprived body, so he'd reacted as any healthy, functioning male might. Yeah, that was all.

As he got into the passenger side of Mrs. Katz's large luxury car, he told her, "She was home."

"Who, Rachel?" The white-haired woman with the Harlequin-style glasses raised her eyebrows in surprise, then turned her attention back to the road. "That's okay."

"It's okay to go into a house unannounced?"

"Sure. This is Ojai. Why is she home, did she say?"

"She hurt her back."

"Oh. Tsk-tsk. Poor thing. I'll give her a call later, see if she needs anything. My husband has back problems, poor man. 'The sciatica,' he calls it. I tell you...."

Mrs. Katz droned on while she drove them through quiet, oak-shaded streets, passing young people on bikes, a couple of joggers, a woman pushing a twin stroller.

The town's pace was a leisurely one. It was peaceful here. He hoped he wouldn't get bored.

His thoughts unexpectedly shifted back to Rachel. Why was she leasing out her house? Moving to another town? Getting married? Maybe she was already married. He hadn't seen a ring, but that meant nothing. She'd mentioned a sister. No husband.

"Is she leaving Ojai?" he interrupted the Realtor in the middle of a sentence about water exercise classes.

"Who? Rachel? No. She'll be living in the guest house out back." They turned into a dirt lane and began to ascend a grove of orange trees. "Now, this place is a little more than you wanted to spend, but there's a stable if you want to keep a horse or two...."

He gazed around him, tried to pay attention to the sales pitch, but his mind kept flashing back to Rachel. If he took her place, she would be living nearby. "Out back." Close. Accessible.

Rachel lying in bed, her dark curls spread out on the pillow, a warm, welcoming smile on her face.

So what? It wasn't as if he was looking to get involved in an affair right now, he assured himself. Anyway, if he were, it would not be with someone such as her, someone who would take an affair much too seriously. He wasn't sure how he knew that about her, but he did.

Hell, she was probably not even available. In fact... Yeah, he hoped she wasn't.

He ordered his mind to pay attention to Mrs. Katz. His task was to lease a house for one year only and to get to work. Stray thoughts of a carnal nature were not what he needed to be focusing on, not at the moment....

Although later, in a few weeks maybe, when he had a little free time, perhaps then he could follow up on what his libido kept returning to today.

Rachel Murray might be interested in a landlady/tenant relationship that was a bit more intimate than usual.

"Oof!"

Rachel grunted as Wanda's fingers probed a sore muscle, then went on with her story. "So then I threatened him with a water glass. Can you believe it? Yikes! That hurt. Sorry, I shouldn't complain when you were kind enough to make a house call."

"I don't mind," Wanda said with a chuckle. "Holler away, release those demons—it's good for you." With that, the chiropractor dug her two thumbs into an especially tender area of Rachel's lower back, just south of her waistline.

"Dear Lord! What are you aiming for here? An exorcism?" Wanda didn't answer, but Rachel's dog barked outside the window. "Phil thinks you're killing me, you know," she said, then groaned some more.

Eventually Wanda's deliberate and unhurried acupressure massage made Rachel's moans quiet and she managed to let go of the grip on her pillow. A blessed minute or two after that, she was actually able to sense when her lower back, which had been strung as tight as a newly manufactured spool of thread, loosened up and something began to flow through her veins. Blood probably.

"Yes," she sighed into the pillow. "By George, you've got it."

"It was a pretty nasty spasm, Rach," Wanda said in that low-pitched, soothing way she had.

As Wanda expanded the deep massage outward toward the hipbone, Rachel returned to the subject she much preferred to discuss: the eternal mystery of the male sex.

"You know a lot, Wanda, so tell me, why is it when you meet an interesting, sexy man, it's always when you've just decided to not put on makeup for one day, or eaten a pound of cookies the night before so that your face is bloated beyond recognition?" She turned her head to the other side. The goose-down pillow felt soft against her cheek. "No, don't answer that, you'll give me one of your Zen tidbits about how things happen because they happen, or how all of life is timing but not necessarily the timing we'd like."

"You've listened," Wanda said with a smile, switching to the opposite hip and digging in again. "And here I thought you always tuned me out."

"Ouch. The pain isn't on that side."

"But it will be if we don't loosen it up."

"Oh...." Rachel sighed. "He was really nice-looking. Kind of...you know, seasoned. Just a little silver in the beard. Not young, not old. Experienced."

"And?"

"And what?"

"Are you planning to see him again?"

"Probably not," Rachel was forced to admit with another sigh. "Given my lousy timing."

"What's his name?"

"Sam something. I can't believe it. The first time I meet him, I'm in bed, in pain. I hadn't even brushed my teeth!"

The sound of a heavily muffled ringing phone startled her. "Where is it?" she said, groping around her head and beneath the covers. "Oh, yeah, it's under the other pillow. Can you get it?"

Immediate relief greeted the chiropractor's removal of her digits of torture. "Hello?" Wanda said, followed by "I'm sorry, she's under the weather. May I take a message? All right.... Thanks." She replaced the phone on the bed table and resumed her massage. "It was your Realtor. Mr. Kovacs wants the place."

"Really?"

"He wants to move in right away and will call you later today. See? You'll be seeing him again, which means your timing and the universe's timing are in accord."

Rachel's heart leaped suddenly, enough to make her feel giddy. "Really?" she repeated, unable to keep the grin from her face.

She felt Wanda rise from the side of the bed. "Roll over," the chiropractor said.

When Rachel was on her back once again, Wanda slipped the ice pack under the small of her back, propped her knees on a couple of pillows and pulled the covers up to her neck. Then she smiled, her kind, unlined face belying her fifty-four years. Inner serenity, Rachel thought. A totally foreign concept in her case.

"Hey, Wanda, thanks."

Her friend squeezed her hand gently. "I'll be back in the morning. Rest now."

"I owe you." Rachel closed her eyes. She was nice and relaxed now, as though she'd gone two rounds with Magic Fingers and had lost gracefully. "He's going to rent the place," she murmured happily. "I really liked him. Gee, I hope I don't drool on him or anything."

She chuckled ruefully and opened her eyes to look at Wanda. "Listen to me, as if anything were going to happen between us. That kind of man never takes a second look at someone like me. Ah, well—" she closed her eyes again "—it's nice to know I can still fantasize. It's been a while."

"Rachel," Wanda said warmly, "you are a lovely woman. Many men have found you so, and you know it. You are perfect just as you are."

"Ha. Tell that to Sam Kovacs."

HE PICKED UP the hotel phone next to his bed and punched in the numbers. After several rings, a muffled-sounding "Hmm?" came from the other end of the line.

"Ms. Murray? Rachel?"

"Hmm? Yes?"

"I'm sorry, were you sleeping?"

"No, it's all right."

She sounded groggy, Sam thought.

And sexy as hell. He pictured her as he'd seen her earlier, her hair spread out on the pillow, the mysteries of her body tantalizingly obscured by a blanket. His own body responded accordingly to the picture.

Hey, Kovacs, why are you going there? He directed the question to his brain and the organ between his legs that was supposed to take orders from his brain, but was singularly unreliable. *Cut it out.*

"It's Sam Kovacs," he said.

"Oh, yes, Mrs. Katz phoned." She seemed more alert now.

"Mrs. Katz also informed me that you're the associate editor of the *Ojai Hello.*"

"Oh? Well, yes, I am."

"That means we'll be working together. I'm the new fill-in editor."

"But the new editor is S.K. Warren. He's supposed to be some hotshot foreign correspondent."

He chuckled at the description. "S.K. Warren is my byline, and I'm not much of a hotshot, promise. I've heard all about you, but not your name. Winston told me you pretty much run things."

What the paper's owner, Winston Carter, had told him was more like "The associate editor is the whole ball of wax—you can't put out the paper without her, so be sure to keep her happy."

Sam hadn't sought the job. But he'd been close to burnout after living the intense, adrenaline-pumping pace of Eastern Europe, Africa, everywhere in the Third World, for fifteen years.

Sam was grateful he'd been smart enough to recognize the signs in himself at the time—too much booze, not enough sleep, a slight hand tremor; hell, he'd even started smoking after five years off the stuff. He hadn't needed a doctor for a diagnosis, he'd made his own call. What he'd prescribed for himself was six months to a year away from the insanity.

The offer from Win, an old college roommate, to fill in for the editor of a small-town rag had seemed a better alternative than the other high-stress positions he'd considered. He figured he needed to feel *settled* for maybe the first time in his life.

Temporarily settled, anyway. Until he went back into the fray.

"That was nice of Mr. Carter," Rachel replied. "What he probably meant to say was that I nag everyone to death each issue, but it gets the job done." She chuckled. "I do tend to do that."

"As long as you don't nag me," he said lightly. "I'll need all the help I can get. So, how's your back?"

"Bone crunchers work wonders. When do you want to move in?"

He glanced around the clean, luxurious-but-impersonal hotel room and thought of Rachel's house, of the narrow bed in the second bedroom with its Native American print bedspread looking as though it had been through thousands of washings, of the kitchen with its chipped yellow tile and the large ceramic pot on the breakfast table that had teddy bears in various poses spelling out "sugar." It was all so wonderfully corny.

"As soon as possible," he told Rachel. "How much time do you need?"

"Can you give me a few days? Where are you staying now?"

"I'm at the Ojai Valley Inn."

"But that costs a fortune," she said. "You shouldn't have to spend money on a hotel. Would you like to stay here? I mean, in the extra bedroom? I mean, until I get my stuff moved out. I mean...."

As she let the sentence dribble off, Sam sensed her discomfort. It made him smile again. The giving, good-hearted type, that's what she was. She'd made an impetuous offer and now regretted it.

Even so, he considered it. He'd had it up to here with hotels, from four-star palaces to dives on skid row, wherever the story had taken him. He considered saying yes, especially when his loins started acting up again at the thought. Hell, they'd been on alert throughout the phone call. Just talking to the woman did it to him, although why, he still wasn't sure. She was nothing like his usual taste, which ran to thin, nervous and unreliable.

Rachel and he in the same house. Days at work and nights at home. So very many avenues of possibilities to be explored at leisure.

But lust aside, he had to face the fact that soon enough, they would not only be living on the same piece of property, but they were to be work colleagues. Bad move to covet an employee, wasn't that what the manual said?

Rachel and he in the same house. Rachel his employee. Working together every day. Company morale. Workplace ethics.

"I'm fine at the hotel," he said briskly. "I wouldn't want to get in your way."

Rachel nodded, but a small dart of disappointment hit her. Darn it. Why had she offered Leah's room to Sam? She barely knew the man. Because he was about to be her boss? No. Because she always did things like that.

Homeless? Here's a home. Hungry? Eat this. Sad? Tell me all about it. Have a dream? Let me help you achieve it.

Not her own dream, of course, everyone else's. Her heart's desire had been placed on the back burner years ago, where it remained to this day.

But to the world at large, Rachel was the original nurturing female, the way her mom had been.

Obviously, Sam didn't need nurturing—he'd said no to her offer. Good, she thought. She was glad. But then, why did she feel so downcast?

Because it was as she'd suspected—Sam hadn't found her as attractive as she'd found him. After all, if he had, he'd have taken her up on her offer to spend a couple of nights under the same roof with her.

"When do you think I can move in?"

Sam's question forced her to zoom back to the present. "Let's see, today is Wednesday. How's Sunday?"

"Fine. I'll be in the office tomorrow, and then there's some sort of party for me Friday night."

"That's right. Oh, shoot, I won't be able to bake. You won't get a chance to taste my cookies."

After a slight pause, Sam sounded as though he were choking back laughter as he replied, "I'll taste your cookies some other time. I won't expect you at either the office or the party. Rest your back, okay?"

"I'll see how I feel when I get up in the morning."

There was another pause, as though they'd run out of topics. Sam broke the silence. "Well, goodbye, then."

"Goodbye."

When she hung up the phone, Rachel remembered how her heart had leaped when she'd learned he was renting the house. And had leaped even higher when he'd informed her they'd be working together.

Her heart needn't have bothered.

THE *OJAI HELLO* occupied the premises of a modest, yellow, wood-framed house two blocks off the main drag. At 6:45 p.m. on Friday evening, Rachel paused at the back entrance and yanked again on the tunic top, smoothing it over her hips in the hopes her elastic-and-Velcro-fastened back brace wouldn't be discernible. It was necessary to wear the thing for a couple more days, to keep her posture in alignment while her lower back finished healing. She wondered how in the world women used to manage to breathe or walk or laugh in stays and corsets, similar instruments of torture.

Her knowledge of corsets, needless to say, was limited to movies and books, in which they usually outlined a slender form with a narrow waist and flaring hips. Not quite her situation. To be fair, Rachel's waist did go in and her hips did flare out; it was the starting point of in and the ending point of out that was the difference. It was a relative thing.

She was five-five and full-bodied, as her mother had been. Breasts and hips on the larger side of normal, a pelvis made for child-bearing, sturdy thighs. The perfect potato picker's body, but hopelessly out of fashion in the thinner-is-better nineties. Rachel had never been thin a day in her life and never would be. Most days she didn't think about it; sometimes, such as this evening, when she wanted to erase what had to be Sam's first impression of her as dowdy, she wished devoutly for a daintier DNA heritage.

When she entered the kitchen, Connie and Bonnie, the twin college students who helped out on the paper, greeted her with huge smiles.

"Hi," they said together.

"We're glad you came early," Bonnie said.

"So you can tell us how everything looks," Connie said.

"Glad to." Rachel surveyed the area.

The house's former living room was now the paper's main work area, off which were three former bedrooms. Two had been converted into several cubicles, one of which was hers. The third bedroom, with its single desk, was now the editor's office. The kitchen was still the kitchen and the party was about to begin.

Sure enough, there was food and beverages on the long table that occupied the center of the living room/ work area. Rachel had tried to coordinate the party on the phone, carefully straddling the line between the Doritos chip crowd and the tofu supporters who made up the paper's staff. She'd vetoed both herbal tea punch and a beer keg, settling instead for soft drinks, bottled water, and white wine.

"It's just fine," she told the twins.

What it was, she thought silently, was passable. E for effort. It just needed a little help.

Within a couple of minutes she had moved the drinks and cups to one end of the table and the blue corn chips and salsa to the top of the copier machine, arranged the pile of napkins into the shape of a fan, reworked the cookie platter so the bakery's butter dreams were layered in a pattern. She put napkins under the breads, removed the plastic wrap from the tray of cold cuts, opened the mustard and mayonnaise jars, and brought the pickles and olives closer to the sandwich fixings. She hummed as she fussed, enjoying herself immensely.

As HE STOOD in the doorway of his new office, Sam observed Rachel's movements. A trained people-watcher, he decided that Rachel was the type who *tidied* things. Which could be annoying, especially if she followed a person around with a dustpan, or fluffed a pillow the moment you arose from a couch. He hadn't sensed either obsessiveness or fanaticism from her yesterday morning, but then, she'd been incapable of tidying much of anything while paralyzed with pain.

It was obvious she was as efficient as hell. Charlie Ross, the sabbatical-taking editor, a round, jolly type, had showed Sam around the paper yesterday and today, and had introduced him to almost everybody on staff. However, whenever he had a question about scheduling or printing or finances, Charlie had cheerfully directed him to "Ask Rachel." Which was proof positive of Win's claim: Rachel ran the place.

Now, smiling, he leaned back against the door frame and draped his arms across his chest, prepared to observe this paragon of efficiency a little longer. He sure did like the view of Rachel from the rear. She wore black leggings, ankle boots and a long, emerald-green sweater that came halfway down her thighs. It obscured most of her shape, except her buttocks, which were outlined nicely, thank you. Especially when she leaned in slightly to adjust something on the table.

He gave a silent whistle of appreciation. Her rear end was round and firm, and not small. Womanly. More than a handful, he thought, and imagined his hands taking hold of her. *Oh, man.* His hormones were on a rampage, and the party hadn't even begun.

"I didn't expect to see you," he greeted her, keeping his voice neutral.

Rachel whipped around, a look of surprise on her face. "Oh."

"I startled you."

"It's okay," she said, her hands self-consciously smoothing her sweater over her hips.

The front view was as good as the rear. She'd pulled her dark curls back off her face so that her cheekbones were more prominent. She had a laughing face, he decided, with those rosy cheeks and dancing eyes. Even with some makeup carefully applied, Rachel still seemed...healthy. Romp-in-the-haystack robust.

The haystack image had a definite physical effect on him. Inwardly cursing the tightness of his jeans, he pushed himself away from the door and walked toward her. A faint scent of rosewater greeted him as he drew nearer. "Well, I'm glad you're here, because I—"

His sentence was cut short by the sound of the front door flying open and the entrance of several newcomers at the same time.

"Rachel! Honey! Are you all right?" This came from a woman named Loretta, whom Sam could only describe as birdlike.

"Oh, how we missed you!" Loretta said, throwing her arms around Rachel and giving her a large hug. Rachel winced slightly, then extricated herself from the woman's arms with a warm smile.

"I'm just fine," Rachel said. "Have you met Sam Kovacs?"

"Oh, yes," she twittered, fixing her bright birdlike gaze on him. "We were introduced earlier."

"Of course," Rachel said to him, assuming the easy air of a hostess. "You've met everyone. Well, Sam, Loretta is not just our receptionist, she also reads tarot cards, and if you ever need any kind of herbs and holistic medications, she's the one to see."

"Good to know," he said, deadpan.

A tall, lanky man joined them. His thinning hair was sun-streaked, and his extremely tanned skin set off eyebrows that were nearly white. Rachel put her arm through his. "Dan," she said. "Good to see you."

"We haven't met," Sam said, offering his hand. "You must be Dan Cummings. You were out on a story the last two days, right?"

"More like out on my koa longboard," Dan chuckled as he shook Sam's hand. "How's it hanging, dude?"

Sam started to smile at the expression, but then realized the man hadn't been joking. "It hangs the way it usually does, I guess."

"Bitchin'," Dan said, nodded, and shuffled off.

When Loretta followed him, twittering about the advantages of holistic sunscreen, Sam looked questioningly at Rachel. "Excuse me? 'How's it hanging, dude?' 'Bitchin'?'" he quoted. "Is he for real?"

"Dan's a surfer," Rachel said a bit defensively. "He used to be a champion. Thirty years ago."

"And when the waves call, he's gone?"

"Ventura Beach is close by, yes. But Dan does his job." He could tell from the way her lower jaw stuck out that his comment had put her defenses up. He'd committed the sin of attacking one of mother hen's chickadees.

He smiled. "A surfer reporter, twin helpers who finish one another's sentences, a holistic receptionist. Sounds like the cast for a TV sitcom."

That got a laugh from her. "In Ojai, we run the gamut. We have followers of Krishnamurti, prep school boys in suits and ties, golfers, horse fanatics, a lot of artists—" Her attention was captured by something over his shoulder and her eyes lit up. "Carmen, you brought the baby."

Sam turned to see the art director, an olive-skinned young woman wearing a front pack that contained a sleepy infant. "Oh, let me," Rachel said, reaching for the child in the sack.

"Rachel—are you sure?" Carmen asked, a faint Hispanic trace in her accent. "With your back?"

"When it comes to my goddaughter Lupe, who cares about a sore back?" As she brought the child to her, a look of utter bliss came over her face as the baby nuzzled her neck.

A twist of something soft in Sam's midsection surprised him. For a brief moment he was no longer the observer. He was moved, and he wasn't used to being moved by the sight of a woman and a child.

Just as quickly, his reporter instinct kicked in again. So, here was yet another facet to Rachel, although it went with all her other nurturing qualities. She was the baby-gusher type. If there was a person or animal under one year of age anywhere in the vicinity, she could be counted on to make a beeline in that direction.

Watching her, the way she murmured nonsense to the child and hugged its small, round form to her chest, he wondered why she didn't have any of her own, wondered if she'd been married. All he knew was that she worked at the paper, had a sister, and owned a house he was about to rent.

He wanted to know more, lots more. As much as he could find out.

"So, you made it, young man."

Sam looked to his right, then nodded. "Turnley."

Rachel watched as Turnley McCallum, leaning heavily on his carved oak cane, limped up to her and Sam. The octogenarian wore his customary plaid shirt and suspenders, and sprouted a long, white beard. In his head, he carried all of the town's history and was pleased to share it at the drop of a hat, which came in handy considering he wrote a weekly column for the *Hello*.

After kissing Turnley's cheek, Rachel left him with Sam, returned little Lupe to her mother, and went to mingle with the rest of the paper's crew and their families. Her usual gaiety was tempered by worry; those few minutes with Sam had given her an unsettling impression. Mainly that he wasn't just going to be another Charlie—easygoing, hang-loose, fatherly Charlie. Sam was a completely different type, not swayed by loyalty or tradition.

As the party wore on, she couldn't shake a nagging sense of fear. The newspaper had been an enormous part of her life since she'd been hired part-time at sixteen years of age to sweep up and answer phones. After high school, she'd come aboard full-time, working her way up from cub reporter to paste-up, to advertising and sales, to her current position. The *Ojai Hello* was Rachel's world. Was her world about to change?

THE PAPER'S SMALL backyard was completely dominated by an ancient towering oak tree, and it was this tree upon which Sam seemed to be concentrating when, a couple of hours later, Rachel observed him through the screen door.

He sat in the old rocking chair, a drink in one hand, a cigarette in the other. Perfect, she thought. The world-weary foreign correspondent and his vices. He even looked the part—faded jeans, navy turtleneck, a well-worn tweed jacket. The beard and mustache were exactly right, including the fact that his hair needed a trim.

She pushed open the screen door, its perpetual squeak making him turn around.

"Here," she said, handing him the ashtray she'd retrieved from the kitchen.

He smiled at her and stubbed out the cigarette. Then he held up his glass. "Want a whiskey?"

She set the ashtray on an orange crate that served as a table. "I thought we only had wine."

"I keep my own stash. It's in the bottom drawer of my new desk." He winked. "That's not for public knowledge."

There was an aura of something about him, she thought. Something dark. Loneliness, she decided. And maybe a deep, soul-killing sadness.

Unless she was letting her romantic imagination work overtime, a definite possibility.

Even so, she turned to face him. "Are you all right? I mean, is there anything I can do for you? Get you to eat?"

"No need to wait on me, Rachel. In fact, where are my manners?" He rose from the rocking chair and indicated it. "Your back. Do you want to sit down?"

She waved off his offer. "I'm better on my feet, and really, I'm okay. Strong stock, you know. Actually, I'm getting ready to leave, so I wanted to say goodbye."

"Oh? Well, then, I'll take you home."

"Don't bother. I'm walking. It's only a few blocks."

"Then I'll walk with you. It'll clear my head. Besides, I need to discuss a few things with you, about the paper."

Giving up, she sighed, "Okay, let's go."

The night was quiet, the streets lit only by the occasional porch light. Someone was burning sweet-scented wood in a fireplace and, as it was only March, there was still a slight chill in the air. Rachel and Sam walked along side by side, just the two of them, not talking at first, through silent, oak-lined, unpaved streets. As they walked, she was aware of two sensations at the same time—the attraction she felt toward him, and the threat he posed. Taken together, they were a definite recipe for confusion.

It was Sam who began the conversation. "Listen, Rachel, I'm going to need your help until I get up to speed."

"You have it."

"And, well, I'm also going to be evaluating some things, maybe making a few minor changes."

"How minor?"

He shrugged. "I'm not sure yet. I just got here."

"I see." As a car passed them, she thought over what to say next, then decided to plunge right in. "Nothing much needs to be changed, Sam, if you are asking me.

The paper works fine. We always get the issue out, make very few typos, and we're in the black. End of story.''

"So, no complaints? Nothing you'd do differently?"

"Nope."

"I'm surprised to hear you say that." He scratched his beard. "Every operation needs some fine-tuning."

"They're my friends, Sam," she said softly. "My family."

He nodded, obviously not surprised by her answers. "Which means you're not sure you can be objective." When she didn't respond, he went on. "So, whatever I decide, I'm on my own?"

"Something like that," she said lightly, then sped up a little, hoping he'd take the hint and let her finish her walk home without him. But the recent rainfall had created a few potholes in the pavement, and she was unfortunate enough to step into a small one.

"Oh," she cried, and would have lost her balance except that Sam was there, grabbing her upper arm with one hand and putting the other around her waist to make sure she stayed on her feet.

"Okay?" he said.

"Yes. Thanks."

"What do you have on under there? Armor?" He winced. "I'm sorry, that was tactless."

She was grateful for the dark night, so he couldn't see the way her face must have been flaming with embarrassment. "It's a back brace," she said stiffly.

"Oh, of course. Sorry."

"It's okay."

Perfect, she thought bitterly as they continued on. Two easy ways *not* to impress a man: meet him when you're in a sickbed, and wear a brace the first time he touches you.

And while you're at it, set up a line of demarcation with your boss his first day on the job, you on one side, him on the other.

It was settled, then. The future held no possibility of a romance with Sam Kovacs. No way it could happen now. The two of them were victims of bad timing and definitely not meant to be.

No, most definitely not.

3

HE WAS NOT USED TO THIS time of the morning—sometimes going to bed about now, but getting up, no. Still, he had to admit, objectively, as Sunday mornings went, this was a fine one. The air was clean with a slight chill, the sky was a clear, pale blue, and the rising sun felt good on his face.

As he approached Rachel's house—soon to be his—he observed how the red-tiled roof seemed solid, even though the white stucco needed a little paint. A driveway ran along one side, a neatly trimmed hedge was on the other. There were flowers everywhere, a riot of them. Good thing he didn't have to worry about their upkeep, because he'd never attended to a garden in his life and had no intention of taking up the hobby now.

Sam balanced the take-out carton in one hand, so he could unlatch the gate with the other. He held on to his parcel for dear life as Phil came dashing around the side of the house, ploughing into him with her customary ebullience. Sam had to chuckle, even as he held his hands high and maneuvered around the dog's enthusiastic nose-butting. As a kid, he'd always wanted a pet, but the nomadic life of an army brat had made that difficult. Lately, the only animal friends he'd made were the half-starved, disease-ridden canine survivors of terrorism and ethnic "cleansing," Third World style. Phil was a real, live, normal dog—a refreshing change.

As the front door opened, Rachel yelled out, "Philomena, leave the man alone."

The dog didn't bat an eyelash at the sound of her voice, but when Sam grabbed the animal's front paws, which were resting on his chest, and said, "Down," she withdrew immediately, sprawled on her stomach, put her face on her paws and, wagging her tail furiously, gave him that "Would you hit an orphan?" look the species seemed to have perfected.

Rachel, her hair in a ponytail, and wearing gray sweats and sneakers, propped her hands on her hips. "No loyalty whatsoever, have you noticed? I tried to teach her 'down' and 'sit,' but I don't think she speaks English."

She smiled a greeting at Sam. He noticed she wore no makeup, but she was one of those women who really didn't need it. Her eyes were dark, her cheeks rosy. Vibrant. There was nothing colorless about the woman, nothing at all.

"Well," she said, "you must be eager to move in. It's not even seven yet."

He crossed the threshold into the house and proceeded to unload the food onto the coffee table. "How's the back?"

"All better."

"Good. I brought breakfast."

"Oh." As he set out two large cups of coffee, cream and sugar packets, two glazed doughnuts, and two apple fritters, she rested a hand on the back of a faded, over-stuffed chair. "Well, that was very nice. Uh, thanks."

A familiar smell made him glance toward the kitchen door. "Hold it. Is that bacon?" When she nodded, he added, "And freshly-ground coffee?"

"And pancake batter ready to go. I was making breakfast. There's enough for two."

"You're on."

He packed up his take-out and followed her into the kitchen. It was a square, old-fashioned room, not updated for thirty years at least, he imagined, and the faded gray Formica-topped table she indicated for him to sit at reminded him of comfortable bygone truck stops. "Do you need me to do anything?" he asked. "Not that there's much I can do in a kitchen."

"Sit," she said, pouring him a cup of coffee from a pot. "I'm all organized."

She most definitely was. He watched her as she poured out the pancakes, melted butter, fussed with plates and napkins. Watched how her body moved, how her generous breasts bobbed slightly as she worked. Even in her baggy clothing, he was reminded of certain women in the Italian countryside, their bodies curved and luscious in their thin dresses, as they walked bare-foot down the road in summertime.

There it was again. The Rachel Effect. He was unable to take his eyes off her, although he was careful not to let her see him observing her. The woman turned him on, plain and simple. Maybe, one more time, he should rethink this non-fraternization policy.

Or maybe, one more time, he should stop thinking with his groin.

When she set down a platter of pancakes and bacon, brought out real maple syrup, and poured him another cup of the best coffee he'd ever tasted in his life, he diverted his lust onto attacking the meal. Safer that way, for sure.

After a few bites he noticed she wasn't eating. "Aren't you joining me?"

"I already nibbled on some bacon. I've been up since five."

"Oh. Well, help yourself to a doughnut."

She hesitated, then said, "Um, no thanks."

"Really?" He chewed on some bacon—crisp and perfect—before becoming aware of the way Rachel seemed to be staring at his mouth. Wondering if he had some food particles caught in his mustache, he licked around it. He added one of the apple fritters to his plate, tore off a piece, and offered it to her. "I feel silly eating alone. Sure I can't get you to have one of these?"

She bit her bottom lip worriedly. "I'm trying to cut down."

"Really?" He popped the piece into his own mouth and chewed happily on it. "I never interfere with women and their diets." He was about to finish the thought with something about how her body was totally, thoroughly, perfect as far as he was concerned, but he kept it to himself. Too personal.

Rachel fidgeted. Just yesterday she'd sworn off any more sugary desserts, and here she was salivating as if her vow had never occurred. She really wanted to get away from the smell of the doughnuts…and from Sam. The pull toward both was way too powerful.

But Lord, the man was hard to ignore, in a blue T-shirt that matched his eyes, a well-worn plaid shirt over that. His jeans hugged his narrow hips, outlined long, sturdy legs.

But it was the way he attacked the meal that did her in. A stupid, silly thing to get all hot and bothered about, she knew, but there it was. He ate with gusto; his bites were large but not gluttonous, just filled with unabashed enjoyment. And she had a real soft spot for a man who loved her cooking.

She couldn't tear her gaze away from him and the way the tip of his tongue captured a drop of syrup at the edge of his mustache. She was hypnotized by the rhythm of his mouth, the way his throat muscles worked as he swallowed, and how, after each bite, he'd run his tongue over his lips to catch any stickiness. And, of course, there was the way he dug into that apple fritter, gave it his undivided attention.…

She wanted to be that apple fritter.

Aware that her cheeks were burning, she smiled brightly. "Ready for more pancakes?"

"Nope. Got to save room for my morning apple fritter. Can't start the day without doughnuts and caffeine."

Elbow propped on the table, her chin in her hand, she watched him chew. "It's not fair."

They smiled at each other then, and the moment filled her with a nice, warm feeling. Then Sam rose, took his cup to the coffeepot, and got himself a refill. Leaning against the counter, he said, "So, tell me what you want me to do."

"About what?"

"I'm here to help you move."

Her hand flew to her mouth. "Oh, but I'm all done. I got started yesterday afternoon and, you know how it is, couldn't stop. I finished up late last night."

"Oh."

Sam felt oddly disappointed by Rachel's revelation, even vaguely annoyed with her. He was not a particularly giving person, didn't usually put himself out much for others, but this morning he'd set his alarm, gone to the local doughnut place, tried to be a good Samaritan.

And not only didn't she need his help, she'd cooked him breakfast.

"So," she asked, "where's your stuff?"

"Don't have a lot—there's two cartons and a suitcase in the car. Some clothes and books, is all. I'll bring them in later."

"How about if I help you?"

"Nope," he said briskly. "I'm going to finish my coffee first."

"I see." She slapped her hands on her knees and rose. "Well, I'll clean up, then leave you to your unpacking."

"Leave the dishes for me. You cooked, I'll clean."

"But—"

"I insist." As he walked back to the table he thought, silently, Rachel didn't need him? He didn't need her.

"Well, okay," Rachel said, but she obviously wasn't pleased about him cleaning up. Tough.

"Hey," Sam remembered to say, "terrific breakfast. Thanks."

"You're welcome." He sat and sipped his coffee. "Well," she said, "goodbye."

He nodded. She stared at him one moment more, then walked out through the service porch.

Dear God, Rachel, she thought as she made her way to the guest house, whatever was she to do with this attraction toward Sam? It was certainly one way, as he'd just showed her in his eagerness to get rid of her. Hadn't she already gotten the message Friday night? That was why just this morning, she'd decided not to do any of those obvious things to get his attention when he moved in. She rarely wore makeup at home, so she hadn't put any on. What with gardening and cleaning, she hardly ever got out of her sweats on the weekend, so sweats she'd worn. She'd made no special effort—no girlish, eyelash-batting, subtle-perfume-type flirtation for her.

Besides, she reminded herself sternly, that would be ill-advised; she and Sam might very well be at logger-heads pretty soon, when he began to make changes at the paper.

Changes at the paper.

She halted at the door to her new home, a second layer of upset forming on top of the original one. Maybe she should march back in there now and confront him—ask him just what were his plans. And how much chaos would they be causing?

No, she decided. She would try to keep work at the workplace, if possible. It was the businesslike way to act. Tomorrow was Monday, soon enough to tackle any new challenges.

But there would be all those hours away from work, hours occupying the same plot of land with Sam. What would she do with all those off-hours? She didn't remember ever feeling this sense of physical yearning toward a man before; it threatened to overwhelm her. The fact that it was not returned put her at a decided disadvantage.

She probably shouldn't have rented the place to him. But it was too late to back out now. Sam was on the premises, and she'd just have to learn to adapt. Adapting was something Rachel did really well.

THE YARD WAS SMALL, Sam noted, but filled with roses and beds of flowers he had no names for. Philomena's doghouse stood against the side wall; an old tire hung from the branch of a tree, and he pushed it once as he passed it. Birds twittered, and next door, someone was mowing a lawn. It was a pleasant, quiet ambience. He was used to noise and chaos and wasn't sure he would be comfortable in all this serenity.

The guest house was a converted garage, a small white stucco replica of the larger house, with a deeply pitched red-tiled roof. The front door was ajar, but he knocked, anyway. "May I come in?"

"Sure," Rachel called. "Just watch your step."

He entered to find himself in one large room. There was a kitchen alcove to the left, with a large wooden table and two chairs nearby; across the way, Rachel was just making up a narrow bed. The other furniture consisted of an armoire at the foot of the bed, a striped love seat and a TV set. And everywhere there were cartons, large plastic bags, shopping bags, piles of books, and plants. Even with the light pouring in from the large skylight over the table, the feeling in here was most definitely cramped.

"Wait a minute." Sam crossed to Rachel. "Let me help do that."

"Almost done," she said cheerfully, smoothing down the corners.

"Should you be bending?"

"Hey, I'm fine. Really. Don't even think about it. What do you need?"

Again, he was struck by how she slammed the door every time he offered assistance. She really didn't want his help, did she? Okay, he could take a hint as well as the next guy. "I was just wondering about a few things—the fuse box, how the stove works, you know."

"Do you mind waiting five minutes? I'm almost finished organizing my clothing."

"No problem." He sat himself at the table, took out a cigarette, then looked at her. "Okay if I smoke?"

"The door's open, so it's all right." He started to put the cigarette back, but she said, "No, it's okay. I quit years ago, but I have to admit I still like the smell. I wish it didn't kill you.''

"I quit, too. Started up again a few months ago. I'm hoping it's temporary.''

As he lit the cigarette, she brought him a round paint-spattered dish to use as an ashtray, then went back to the armoire.

Sam gazed around the room. "Are you sure you'll be okay here? It's so much smaller than you're used to.''

"Isn't it sweet? It used to be Dad's studio. He died a while ago.''

"I'm sorry. And your mother?''

"She died before he did.''

"That's rough.''

"It's okay, it happened years ago.''

"How about your sister—the one who's at school? Where's she going?''

He wondered if she minded talking about herself, but figured if she did, it was up to her to let him know. He always asked questions; any reporter worth his salt had Curiosity for a middle name. The only problem was, he usually remained detached when people unfolded their sad stories. Detachment, for some reason, was difficult with Rachel. She got to him, moved him, in a way he was not used to being moved.

"Humboldt Community College,'' she told him. "It's a two-year college, but after that, Leah can transfer to a state university.''

"So, she's pretty young, then.''

"Actually she's twenty-two. She's just not sure about

what she wants to do with her life. I worry about her a lot." She riffled through a carton, then pulled out a straw basket. Walking over to him, she smiled. "Look—I noticed you have a button on your shirt that's about to come off. Here's my sewing kit. Let me fix it for you."

He glanced down at his shirt and, sure enough, one of the wooden buttons dangled by a single thread. "No, thanks."

"It'll just take a second." She reached toward his shirt, but he caught her hand before it landed on the fabric.

"Not necessary," he said firmly. "You've done enough for me today. I actually have a needle and thread somewhere—I'll take care of it later."

At first she seemed taken aback by his adamant response, then she gazed down at their joined hands, and so did he. He was gripping her fingers tightly, too tightly, so he let up on the pressure. But he didn't release her.

Her hand was graceful, he observed, the fingers straight and nicely formed, her nails even and clean, no polish. Her skin felt satiny soft beneath his palm, and he caught a faint whiff of that rosewater again. Skin lotion, he decided. Her hand felt good in his. He felt a strange reluctance to release it.

As though obeying a silent command, they both looked up at the same moment and stared into each other's eyes. The room seemed so quiet, so still. Sam found himself totally caught up in what was going on in her expressive eyes. There was a quick flash of hunger in their brown depths, followed immediately by…what? Trepidation? Then she blinked, as though waking from a dream.

Yanking her hand from his grip, Rachel smiled uneasily. "Hey, okay. Sure. I don't need to be told twice. I won't mend your button."

Button? he thought, then remembered what they'd been talking about. They'd been discussing his shirt, but they'd been experiencing something totally different.

He yanked at the collar of his shirt. For some reason, it suddenly felt way too tight. "Thanks for the offer, anyway," Sam said. "Really."

"No problem. Look, let's go back to the big house. I'll show you where everything is."

IT WAS NIGHTTIME and she was finally settled in. The tiny kitchen and bathroom were organized, lamps were plugged in. Rachel sat on the cushioned window seat, beneath which used to be toys, art supplies, stuffed animals and dolls. Right now it accommodated all her linens.

Knees drawn to her chest, Rachel stared out the window, across the yard. One light burned in her—no, she corrected herself—Sam's bedroom. The mournful sound of Miles Davis was barely audible from that direction.

He was probably in bed. The bed she'd occupied only last night. A strange mixture of emotions welled up inside her. Heat and yearning for Sam…and a sense of loss. Her house was no longer her house.

Her house. Home. Where she'd devoted her entire life to raising her younger sister.

"She's all yours now," her mother had said a few months after Leah's birth. Rachel had been thirteen at the time, and her mother had been sick as long as she could remember. She'd handed the baby to her older daughter, smiled sadly and said, "I'm so sorry, sweetheart."

Her mother had died two weeks later. Devastated, her father had never really recovered, but bless him, he'd hung on for four more years, through Rachel's high school graduation, then died that summer. All he'd left was five hundred dollars and the house. Rachel had gone right to work—she had a child to raise; indeed, she'd been raising her since infancy, anyway.

Now Rachel was saving money for her own personal dream, to own and run a toddler day-care center. She'd been planning it for years. Not only did she love children, but her home—on a quiet street with a nice backyard and a separate playroom—was a perfect setting.

Over the years through extension classes, she'd completed most of the units required for a B.A. She only needed twenty more units, then one year of intensive study, to become accredited in Early Childhood Education.

However, when Leah had announced her resolve to return to school to study art, Rachel had put her dream away for a while longer. This was more important, she told herself. When Leah seemed more settled, on a straight path toward *somewhere,* Rachel would pick up her dream again.

So, she'd sent her baby sister off to Humboldt. Leased out the house to earn extra money for Leah's living expenses. Prayed, again, that this time it would work, that this time her little sister—more like her daughter—wouldn't lose herself in low self-esteem and bad company.

And through it all, there had been affection and hugs and long, intimate talks. The sisters loved each other, sure. But sometimes Rachel was terrified for her little sister, and sometimes she wanted to wring her neck.

Her musings were interrupted by the light in the big house going off, leaving the backyard in total darkness. Outside her window, a mockingbird called out for its mate, a nightly ritual. A few early spring crickets began a symphony. A deep longing arose in her throat, a hunger for the feel of a man's arms around her.

There had been a few minor relationships along the way, but she'd had her hands too full on the home front to ever make falling in love a priority. Mom had handed Leah over, and Rachel had done the best she could. But still, there were times, such as tonight, when she wondered if it would ever be her turn.

She lowered the blind on the window, crawled into bed, pulled the covers up and stared at the ceiling. Tomorrow was Monday, the first day of work under a new editor. A new editor who might turn the workplace into a storm center.

And, irony of ironies, it was that editor's arms she

longed for tonight. The realization brought more confusion to her already overloaded brain. She prayed that
sleep would shut down all the chatter; if not, she was in
for a long, long night.

SAM WAS SEMI-PREPARED for his first solo day at the
paper. Charlie had walked him through last Thursday,
the day when stories and photo shoots were discussed
and assigned, the ad pages blocked out. This past Friday,
he and Charlie had gone over the layout and printing
schedules, the computer system. Sam had brought home
a lot of work over the weekend.

And now it was Monday. Monster Monday. D-day
minus one. The day before the paper was put to bed was
always the second-most chaotic day in a weekly's schedule. The flurry of nerves and excitement that permeated
the premises of the *Ojai Hello* took him by surprise at
first. However, the ability to think on his feet and work
quickly, ingrained in him after all his years in the
world's hot spots, enabled him to adjust fairly quickly
to the chaos.

While Charlie was happily on his way to Maui, Sam
was calling reporters to check on the progress and length
of their stories. As editor, it was Sam's job to review,
edit and shorten the copy that was coming in. He had
photos to approve, lead-ins to write. In the large main
room, Carmen had begun to assemble pages onto layout
boards; the long slanted shelves along both sides of the
room were already crowded with them. Sam checked
each over several times during the day.

Through it all, Rachel was there, suggesting another avenue when a story fell through, assigning someone to check a fact, filling him in on how to work the computer, whom he was talking to on the phone. When he forgot to eat, she brought him lunch at his desk. Most important of all, she kept the coffeepot going all day. She seemed to second-guess his every need, a combination editor/secretary/den mother. He could not have gotten through the day without her. As Winston had said, she was the heart of the paper.

As far as making any personnel changes, he realized it would be another couple of weeks before he could give that his attention. For the present, he had some trouble telling Bonnie from Connie. Giggling, they informed him that Bonnie's nose was more pointed, but they looked like mirror images to him. Carmen brought her baby to work, and the child slept soundly in the midst of all the uproar, except when Carmen nursed her. This she did openly at her desk, which no one seemed to mind or even to notice. It stopped him short the first time, then he shrugged and got caught up again in the activity.

At nine that night, after his first full day as editor, he was wiped out but oddly contented. Earlier, he'd heard people calling "Good night" and "See you tomorrow," so when he opened the door of his office, he fully expected to find the place empty.

There was still one person there.

Rachel sat on a high stool in front of the slanted paste-up shelves. The harsh overhead light cast shadows as she moved bits of paper around on the blank space in front of her. He paused in his doorway to gaze at her.

She wore a long skirt, an overblouse with a vest, and boots. Her unruly hair was pulled back off her face with two gold barrettes, and she had ink smudges on both cheeks. Again, she struck him as someone who glowed with a visceral life force.

In the past few years he'd seen so much death. At the moment Rachel was the antidote. He wanted to feel some of that life force, wanted to be inside that life force, surrounded by the inner strength of that life force.

He wanted her, plain and simple. No denying it.

So what? he told himself. Being a grown-up meant not dwelling on the things you couldn't have. Being a grown-up was getting past disappointment and getting on with your life. He would continue to keep their relationship friendly, without ever approaching intimacy.

"Shouldn't you be home by now," he said lightly, "like everyone else?"

She looked up, distracted, from her work, then smiled at him. "Pretty soon."

"What are you working on?"

"I need to put together the Life and Arts section."

He could have left then. Probably should have left then. But he was an editor and needed to know everything he could about the paper.

He walked over to her and peered over her shoulder. "Isn't that Carmen's job?"

"I told her to go home—her older son has a cold.

Besides, I like this time alone here. Look, I've just come up with this—''

Leaning one hand on the table and the other on the back of her stool, Sam bent closer now, his face an inch from her neck. He could smell that rosewater again, and something minty. Gum, maybe. He inhaled Rachel's fragrances with appreciation as she directed his attention to a photo of a seal facing a toothless old man with a pointed nose, whiskers and very little chin. In profile, the two looked amazingly similar.

''I'm trying to come up with a caption,'' she said, ''and so far all I have is 'Who'd you say your father was?'''

He smiled, thought about it for a moment, then said, ''Looks like we used the same plastic surgeon.''

Angling her head, she smiled up at him. As she did, it seemed to register just how close he was, and the smile on her face faded. A look of vulnerability came into her expression, and her lips parted as though she wanted to say something.

Oh, that mouth, he thought, with its faint suggestion of lipstick. And, oh, those lips. Full and tempting. He couldn't take his eyes off those lips. That quickening in his bloodstream started again, as did the need to touch her mouth, to feel her skin against his own.

How long the moment lasted, he had no way of knowing. He did know that he'd firmly decided against intimacy with Rachel. Where was he heading with this?

She took the question out of his hands—for the moment, anyway—by averting her gaze from his and looking back down at her work. "Thanks," she said, her voice a little hoarse.

She felt it, too, and he knew it. This kind of chemistry was rarely one-sided. A pulse beat on the side of her neck. He wanted to place his mouth on that pulse.

Get out of here, he told himself. But not strongly enough. He pulled up a stool and sat next to her, watching as she penciled in the new caption under the photo.

"So, how'd the first day go?" she asked, not looking at him.

She was going to pretend that look hadn't happened. All right, he thought. He could handle that.

"Fine. I spent yesterday reading back issues. It's a good paper."

She seemed pleased. "I'm glad you think so."

And it will be even better, he thought, with a few well-thought-out changes. He wondered how she would react to any personnel shifts and could almost picture her circling the wagons around everyone on staff.

The thought made him smile. Shifting in his seat, increasing their distance even more, he leaned an elbow on the edge of the table. The sexual tension in the air was less overt now, which was good. He would be working with this woman for the next year and he wanted to keep their relationship collegial. "I know Win offered you the job of filling in for Charlie. Why'd you turn it down?"

Rachel hesitated briefly before answering. Her mind was still trying to settle down after that sudden, completely unexpected moment when she'd looked at Sam and knew, for the first time, that he wanted her. A whole bunch. The heady moment had made her spirits soar, but had scared her, too, so she'd found herself backing off.

She gazed at him. At his very blue eyes—darker than cornflowers, she decided—with those sad lines of fatigue radiating out from each corner. At his nicely shaped beard and mustache. At the well-worn tweed sport jacket and T-shirt. At the jeans he seemed to favor wearing all the time. Did he have several pairs? she wondered. Or did he wear one until it wore out?

"I think," she told him, "I'm one of those people who's better as a second-in-command."

He slanted her an amused yet cynical look. "Sure you're not short-changing yourself?"

"I don't think so. I know my strengths—put someone else in charge, and I'll make it work."

His gaze assessed her, then he nodded slowly. "Most people wouldn't admit that. You must be comfortable with yourself, with who you are."

Yes, she thought. And no.

"Mostly I am," she said aloud. "May I ask you a question?"

"Fire away."

"Why are you here? I mean, why did you give up reporting? Unless that's too personal."

"No, it's okay." A weary grimace twisted his face. "The short answer is that, after a while, it gets to you, and you either become less and less human or you shatter into pieces. I was getting close to one or the other, not sure which, so I thought a little time off was in order."

"Do you miss it?"

He shrugged. "Some. But it's not forever. I think a year is long enough to do the trick. But look—" he stood abruptly, cutting off further discussion "—it's time both of us called it a night."

"As soon as I put this section together."

"How about if we get to it early tomorrow?"

"But—"

"I mean it, Rachel." He offered a hand to help her off the stool. Without thinking, she placed her hand in his and stepped down.

Somehow she landed right up against him, chest against chest. Somehow he kept their hands joined, but at their sides. Somehow they were now face-to-face, and he was gazing at her with an expression that seemed close to anger.

"Damn," he said darkly. Letting go of her hands, he cupped her face in his broad palms. "This wasn't supposed to happen."

And he brought his mouth to hers.

4

HE'D MEANT IT to start out easily, a getting-to-know-you kind of meeting of mouths. But the moment their lips met, the moment he made contact with that soft flesh, his male reaction mechanism zoomed into overdrive. The hands that had been cupping her cheeks moved over her shoulders and around to her back, pressing her body closer to his. He felt her arms wind themselves around his waist, and he heard a small groan, but wasn't sure from which of them it had come.

He angled his head so he could deepen the kiss, sought her tongue with his, stroked her back. She seemed to melt into him. Her breasts felt as full and as welcome against his body as he'd fantasized they'd be. Even through his shirt and her own clothing, he could feel the hardened points of her nipples against his chest.

He wanted to kiss her silly. Kiss, hell. He wanted to lay her down on the long worktable in the center of the room, shove aside all the photos, pens and rulers, and take her right there. The impulse was very strong. Too strong. Out-of-line strong.

Breaking the kiss, he grabbed her shoulders and held her away from him so he could look at her face.

Her eyes were closed, but when she slowly raised her eyelids, as though awakening from a dream, their warm, brown depths telegraphed surprise, desire, confusion, all mingled with one another. Oh, how he wanted to kiss away the confusion.

But first...

He eased her back onto her stool, then pulled his own up and sat, facing her. He could barely catch his breath. Clenching his hands into fists, he rested them on his lap; they were shaking too hard for him to let her see.

Rachel was breathing hard too, gazing at him with a question in her eyes. The pulse at the base of her neck beat rapidly as she swallowed; he noted the slight flush in her cheeks, forced himself to ignore her full, luscious mouth. Heady intoxication filled every pore of his skin.

Sam was used to passionate, if brief, liaisons—a journalist always on the go didn't get a chance for anything more than that. And right now, what he knew was that he'd *really* like to begin one of those with Rachel. It would be passionate, for sure, and—if it turned out the way he suspected it would—a little longer than brief.

"You okay?" he asked, gulping for air.

She bit her bottom lip, heaved a huge sigh, then said, "I think so. Give me a minute." Then she shook her head. "Wow."

"Yeah." He considered her for a moment, then made up his mind to attack this directly. "Look, here's the thing. I want to take this a lot further..." He left it dangling.

She didn't react for a moment, then nodded slowly. "I sense a 'but' in there someplace."

"Yeah, well, there're a couple of problems. The first one is obvious—we work together, live on the same plot of land. It could get sticky. I'm your boss, you're my landlady. Two business relationships. You know the drill."

She continued to meet his gaze, waiting. "Yes."

He swallowed the sudden burst of saliva in his mouth and wished his heart would slow down because now he had to really lay it out for her. "Number two is even more important."

Everything that Sam was saying seemed to be coming from a distance. Rachel knew she was still in shock from the sudden kiss and the overwhelming physical and emotional reactions it had produced. She knew she was at the paper, that it was late at night, but aside from that, all kinds of wild, exciting notions whirled around in her brain.

She had proof now. He wanted her. *Really* wanted her. The way she wanted him, but had been trying not to admit. Even after that little scene when she'd offered to sew on his button, even then she'd assumed her attraction to him was one-sided. But she'd been completely, totally, one hundred percent wrong. How had she missed the signs?

"Number two?" she heard herself asking, amazed at how normal her voice sounded, how in control she appeared.

"The second problem." His eyes were blue lasers, piercing her with their intensity. "Cards-on-the-table time?"

Uh-oh. A sudden sense of dread flooded through her, but she nodded.

"I'm not the forever type, Rachel. If you're into daydreaming, promises and planning futures, I'm not your man. You need to accept that. And," he went on without smiling, "if you're thinking any of those I'll-agree-now-and-reform-him-later type thoughts, forget it."

His vehemence made Rachel bite back a nervous laugh. "My, my, you sure do know how to sweep a girl off her feet."

"I'm trying to be honest with you."

"Okay," she said slowly. "I can appreciate that."

He grabbed her hand, looked down at it, and ran a fingertip along the vein near her wrist. The heat shot right to her breasts and made the muscles between her thighs clench with instant need. Had she ever felt this way before? This on fire?

"But, dammit," Sam went on, his actions completely contradicting his previous words. "I really want you. You got under my skin the minute I saw you."

Rachel's mouth dropped open in amazed pleasure. "You're putting me on."

"No." His smile was brief and reluctant, then he stared down at her arm as he continued stroking it. "I wanted to crawl right into that bed with you and make you forget all about your damn back."

The pleased flush on her cheeks had to be a dead giveaway, she knew, but, oh, how welcome were the words he was saying. And how quickly her body reacted to his touch! "Honestly, I had no idea."

"How could you have missed it? I knew you wanted me."

She felt foolish now, so she covered it with a shrug. "Well, sure I did. I mean, foreign correspondent, a man of romance, mystery, used to living in exotic foreign lands. How could I resist?"

His expression was amused. "Romance? Mystery? Hardly." He shrugged. "Anyhow, I just wanted to get all this straight up front."

Hold it, she thought. There was something she was missing. "Do you always discuss sex this much before you actually, uh, get down to it?"

He let go of her hand, and his eyes narrowed. Had her question made him angry? It had certainly taken him by surprise. Then he smiled, mocking himself this time. "Not usually, no."

"Are you trying to warn me off?"

He seemed to consider it, then shook his head. "No."

"Then that means the offer is, shall we say, still on the table." She watched his reaction closely, still trying to figure him out, but on less-shaky ground now herself.

He seemed uncomfortable with her directness—even though he'd been nothing if not direct. "Yes, it is."

"So, what you're saying," Rachel went on, "is, you'd like us to have a no-strings, sex-only kind of thing."

After a brief pause he pursed his lips together and nodded. "Yeah, that's what I'm saying."

It sounded exciting, she had to admit. All kinds of pictures of lovemaking in unusual places flashed through her mind—naked bodies on mountain tops, in dark corners, in front of a fireplace. The chance to act out her fantasy life, her daydreams, with a man who couldn't have fit the bill more perfectly if she'd ordered him up from Central Casting.

But could she follow through? Could she indulge in raw, uninhibited sex with someone who had just informed her, in no uncertain terms, that he wouldn't be around forever? That there was no possibility of any future for the two of them?

Rachel was a throwback, horribly old-fashioned. She had never been casual about anything to do with sex. But just this once, she told herself, just this once she should consider going for it, anyway.

He didn't give her the chance.

"Look," he said briskly, his hands waving away the whole setup, "if you even have to think about it, it won't work."

"Huh?"

"The truth is," he went on, "as much as I want you, I also had a bad feeling about it from the beginning. Which was probably why I talked so much just now." He shrugged, stood, adjusted his jacket then yanked at his collar. "These things happen or they don't, and I think maybe this one's not supposed to."

Sam felt proud of himself. He was not being dictated to by his hormones, he was using his gray matter, being a grown-up, even being generous to another human being. As he'd thought, Rachel was the "forever" type. He'd gotten that about her right away, but had chosen to ignore it. If they'd embarked on this…thing, he would wind up breaking her heart. And, he told himself nobly, he really liked her too much to do that to her.

He smiled at her, but Rachel didn't smile back. Still seated, she continued to gaze at him, her expression mystified. "Sam?"

"Hmm?"

"Let me run this by you for just a moment, see if I got it straight. You did just invite me to bed?"

He nodded. "Yeah."

"And you did just take it back?"

"Yeah."

"Before I answered the invitation." It was not a question, and he knew it.

"Yeah. I made up our minds for us."

Her gaze narrowed, then she, too, rose from her stool. "Damned noble of you," she said, unconsciously echoing his earlier thought.

As he watched her turn and storm out of the room, he wondered why, coming from Rachel's mouth, it sounded so ludicrous.

SHE WAS ANGRY with him this morning. Very angry. Oh, boy, was she angry.

During a long, sleepless night, she'd been through all the emotional steps that preceded a good healthy rage—denial, self-doubt, disbelief, insecurity. By the time the sun had attempted to poke its head over the cloud-filled horizon, she was thoroughly irate at Sam Kovacs.

As she dressed, Rachel stomped around her small room, slamming drawers, yanking too hard on her hair as she attempted to tame it into something sleek. How dare he offer and retract? How dare he tantalize, then take away, like a waiter displaying a tray of rich French pastries, then yanking it out of reach?

She pulled on her rain boots with vehemence. And how dare he make up her mind for her? Who was he to her, that he could take the decision out of her hands? She'd been making her own decisions—and pretty darned good ones—for a lot of years. Even if she hadn't actually made up her mind about what to do, he'd removed any possibility of her finding out! It wasn't fair.

By the time she got to the paper, not only was she still miffed, but her hair was impossibly curly from the humid drizzle. What she wanted to do was barge into his office and let him have it. However, she told herself, if she was a scorned woman, she was also a responsible, in-charge associate editor who had a job to do. So even though something inside rebelled at the thought, she would put her emotions on hold, at least while she and Sam were at work.

With great effort, Rachel kept her attitude businesslike and efficient. Which was good, because Tuesday was the worst day of the *Hello*'s week. Terrible Tuesday, they called it, the day following Monster Monday. Everything had to be in and assembled by nine that night—no excuses, no delays—when the proofs were to be delivered to a nearby town to a printer who provided the same service for all the small papers in the area. If they missed that deadline, there would be no paper this week.

For several years Rachel had suggested they set up their own presses, but the owner had deemed it more cost-effective to continue as it was. And, indeed, in the eighty-one years of the *Ojai Hello*, they'd never missed an issue.

This morning, the staff had had to scramble because of a breaking story. The previous night there had been a home-invasion robbery that involved hostages and a car chase along the back roads near the river. The good news was that no one had been hurt, and the perps were in jail. The bad news was that the whole front page of the paper had to be scrapped, other pages reassembled.

By noon, the Classifieds were closed. The ads were all set, and last-minute changes to stories had been made. A panicked spell-check on a photo caption—in which it turned out that Bvdk was the actual spelling of someone's last name—resulted in Carmen's apology to Bonnie for having yelled.

Throughout the day, when Sam needed information about the town, Rachel supplied it. When he had a question or needed a fact checked, she answered him. But, by heaven, she did not bring him coffee, did not offer

any of the cookies she always baked on Monday night—
and this Monday, despite her bad temper and the cottage's barely adequate oven, had been no exception.
She'd left the plate of lemon bars next to the coffeepot.
If he wanted either, well, too bad. He was on his own.

At nine that night, Harris Clay, a local potter who did
odd jobs for the paper, drove off to the printer, his precious cargo in his van. Rachel left the premises shortly
thereafter, calling out a cheerful goodbye to everyone
still there, with the exception of Sam.

HE KNOCKED on Rachel's door at 10:00 p.m. He'd tried
to talk to her all day, but his efforts had been unsuc-
cessful, she'd either brushed him off or someone else
had been nearby. There was no excuse now, nor would
he accept one. He knocked again, louder this time.

Philomena barked from inside.

"Rachel? It's Sam."

"Shush, Phil. Go away, Sam."

"No." He waited.

After a moment he heard her belligerent response.
"What?"

"Will you open up?"

"I don't feel like it."

He sucked in a deep breath then expelled it. "We need
to talk, Rachel."

"Actually, we don't."

Now he felt his teeth grinding. He was trying to be
reasonable, but what he really wanted to do was smash

the damn door down, which was probably not in his best interests. Okay, he thought, he'd say what he had to say through two-and-a-half-inch wood. "Then listen, okay? Maybe I didn't handle things too well last night. I admit it. Satisfied?"

He waited for her response but none was forthcoming. Did she want him to say he was sorry? Well, he didn't feel sorry. Unsettled was what he felt, and in bad temper, although he wasn't exactly sure why. "Look, ignore *how* I said what I said, and listen to *what* I said. It won't work. Think about it, Rachel. You're too emotional. I mean, look what happened today. You were so pissed off at me, smoke was coming out of your nostrils."

"What an attractive image."

"I know you were trying to hide it, but, hell, you telegraph everything you're feeling, so it was impossible to miss." He plowed on with determination. "It's that kind of thing that makes it impossible to work together, to practically live together, to have an affair and keep it light."

"Who wants an affair?" she snapped. "I certainly don't."

"See? Smart-ass remarks. Hurt feelings. What if we got together, and it didn't work out? There would be wounded egos—I would get short-tempered, you would give me the silent treatment, or you would break into tears. What if I started dating someone else, and you saw me bring her home? Or the reverse—I saw you bring someone home? It can get sticky. Think about it."

No answer. But dammit, he was going to have his say—all of it. "Or what if we just had a fight and screamed at each other in front of everyone at the paper? See how it would interfere? It would be totally inappropriate behavior. I'm making sense, and you know it."

Scream? That's what Rachel wanted to do right this moment. At Sam. The stupid man kept talking about what could go wrong, she thought. But what if it went right? What if they got together and found they liked it? Apparently the concept of a working relationship was not within Sam's realm of possibilities. Still, she cut off her next sarcastic rejoinder and, hugging her robe tightly around herself, considered what he'd said.

Okay. He was at least partly correct, she had to admit. She was much too emotional, always had been. Yes, she'd tried to cover it all day, but she knew she'd acted like a child who'd had her toy taken away. And all they'd done was kiss. Truth was truth. Yes, there probably was no place in their relationship for an affair.

But, darn it, *she'd* wanted to be the one to say that, not him. And, yes, it hurt. She'd had a glimpse during that one wonderful kiss last night... A glimpse of a world she wanted to enter, a man she wanted to know and be with and make love with. It hurt that she couldn't have that world.

But she'd roast in hell before she'd let him know it.

"Rachel? Are you there?"

Leaning her head against the door, she felt close to tears. "Yes."

"Then can we start over? Maybe be friends?" When she didn't answer right away, he added, "You know we click at the paper. We get along. And—" He paused for a moment, then added, "And I... Dammit, I like you, Rachel. I mean, apart from any man/woman thing. So, what about it? Friends?"

Tears of frustration welled up in her eyes. Oh, great. Just what every woman wanted to hear from a man she was attracted to: can we be friends?

But she found herself softening nevertheless. His last words had had a different tone to them, a lessening of his customary detachment. He'd reached out, asked her to be his friend, and she had a feeling he didn't do that very often.

"All right," she said into the door. She would not open it. Not only was she wearing that same ratty chenille robe, but she was afraid if she did open it, she would do something stupid. Such as sob in his face. Or grab him, fling him down on the ground, and kiss him silly.

That thought made her smile. Sex on the grass. Talk about inappropriate behavior. Resting her cheek against the cool wood, she said tiredly, "Okay, we'll be friends. Now go away."

She heard him chuckle. "I'm gone. Good night, Rachel. See you in the morning."

HE WAS SETTLING IN, Sam thought on Thursday of the following week, feeling less like an alien from outer space. In the past several days Rachel had been a good guide around Ojai.

However, their friendship hadn't exactly blossomed. Too many undercurrents, he figured. Sex and friendship rarely mixed, yet he still lusted after her. That hadn't changed at all.

He glanced at his watch. Lunchtime. He was famished. Needing to wash his hands, he headed for the paper's unisex bathroom. On the way, he heard music coming from someone's radio, one of Brahms's string quartets. He smiled to himself, remembering sitting in a Baroque concert hall in Vienna and hearing the same piece, all the while keeping an eye on an important politician who'd run on a platform of "family values" but was there with his mistress. The minister thought he was incognito in his false beard and glasses. When Sam broke the story, the scandal reverberated for days, until something juicier pushed it out of the news and people's consciousness.

Those days were over, Sam thought, at least for the present. And funnily enough, he didn't really miss them. For the present, anyway. He'd needed this time away from the firing line, and his duties at the paper kept his brain functioning. How long it would be before the restlessness set in again, he had no way of knowing. Because it would. It always did.

When he pushed open the bathroom door, a strange sight greeted him: four stringed musical instruments and four people playing them, two of the paper's employees and two people he'd never seen before. All four looked up from their music stands and put down their bows at the same time.

"Oh, sorry," he said.

Ken Yamamoto, a part-time reporter currently perched on the closed commode, removed the violin from under his chin. "No, it's okay, Sam. Do you need us to leave?"

"Not really. I just want to wash my hands."

"We practice here at lunchtime every other Thursday," Ken told him. "The acoustics are perfect."

"No, no, go ahead. I'll use the sink in the kitchen."

Chuckling, he walked out, the music starting up again as he closed the door. Oddball bunch of people here, he thought, half of them eccentrics and the other half on their way to being so. He made a mental note to ask Rachel about the quartet, who, he had to admit, were not bad for amateurs. He wondered if they gave concerts. Maybe he and Rachel could go together.

Maybe not. Frowning, he stopped in the kitchen doorway. Maybe it was best if he and Rachel continued to keep their distance. The way they had this past weekend. Coming and going on their own, waving as they passed each other. He'd gone to the bookstore, had explored the surrounding hills in his new sport utility vehicle; she'd been gone most of the time with what, he assumed, was a busy social life.

She was a people person, he was a loner. Always had been. Which was why he never minded new assignments, why he was able to adjust so well to strange surroundings, strange beds, strange people in strange lands.

So, in this past week and a half, he and Rachel had kept things polite, not personal. It was better that way, he told himself as he poured dish lotion on his hands and scrubbed at the ink stains on his fingers.

FOR SEVERAL SECONDS after hanging up from her sister on Friday afternoon, Rachel stared at the phone. It hadn't been as bad as it could have been, but it hadn't been good, either. Rachel was so lost in contemplation—Leah was getting ready to quit school again—that Sam's voice startled her.

"Can I see you for a moment?" He leaned into her room, one hand on the door frame.

"Sure."

He turned on his heel, and she followed him out the door and into his office. "Close the door behind you," he directed, sitting in his desk chair, his expression serious.

"What?" She perched on the edge of the chair across from him, but did not lean back.

"First of all, I really appreciate everything you do here, and I want you to know that."

"Thank you." She waited, watched him shuffle a couple of papers.

He sat back in his chair, rested his elbows on the arms and steepled his fingers. "I've taken these past couple of weeks to evaluate, and I'm going to make a couple of changes.

"One of them," he went on, "has to do with Dan. I wanted you to know first. He has to go."

"Why?"

"Because he has the work habits of a second-grader."

She felt her posture stiffen. "He's a good writer."

"When the waves aren't calling. And when he turns his column in. Don't think I don't know that you keep covering for him."

Leaning forward, he folded his hands on his desk and gazed at her. "But you're too protective, Rachel. These past few weeks I've watched you. You cover for Dan. You rewrite Turnley's column ninety percent of the time. While Carmen's nursing her baby, you do paste-up. You sell ads, help the bookkeeper balance the books. You bake cookies every Monday night so everyone has something homemade to eat on Tuesdays. You stay here way after everyone else has left."

"So?" Why did she feel defensive about her actions? Why was he making her feel defensive? "Am I complaining?"

He continued to gaze at her, a puzzled frown between his brows. His voice was quiet when he asked, "How can you carry so much responsibility on your shoulders?"

"I like responsibility," she proclaimed. "I'm used to it."

"No wonder your back goes out. Being Atlas is damned exhausting work."

Hurt flooded her, but she covered it by snapping, "What I do is my business."

"And running this paper is mine.

"I'm giving Dan two weeks notice today," Sam said. "Ken Yamamoto is coming on full-time. He's grateful for the work, and he's damned good." He shrugged. "Sorry, but that's the way it is."

5

No washer. Your body goes hot, damp, then ice-chilled exhausting hot.

Chet flooded her, but she resisted it by pumping...

"What's in it my business...

"And ruining..."...

"I'm sorry, I can have with hotel another," Sam said then, "minutes to entering's full rise, they get in...

SATURDAY MORNING Rachel was not pleased to see Sam waiting at the end of the driveway as she walked toward her car, dressed in her weekend sweats—kelly-green this time—and balancing a loaded laundry basket on her hip. She would avoid him, she decided, but he stepped right in front of her, blocking her path.

"Use the washer and dryer in the house," he said easily.

She shook her head. "It's not part of the agreement."

"I'm making it part of the agreement." He offered a small smile. "It's all right if we both bend a little, Rachel. What do you say? I promise to lighten up if you will."

He reached for the basket, but she tugged it back. When he released his hold, the basket upended, and all the laundry tumbled out onto the driveway. They both bent at the same time and bumped heads.

"Sorry," they said in unison.

A giggle rose in Rachel's throat, which horrified her, so she distracted herself by rubbing her forehead. Why was this man in her face this morning, when all she wanted to do was to forget his very existence? And why was laughter—albeit nervous laughter—threatening to erupt out of her mouth? He seemed to have this crazy effect on her, and she resented him deeply for it.

"Did I hurt you?" Sam asked, concern on his face. "I'm sorry."

Biting her lip, she shook her head. "No, it's okay."

He helped her load the laundry back into the basket, and she didn't protest. Among the sheets and towels were a few articles of her underwear, and when he picked up a diaphanous pale-lilac bra, she actually groaned with embarrassment. It was her one weakness— silky, sheer, ultra-feminine lingerie.

He gazed appreciatively at the bra. "Nice." When she grabbed for it, he let it go, but added, "*Very* nice."

His smile should have made her furious; instead what she wanted to do—again—was to burst out laughing. This whole scene felt like something out of a movie. Totally unreal. Forcing herself to meet his gaze straight-on, she mocked, "Don't tell me—you're a cross-dresser."

He raised an appreciative eyebrow. "Not even close. But I do have a healthy masculine appreciation for sexy lingerie." He grinned wickedly. "Sue me."

Finally she just had to laugh, so she did. If a man was irresistible, who was she to resist? Her jumpiness evaporated, just like that, and Sam must have sensed it, because he loaded the rest of the laundry into the basket, picked it up, and jerked his head toward the house. "Come on. Let's do the wash."

She followed him through the back door onto the tiny

service porch just off the kitchen. She hadn't been inside here in the two weeks since she'd moved out, and she couldn't help wondering if he'd made any changes. It was his house now, she reminded herself. None of her business.

After she'd added soap and fiddled with the dials, she closed the top of the machine and turned to face him. She owed him an apology and, as she felt more self-possessed now, this was as good a time as any.

"Listen," she said, "about Dan. I was wrong."

"No, you were loyal. It's understandable."

"But you were right. I had no idea he'd be glad to be fired. Did you know he'd been thinking about quitting so he would have more time to surf? And that he wanted to write a novel? And that he was grateful you'd made up his mind for him?"

"No, I didn't know. But I'm not surprised. Most people who want to leave a job make it pretty obvious."

"Well, anyway, thank you for not saying 'told you so.'"

He shrugged, as though to say that wasn't his style, and she experienced a sudden urge to hug him for being so generous. She liked to hug people; it was her nature.

But she didn't give in to the urge. Instead she took a step back and rested a hip against the dryer door. "I'm going to miss Dan. He's part of the family."

"And family is real important to you, isn't it?"

"It's the most important thing in the world," Rachel answered with more raw emotion than she'd intended.

All her life she'd needed to belong, to be part of a

greater whole—a sense of family to wrap herself in for warmth. With the death of both parents, her genetic family was down to one sister, but she'd always had her neighbors and all her friends at the paper to fill in. Now Charlie was gone, and Dan was on his way out. Everything was changing.

Overwhelmed by another strong wave of emotion, again Rachel had to fight an urge to move toward Sam, this time to lay her head on his chest and let him hold her in those strong arms of his. What was the matter with her today? It was as though she were a child who craved comforting, a small, scared little girl seeking a safe haven.

It was all Sam's fault. From the moment Sam Kovacs had hit town, Rachel's entire world had turned upside down.

THE LAUNDRY WAS FOLDED and put away, her bed linens changed, bills paid. Her one small room had been scrubbed clean enough to pass a military inspection. Now that Saturday chores were completed, Rachel sat at the table, the fingers of one hand drumming a tattoo on the scarred wooden top, the other absentmindedly scratching Phil behind the ears, and wondered what to do with the rest of the day. Rachel was no fool; she was aware that the furious activity of the past few hours had been an attempt to work off her inner turmoil.

Consequently, about two in the afternoon—a sunny one, for a change, considering the unusual spring rain of the past week—Rachel wound up at Bart's Books.

There, she browsed in the cozy, eclectic Cookbooks section for a long while, imagining the tastes of all the exotic recipes she read about. After a while, she meandered over to Mysteries, to see if any new favorites had come in. As she always did, she began at the beginning of the alphabet, with A, which today was Aird, Catherine.

SAM WAS AN AVID READER. Politics, history, biography—anything to do with how the human race had managed to survive, given its warlike, destructive nature—fascinated him. So Bart's was like a dream come true. He'd opened a charge account and had spent part of last weekend there, wandering happily along the warren of pathways, an entire universe of books. Today he was back. He had compiled a stack of several tomes, which he left on the big front counter, before he decided it was time to hit Mysteries.

He began, as he usually did, at Z, which required getting down on his haunches and cocking his head at an odd angle so he could read the spine of each book. He was through the R's and back down on his haunches when he noticed it—a faint, familiar whiff of rosewater. At first he thought he might be imagining it, but it grew stronger, so he glanced to his left to find the source. He was eye level with the sight of scuffed tennis shoes and the elastic bottoms of Kelly-green sweatpants. A funny stirring of anticipation hit his midsection as his gaze made its way up the form.

It was Rachel, her hair loose around her face, her nose

buried in an old paperback, thoroughly engrossed as she flipped through the last pages of the book. He felt warmed by the sight of her, although he hadn't felt chilled before.

"You the type who has to know who did it first?" he said.

The sound of his voice made her jump. She looked down at him, said "Sam!" and dropped the book onto the floor at the same moment.

Scooping it up, he rose to a standing position and handed it to her. "I keep making you drop things, don't I?"

"It's just that I get so lost when I'm reading."

"Yeah, I know what you mean." He cocked a hip against an entire shelf of Ngaio Marsh and grinned at her.

This was an excellent opportunity to put into practice what he'd decided that morning—Rachel and he were going to be friends, whether she liked it or not. After their exchange that morning over her laundry, he already felt much more at ease with her and hoped the feeling was mutual. "Fancy meeting you here, or something like that."

Returning his smile, she said, "I can't seem to escape you, wherever I go."

At that moment a serious-looking young man with thick glasses came around the corner. As the stacks were built tall and close together, Rachel moved to make way for the new arrival, but space was tight. She tried to maneuver her way around Sam, which brought her into direct contact with him.

Frontal contact.

Her breasts brushed against his chest as she shifted to his other side, and with that one brief touch, his body went on all-points alert. In the space of a heartbeat, blood pooled in his loins. His hands itched for the touch of her skin, longed to cup those breasts, to bring those nipples to sharp, aching points with his thumbs. Surprise, surprise, he thought wryly. His treacherous body was doing it again, taking his brain in an entirely different direction than the one he'd ordered.

"Sorry," Rachel mumbled. "There's no room."

"Excuse us," Sam told the young man. He grabbed her hand and maneuvered them both out onto the open patio where reading tables were set up, and where one solitary orange tree grew toward the sky. Sam needed air, needed it desperately.

Damn. All that energy he'd invested in keeping their relationship platonic, then one whiff of rosewater, one brush of those generous breasts against his chest, and he was a goner, lost in Lust Land again. It hadn't been this strong, this potent, since he was a teenager.

Hell, since being a teenager, he hadn't reacted this way to a female without doing something about it. He'd been dealing with mature women who were too involved in their own careers to be interested in anything other than a teeth-rattling fling, women who, like him, were not looking for anything long-term or too emotionally intense.

Women who were the exact opposite of Rachel.

But this damned *wanting* that came with her presence was killing him. He dropped her hand, and shoved both of his into his back pockets. "I'm just about finished here. If I stay any longer, I'll buy out the place. How about you?"

"Yes, I guess I'm through for the day." She looked up at the sky, visible through the stacks of books all around them. "We're in for some more bad weather, I think."

"Doesn't bother me."

"Me neither. I love to walk in the rain."

Sam did, too—did some of his best thinking that way, had all his life. Very few women had that in common with him; something about their hair was the usual problem. He would love to walk in the rain with Rachel, could picture her thick mane curling, even frizzing around her face like a dark halo. However, he told himself, right now it was probably a smart idea to say goodbye.

Instead he found himself saying, "Can I interest you in an O-Hi Frostie?"

"How did you know?"

"What?"

"That I was just about to go there myself?"

"Great minds," he said. "Let's do it."

Sam's sudden appearance at the bookstore had thrown her, and Rachel hadn't had time to build up a defense. Instead, as she gazed into those electric-blue eyes with their sexy outward-radiating lines, she swore both her brain and her bones were melting. When they left Bart's, she took Sam up on his offer to add her three small paperbacks to the well-worn burlap bag he'd brought with him, which also contained all his newly purchased books.

As she walked along beside him, one part of her brain observed the passing weekenders on Ojai Avenue; another part struggled to come up with an attitude toward him, anything but this sense of powerlessness. By the time they'd each gotten a vanilla-chocolate swirl at the ancient O-Hi Frostie and had seated themselves at one of the picnic-type tables nearby, she felt much more self-possessed.

"So," she said with a bright smile, "how's it feeling, at the paper? All adjusted? Any other plans I should know about?"

Raising an eyebrow, he studied her for a moment. "We're going to talk shop, are we?"

"Not if you don't want to."

"Sure." He shrugged. "Why not? As a matter of fact, I'm going to call a meeting next week to discuss a few more changes I'd like to implement."

"What kinds of changes?" she asked lightly, even as the back of her neck prickled with apprehension. "If you don't mind my—" she began, but when she glanced over at Sam, he seemed to be gazing at her with a strange, intense look on his face, his eyes focused on her mouth. She was reminded of that day in her kitchen—move-in day—when she'd been unable to stop watching him eat. Now he was doing the same to her.

Had she smeared some ice cream on her nose? Did she look somehow awkward eating a cone? Nonsense, she decided. She'd been devouring O-Hi Frosties all her life, and considered herself an expert.

Still, she patted the napkin around her nose and mouth to make sure. That seemed to break Sam's concentration. He started on his own cone, but a puzzled frown remained between his brows.

"What?" she said.

"Huh?" He looked up at her, through her, distracted. "What kind of changes?"

He blinked a couple of times, then seemed to come back to earth. "Sorry," he said with a small chuckle, "I went away there. Anyhow, here's what I think...."

They moved easily into a discussion of his plans. Sam wanted to give the paper a face-lift. The town's demographics had changed—there were fewer starving artists, more upscale weekenders and young families escaping the city—which meant the newspaper had to be different, too. "Big bucks means big changes," he told her.

"Sad but true," Rachel agreed.

The *Ojai Hello* was the center of her life, and she wanted to make sure her own input and suggestions were heard. But throughout their discussion, that separate part of her mind that seemed to deal with all matters pertaining to Sam-the-object-of-desire—as opposed to Sam-the-tenant-and-editor—was busy exploring a whole other topic. Had that been hunger she'd seen in his eyes as she licked her cone? Not hunger for ice cream, but for her?

Was it possible, she wondered with a small thrill of excitement, that he was still attracted to her? Since that one kiss, nearly two weeks ago, Sam hadn't really given her any indication that he was. She'd assumed he was one of those people who could just turn off, the kind of man who decided not to feel something and then, simply, ceased to feel it. Sometimes she wished she were like that, then the volatile emotions she was so prone to might not get in her way.

"—so, I've been playing around with a seasonal Best Of Ojai issue," Sam was saying. "You know, Best Coffee, Best Bagels, Best Gallery, and so on."

Rachel brought both parts of her brain back to the discussion. "Best of," she repeated. "Really? I know it's a popular thing to do, but I don't care for it."

"Why?"

The adjacent table to theirs was suddenly invaded by a mother with three small children, all clamoring for different flavors. Rachel had to raise her voice slightly to be heard. "I don't know. I guess I just hate 'Best of' anything. Why can't there be room for everyone? Why does everything in modern society have to be a competition? It's such a darn—" she flung her hand in the air for emphasis "—testosterone view of the world. Having to be the best. It's why there are wars and starvation—people always having to be number one."

One side of his mouth quirked up. "If women ruled the world…?"

"Maybe."

"They'd become more like men. There's something magical about power and winning. Sorry, that's reality."

"You're probably right. I just—" With a shrug, she said, "I don't know."

"You just want everyone to be happy, Rachel. It's your nature. And," he added softly, "it's a nice nature."

The compliment embarrassed her, but it felt good, too. Sam's approval made her glow inside. He liked her.

But did he still *want* her? "What about your nature?" she asked.

"What do you mean?"

"You told me you can tell everything I'm feeling, and, yeah, I guess I am kind of transparent. But I have a hard time figuring you out. I can't...you know, get a grip on just who you are."

"What do you want to know?"

A child at the next table began to cry. Rachel checked to make sure the mother was handling it, which she was, then returned her attention to Sam. Resting an elbow on the table, she cupped her chin in her hand. "Tell me about you. If you were writing a piece on Sam Kovacs, what would it say?"

"Age thirty-eight, army brat," he said offhandedly. "Only child. Parents still living in Omaha. On my own since seventeen. Put myself through college, got a job on a paper, and haven't looked back since."

"Those are statistics. What else? Who are you, inside?"

He raised his eyes to the heavens. "Why is it that

every woman wants to know that about every man she meets?''

''And why is every man reluctant to answer it?''

He grinned. ''Testosterone again, probably.'' He tossed the rest of his cone into the garbage, and draped his arms across his chest. ''Okay, here's who I am, to the best of my ability. A reporter, first and foremost. An observer of what I see. It's like I have my own personal camera in my head, taking pictures all the time.'' He paused, obviously thinking. She liked him for making an effort.

''A loner,'' he went on. ''Mostly an outsider. Driven by wanderlust. Always sure there's something else, something better, different, in the next pasture, over the next barbed-wire fence.''

''So, you've never wanted to settle down?''

''Nope.''

''Never wanted to stay in one place and grow old along with the willow tree in your yard.''

''Never.''

Rachel's previously glowing, hope-filled mood took a decided downswing at his answer. If she'd begun this to discover if Sam was still attracted to her, she'd wound up with the answer to a whole other question.

''We really are totally different,'' she said, ''aren't we?''

''In some ways. Not in others. We both love our work, and books, and walks in the rain.'' His attitude was friendly, encouraging.

But not in the least bit suggestive or sexual. Dead end, she thought. Give it up.

"I guess so," Rachel said without enthusiasm.

Even though she smiled at him, Sam sensed a cooling at the table's atmosphere. Suddenly it seemed the two of them were out of conversation. Up to now they'd spoken easily, bantered some, batted words around like pinballs in a championship game. Now, there was silence.

As Rachel gazed at the passersby, he asked himself, with his customary detachment, Why? But he already knew the answer—he didn't fit her mold. More proof, he told himself, why he needed to avoid getting physically and romantically involved with her. Rachel needed permanence; he ran from it.

But, damn, he liked this woman, liked just plain being with her. And, yeah, he wanted her. Still. She'd gotten under his skin. He pulled at his T-shirt collar with two fingers; it felt tight all of a sudden.

A hell of a case of lust, that's what this was, he assured himself. The way she'd licked that cone, her tongue movements slow and deliberate, made him want to howl. He'd wanted to lick *her*. All over.

Lust. Sure, that's what it was. A small sexual spark, non-consummated, had become a driving need. At work, at home, on their off-days, that not-too-subtle undercurrent of unspoken attraction between them was always there, like annoying background music. It was hard to escape; hell, they were practically in each other's pockets twenty-four hours a day.

He needed to get away from her. Maybe he should check out one of the hang-out bars in a neighboring town sometime this week, meet someone who wanted physical relief with no strings. Get it taken care of.

Why, he wondered, didn't that sound real appealing?

Rachel glanced at her watch and again at the sky. "It's about to pour."

He followed her gaze. Fat gray clouds obliterated most of the previously blue sky, and the wind had picked up in the past few minutes. He rose and offered his hand. "I'll walk you home."

"Thanks, but it's not necessary. I'm going to a friend's house first. She's just a block away."

For some reason, he waited for her to invite him along. Which was stupid—why would she? And anyway, hadn't he just decided they needed some separation, to not be in each other's faces all the time?

"Okay," he said easily. "I'll leave your books by your door."

Right, he would head for his place, read about some land he'd never visited—not that there were many of those. Try to lose himself. All this getting to know Rachel more and more as a person, well, it was messing with his head.

THE STORM BROKE with a vengeance late that night and continued unabated into Tuesday. On Monster Monday, the *Hello*'s power went out twice, but the emergency generator kicked in both times. Even so, the computers weren't happy with the electricity interruption, and retrieving lost or contaminated files took up a lot of the staff's day.

Late Tuesday afternoon, they got word that a flood had closed Highway 33, the route Harris usually took to the printer's. He would have to go the long way, over back roads, so, to be safe, the paper needed to be ready an hour early, by eight. There was no problem at the printer's; they had all kinds of electrical backup.

At 6:00 p.m. they got word that even the long way was impassable due to mud slides. The El Niño-caused steady rainfall this past winter had been the worst in recorded history, and the surrounding mountains were soaked through and through. As if that weren't enough, Harris's van developed transmission trouble.

Rachel did everything she could think of—called the town's sole printer, who couldn't accommodate her, researched running off thousands of stapled copies of regular 8½-by-11 sheets of paper, but the graphics, the ads, the personals, the classifieds were all on different computer programs and would be impossible to reformat in time. For the first time in the history of the *Ojai Hello*, it seemed there would be no paper.

Rachel felt responsible for the failure. Somehow, someway, she should have found alternate printers, methods. Somehow, she should have made it happen. She tried to shrug off the feeling before she went into Sam's office to give him the bad news.

He was on the phone when she entered. "Yes, thanks, I appreciate it." He hung up, then said, "There's a fax coming in about now. A whole bunch of highway ordinance maps. We're going to need them.''

"I came here to tell you—"

"That the roads are closed. I know."

"But how did you—"

He indicated a radio on his desk. "I've been listening to the police reports. It's up to us."

"But—"

"Not to worry." He rose from his chair, grabbed the parka hanging on a coatrack, then came around his desk and grabbed Rachel's hand. "Come on. I've got a brand-new four-wheel drive, and I've been wanting to take that baby for a spin. This seems to be the moment."

LATER ON, she would wonder how on earth they made it. While they bumped and slid and swerved dangerously along and around the water-soaked terrain of the surrounding mountains, Rachel deciphered the maps, which indicated fire and logging roads. With the aid of a flashlight, she served as navigator to Sam's pilot. Trees, potholes, boulders—he conquered them all, in the mad dash to make sure the *Ojai Hello* got printed.

The wind screamed outside the vehicle. Their vision was nearly nonexistent even as the windshield wipers worked furiously. Rachel knew she should have been terrified, but for some absurd reason, she wasn't. She should have been more concerned about Sam's driving, but she wasn't. She felt confident he would get them there and confident in his abilities to get them there in one piece.

"Tell me again," Sam shouted over the roaring wind and rain, "why we don't print the paper on the premises."

"It's not cost-effective," she shouted back.

"Guess what? It just became cost-effective."

Rachel found that very funny and giggled, which set Sam to laughing, too.

"Sam?" she said a few minutes later, raising her voice to be heard over the wind. "We're supposed to turn left in about a quarter of a mile. There should be a path between two huge boulders!"

"Are you kidding? I can't tell if we're seeing boulders or skyscrapers. Can you?"

"No. But—"

Her sentence was cut short when the four-wheel drive dipped into a huge indentation. The wheels spun furiously for a few moments while Rachel held her breath. Then, as if by magic, they were out of there and moving on.

Windows rattled as a huge gust of wind hit them. "By the way," Rachel shouted, "do you have any experience driving in this kind of weather?"

"Nope. There were several times when I had to scramble pretty fast to dodge bullets, avoid land mines, crazed crowds and advancing armies. Does that count?"

"It's a start," she quipped.

After what seemed an eternity, they finally descended from the mountains onto a level road. Sam emitted a sigh of relief as they drove through the deserted, rain-soaked streets of Meiner's Oaks and spotted their destination. The printer's lights blazed in welcome.

They managed to unload all the page proofs, shielding them with their bodies even though they were wrapped in thick plastic for protection. Then he and Rachel were shown to a small bathroom with a wall heater, to dry off.

Hair, clothing, shoes, all were streaming wet, and as Sam looked at Rachel and she looked at him, they both broke up. If their laughter was a tension-easer and tinged with hysteria, so what? The sense of relief was enormous. She leaned against him, weak with laughter, and he put his arm around her shoulders, chuckling.

Then something changed. His arm tightened, the chortling stopped.

He wasn't sure who started it, only that his mouth found hers and he was kissing Rachel with a fierceness that he'd never felt before. It was as though they were celebrating a successful passage from near-death to life. Her hands reached under his wet clothing, and, with a loud groan, his reached under hers in his driving need to touch her, to make sure she was real. He cupped those large, luscious breasts in his hands. Perfect. Nirvana. Her nipples were hard and cold from the chill, but they heated up under his thumbs.

His head swam with a dizzying sensation. Tongues dueled, breaths mingled. His pulse throbbed with deep, intense need for her. What he wanted to do was to rip down his zipper and take her, right there, wanted to get as close to her as he could, to intermingle his body with hers so that he couldn't tell where he began and she ended.

A knock sounded on the bathroom door. It had the effect of a pail of cold water on two mating dogs. As Rachel pulled away from Sam's embrace, she backed up to a wall. Her hand flew to her mouth, an embarrassed flush blossoming on her cheeks.

"Rachel?" Sam reached a hand toward her, his breath coming out in quick, short gasps.

She busied herself adjusting her clothing, but wouldn't look at him.

"Hey," he said, "are you okay?"

The knock sounded again. "You two gettin' dry in there?" someone called from the other side of the door. "How about you lend a hand? I'm short two helpers."

Without making eye contact with Sam, Rachel turned and opened the door. "Glad to. Show me what to do," she told the printer and walked away.

6

"SO, WE GOT THE PAPER done and drove back at dawn," Rachel told Wanda. "We practically didn't talk the whole time. I think he was as uncomfortable as I was. He tried to make conversation, but I didn't. I think I was afraid of rejection. Good tea, by the way. What's in it this time?"

Rachel, slumped despondently in a chair, was visiting with her chiropractor friend between clients on Thursday. Wanda leaned against the treatment table, her long, gray-streaked braid draped over her shoulder. Both were drinking one of Wanda's herbal tea mixtures, hot, aromatic and soothing.

"Licorice root, chamomile and clover honey," Wanda answered. "Why were you afraid of rejection, Rach? He's made it pretty clear he wants you."

"Sure he does. And I want him. But then what? What if we make love and then Sam says to me, 'Hey, great, but remember, I'm not a forever-type guy, so don't expect anything'? He could, you know, probably would, and that's rejection. Call it by any name you want. I mean, I'm not asking for guarantees, but—"

"But you're asking for guarantees. Before you sleep with him, you want him to fall in love with you."

"Do I?" she asked, momentarily taken aback. Then she took another sip of tea and considered what her friend had just said. Finally she nodded. It was the truth. "Well, why not?"

Rachel sat straighter in her chair, suddenly indignant. "I mean, I'm a nice person, and a good cook, and we laugh a lot, and we both love the newspaper business and books. And he says—no, he more than says, he's *shown*—he's attracted to me, and I sure as heck am attracted to him. I mean, why shouldn't he fall in love with me?"

"No reason at all."

She slumped again in the chair. "Yeah, but I don't think Sam lets himself fall in love. Not from what he's told me about himself." After another sip of tea, she set the cup down and brooded. "I wish he were different. No, that's not true. I like him just as he is. Except, well, I wish he needed me more. He's so self-sufficient, so much of a loner. I want the kind of man who wants roots and a home. And kids. I want kids, Wanda."

Her friend smiled softly. "And you, of all people, should have them. You should also have that little day-care center you've talked about for years. You should be surrounded by children, Rachel. You are the original Mother Earth."

"Yeah, well, Mother Earth is getting a little dry from lack of watering, pardon my analogy."

On Wanda's chuckle, Rachel rose from the chair and began to pace the small office. "But, okay, say Sam isn't in love with me," she went on, thinking aloud, "and this is pure lust on his part. What's the matter with that? I keep saying I want him to be different. Maybe it's *me* who should be different—you know, more like Leah. She's so much more casual about men and sex, so much less intense about her love affairs. You know me, I'm always so *serious* when I'm in a relationship."

"That's how you're built," the chiropractor said simply. "Leah is Leah. You are your very own, original, perfect Rachel."

"You're just saying that because you're my friend."

"I'm saying it because it's the truth. And how's this for another truth? It's time to stop mothering Leah and tend to yourself."

"Ha. Easier said than done."

"So you keep saying. Shall I tell you one more truth? About Sam Kovacs?"

"What?"

"You're already in love with the man."

She stopped pacing and glared at Wanda. "I am not."

Wanda smiled knowingly. "All right, you're not."

"But maybe I am. Oh, God, what am I going to do?"

The intercom buzzed before her question could be answered. "That's my next appointment, Rach. Sorry. Does this have to be decided today?"

"No, of course not." She emitted a loud sigh. "Thanks for listening, Wanda."

The two friends hugged, then Rachel headed for the door. With her hand on the knob, she paused. "The Oak Tree Awards Ball is a week from Saturday," she said, referring to the yearly black-tie affair the *Hello* sponsored at the Ojai Valley Inn. "Under ordinary circumstances, I might say, casually, to Sam, 'Why don't we go together?' You know, editor, associate editor, representing the paper. But there's this other layer now, this push-pull, and I feel self-conscious." She turned to face her friend. "Tell me what to do. Give me one of your Zen pearls of wisdom."

Wanda smiled. "I have no answers, and you know that. But I would suggest a little patience."

"Me? Patient? Ha. You might as well ask Mount St. Helens to show a little restraint."

"All your fretting won't make anything better," her friend said calmly. "Let whatever is supposed to happen unfold in its own time. Stop trying to help it along."

"I'm not sure I know how to do that."

"This is as good a time as any to practice."

As HE STROLLED along the narrow pathway that led away from the valet parking, Sam fidgeted with his bow tie, wishing again he'd gone with his first instinct and bought a clip-on instead of letting the tux salesman talk him into the old-fashioned type you had to knot yourself. Not for the first time, he fussed with it and fussed with it, but it still had a way of tilting slightly, which seriously pissed him off.

He absolutely hated dressing for formal affairs. He'd done it often enough—awards banquets, society weddings, all the big political affairs a reporter had to attend—but he found the clothing and all the rituals confining.

Tonight, however, he had to be here. The *Ojai Hello* would be handing out Oak Tree Service Awards to the town's leading volunteers. And so, here he was at the Ojai Valley Inn, a posh hotel and golf resort tucked away in the mountainside outside of town.

He ducked under a vine-covered bower and entered the Shangri-la Pavilion, with its white-paneled walls and wide windows overlooking the whole valley. Sam waved to Turnley and his equally elderly wife, Mary Ellen, both of whom looked quite spiffy, then stopped off to chat with Carmen's husband Roberto about how much each disliked tuxedos, but "Boy, did the women look great." He shook a few hands, remembered more names than he would have thought, and kept glancing around the cupolaed ballroom, looking for Rachel. She would have arrived early, of course, because she'd been in charge of the whole event.

Nowhere in sight. He hadn't seen much of her, outside the paper, all week. Rachel had been avoiding him since that rainy Tuesday night when they'd practically done the deed on a bathroom floor. The aftereffect of which being that they still were not lovers and, it seemed, were no longer friends. Which put him in an even more piss-poor mood. He tugged once more at his bow tie.

He was heading for the bar, his favorite hangout at these types of functions, when he finally caught a glimpse of Rachel. It made him halt right there in the middle of the dance floor.

What in the world was she wearing—or almost wearing? A long gown with thin straps, revealing bare shoulders and gently rounded arms. The ankle-length dress dipped into a deep vee, exposing one hell of a lot of cleavage. Her high, spiked heels were the same tint as the dress, a burnt-orange color that brought out the vividness of her cheeks and made her brown eyes glow with warmth. Her lustrous dark curls were piled on top of her head.

Couples danced and twirled around him but he was scarcely aware of them. How had he failed to notice how long and graceful her neck was, how…statuesque—yes, that was the word—Rachel could be? Not only statuesque, but drop-dead sexy.

He had never seen her this way, not as drop-dead sexy. Sure, he'd thought of her with lust and longing, he'd approved of her full woman's body; hell, he'd wanted to possess it from day one. But he had never thought of her as a woman whom every other man in the vicinity with a still-functioning libido would pant after. And he didn't much care for the fact that, at the moment, that was exactly what seemed to be happening.

They were circling her now, on the far edge of the dance floor. Three of them. One old enough to be her father, one young enough to be her sister's age, and one perfectly age appropriate. He hated them all, with a gut fierceness that took him aback.

He continued on to the bar, got himself a stiff one, and watched through lowered lids. *Detach,* he told himself. *Study, assess, get it under control.* The way his body heat was building, he was in danger of going up to Rachel, grabbing her and transporting her to the cloakroom, where he would take her standing up against a rackful of other people's coats. Downright primitive was how he felt. He wanted to mark her as off limits, wanted there to be no doubt in the minds of any of the men surrounding her, or any that might surround her in the future, that she was his.

His?

He frowned. But she wasn't his. It had almost happened, came real close last week during the storm, but they'd been interrupted, and she'd pulled away, both physically and emotionally, since then. And so had he, truth be told. The incident had thrown him, confused him, so he'd swept it under the rug and lost himself in hard work.

No, Rachel wasn't his.

Why isn't she? asked an insistent inner voice.

As he sipped his Scotch, he tried to remember all the reasons, something about not fraternizing in the workplace, and about him sparing her a broken heart. It all sounded kind of weak at the moment, with blood pounding in his ears like drummers gearing up for a battle. The sound drowned out any logical thought.

Have another drink, he told himself. *Two's your limit.* Have the second, he thought, observe some more, remember that you're here on business, to hand out some damned awards.

THERE WERE five of them, all men, in Rachel's current circle of admirers, and each kept sneaking peeks at her revealing neckline. One stared blatantly. Old Hank Swofford, bless him, one of Turnley's cronies. Eighty-five and still eyeing the ladies. She enjoyed the attention, found herself basking in it, actually. It gave a woman a sense a power to hold men in sway.

Rachel always used the Oak Tree Awards Ball as her once-a-year excuse to go all out in the "dress to the nines" department. This year, as usual, she'd used her long-standing agreement with the paper to barter advertising space for a complete makeup job and hairdo. However, this year, she'd also splurged on a new gown. Its neckline was a lot more daring than she was used to. She usually didn't advertise; she had always somehow been uncomfortable announcing to the world that, yes, she'd been generously endowed by her Creator, and yes, she thought of herself as a desirable woman. But, hey, it was the truth, or at least it was tonight. She felt pretty and sexy, *voluptuous,* a good word, and not a bad thing to be. Judging by the men at hand for the past hour, her assessment of herself had been right on the money.

There was one man, however, who didn't seem inclined to join her circle of admirers. Sam stood at the bar, his back to it, his elbows on the counter, one knee bent, his foot resting on the brass foot rail.

And he watched her. Never took his eyes off her. He didn't come over, didn't join in. Just watched her, hawk-like, not a glimmer of a smile on his face. If his body language was casual, she knew from the aura of tension that emanated from him that he was feeling far from relaxed. Once in a while he reached for his drink, took a sip, then went back to watching her.

It was unnerving. Well, sort of. She also loved it, preened for him without looking at him, and felt absolutely wonderful. Why not show the stupid man what he was missing? A female could get real used to all this masculine attention, Rachel decided. Real used to it.

Even though there really was only one man's attention she craved.

DRINK TWO was now circulating through Sam's blood-stream. He considered ordering Drink Three. But that number, and several more, had spelled trouble two years ago in Afghanistan. While under the influence, he'd gotten into a fistfight, smashed up a car, come perilously close to losing it altogether. Which was why, he reminded himself, he was here, in Ojai, away from the world's battlegrounds, in a non-stressful situation.

Non-stressful, hell. Watching Rachel, he knew if his muscles, most especially in his groin area, got any more stressed, he'd very possibly make a fool of himself. And somehow, dressed in a tux, surrounded by elegance, he didn't think it was a fine idea for the new editor of the *Ojai Hello* to act like an ass.

Do something, he told himself. *Stop fantasizing. Act.*

Pushing away from the bar, he headed for the small cluster that had Rachel as its center. He could practically smell the pheromones from here, but he'd be damned if hers would be aimed at anyone other than him.

"They're playing our song," he said, nodding to the others while taking her hand.

"Excuse me?"

"Our dance. Shall we?"

Without waiting for a reply, he swept her onto the dance floor. As the band played something old and dreamy, he pulled Rachel close and moved with the rhythm. She didn't protest, and she fit perfectly. He hadn't seen the back of her dress, but as his hand smoothed over bare, silken skin, he realized that it was lower than the front.

There were several other couples on the dance floor, but Sam was only aware of Rachel. Her cheek rested lightly on his shoulder, and whatever perfume she wore tonight—French and expensive—did its job. Madness-inducing, he thought, then closed his eyes and gave in. He breathed in the scent of her, let his palms absorb the softness of her bare flesh, let the pulse of the music dictate his own movements, and made himself remember that they were in public and were dancing, not engaged in another, much more intimate activity. The thought made him groan.

Rachel lifted her head from his shoulder and looked at him. "What?"

He shook his head. "Nothing. By the way, hello."

"Hello," she returned softly.

"You look absolutely beautiful."

She lowered her gaze for a moment, then looked back up. A faint blush rose on her cheeks. "Thank you. So do you. I love the sight of a man in a tux."

"Why do you think that is?"

"Something to do with opposites. A starched shirt-front, bow tie just so, everything precise and in place. A proper, formal covering for...well, what's underneath."

"Our basic animal nature?"

"Something like that."

"Tuxes turn you on, do they?"

"Some tuxes," she said, noncommittally. "By the way, your tie is crooked."

"I know."

"I'll fix it later," she said, and returned her head to his shoulder.

But not before he observed what had happened to the front of her dress. Her nipples had hardened and now stood out in full, round peaks against the soft fabric. Either she wasn't wearing a bra or there was one built in to the gown. Who cared? he thought, as an unbidden shudder of desire overtook him. He loved her breasts. They were magnificent. The memory of how they'd felt in his hands on that rainy night made him groan.

Tightening his hold on her, his hand dipped lower on her back, his fingertips inching beneath the gown's fabric to caress the subtle curve of her hip. He heard her sigh. As he urged her closer, pressed her into him, he knew there was no way she could not be aware of his arousal. But she didn't pull away, didn't seem flustered or embarrassed, as she had that night in the rain.

Sam knew it then, for certain. On this night there would be no pulling back, by either of them.

IT HAD ALMOST been a duel between the two of them, Rachel thought with a slightly tipsy smile as Sam helped her on with her wrap. All evening, throughout dancing and dinner, during the awards ceremony, a silent battle had waged as to which of them could turn the other on the most, without appearing obvious, and without—she hoped—anyone else at the reception catching on.

Even now, near the cloakroom, while others gathered their coats and chatted, while smiles and handshakes and good-nights were going on all around them, the battle continued. Rachel chatted with Mary Ellen while Sam, behind her, lifted her heavy wool cloak onto her bare shoulders. She felt his warm breath on her ear, noted the way he brought his hands around to fasten the large hook at her throat, how his fingertips casually brushed her collarbone, sending small tremors all through her body.

She laughed at a comment that Harris Clay made as he went by, all the while experiencing a tingling, shivery sensation that traveled rapidly along her bloodstream and reached her nerve endings. My, but she felt daring tonight. Reckless. Backing up, ever so slightly, she moved her hips, ever so subtly, and was gratified to hear Sam's small moan of desire as her buttocks pressed briefly against his arousal.

"Better not," he whispered, his breath hot on her ear.

"Better not what?" she murmured innocently, smiling in secret delight as she moved her hips just a little more.

"Great dress, Rachel," Bonnie told her, giggling as the result of just a little too much champagne.

"So's yours," Rachel replied gaily, stepping away from Sam and hearing another nearly inaudible moan of disappointment.

Connie stumbled against her. "Oops, sorry, Rachel." She giggled, which set Bonnie off again. The twins had had too much to drink and were being escorted home by Carmen and her husband.

"Come on, you two," Carmen said sternly, "it's nighty-night time. Good night, Rachel. Good night, Sam."

"Good night, Sam," Connie said.

"Good night Rachel," Bonnie said.

"Sleep tight," they said in unison, then giggled again before being shushed and ushered out the door. At the last moment, Carmen turned her head and winked at Rachel before disappearing into the night.

Had the mutual lust between her and Sam been obvious, after all? Rachel wondered. Did she care?

When she turned to find him, their gazes met, locked

briefly. Silent, unmouthed messages passed back and forth with lightning speed. No one else existed, not the cloakroom attendant or the partygoers, not the rest of the town or the valley. They were alone on a planet, surrounded by a cocoon of longing, a sensation so strong it practically set up its own vibration in the universe. Tonight, it was hard to tell where reality began and ended; tonight she didn't care.

"Come on," Sam growled. She sensed the irritation and impatience in him as he put his arm around her shoulders, gripping hard, and led her along the winding pathway to the parking lot. After he'd handed his ticket to the valet, he asked her, "Did you bring your car?"

"No," she said. "I came early with Loretta. She left an hour ago."

"How were you planning to get home?"

She shrugged. "I knew someone would take me."

"Anyone in particular? I noticed several who would have offered."

He was jealous, she thought, and bit back a smile of joy. Jealous, possessive. Yes! "But," she purred, "it looks like it's you I've ended up with."

He pulled her closer. "Damn right," he muttered.

She thought briefly of Wanda's advice to let things unfold in their own time.

Oh, Wanda, she thought silently, they're unfolding, right about now.

When his car was brought around, Sam tipped the valet and walked her around to the passenger side. He opened the door, turned her so she faced him, and gripped her upper arms. Hard. He was squeezing her almost tight enough to hurt. In the soft lighting of the parking lot, he stared at her, and there was so much fiery intensity in his gaze, Rachel found herself gasping at the onslaught of sensations whipping through her. He wanted her, burned for her as she had burned for him, it seemed, for a lifetime. The jaw muscles beneath his beard clenched and unclenched, and his nostrils flared slightly. The pure animal beneath the formal dress was making itself known.

"Look," he said fiercely, "let's get this straight."

"Oh, no," she said with mock horror, "am I going to get another lecture about how you're not the forever type?"

"No, dammit. Right now, I have no idea what type I am, only that—" He frowned, shook his head, muttered a curse. "No more talking," he growled. "Get in."

The ride home took ten minutes, and they didn't speak the entire time. But Sam took her hand and placed it on his knee, then cursed under his breath every time he had to shift gears. Again, she smiled to herself. His impatience matched hers, but his was more obvious—and she reveled in it. Slowly, steadily, she moved her hand up his leg to the junction of his thighs. When she felt the solid, rock-hard bulge of his arousal, she gasped, glorying in the evidence of just how much he craved her. Feeling tipsy again, she used her fingernails to stroke him through his pants.

As she heard his breathing increase she thought, Tonight, she would be like Leah. Tonight, she would surrender to passion.

He roared into the driveway of the house, turned off the ignition, and pulled her to him. When his mouth possessed hers in a long, sensual kiss, nothing else existed but the surge of heat through her bloodstream, the sound of her own heart beating in her ears. Whatever jealousy Sam had been feeling, whatever desire had been building during their long evening of networking and socializing and dancing, it all seemed to have gathered into a large mass of almost-angry passion. His mouth possessed her mouth, his tongue sought hers, sweeping, plundering, putting his stamp on her, branding her with urgent, moist fire.

As she met his passion with her own, he angled his head for even closer contact, reaching under her cloak and massaging her bare back with broad, restless strokes. Then he pulled her straps off her shoulders, cupped her breasts in his hands, and groaned again. When his fingernails flicked at her nipples, now standing in stiff peaks and exquisitely sensitive to his touch, she almost screamed.

Rachel pulled away and wrapped her cloak tightly to her aching body.

"What?" Sam seemed startled, his breath coming out in swift, harsh gasps.

"Not in the car, Sam. Not when there are beds so

close by." Her own breathing was strained; she felt barely able to gather the oxygen her lungs required.

"You do know you're driving me crazy."

"Yes. I want to."

"You may regret you said that." He shoved open his door, then came around and yanked open hers. "Come on." Grabbing her hand, he headed for the back door.

"I take it we're going to your place," she quipped over the beating of her heart, "not mine?"

"You got it. I have all the protection we'll need next to my bed. Besides—" he turned to her as he put his key in the door "—your little cot in there won't hold us. Not with what I intend to do to you tonight."

7

PROTECTING RACHEL was the last logical, coherent thought Sam had. After that, all he was aware of was a desperate need to be inside her, a need that drove him with a ferocity that seemed to come from deep within. Grabbing her hand, and without turning on any lights, he steered her toward the bedroom, ripping off that pesky bow tie and discarding his formal tux jacket onto the dining room floor. By the time he reached his bedroom, the rest of his clothes had been removed. He was a man in a hurry. If he didn't join his and Rachel's bodies soon, if he couldn't bury himself inside her, couldn't sink deeply into the warm, wet mystery of her within the next few moments, he would explode. Or implode. Or whatever.

A full moon shone through the sheer gauze curtains over the windows; it was the only light available, but it was enough. Oh, yes, it was enough. Rachel stood at the foot of the bed, available for his viewing pleasure. She had dropped her cloak somewhere, and the straps and bodice of her gown were already at her waistline. She was revealed to him in all her stunning glory—that high, long neck, those creamy shoulders, and, most tantalizing of all, the pearly twin globes of her breasts. They were perfect, large and firm. He just had time to admire the way they stood tall and proud, begging to be touched as they rose and fell with every labored breath she took, before he groaned and moved quickly to stand in front of her. Cupping her breasts in his hands, he leaned over and took one of her pouting, puckered nipples into his mouth.

Rachel gasped, her back arched, and she clenched her fingers in his hair.

"Sorry," he murmured.

"For what?" It came out in a strangled whisper.

"Am I going too fast? I can't stop."

"Don't stop," she groaned. "Don't ever stop."

He knew she was on fire, knew she was feeling as wild, as out of control as he was. But he wanted to drive her even wilder. He brought her breasts close to each other and suckled first one nipple then the other while Rachel managed to work her dress down over her hips, so that it finally pooled around her ankles.

Tearing himself away so he could gaze at her, he felt like shouting hallelujah at the picture she presented. She was like a gift to a sailor too long at sea. Her hair had come undone and now flowed around her shoulders in soft curls. The rosiness of her skin was revealed in her waist-up nudity; below, a lace garter belt, see-through bikinis, thigh-high silk nylons completed the picture. With her shapely legs, her abundant, generous curves, there was nothing boyish about her body in the least. Rachel was old-fashioned pinup material.

He could gaze at her for an eternity, but his aching body had other ideas. Her full, sensuous mouth, her pouting breasts and, most of all, the mystery between her thighs beckoned him. He had to have her. Now.

He eased her onto the edge of the bed, so that her legs hung over the side. Groping in the drawer of the side table, he found the package of condoms.

"Sorry," he said again as he readied himself with shaking hands. "I have to get inside you."

"Stop talking," she said, spreading her legs to welcome him. He tore away her sheer bikini underpants, then used his hand to ascertain that, yes, she was as ready for him as he was for her; moisture coated his fingers as he inserted one, then one more. Arching back, Rachel lifted her legs so her toes gripped the edge of the bed. Then she reached for him and guided him into her.

"Oh-h-h-h...." The sound erupted from him in one long vowel as he felt her muscles and heat and womanly essence close around him, greeting him, sheathing him. For a moment, he stilled his movements, wanting to celebrate being inside her, to bask in the sense of being joined with Rachel in that mysterious, powerful, age-old ritual of mating. But he was too impatient, and so was she.

Capturing her hands, he raised them over her head and held them there. Then he began to ride her, hard, and she met his thrusts with her own. Their rhythms were a perfect match, slow and steady in the beginning, then gaining in momentum. They moved as though each were privy to the same silent music. Together they crescendoed at the crest of a high mountain. Their cries of exhilaration echoed into the night as they reached the summit and slid slowly down the other side.

WITH HER HEAD ON SAM'S shoulder and his arm clasping her to him, Rachel lay still, listening to the sounds of their breathing. In the past few moments their duet of desperate gasps for oxygen had slowly evolved into a quieter, steadier cadence. Wasn't it amazing, she asked herself drowsily, how the body recovered so quickly from such a terrific onslaught of physical sensation?

Especially that first time—their coupling had been fierce and desperate, definitely not for high-blood-pressure types.

But then, after that, she thought, laying her hand lightly on his chest and fingering the fine sheen of sweat there, there had been the second time. Even now, her pulse thrummed at the memory. Sam had insisted they take it more slowly that time, and he'd made love to her tenderly, exploring her body in a leisurely fashion, stroking her slowly and deliberately, arousing her to a fever pitch several times before allowing her release. He'd been in charge, and he'd feasted on her.

Maybe their next encounter—number three, she thought with a smile—it would be her turn to feast on him. And feast she would. If she had the strength now, she would nibble a little.

But who had strength? The man had thoroughly exhausted her. She sighed, utterly contented. What a marvelous, magical way to become exhausted. She felt peaceful, fulfilled, and not just physically. That second, slower time, he'd murmured in her ear steadily, telling her how much and for how long he'd been craving her, how perfect her body was. How, with her in his arms and in his bed, he felt he had died and gone to heaven.

Oh, but she loved the attention, loved being fussed over and made to feel totally special. She'd been starved for this—not just the sex, but the attention, too—forever. Or so it seemed. And now, here was Sam Kovacs, world-weary journalist, who had been sent to this small town fifteen miles inland from the California coastline, and set down in the middle of her life, to bring her the gift of love.

Because, of course, Wanda was right. Rachel was in love with Sam Kovacs. And if he wasn't yet in love with her, he soon would be. Tonight their joining had involved more than just bodies. Their minds and souls, too, had made love to each other. The act had not been purely physical; she might not have had the amount of experience Sam had, but she knew the difference.

Turning onto her side, she snuggled her back into the curve of his body. Murmuring something incoherent, he brought his arms around, cupped her breasts in his hands, inserted one knee between her legs and kissed the back of her neck.

"You okay?" he asked sleepily.

"Couldn't be better."

They were perfectly entwined now, a couple, and she dropped off to sleep with a smile on her face.

IT WAS PHIL'S BARKING that woke her. Full daylight flooded the room, and, for the moment, she was confused by her surroundings. Where was she? Oh, yes, she finally realized, she was in her old room in her house. The clock read 8:00 a.m. She glanced over her shoulder to see if Sam was awake, but he wasn't there. He'd left a note for her on the pillow. *Didn't want to wake you. Back soon. Sam.*

Phil's barking stopped. Rachel laid her head back on her pillow, wishing Sam were here with her, wanting a little morning-after snuggle with him. Maybe more than a snuggle. She missed him.

It was a strange feeling to be back in her old bed. Of course, it was no longer hers. At least temporarily, it was Sam's. Originally, it had been Mom and Dad's. Then Dad's alone. Even after he'd died, Rachel hadn't taken over the master bedroom right away. She'd remained in her own girlhood room for years afterward, only moving in here about ten years ago.

Turning over, she clutched the other pillow—Sam's pillow—to her face and inhaled deeply. It smelled faintly of Old Spice, she thought. A good, solid, untrendy brand of aftershave. Sam's aftershave. Her lover's aftershave. What part of his face did he need a razor for? she wondered. The cheeks down to the beard, she supposed, and under his neck. She couldn't wait to watch him shave.

Oh, she liked that beard of his, and that mustache. During their lovemaking, the soft bristles had added an extra dimension of sensation to her skin—all over, she thought with a blush. A nice little thrill swept through her body as she realized she was ready for more of his lovemaking, lots more. Encore, please.

Phil barked again, briefly, reminding Rachel that it was the dog's breakfast time. When she rose and grabbed a robe of Sam's from his closet, she couldn't help noticing how little clothing there was hanging there. Some jeans, sweaters, T-shirts, mostly old and well-used. A couple of sport jackets. Two dress shirts, three ties.

She wondered if he would mind if she explored the house a little. Not that she would pry, no looking in drawers, or any of that. Well, of course, he wouldn't mind, she told herself. Not after they'd explored each and every inch of each other the night before. Heck, how much more intimate could you get?

Funnily enough, the house was practically the same as she'd left it. No personal touches. One photo on the fireplace mantel of a group of casually dressed people, all looking exhausted but grinning gamely for the camera. In the background was overgrown jungle vegetation. Other reporters, Rachel assumed. They had the look.

There were a few books in one of the bookcases, but the rest of the shelf space was bare. There was a definite absence of knickknacks and plants. Nothing. The kitchen looked clean, but no different from when she'd lived there. Even the basket of dried flowers she'd left for him on the table as a housewarming present was still in place. The entire house was neat, but didn't seem lived in. What kind of a person rented a three-bedroom home and put no personal stamp on it?

Loner. Observer. The words Sam had used to describe himself came back to her. *Wanderlust. Outsider.* There was no evidence of anything even close to a nesting instinct here in the house, for sure. Was that just the way he was made? she wondered. Or was he afraid, afraid that if he put his mark on something, someone, he'd have to care? And maybe he didn't want to care.

Her upbeat, happy mood diminished as a chill of warning rippled through her and landed in her stomach. Uh-oh. Here she was, all lost in fantasy, using words such as love and planning future times together with Sam, when she'd been warned that she wasn't to do that. She was not to expect any kind of commitment from him.

It was too soon for that, she knew, but, oh, how she wanted one. Would he give her the chance? And if he didn't, how hard would she be willing to fight, to change his mind?

OUT OF BREATH, Sam reached the top of the hill and pushed his way through some low-hanging tree branches.

Shading his eyes with his hand, he peered out at the vista. Below him stretched a wide valley, lush and green from the recent rain, occasionally dotted with homes, a ribbon of a river running through its center.

It was a great view, he knew, and he wished he could appreciate it. But he hadn't come up here to check out the scenery. He'd come because he'd wanted—no, craved—the solitude. Despite all the previous night's aerobic activity, his eyes had snapped open at six this morning, followed by a strong impulse to go running. How he had the strength after last night's little workout, he didn't know.

All he'd known when he'd woken up next to Rachel was that he'd had to get away from her and the pull she exerted on him.

He'd already seen the sunrise. Now, shivering in the early morning chill of mid-April, he perched on the flat surface of a large boulder. His fingers felt around his fleece-lined jacket for a cigarette. He was down to five or six a day, which was an improvement. He found one, lit it and inhaled deeply. Rotating his shoulders, he wondered why he wasn't more sore. What his body felt was total satiation, as though relieved to have been released from its bondage of lust.

However, inside his head, it was a different story.

Discomfort, edginess—all kinds of feelings were stirring in there, feelings he didn't much care for. And, of course, they were all tied up with Rachel. He yanked at the collar of the jacket, even though it wasn't tight. What exactly was going on with him this morning? he asked himself. No clear answer presented itself.

Instead, snippets of memory kept popping up in his head, stuff he hadn't thought about for years. His mother with her high-pitched whine and smothering ways. His father's bursts of temper and long absences from home. Sam was like his dad, had always been like him. Even as a kid, he'd hated to be fussed over, resented rules and bedtimes and feeling tied down.

The apple didn't fall far from the tree, his mother had observed many a time. To this day, like his dad, Sam avoided intimacy, was downright allergic to the idea of depending on anyone, of needing anyone—because there was always a price to pay. So far, in his thirty-eight years, he'd managed to escape all that nonsense.

But last night, lying next to Rachel, her warm, full body wrapped around his, or his wrapped around hers, all kinds of ridiculous notions had surfaced. Homey, *domestic* notions, with Rachel always in the picture.

He took another drag on his cigarette. Yeah, last night had been special. He'd never felt so connected to a woman, both physically and otherwise, in his life. So? What did that mean? Did he have to do anything about it? What was expected of him?

Fear hit him with that last question. In fact, fear was the primary emotion this morning. Fear of the unknown. Hell, he had no experience with this relationship stuff, or very limited experience, anyway. He usually bedded a woman first, got to know her afterward. This time had been different. He and Rachel had gotten to know each other beforehand, making the sex act so much deeper somehow. He knew the woman now, knew her quirks, her passions, her vulnerabilities.

He dragged again on his cigarette, then let it drop and ground it out with his heel until there was no chance of starting a fire. Dammit, he *liked* Rachel. Liked her mind, admired her skills with people, worshiped her body. She was a real person to him now, so there was something more at stake.

Like it or not, he supposed he and Rachel were now involved. It would seep into their work situation, and she would start wanting more from him than he could give. When he left at the end of the year—which he would do—he would break her heart, and maybe even his own.

He stood, kicked at some pebbles, and watched them arch over the side of the mountain. Damn, why had he allowed it to get this far? Because there had been no choice, that was why. Their lovemaking last night had been inevitable from day one.

But that didn't mean anything else was inevitable. It wasn't as if the outcome was written anywhere. It didn't mean he couldn't call a halt to it right now.

But did he want to? That was the question.

BY THE TIME he returned to his place, he'd decided nothing and his mood was even darker. He didn't want to feel backed into a wall this way, trapped. But because he didn't know who was doing the trapping—himself or Rachel—he felt downright surly.

As he pulled into the driveway, he asked himself why in the world he had rented a three-bedroom house. It was way too big for one person. He remembered that he'd had some sort of stupid fantasy about setting up an office in one of the bedrooms and using the other as a guest room. For whom? What guests? Friends? He had no friends, not really. He had colleagues, other reporters who passed each other on the way to deadlines. Why had he rented this place?

When he opened the door to the bedroom, he half expected to see Rachel still sleeping in the bed. But, no, she was gone, although—what a surprise—she'd picked his tux up off the floor and had made the bed. Her perfume lingered in the air, and he resented it deeply.

He took a shower, stayed in there for a while, letting the hot water soothe him, hoping it would wash away the indecision. When he got out, he slipped into a pair of jeans and a clean T-shirt and was on the way to making coffee when a knock on the back door made him stiffen with apprehension. It was Rachel, had to be. Taking his time, he went through the kitchen and opened the door. Sure enough, she was there, wearing an Indian-print, ankle-length caftan. In her hand was a plate of cookies, on her face, a look of uncertainty.

Dammit, he thought, why did she have to be so giving? Why did she wear her heart on her sleeve? And why in hell did she have expectations of him? Because that's what she had, it was there in the softness of her clothing, there on her open face, in her morning-after offering of a gift from her kitchen.

Her smile was both hopeful and shy at the same time. "Good morning."

Afraid to speak, he just nodded. He was so pissed off he wanted to hit someone, but his anger wasn't directed at Rachel, and he knew it. It was at the situation he'd gotten himself into.

She held out the plate. "I brought you these. White-chocolate chip. I baked them yesterday morning."

"Thanks." He stepped aside to let her in. "I was just about to make coffee. Want some?"

"Sure." She floated past him and as she did, a whiff of that rosewater scent she wore assaulted him, making his body whip right into "need" gear, even as his head still raged.

"Where did you go?" she asked, setting the cookies on the table. "I woke up, and your side of the bed was empty."

Your side of the bed. God help him, she was already assigning them sleeping positions. Leaning against the kitchen door, he folded his arms across his chest. "I went for a run," he answered curtly. "I needed to think."

Her back was to him, and he saw her shoulders stiffen momentarily. Hell, he didn't even have to look at her face to know what was going through her mind—she didn't like what he said about needing to think. She was so easily readable, he thought with irritation. Rachel could have been the original model for a treatise on body language.

"I see," she said.

She turned around then, lowered herself onto a chair and faced him. But she said nothing. Her gaze was— what? Not hurt or fearful, as he'd expected it to be. No, she seemed to be waiting. To her credit, she did not ask him where he had gone for his run, or what he had thought about, or even what he had decided.

So, she was going in for subtlety this morning, waiting for him to start the conversational ball rolling.

The problem was, he had no idea what to say.

Being with you was so different, so exhilarating, that I'm terrified was what he could have said. *Scared spitless. I want you to go away so I don't have to deal with you. I want you to stay and let me hold you again. For the first time in a very long time, I have no idea how to handle something, no idea at all.*

Saying nothing, he strode over to the coffeemaker to prepare his morning dose of caffeine.

As morning-afters went, Rachel thought glumly, this one could be greatly improved upon. Sam was not hugging her, wasn't stroking her hair and murmuring about how special last night was. This morning-after was not filled with warmth or renewed ardor.

However, he wasn't telling her to get lost, either, which, judging by his attitude, was what he wanted to do. Sam was upset, that was plain to see. Angry, even. She had a feeling he didn't like displaying his temper, didn't like losing control. So, she made him lose control? Good. Chalk one up for her side.

What he was doing, she figured, was trying to barricade himself behind an invisible fence that said Do Not Enter. But he was too late. He'd already invited her in, which meant, at least, there was a chance.

Unless she was in one of her Pollyanna modes this morning. "It will all work out, just you wait and see," she'd used to tell Leah when things looked bleak and hopeless.

As she watched his back, observed the movement of his arm muscles and the nice way his jeans cupped his cute, small butt, she wondered if she'd played this wrong. Maybe she shouldn't have brought over the cookies, should have acted cooler. Showing up at her new lover's back door was not what Leah would have done; Leah would have made sure he had come to her first.

But, heck, weren't she and Sam beyond games? Shouldn't they be? Hadn't something life-altering happened to both of them last night?

Of course it had.

Then why wouldn't he admit it? In fact, why was the man, instead, in a totally foul mood? All of a sudden Rachel found herself growing indignant. Why did people have to play games? Why didn't people—no, why didn't *Sam*—rush to embrace love instead of run from it?

Patience. She could hear Wanda's voice in her ears. *Let it unfold as it's supposed to. Don't push it.*

She tried, really she did. But Wanda was Wanda and Rachel was Rachel, so it came out, anyway.

"Last night," she blurted while he made coffee, "was wonderful."

This is a test, she wanted to say. *This is only a test.*

He was in the middle of pouring water into the well of the coffeemaker when she spoke. He hesitated for a brief moment, then went on pouring. "Yeah," he said.

She waited for more, but none was forthcoming.

That was it? *Yeah?* Her indignation meter rose several notches; maybe some of his anger was infecting her. No, she told herself. Switch gears. When in doubt try humor.

"I meant the party, of course," she said lightly, "not what came afterward."

His head whipped around in surprise, then he got that she was joking, but didn't smile his appreciation of her humor. He went back to making coffee.

"What came afterward," Rachel forged on, "was sensational."

He froze again, glanced over his shoulder briefly, averted his gaze, turned back to the coffeemaker again, grunted. "Yes, but—"

He didn't finish his sentence, just shrugged.

Shrugged!

She waited. Lord, how she hated yes-buts. *Hated* them. They always meant someone was going to give an excuse to weasel out of something. And there was no way Sam was going to do that to her. No way she'd let him get away with it.

"I'm so glad we had that night, Sam," she found herself saying sweetly. "Because there won't be any more."

That got him. He nearly dropped the coffeepot, which was what he deserved, she thought. He gripped the handle tightly and whirled around to face her. "There won't?"

His face, which was usually carefully arranged in detached, listener mode, now registered shock, followed by relief, then regret, then relief again. More emotions, she was pretty sure, than he wanted to reveal to anyone.

"No," she said evenly, savoring the small moment of triumph. "You were right—it could be disruptive at the paper. And we're too different, our needs, I mean. We don't want the same things out of life, so why start something that will only end badly? But I sure did have a great time last night, Sam. Thanks."

As he continued to stare at her, the hand that was not clutching the coffeepot reached up and yanked at his T-shirt collar.

"Why do you always do that?" Rachel asked him.

"Do what?"

"Pull your shirt away from your neck, like you're choking. I mean, it's not as though you're always wearing a tie or anything."

He seemed thoroughly confused by her question. "Do I do that?"

"All the time. Why?"

"I have no idea."

"Oh." She nodded. Then, with all the dignity she could muster, she rose from the table. "I'd better get going. I have a ton of things to take care of. Thanks for the offer, but I don't think I'll have that coffee."

She removed a napkin from the ancient yellow-plastic napkin holder on the table, spread it out and placed the cookies on it.

"I'll take my plate back," she added. For some reason, that seemed to be an important thing to say.

Then, head held high, she walked out of the room.

8

MONDAYS WERE A BITCH.

Sam inhaled deeply on his tenth cigarette of the day. Especially here at the *Ojai Hello* and especially this Monday. As he leaned on the porch post, he watched a couple of neighborhood cats roll around in the dirt near the hyacinth bush. In the late afternoon light, the tall oak trees cast interesting shadows. He wished he could get his mind to drift with the warm breeze; instead, he replayed the day so far.

This was the paper's busiest week of the year—the annual Ojai Music Festival in Libbey Park was coming up this weekend. There were extra pages and articles, ads were up two hundred percent in honor of the tourists who were already pouring into town. On top of which, the new "Best Of" lists were ready to go, there were more modern graphics for the Life and Arts section, and the usual glitches to deal with when introducing any change in format. Since eight that morning, Sam had been up to his eyeballs in decision-making, putting out fires, issuing orders, and paperwork.

For which he was grateful, because up to this moment,

there hadn't been time to dwell on Rachel. However, she was now back in his head, stronger than ever.

For the past three weeks the two of them had passed each other on the run, and only spoken when work demanded it. At home, they came and went separately—they could have been living on opposite sides of town for all the contact they had. But that didn't mean she was out of his thoughts. Far from it.

He had to ask himself again. If she'd been the one to end it before it got sticky—for which, he assured himself, he was grateful she had—then why did he feel guilty? He never indulged in guilt, but it had been dogging him for three weeks.

When Rachel had walked out of the kitchen that Sunday morning after the ball, head held high, she'd almost had him fooled. But the next day at work, he'd seen traces of red in her eyes, puffy lids, which meant she'd cried. Women did that, got that emotional release, and Rachel was nothing if not an emotional woman.

Okay, so her whole exit had been pure bravado. So, she'd cried, so she was upset; hell, he was, too. Why was he guilty? At least she'd walked out in style, he told himself, inhaling again, and wishing the smoke would smother the feeling of disquiet in his gut. Yeah, she'd been the one to put the brakes on, and he was glad it had been her. Hell, he wasn't even sure he'd have had the strength.

He took one last puff, then threw the cigarette in the dirt and followed the smoke as it rose in the air. Three weeks. Shouldn't he be feeling less uncomfortable by now instead of more? He'd lost Rachel, not that he'd ever really had her.

Except on that one night. Even now his body reacted to the memory. Yeah, the two of them had been magical together, as he'd known they'd be. As she'd said, sensational. He muttered a curse. If only there was some way to keep those kinds of nights going without all the other complications. Complications that women always bought to affairs. Absentmindedly, he reached up and yanked at his shirt collar.

"ENOUGH!" Rachel declared about 5:00 p.m. She'd been at it for hours on end, and she had to get a minute to herself, *had* to, or she would scream at someone. But there were people everywhere—all the regular staffers, all the part-timers—scurrying, complaining, whining. It really was too much.

"I'm taking a break!" she shouted into the general chaos and headed for the front door.

"But, Rachel—" someone began.

"Five minutes, promise," she lied, intending to take at least fifteen as she dashed out the door.

She would *not* think of Sam, she told herself as she hurried along the two blocks to her destination. He had been the cause of way too much thought for weeks, when she was alone, anyway. It was a constant struggle to shake the sadness, the sense of deep disappointment that she'd been left with after she'd walked out on him. She'd spent way too many tears on him, too. And for what? For three weeks she'd waited for some sign from him that he regretted what had happened, even that he missed her.

But she got nothing from him except polite requests at work from a face that registered nothing. The man was a stone. She'd been stupid enough to fall in love with a man who was incapable of loving back.

Well, too bad, she told herself as she marched toward Ojai Avenue longing for an ice-cream cone. She had too much on her mind, too many other parts of her life that needed her attention, to dwell on Sam "Yes-but" Kovacs, and his surly behavior on what should have been a simply lovely morning-after.

When she finally returned to the paper, Rachel wasn't quite through with her cone. What sounded good right now, she thought, was another couple of minutes of peace and quiet on the back porch rocking chair. She swept past the front door and turned the corner. However, just as she was about to unlatch the back gate, she noticed the back porch was occupied. Sam stood there, in profile to her, one shoulder propped against the post, smoking a cigarette and staring out at nothing.

She stopped short, her heart suddenly cracking with pain at the sight of him. *Oh, Sam,* she wanted to say as emotion flooded through her, *It could have been so wonderful.* Tears filled her eyes, a lump formed in the back of her throat.

Stop, she ordered herself. *Just stop right now. Don't waste your time. Forget Mr. Stoneface.*

Taking a deep breath, she tried to shut down her emotions, but that was ludicrous. That would be like asking rabbits to stop procreating. All right, she would just have to tough it out, breeze right by him. Assuming the air of woman-on-a-mission, Rachel hurried up the path, heading for the back door.

Suddenly Sam shifted the angle of his head and his eyes locked on hers. There was a moment when neither of them spoke, but Rachel could have sworn the air was heavy with messages—what kind, she wasn't sure.

Then the side of Sam's mouth tilted up slightly. "O-Hi Frostie?"

She nodded. "What else?"

"Looks good."

"It is," she said, having to stop herself from automatically offering him a taste—it was what she did, it was who she was. But not today, not with Sam, anyway. No taste for him.

Licking her cone with great gusto, she walked up the two broad wooden steps that led to the back door. His hand on her shoulder stopped her from going in. "Wait," he said. "Take a minute more."

"I can't."

"I'm leaving, anyway."

That stopped her. "There's no need to do that."

"Sure?" Without spelling it out, he was asking for permission to remain in her presence, letting her know he was sensitive to the pain she must be in.

Oh, yeah? she thought. Two could play that game. Turning to face him, she said firmly, "Of course I'm sure. Stay. You need a break as much as I do."

"We've both been working our butts off today, haven't we?" he said easily. "Sit, why don't you?"

Something in his tone alerted her. Maybe he wanted to talk, she thought, a faint glimmer of hope erasing her previous antagonism. Maybe he wanted to go over what had happened three weeks ago. The two of them couldn't keep on like this, walking on eggshells, avoiding each other with a studiously polite air.

She lowered herself onto the dear old rocking chair, which squeaked as she eased it back and forth, and finished her cone. Ever the hopeful fool, she waited for him to start the conversation. Instead, Sam took up his vigil again, his back to her, staring out at nothing, smoking his cigarette. Stone face, stone back, she thought. What was going through his mind? she wondered as the two of them remained on the porch, not talking, the only sound the loud creaking of the rocking chair.

Don't give him the satisfaction, she thought. Stay cool. "I'm going in now, Sam," she muttered, irked by his silence. "I have a lot of work to do."

She yanked open the screen door, walked through, and let it slam loudly behind her.

SAM LOST TRACK OF TIME, but when he next looked up, the clock in his office said eleven-fifteen. And still Monday, by forty-five minutes. He'd been there sixteen hours. He wiped his hand across his face, rubbed his tired eyes. There was no sound from the other rooms, so he assumed he was alone. The issue was coming along well, but he'd probably be better off leaving the rest of it for tomorrow. He rose from his desk, grabbed his jacket and thought he'd check on the boards before turning out the lights.

As it turned out, he was not alone. Rachel—surprise, surprise—sat on a tall stool facing one of the slanted paste-up shelves that was covered with pieces of paper. One bright overhead light illuminated the work area, but Rachel wasn't aware of it. Her eyes were closed, and her chin rested on her chest, which rose and fell with a slow, even pace. She was fast asleep.

As he stared at her, the sight kicked up all that damn inner turmoil again. Yearning. Regret. Guilt—again. It was because he was so tired, he told himself. Had to watch those emotions that arose from exhaustion.

Obviously, Rachel was exhausted, too. What a trouper she was. And how hard—too hard—she worked. As he walked toward her, he had to fight the urge to wake her up by running a finger along that soft cheek of hers. Instead he shook her shoulder.

"Hey," he said quietly.

"Huh?" With a start, she sat up and looked around, as though getting her bearings. "Oh, God, I must have fallen asleep." She rubbed at her eyes, leaving a long smudge of mascara on the lower lids. "Sitting up! Can you believe it?"

"Sure can. Go on home," he said. "Save it until tomorrow."

Stifling a yawn, she bent her head to her work, avoiding his gaze. "No, no. It's okay. I have to do this."

He swept the proof away from her. "Rachel, you can't

keep pushing yourself like this. Go home. Get some sleep.''

Angling her head, she glared at him. ''Excuse me, you may be my immediate superior, but I don't remember appointing you my father.''

Her displeasure with him was obvious. ''Listen,'' he found himself saying, ''why don't we call a truce on this thing?'' *This thing*, he'd said. Bad choice of words. ''I mean, can we forget about…what happened between us and go back to being friends?''

His request seemed to take her aback. She studied his face for a moment, then said, ''I don't think so.''

''Oh.''

He was amazed at how badly that made him feel, and it must have shown on his face because her expression softened and she sighed, pushing a stray curl away from her face. She had such a nice face, he thought, such an open face. And beautiful warm brown eyes, beautiful even with that black stuff under them.

''Oh, Sam.'' She sighed. ''I… Sure, okay. I mean, we can try, I guess.''

It was tentative as hell, but it was something, he told himself as he perched on the stool beside her, his spirits lifting. ''Good. Take a minute. Talk to me.''

Rachel looked down at her work, seemed to come to some sort of decision, then faced him again. ''I was thinking about my sister,'' she began, then seemed to change her mind. ''No,'' she said with a wave of her hand, ''I won't bother you.''

She already did bother him, but that was a whole other

matter. "It's okay," he said encouragingly. "We're friends, right?"

She sat back on her stool, gazed at him for while, then offered an apologetic smile. "I worry about her. She goes from man to man, school to school, job to job. There's something basically unhappy about her, restless."

"So I've heard."

His comment seemed to make her shift gears into protective-mother-hen mode. "Not all the time," she said, her chin jutting out slightly. "You don't know her, but sometimes she can be so great, and committed, and right there, you know?"

He shrugged. "She's young."

"Twenty-two isn't young. At twenty-two I was holding down two jobs, paying bills, making sure she had hot dinners and healthy breakfasts, and did her homework." Wrinkling her nose, she shook her head. "I don't mean to sound like I'm complaining. I'm not. I did it all with love."

"Sure you did. But you were a mature twenty-two, and she's an immature twenty-two."

She didn't like hearing that one, he could tell, didn't like it at all. But to her credit, she thought it over for a moment, then nodded. "Yeah, I guess she is." She slumped in her chair. "And I'm so worried about her."

"You worry about a lot of people."

Her chuckle was self-mocking. "Yeah—it's the worry gene. I got it from my mother, lucky me. Leah managed to escape it completely.'' She offered another, brief smile.

She seemed so tired, Sam thought. And wound too tightly at the same time. He fought the urge to wrap her in his arms and ease her head down onto his shoulder. As her friend, offering comfort would be okay, wouldn't it?

Rachel made the decision for him by reaching for one of the proofs and pulling it toward her again. ''So, that's it. Back to the salt mines.''

Let her work, Sam thought, if that's what she wants to do. *Go home,* he told himself.

But, out loud, he found himself saying, ''Has your whole life always been about Leah?''

She shot him a glance that was both wary and defensive, so he held up his hands, palms out. ''I'm not criticizing, promise. I'm just curious. Did you ever want anything for yourself, something that had nothing to do with Leah?''

A frown formed between her eyebrows, then she raised her shoulders slightly. ''Well, sure. I want to finish college—I've been going to night school.'' When he nodded encouragingly, she went on. ''I want to get my master's so I can open a child-care center. I love kids.''

He smiled. ''I noticed. So I guess you won't be staying at the paper forever.''

''What I want is way in the future, Sam. I love it here, so I'll be around for a while longer.'' She rubbed tiredly at her eyes. ''Okay? Can I go back to work now?''

Not yet, he thought. One more thing. "Rachel, will I incur your wrath if I offer feedback? About Leah?"

Once again, her expression turned wary. "It's possible."

"Okay." He hopped off the stool. "As I said, it's none of my business."

She put her hand on his arm to stop him, then removed it quickly. "I changed my mind. I guess if I can introduce a topic, I can sit still and listen to what you have to say."

He sat down again, leaned an elbow on the table, and looked her straight in the eye. "Let her go."

"What do you mean?"

"Let her find her own way. Don't be there all the time to rescue her. Don't try to fix her or do anything about her."

Rachel's mouth dropped open, as though he'd just announced there was no such thing as air. "I know I need to stop mothering her, but let her go? Impossible. Has anyone ever been so important to you that their pain hurts you? That their pain feels like your own?"

Zap. Got him, he thought, got him good. Still, he made himself answer truthfully. "I guess not."

She nodded. "So, how can you tell me what to do? You haven't been there." She got off the stool and walked over to the long window that faced the dimly lit street beyond. "You have no idea," she said quietly, but he could hear her, could sense the intensity behind her words, "how it is to raise someone and see them troubled. You've been footloose your entire life, committed to nothing and no one, so how can you tell me what to do?''

He stared at her back, said nothing. There was nothing to say.

''It's always people without kids who are filled with advice for people with them, ever notice that? And furthermore—'' she turned around to face him head-on ''—let me tell you something. I'm on to you.'' She stood tall, her hands on her hips. ''You're very good at what you do. You're a fine reporter, and you've proved yourself a fine editor. You're even a good tenant. You ask nothing, you need nothing. A great guy. But the bottom line is—'' she pointed her finger at him ''—you can't really be my friend because you are absolutely terrified of caring for another person. I may worry too much, and I may even have screwed up raising my sister, but at least I was in there trying. At least I let myself love someone.''

With that, she headed out of the room.

Her words took him by surprise...and they stung. Without thinking, he followed her, countering, ''Hell, you seem to love everyone.'' He realized as soon as the words were out how resentful they sounded, but it was too late to recall them.

''Oh, really? Well,'' she said, whirling around as she reached the front door, ''that evens things out—doesn't it?—because you seem to love no one.'' She grabbed her purse from the nearby coatrack. ''I'm going home now. I'll be back at the crack of dawn.''

She walked out the door, letting it bang shut behind

her. Second time today, he thought, apropos of nothing, the woman had done that to him, slammed a door on him.

He felt as though someone had gut-punched him. Somehow he'd managed to botch it, had totally screwed up the whole thing. And, because everything she said was the truth—he had never loved anyone, was completely at a loss when it came to connecting with other human beings at a deeply personal level—he had no idea how to fix it.

EARLY THE NEXT MORNING, Terrible Tuesday, Rachel's eyes popped open, and immediately she thought about all she had to find time to do today at the paper. On top of which, she had no car. On Sunday afternoon, after she'd helped Turnley and his wife organize their garage sale, she'd been on her way to buying a baby shower gift when her eleven-year-old Civic had refused to start. She'd gotten Willie at the service station to give it a tow and to drop her home.

She'd walked to work and back yesterday, and the paper would take up all her time today. But tomorrow was the *Hello*'s light day, and she had so many errands to run. She needed a car. Maybe she would borrow one.

Or maybe she wouldn't. Her mouth opened in a huge yawn. Then another. Good Lord, she was tired. Recently there'd been so many nights of restless sleep or no sleep at all. She wished she could stay in bed this morning— actually sleep in. Take a day off work, the way normal people did.

Ha! Not show up? On a Tuesday? With all that needed to be done for this issue? She couldn't—wouldn't—do that to everyone else.

She shuffled into the bathroom, looked in the mirror. A real horror show greeted her—there were heavy, mascara-tinted bags under her eyes, and her hair stood out as though waiting to receive messages from outer space.

She opened the mirrored cabinet and checked inside for something to make her feel better. Aspirin was what she needed. Aspirin fixed everything. Why on earth had she bought the type with a childproof cap? she wondered as she struggled to get it off. There were no children in the house, hadn't been for years. Habit, she guessed.

Aha! She finally got the little arrows lined up and pushed upward with her thumb, a little too heartily. The cap went flying off into the air, arched, then fell at her feet. Muttering imprecations at drug companies, she bent to retrieve the white plastic cap, and felt that sudden, sharp, searing pain shoot across her lower back.

9

"ARE YOU SURE you don't know where she is?"

Sam stood at Loretta's desk, and the birdlike woman with the bright red hair sat back in her seat and sighed. "Sam, I swear it."

"She hasn't called?"

"I told you. No. And she's not answering her phone."

Muttering a curse, he strode into his office, picked up the phone and punched in Rachel's home number. After several rings, the machine picked up. He slammed down the receiver, sat, played with a pencil, and tried to think straight.

Terrible Tuesday. Ten o'clock. No Rachel. When he'd left at seven this morning, her car hadn't been in the driveway. Come to think of it, her car hadn't been in the driveway since Sunday evening.

He let go of the pencil and raked his fingers through his hair. Where was her car? Where was she? What in God's name was going on? Something must have happened to her, something pretty awful. No way she'd leave them this way, today of all days, unless it was a matter of life and death. That thought got him up from his chair in a hurry.

"I'll be back," he called to Loretta, dashing through the premises and out the front door.

He pulled into the driveway with tires squealing. Phil yapped when she saw him and pranced around him all the way to Rachel's door. It was unlocked.

"Rachel?" he called before he went in. "Are you here?"

No answer. Opening the door, he peered around the room. It was dark, the shades drawn.

"Rachel?" There was only one room in the whole place. Where the hell was she?

Just as images of her broken body lying on a deserted road flashed in front of his eyes, he heard a weak-sounding "Sam?" coming from the bathroom.

He was across the room in three strides, stood in the doorway and looked down. Rachel was lying on the floor, on her back, her knees bent. She wore a faded blue robe, but her legs and feet were bare. She fluttered a couple of fingers at him by way of greeting.

"Hi."

"What the hell are you doing down there?" he barked without thinking.

"Posture exercises?" she said, then winced.

"Of course, it's your back." Muttering a curse, he got down on his haunches. "Is it bad?"

"Not really. How is everything at the paper?"

"Have you been here all night?"

"Only since this morning. Will you get the issue out okay?"

"Rachel, forget the damned issue. Why didn't you

call for help?'' He smacked his forehead with the palm of his hand. ''I'm an idiot. You couldn't get to a phone, right?''

She managed a small smile. ''It would have been difficult. So, I stayed where I was, and then I fell asleep.'' Her voice cracked. ''Right here, can you believe it? Good thing this rug is here, huh?'' As though she just couldn't keep up the brave front anymore, her lower lip trembled. ''Oh, Sam,'' she said, her eyes filling.

Damn, he thought. He'd never been much good with women who cried, but at present, his relief that Rachel was alive mixed with the sight of her eyes tearing up was turning him inside out. ''Are you in a lot of pain?''

''Only when I try to move.''

''Should I call an ambulance?''

She shook her head slowly. ''No, really, it isn't that kind of thing.'' Her eyes brimmed over, a few teardrops made their way over her cheeks and onto the rug.

He lifted his hands and dropped them. ''What can I do? Tell me.''

''You can get me some ibuprofen from the medicine cabinet. Three of them.''

Grateful to be of some use, he got the pills, filled a glass with water, bent again, and lifted her head up to help her drink. When a little water dribbled out of the side of her mouth, she wiped at it with her hand, then made a disgusted face. ''Can't take me anywhere.''

''What else?'' Sam asked when she was done. ''Sure I shouldn't call an ambulance? Just how bad is it?''

''It's only a spasm, Sam. It looks worse than it is. I'll

be fine in a day or two. Look, why don't you get me some ice from the freezer, and I'll crawl back into bed.''

"I'll help." As he reached for her, she put up both hands, as if to fend him off.

"No."

"Rachel, you can't move, so how can you crawl?"

"I think it's loosened up a little."

"But—"

"Sam," she said, emphatically cutting him off. "I'm embarrassed, okay? I don't want you to see me. First, I have to turn over onto my side, then get up on my knees with my butt sticking up in the air—" she made another face of disgust "—and it looks awkward and I feel awkward and I don't want you watching." With another lightning-swift mood swing, her eyes filled again, and she wiped at them impatiently. "I'm sorry. I don't seem to be able to stop crying. I never do that. I mean, not this much."

Once again, Rachel's tears were difficult for him to cope with. He stood, backed into the doorway. "Look, you do what you have to do, I'll get the ice."

He kept his gaze averted while she made her way from the bathroom into her narrow bed. But he heard the steady sound of shuffling, the labored breathing as she exerted herself. It took her about ten minutes, and he parted the scalloped curtains that covered the small kitchen window and gazed out, unseeing, the whole time.

It was hard for Sam to do nothing. Real hard. But

Rachel's plea for privacy was something he understood very well, so he figured he needed to respect her wishes.

When she finally called, "Okay, all set," he turned around. She was in bed, the covers pulled up over her chest. She was panting, her face was pale; her entire countenance spelled sheer exhaustion.

He helped her settle the ice under her lower back. "Thanks," she said weakly. "Could you hand me the phone? Then get going."

"I can't leave you."

"Sure you can. It's Tuesday." Her lower lip quivered. "Tuesday! I have so much to do!" She broke down again. Obviously she had no more reserves of strength left. "How could my body have attacked me this way?" she sobbed. "Am I being punished?"

Sam stood over her bed, staring down at her, again feeling male helplessness in the presence of a woman's tears. But there was more to it, and he knew it. These were not just any woman's tears, and this was not just any woman. This was Rachel.

God, how frail she seemed today. He'd always seen her as capable—durable, even—and strong in the face of adversity. Emotional, sure, but never this fragile. Break-apart fragile.

"Why did this have to happen today of all days?" she wailed, her hands over her eyes. "Why couldn't it have waited one more day till the paper was out?" Turning her head so she faced the wall, she waved him away. "Please Sam, go away. I feel so weak and stupid. Leave, go away. I mean it."

"But—" Ignoring her words, he sat on the edge of the bed. Unfortunately that made the mattress dip and Rachel yelped with pain. He shot right back up to a standing position. "Sorry."

Sam was completely, totally, at a loss. Rachel felt awkward and stupid? He could match her, easily. He understood that his presence was distressing her, but how could he leave her? And why was she pushing him away so hard, dammit?

He grabbed a box of tissues from the bathroom and handed them to her. After plucking out several, she held them over her eyes. "Thanks," she said, sniffling.

"Have you eaten?"

"I'm not hungry. Go."

"Okay, okay, you've made your point."

He looked around the room for something, anything he could do for her. But nothing came to mind. He backed up toward the door. "Last chance. Do you need anything?"

She sniffled, dabbed at her eyes. He saw her swallow a couple of times, saw her make the effort to get control. "Maybe later tonight—" more sniffling "—when you come home, you can make sure Phil has some water."

"Sure."

He waited, but she said nothing more.

Reluctantly he opened the door. Bright sunshine greeted him, making him blink. He thought of one more thing.

As he turned to speak to Rachel again, a shaft of light seemed to dissect Rachel's dark little cave. "Shouldn't someone be with you? How about your friend, what's-her-name? The chiropractor?''

"I'll call her. Promise. Please, Sam. They need you at the paper. Go.''

"All right,'' he said. "I'll check on you later.''

He stepped out into the light, closing the door behind him. The moment he did, he could hear Rachel, from within, giving in to a real, old-fashioned weep-fest. It hit his gut, hard. She sounded as though her heart were breaking. Strangely enough, he swore he could feel her pain.

WITHOUT RACHEL, Terrible Tuesday was a living hell. Everyone seemed to develop some sort of insurmountable problem that only she could solve. But they had to make do with Sam. One after the other, they approached him.

"What shall I do about the—''

"How do you—''

"Where is the—''

He tried to be patient, but there were limits. After attempting to answer one more question, he finally snapped at Connie, "Hey, you guys do this every week. Work it out.''

"But there's all this new stuff!'' she wailed.

"Learn to adapt!''

Good God, he thought. He'd known Rachel was the hands-on type, but this was ridiculous. The staff, all of them, were way too dependent on her. It had to stop.

In early afternoon, Carmen came rushing into his office, the baby strapped to her chest and sleeping peacefully. "The Life and Arts section isn't done!" she said.

"So do it," he said absentmindedly, jotting down an idea for next week's issue.

"But Rachel always does it," the art director complained.

"Well, seems like she didn't get to it." He looked up from his pad. "Better get a move on. It's your department."

She stared at him for a moment, then the look of near-panic faded and acceptance took its place. She nodded slowly. "Yeah, it is. I guess I got out of the habit because Rachel was always there."

"Rachel is entirely too much 'always there.'" Frustrated, Sam dragged his hand through his hair. "What happens when she goes on vacation? She does take vacations, doesn't she?"

Carmen shrugged. The baby squirmed and she patted her back as she answered, "Oh, sure. Two weeks a year, like the rest of us."

"Whew. Good, I was starting to worry."

"But she never goes far—maybe to Santa Barbara for a weekend, like that. The rest of the time, she stays at home, calls in a couple of times a day."

"Figures," he muttered. "Well, look, Carmen, tell everyone to pretend Rachel's on vacation, on another planet, and there's not a phone in sight. Got it?"

Smiling, she gave him the thumbs-up sign. "Got it."

Sam called to check up on Rachel several times, and each time she told him she was doing fine, which he doubted. She would pepper him with questions about the issue. He would bark at her to take care of herself.

By midafternoon, he found himself unable to concentrate on his work because he was thinking about Rachel, picturing her in that narrow bed, writhing in pain. Again, he swore he even felt a twinge in his own back.

He picked up the phone and called her again. "What do you want for lunch?"

"Nothing," she grumbled.

"With or without mustard?"

PHIL GREETED HIM with a happy little dance. The dog's food dish was empty. Sam tapped quietly on the door of the cottage. No answer. Careful not to make any noise, he entered and tiptoed over to the bed.

The small lamp by her bed was turned on, but Rachel was asleep, her hands folded over her midsection. In the dim lamplight, he observed the tracks of dried tears running down her cheeks. The sight caused a funny kind of twisting in his heart that he had no name for. Then he turned off the lamp, quietly set his take-out package down on the table, found the dog food, and fed Phil.

After that, he raised the blinds so the room wouldn't seem so gloomy, and opened the window to let in some fresh air. Finally, with a sense that he'd been of some use, at last, he went over to the bed and shook Rachel gently. Her eyes fluttered open.

"Hi," he said.

"Why are you here?" she muttered, her lids heavy. "Who let in the light?"

"Elves, I guess."

"W-what are you doing?" she asked groggily as his hand groped under the covers for the no-longer-frozen ice pack. "Oh," she said.

At the kitchen alcove he filled the pack with fresh ice, then slid it once again under her lower back. As he smoothed down her covers, she followed his movements with a frown between her brows. "Did you take some sort of nursing course since I last saw you?"

Ignoring her grumpy sarcasm, he announced, "Lunchtime." He unwrapped his package, put one half of a thick turkey sandwich on a paper plate, brought a chair over next to Rachel's bed, and set the plate down on her stomach. "Eat," he ordered.

Seating himself on the chair, he bit into the other half of the sandwich. It tasted delicious, but then, he was ravenous, so he was in no position to judge its actual worthiness.

Rachel eyed her plate, then slanted him another suspicious look. "Why are you being so nice to me?"

"Because you need someone to be nice to you."

"Oh."

He took another mouthful of turkey sandwich, then noticed she wasn't touching her food. "Eat, I said."

"Don't want to."

She sounded petulant, like a little girl who was being forced to share her toys. Her entire attitude toward him, in fact, was so absurdly childish, it was almost funny, but he didn't think now would be a good time to laugh.

He studied her for a moment. "Tell me something,

you're always taking care of the whole world, but who takes care of you?''

''No one,'' she answered. ''And I don't need any taking care of now, thank you.''

''Oh, yeah?'' He picked up her sandwich, put it in her hand, closed her fingers around it. ''Listen to me,'' he said firmly. ''I'm here to make sure you get better, got it? No more back talk. Your job is to get well, so you can come back to the paper—the damn place is chaos without you.''

That got a small, pleased smile out of her. ''Is it?''

''Oh, I get it. You like being indispensable.''

Rachel shrugged, but had the grace to look shamefaced. Then, with a sigh, she took a bite. With her mouth full of rye bread and turkey breast, she said, ''Thanks.''

''You're welcome. By the way, I fed Phil.''

She swallowed. ''Did you add a little water to the dry food?''

''Why add water to the dry food?'' he asked. ''Then it's not dry.''

''She likes it that way.''

''I'll remember next time.''

They ate in companionable silence for the next few minutes. Then Rachel's face took on a look of sadness. ''I hate having to ruin your day like this.''

''Hey, Rachel…'' he said, ''it's okay, really. You're someone who thinks she can't depend on anyone else, so she does it herself.'' Without planning his next words, he found himself saying, ''I'm here now. Depend on me.'' He meant every word, knew it the moment he said it.

She stared at him, her eyes wide and anxious. "I'm not sure I know how."

"Fake it," he said with a grin. "Now eat."

IT WAS HARD TO ADJUST to Sam's presence in her small house. She felt uncomfortable with him fussing over her—not that fussing was the right word to use with Sam. He was just *there* and refused to leave. As she couldn't do much else, over the next couple of hours, Rachel observed him while he brought her a glass of water and more pills, while he went over some newspaper copy at the table, scratched Phil behind the ears, spoke on the phone with the paper's staff. He was mostly patient with them, but firm, insisting they make decisions and come up with solutions, and praising them when they did.

He was good at this. She'd known that from the first time he'd conducted a staff meeting all those weeks—nearly two months—ago. But now she understood just how different his managerial style was from hers. Sam was a delegator, which was what all good managers should be. Rachel didn't have the word delegate in her vocabulary.

Which was why it was so hard to lie in bed and let someone else do everything for her. But, this was Sam. And she was still in love with him.

It had never gone away, of course, in the weeks since that night they'd spent together. She'd tried to put it on the back burner, to ignore the truth, but it was there, staring her in the face. She loved him.

For his part, she figured Sam liked her a whole bunch. He even valued her. He was here nursing her back to health so she could return to work. But he didn't love her. It was depressing enough being down with a bad back. Being the only person in love in a two-person relationship was the pits.

Uh-oh, Rachel warned herself, watch that self-pity.

Sam had just fluffed up her pillows for her when she sighed, "Oh, Sam."

He straightened and looked at her. "What now?"

"Here you are being so good to me, and I yelled at you last night."

He shrugged. "I made you angry."

"I'm not a nice person."

Chuckling, he sat on the bedside chair. "Bull. You're about the nicest person I've ever met. Let up on yourself, okay?" He studied his thumb for a moment. "Listen, what you said about me—"

Quickly she cut him off. "I had no right,"

"Sure you did." Raising his head, he met her gaze directly. "Hell, if anybody has the right, you do." He didn't mention that one night they'd spent together, but both of them knew that was what he was referring to. "And you were on the nose. How can I comment on emotions I haven't experienced?"

And never would experience, Rachel thought silently.

"Leah's lucky to have you, Rachel," he went on ruefully. "You're fierce when it comes to protecting some-one you love—one more thing I've never experienced."

Oh, Sam, she thought sadly. What a waste....

He put an end to the conversation by slapping his hands on his knees and rising from the chair. "And now, I have to get back to the paper before I have a rebellion on my hands."

"Give my regards to them all. Tell them I miss them."

"You miss them? Hell, they're going nuts without you."

WANDA CAME OVER later that afternoon and gave her an acupressure massage. Rachel thought she'd seen the last of Sam for a while, but he surprised her by returning that night—after Harris had driven off to the printer's—and this time he brought flowers.

On Wednesday morning, he drove her to Wanda's office for another treatment.

On Wednesday evening, he entered her cottage, bearing a dish. He wore a large white chef's apron, spattered with all kinds of interesting colored spots.

"What's this?" Rachel asked him.

"Beef stew—I figured I knew how to cut up some onions and potatoes, and it doesn't take a brain surgeon to follow a recipe."

He sat next to her while she took a bite, chewed for a while, then chewed some more. It was tough and stringy. "What kind of meat did you buy?"

"I don't know. Meat. Is there a right kind?"

Without answering, she forced herself to swallow it down. "It's delicious," she lied.

He grabbed her fork and took a taste. "Actually," he said, "no, it isn't. But it's passable."

"Maybe next time," she said with a helpful smile, "a bay leaf, some salt?"

"I'm pretty sure there won't be a next time."

"Did I hurt your feelings?"

"Hardly." One side of his mouth quirked up. "Hey, some of us cook, some of us call take-out. I'm fine with it. Stop worrying about my feelings, Rachel, just get yourself well, so you can get back where you belong."

ON THURSDAY AFTERNOON, Sam sat on the same chair and watched Rachel as she slept. She looked so pretty, he thought. Peaceful. That lovely full mouth of hers was curved up slightly in a smile.

For three days he'd fed her pain pills and food, he'd changed the ice pack, he'd kept her company. And it showed. The tightness around her mouth and eyes was gone. For three days he'd taken care of her, something he'd never done for another human being in his life. For three days Rachel had needed him, still did.

As much, he was starting to realize, as he needed her.

Not need in the usual way—he was a self-sufficient guy, after all. But he needed her smile to make him feel warm inside. And he needed that look of concern for his feelings, the knowledge that someone else in the universe gave a damn about him.

And of course he needed that body of hers, and that

mouth. And that mind. She was like the perfect other half of him. Each of them filling the other's empty spaces.

Love.

The word came floating into his mind, fluttered a little and landed. He was in love.

Closing his eyes, Sam sat still and let the sensation wash over him. It started in his heart and spread upward, downward and outward at the same time. It was a warm, welcoming light, a creamlike substance, invading all parts of him, and going even deeper into the vast recesses of his soul. It washed him, completed him.

And didn't destroy him. Didn't bring up the need to run away, far, far away. Didn't strangle him, or make him yank at his collar because he felt as though there wasn't enough air in the room—Rachel had pointed out that little mannerism of his, and he'd since recognized it as something he'd been doing his whole life.

Love. A wonder he had never felt before, not even on a Tibetan mountain at sunrise, or at the sight of a glacier taller than any skyscraper in the world, filled him. This was a wonder not based on what his eyes could see, but on what his heart could feel and accept.

Son of a bitch, Sam thought with a smile. For the first time in his life he was in love.

When Rachel opened her eyes, the first sight she saw was Sam gazing at her, an odd, strange light in his eye. "Still here, huh?" she said.

"Still here."

"Why?"

He chuckled. "When are you going to stop asking me that?"

Embarrassed, Rachel wrinkled her nose. "Sorry. It's a habit."

Without speaking, Sam continued to gaze at her, then stroked her hair off her forehead. She followed his hand movement with her eyes. There was something...different about him, about his attitude. It was so much more accessible. It was the way she'd once told Wanda she wished Sam would be.

Then why, she wondered, did a small shiver of trepidation dart down her spine?

"How's the back?" he murmured.

"Just about all better."

"Could it tolerate a kiss?"

"Huh? You want to kiss my back?"

He grinned. "I'll start with your mouth."

"Oh." As the heat rose to her cheeks, she realized she felt nervous, on edge. "I'm...not sure."

"How about we find out?"

Without waiting for an answer, he leaned over, propped a hand on the sheet just above her head, and lowered his mouth to hers. His lips were warm. Nice. The soft bristles of his mustache tickled her, but in a soothing way. "Mmm," she found herself saying.

Lifting his head, he smiled at her. "You okay so far?"

Yes, she almost said. And not really. What she was was thoroughly disconcerted. Sam was being so sweet, so soft. So not Sam. His gentle concern made her feel like crying again. Swallowing the urge, she said cautiously, "Okay so far."

He surprised her by pushing aside one flap of her robe. "Beautiful," he murmured as he curved his hand around her breast. Leaning over, he kissed the nipple, then licked it, once.

"Oh!" Instant heat shot all through her, making her back arch sharply, which made her wince. "Ow."

He pulled back. "What?"

"I think not," she said, as arousal warred with back pain. She had not been prepared for the physical onslaught of sensation caused by one small flick of Sam's tongue. She had not expected to be the object of Sam's desire, ever again.

He, too, had had an immediate reaction, she could see it. It was there in the way his chest rose and fell, in the small poofs of his rapid breaths. "Damn," he said.

"See, the thing is," she explained, closing the flap of her robe over her naked breast, and willing her heart rate to return to normal, "when you touch me like that, I have to move. So I did. And it hurt. Not that I planned to move. It's kind of automatic. You know."

"I know."

"So we can only, uh, get physical, if I don't, well, move." She was blabbering away, knew it, and couldn't do a darn thing about it.

"I see," he said, nodding. A twinkle of amusement lit his eyes. "And I take it there is no way you *can't* move."

"Unless we put me in traction and let you have your

way with me.'' She bit her bottom lip. ''What do you think?''

''It's a thought.'' He nodded again. ''Maybe sometime in the future?''

''Hey, whatever turns you on.''

He smiled at her, and she smiled back. Then they both started to laugh. Yes, Rachel thought. This was better. It felt so good to release her tension. And it didn't even make her back hurt.

When the laughter died down, Sam seemed to study her for a moment, a look of bemused concentration on his face. Almost distractedly, he brushed the back of his hand over her cheek, ran his thumb along her bottom lip, then took one of her hands and placed it in his.

''Know what?'' he said.

''What?''

''I love you.''

She froze at the words. It was as though every working part of her body ceased to function.

''It came to me,'' he said, ''while you were sleeping. Yeah, I love you.'' He squeezed her hand, smiled. ''I should be scared to death, but I'm not. I love you.''

Stunned nearly speechless, she managed to say, ''Oh.''

''And, in case you're interested, I've never said those words to another woman in my entire life.'' He raised one eyebrow. ''How do you like that?''

He waited for her reply, but she couldn't seem to come up with one.

''Rachel?''

Obviously, Sam expected some sort of answer from her, some reaction, something. But she felt unable to say or do anything. What was the matter with her? Sam had just said the words she'd wanted to hear from him for weeks. He had declared his love for her.

And what she felt in return was sheer terror.

10

"No, you don't," she finally blurted.

Her protest made Sam jerk his head back in surprise. Still holding Rachel's hand in his, he looked at her, unsure just what she meant.

"Yeah," he said with a nod, "I do."

"No, you can't love me." She pulled her hand from his, averted her gaze and fussed with the edge of the blanket. "You're confusing love with, I don't know—lust. Or need. You can't run the paper without me, so you mistake that for love." She spoke rapidly and was, he thought, verging on hysteria.

He made himself speak slowly, calmly. "Rachel, that's not what I'm doing."

"Yes, well, you think you love me," she went thundering on, "but this isn't me. This weak, weepy woman lying here in bed isn't me, not who I am. I know that helpless kind of thing turns a lot of men on, but I'm not really like that. You'll be sorry. So if you think you love me, well, this isn't really me—"

"Rachel—" he tried to interrupt, but it seemed nothing was going to staunch the flow of words.

"And besides, you're a wanderer." She raised her

head, glared at him accusingly. "You told me all about yourself, remember? You'll be leaving, not staying in Ojai, and Ojai is my home, and I have absolutely no intention of getting used to your presence because one day you'll be gone, and then what will I do?"

With that last run-on sentence, she seemed to run out of steam. Tears welled in those large brown eyes, and he knew she was spooked, that something in his declaration had deeply unnerved her.

This was not great news. Sam felt disappointed. And hurt. After he admitted his feelings for her to himself, then to her, he'd assumed it would be smooth sailing. He'd thought she'd open her arms with welcome and tell him how much she returned his love. Then they would talk about it, make some plans.

But Rachel had scrapped that little scenario by not thinking or reacting logically in the least.

In these past few days she'd shown him a hell of a lot of facets to her personality, sides to her that he'd only been vaguely aware of before. He knew now that, with all her superwoman skills, she could also be fragile, bad-tempered. And irrational.

He still loved her. In spite of—no, because of—all that she was.

Instinctively, Sam sensed that something important hung in the balance. But he had to tread carefully here. As he'd admitted, he wasn't real comfortable with man-woman relationship matters, and he wasn't sure just what the next move should be.

Leaning in, he rested his elbows on his knees and met

her teary gaze. "Why are you fighting me so hard, Rachel?"

Again, she looked away, played with the blanket, rolling the edges between her fingers. "I'm...not sure," she confessed in a small voice.

He stared at her for a moment more, then reached for her hand, but she batted it away before he could take it.

"No—go away," she said petulantly, the little girl once again. "I don't want you here."

She must have realized how unkind that sounded because she covered her mouth with her hand as if to take the words back. After blinking a few times, sniffling some more, she finally said in a ragged breath, "I'm so sorry, Sam, I don't want to hurt you. But please, just go."

Helpless, he stared at her for several long minutes while his insides took in the situation and protested loudly. She might not have meant to hurt him, but she'd done a damn good job of it. He hated the sensation—he felt way too exposed.

Reaching for his reporter persona, he sought refuge by counseling himself to pull back, detach, observe. But he was only partially successful; he could tell by the way he rose unsteadily to his feet, by the way his hands fisted at his sides and his jaw tightened, that his detachment was a joke. If hurt often led to anger, this moment was turning into a classic example.

"For the last three days," he said, careful to keep his voice from shaking, "you've been telling me to leave. Know what? That line is starting to get old."

He would have said more, but he no longer trusted himself to speak. Instead, he turned his back on her and walked out the door.

If Rachel had felt a rising panic before when Sam had declared himself, now, as he turned his back on her, it blossomed into a full oxygen-robbing, heart-thumping anxiety attack. As the door closed behind him, she wanted to call after him, to tell him to come back, but she wasn't sure what she would say. And she couldn't seem to catch her breath. Oh, God. What had she done? Why had she done it? Why was she letting Sam go?

Folding her hands over her rapidly beating heart, she pressed hard and told herself to calm down, to let the air in and the carbon dioxide out. But her head was doing a dance in outer space, and it was hard to concentrate on much of anything other than feeling thoroughly, totally, awful. And thoroughly, totally, scared to death.

The ringing of the phone pierced the small room. Could it be him? He'd had time to get to the house. Yes! she thought. Sam! They would talk it over. She would make it all right. Somehow, she would fix it.

The phone was lying next to her pillow, and she spoke breathlessly into the receiver. "Hi."

"Hi, Rach."

Her spirits plummeted back to earth. It was not Sam. It was Leah, and she sounded down. Rachel sniffled a couple of times, then said, "Where are you calling from?"

"Up near Santa Cruz. Do you have a cold?"

"It's my back."

"Oh." She thought Leah had accepted the non sequitur until she went on, tentatively, "Are you, I mean, is everything okay?"

No, she wanted to say. *Everything is not okay. My world just fell apart.*

But she didn't usually unload her pain on her baby sister. Besides, at the moment, Leah sounded pretty lost herself. "Everything's fine," she made herself reply. "What's going on with you?"

"I'm kind of bummed."

Rachel swallowed down the last of her tears. "So I hear. Talk to me."

"Oh, Rach, I just feel so…lost. I don't know what to do with myself."

Several suggestions—the usual ones—gathered at the tip of Rachel's tongue. Get a job, try some counseling, go back to school, finish something. Anything. Just see it through.

But this time the words remained unspoken. Instead she said, "That's tough, Leah."

There was a pause in the conversation. Leah, she knew, was waiting for her to continue. But Rachel was, uncharacteristically, not jumping in to soothe, to nurture. She had little left to give.

Leah broke the silence. "Maybe I should come back home? If Sam's still in the house, maybe you and I can rent a little place together?"

As she'd done all their lives together, Rachel felt all of her sister's uncertainty, plugged right into the fear at the heart of Leah's soul. Quietly she said, "So I can take care of you?"

"Hey," Leah replied with a sad little laugh, "you've been doing it ever since I can remember."

Rachel's heart felt as though it were breaking. Suddenly Leah was six again with a skinned knee, eleven and not chosen to play the princess in the school pageant. "Oh, sweetie," she sighed, "I'm sorry. I'm sorry you feel so lost, and I love you with all my heart. But I don't think coming back here is the best thing for you to do."

"You don't?"

"No. You're a terrific person, with a good brain and a gift. You're an artist, Leah—you need to explore that, maybe back in school, maybe somewhere else." Surprised at how the words seem to take on a life of their own, she went on. "But I can't do it for you, and I can't fix you when you're broken. As much as I wish I could, I can't. You'll have to do that yourself."

"Oh." Leah sounded baffled, lost.

Again, Rachel's instinct was to tell her to forget what she'd just said, to come on home, she would make it all better. But Sam's words of advice echoed in her head at the same time. *Let her go,* he'd said. *Let her find her own way.*

And those words—stronger, better words, for both Leah and her—drowned out her automatic, instinctual response.

"You can always count on my loving you, sweetie," she said with feeling. "I hope you know that."

After a moment, and a deep sigh, Leah said, "Yeah, I do. And I love you, too, Rach. Take care of yourself."

Take care of yourself. The sentence reverberated in Rachel's head long after Leah and she had said their goodbyes. She had a feeling it might be a while until she heard from her baby sister again. But she also knew she'd given that baby sister the best gift she could— independence.

Take care of yourself, Leah had told her. Rachel had been doing that all her life.

Except for the past three days, when Sam had been here. He'd nursed her, bullied her, fed her, taken care of her, the way she had taken care of so many others—her father, her sister, her co-workers, her friends—all her life.

At first she'd hated Sam hovering over her, making her do things she didn't want to do just so she'd get better. But, then, she'd gotten to kind of like it, even though she hadn't told him so. Maybe being taken care of once in a while wasn't the worst thing in the world. Especially if Sam was the one taking care of her.

Through the open window she heard the sound of a car engine revving up, then driving away.

Sam.

Her hand flew to her heart. Oh, God. What had she done? The panic started up again. Sam had told her he loved her, and she'd pushed him away. For the first time in his life, Sam had declared his love for a woman— her!—and she'd thrown it back in his face, as though it were an unwanted gift. As though it were garbage.

Clasping her hands together, she brought them up to her mouth. Leah's phone call had interrupted her train of thought, but she was back on the tracks now, and the ride was a bumpy one. Why had she done that to Sam? What on earth had possessed her?

Insecurity, that was what had possessed her. She'd reacted because—admit it—she'd felt totally, horribly inadequate. Not up to snuff, not her familiar, capable self. Lying in bed in that awful robe, completely devoid of her usual high spirits and strength. Having to lean on someone else. Weeping and moaning and complaining, like some elderly patient in a nursing home. She didn't like herself this way—didn't know how to just *be*.

So, then, here was the truth at last: she had always played the role of caregiver and was unsure of herself in any other capacity. What an awful realization.

She lowered her clasped hands onto her lap. Still, even at her worst, Sam had said he loved her. Of course, he hadn't seen her at her *worst* worst, crawling on the floor with her more-than-generous rear end sticking up in the air.

But he liked her rear end. That night they'd spent together, he'd extolled the virtues of her body—every part of it—declaring her full figure perfect, sexy, utterly desirable. She'd believed him, too, that night, knew he'd meant every word of it.

But today, had he meant what he'd said? Did he really, honestly, actually, *love* her? The answer clicked into place with the speed and certainty of an arrow hitting a bull's-eye. Of course he did. Sam had never lied to her about his feelings, not once since she'd known him. As she had on that lovely night they'd spent together, she recognized truth when she heard it.

Sam loved her.

Rachel's hands relaxed, the tension in the rest of her body eased up a little more. Finally, now that she was alone and her head was clearer, she allowed the fact to register in its entirety. And it was a downright thrilling fact. Sam loved her.

But even the sweet, heady sensation of being loved was short-lived as a new realization rose to consciousness. Sam! She'd driven him away, made him angry, hurt him! She had to fix that, right away.

Grabbing the phone, she punched in his number, let it ring several times. Through the open window, she could hear the ringing phone in the big house. It sounded like a tolling bell. Gone…gone…gone.

She threw her bedcovers off and was about to leap out of bed when she remembered Wanda's words of caution. She was to get up and down slowly, always bend from the knees, stretch often, and she would not wind up a cripple with a bad back the rest of her life.

She had to take care of her back, she told herself firmly, so she could fully enjoy being with Sam.

Slowly, she rose from the bed, stretched with care, then removed her robe, found her brace, and strapped it on. As she slipped a loose caftan over her head, she mused on Sam's whereabouts.

It was still early yet, not quite five, he'd be at the paper. She'd go to the paper.

Grabbing her purse, Rachel walked slowly to the door, opened it, looked out. Her yard was in full bloom, everything was green and smelled sweet. The late afternoon sun was an hour or so away from disappearing over the Wincellers' rooftop. The air was wonderful; after three days in that small room, it felt so good to inhale fresh, clean air.

Phil wandered out of her doghouse, stretching after a nap, then walked up to her, tail wagging. Supporting herself with her knees, as Wanda had demonstrated, Rachel bent to scratch behind the animal's ears.

"Sam?" she called out, just in case, then glanced at the driveway. His car wasn't there.

But neither was hers. Then she remembered. Her car was still in the shop.

Should she walk to the paper? Could she? Sure, Rachel, terrific move. Make your back worse than it is already. *Learn to take it slowly*, Wanda had said. Rachel didn't know the meaning of the word.

Sudden despair made her sink down onto the grass at the base of her large oak tree. She lay flat, looking up at the sky through the branches. It was powder-blue and clear, a few white wisps drifted by. A perfect day in May.

She had no car, she thought sadly. And no way to reach Sam. And, after so much time spent in bed, not a lot of strength, either. However, she did have tears. Oh, yes, those she had in abundance, enough to make up for years and years of being strong.

WHEN SAM PULLED INTO the driveway and saw Rachel lying on the grass, he was out of his car and at her side before he allowed the fear to catch up with him. "Rachel?" he cried, falling to his knees beside her. "Why are you lying here like this?"

Her eyes popped open, and she stared at him as though he were a ghost. Then he watched as her face lit up with the sweetest, most welcoming smile he'd ever seen on any face. "Sam," she said, opening her arms, "you came back."

Without thinking, he put his arm under her shoulders and gathered her up close to him. Suddenly he halted. "Your back. Am I hurting you?"

"No, it's okay." Draping one arm around his neck, Rachel pulled his mouth toward hers.

He obliged, kissing her lips tenderly. A feeling welled in him that was overpowering. A sense of homecoming, of belonging, that he'd never known but must have been missing all his life.

He moved his mouth over her soft cheek, along the smooth column of her neck. "Rachel," he murmured into her hair, smelling the rosewater, female essence of her. He would never get enough of her smell. Never.

Leaning back against the thick tree trunk, he settled her between his legs, on her side, her head lying on his chest. "Rachel."

"Sam," she murmured back, wiggling into his embrace.

Phil joined them, licking both their hands until Sam told her to get lost. The dog, not one to take rejection personally, lay down next to them, her face on her paws, watching them.

After a while, Sam found his voice. "Changed your mind, did you?"

"About what?" she said innocently.

Smiling, he cupped her chin and forced her to look at him. "I'm on to you, you know."

"Are you?"

He nodded. "Yep. See, I've been running my whole life, but so have you. It just came out differently, that's all. If you've been terrified of being dependent on someone else, so have I. If I've never let myself need anyone before, neither have you. Inside, we're the same."

"Interesting concept," she said.

"You need me, admit it."

"Do I?"

"Say it."

"Okay, I need you," she said grumpily, but he knew she wasn't serious. "Happy now?"

"And you love me. Say it."

"Oh, Sam, of course I love you. You knew that already, didn't you?"

"Yes, but I needed to hear it."

"I love you." She moved up his body slightly, snuggled her face into his neck.

A hummingbird buzzed by, sighted the feeder that hung on a branch, and dived for it, its tiny wings flapping. Out on the street, a car with a muffler problem drove by, blasting loud music into the quiet neighborhood. Then it faded into the distance.

They stayed under the tree for a while longer, watching the fading sun cast longer and longer shadows over the backyard. Rachel felt contented, totally relaxed, totally at peace, for the first time since—

She had to think. Oh, yes, since before she'd set eyes on Sam Kovacs, world-weary foreign correspondent. He'd roared into town and wreaked havoc with her daily existence from the start, that was for sure.

But right this minute there was nothing wrong in the entire universe. Her sister was off on her own journey, and Rachel was being held by the man she loved. For once, thank you, the timing was working out quite nicely.

The sound of Sam's chuckle made her angle her head to gaze up at him. "What?"

"This whole scene—" his hand gesture took in the yard, the tree, the day "—you and me here together, it's amazing."

"I was just thinking the same thing."

"Before, when you threw me out of your place—"

"Oh, Sam, I'm sorry—"

He put a finger over her mouth to stop her apology. "Quiet. I'm talking."

"Yes, dear," she said with mock servitude.

"Anyway, I hopped into the car, ready to take a strip off a back road. I got about a mile out of town, then turned right around, because I wasn't going to allow you to get off that easily. I was determined to come back and tear a strip off you. I was pissed."

"Yes," she said meekly. "I imagine you were."

Smiling, he waved a hand in the air. "But that's history. No more anger. Gone—" he snapped his fingers "—like that. So here's what I think. We both need to do some changing, right? I figure I'll help you stop wearing yourself out giving to everybody else, if you'll help me stop running so hard."

Rachel sighed contentedly. "Sounds like a plan."

Sam's expression turned serious, his blue-eyed gaze on hers intense with emotion. "As far as my leaving, I'm open. We could travel, or stay right here. You could go back to school, get that degree, open your day-care center. Maybe when Charlie comes back, I'll do some free-lance articles, or write a book. As long as you and I are together, I don't know and don't care."

"And all because you love me?" she said, her voice filled with wonder.

"Yes. And because you love me."

Again, she emitted a contented sigh. She felt delicious. "That I do."

"I'm through running, Rachel," Sam said somberly as he traced the outline of her mouth with the pad of his thumb. "No more living out of suitcases, no more staying detached and alone. I want to— No, I *need* to be with you. You are my home."

A lump formed in the back of her throat. "Oh, Sam, you're going to make me cry again."

"Then I'll change the subject. I can't stand it when you cry." Bending his head to hers, he kissed her again, slowly, while he stroked his fingers along her collarbone, curved his hand over a breast, then stopped at her rib cage. "What the hell—? Oh, you're wearing that brace thing again."

She felt her face reddening. "I was looking for you. I was coming to find you."

He expelled a long, loud, relieved breath. "Thank God."

As they shared another kiss, a deeper one this time, Rachel perceived the change in Sam's body. It would have been difficult to ignore under normal circumstances, but practically lying on top of him as she was, she couldn't miss it. Mmm. She was tempted. Her back felt fine, but she knew she shouldn't be pushing it.

As though he'd read her mind, Sam raised his head from the kiss, touched his forehead to hers. "Damn, I want you. Real bad."

"Tomorrow. I promise I'll be better tomorrow."

He took a moment to get himself together, then said, "Okay. Back to bed for you. Alone, I regret to say."

"Excuse me. Was that an order?"

"Yes."

"Don't get used to it, buster. You got that?"

He chuckled. "Trust me, I got it. Come on."

After helping her to her feet, he put his arm around her and steered her toward his place. Rachel jerked her thumb in the opposite direction. "Sam, my bed is back there."

"But mine is larger. You'll be more comfortable there."

She opened her mouth to protest, but what he said made sense, so she closed her mouth. They walked on, up the back steps. As he pulled open the door, he said casually, "You'll move back in here, with me, won't you?"

"Excuse me?" She did a double take.

"In fact," he went on easily, "if we got married, we could—"

"If we what?"

She stopped, stared at him, felt her mouth drop open in amazement. He was throwing out suggestions like fastballs, and she wasn't sure she could keep up. "Who are you," she asked, only semi-joking, "and what have you done with Sam?"

"Yeah, I kind of shocked myself there, too," he said with a grin. "But now that I'm on a roll, let's see where it goes, okay?"

He ushered her into the house, closing the door behind them. They were in the kitchen now—her dear, beloved kitchen that she'd missed more than she'd wanted to admit. She stood facing Sam while he propped a hip against the counter, nodding.

"Marriage. Yeah, feels right. This proposing thing is another first for me," he said, scratching his beard, "but what the hell? This is a day of firsts."

She shook her head in disbelief. "Boy, when you get an idea in your head, you run with it."

"You haven't answered me."

"What was the question?"

"I asked if you'd marry me. The way I figure it, if we got married, I'd feel better about the whole thing.

Living in sin is fine for casual affairs, but I have a certain image to maintain.''

''Image?''

''Editor of the paper, even if it's only temporary. Future father of our future children. Dog owner. You know.''

Rachel's knees felt weak. Torn between tears and laughter, she backed up and lowered herself onto a chair.

''Children?'' she croaked, steadying herself at the table. Despite the sensation of total joy leaping through her bloodstream, she said, ''Hey, you aren't going to turn conventional on me, are you?''

''Don't you want to have children? Don't you want to get married?''

She shrugged, knowing she was fast losing all control of the conversation. ''Well, Sam, of course I do, but—''

He shrugged back, a corner of his mouth in a mischievous, upward tilt. ''Then what's the problem?''

Rachel could have said he was going too fast. That she needed time to take all of this in. In the space of a few moments, all of her dreams were falling into place. She could go back to school, open her day-care center, live with the man she loved, bear his children. She no longer had to take care of the world—unless she wanted to—and there was, for the first time in her life, someone with strong enough shoulders to lean on standing right in front of her and telling her it was okay to lean.

''What's the problem?'' Sam asked again, pushing himself away from the counter and walking toward her. Rachel could have said she was on love overload, that she needed to get used to one idea before tackling the next.

Instead she stared at him, at this wonderful man with the beard, this formerly detached reporter of other people's lives, currently the fully engaged, emotional, giving man of her dreams as he approached, a look of love and laughter on his dear face.

Rising from her chair, she opened her arms to him. "There *is* no problem, Sam. Things have unfolded nicely."

"Unfolded?" he repeated.

"Never mind. Kiss me."

"Yes, ma'am," he said emphatically and proceeded to do just that.

LOIS GREIMAN

From Caviar to Chaos

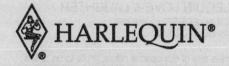

HARLEQUIN®

TORONTO • NEW YORK • LONDON
AMSTERDAM • PARIS • SYDNEY • HAMBURG
STOCKHOLM • ATHENS • TOKYO • MILAN • MADRID
PRAGUE • WARSAW • BUDAPEST • AUCKLAND

Dear Reader,

From Caviar to Chaos...that's my life. Well, okay, not the caviar part. Fish eggs aren't my thing, but chaos is me all the way, so I relate to Daniel and Jessie on a very personal basis. Our lives have decided similarities...and a few differences. (Please feel free to use your imagination to decide which is which.) I'm a farm girl from North Dakota who spent several years training horses, married the cutest guy ever to graduate from veterinary school, then proceeded to buy a farm and fill it with kids and horses and pets. Since then my life has been...well...chaotic. I hope you have as much fun reading about the chaos as I have living it.

Sincerely,

Lois Greiman

Books by Lois Greiman
HARLEQUIN LOVE & LAUGHTER
48—COUNTERFEIT COWGIRL
64—HIS BODYGUARD

To Nora Braun, whose company always inspires me,
but never more than on our trip to Wisconsin.
Thanks for the friendship and fun—
oh, and for this plot! You're the best.

Prologue

"CECIL?" Daniel asked.

"Huh?"

"Is this—"

"This is Cecil MacCormick. Who's this?" the old man shouted through the receiver.

"It's Daniel." He paused, waiting for recognition to dawn. But apparently dusk had settled in for perpetuity in the small town of Oakes, Iowa. "Daniel MacCormick."

Silence.

"Your nephew?" He hadn't meant to make it sound like a question.

"Danny? Is this Danny? Willy's boy?"

Of course, Willy's boy. How many nephews named Daniel did the old man think he had? "Yes."

"Danny boy! Ain't heard from you in a month a Sundays. Been wondering 'bout you. Just the other day I thought to myself, I thought, wonder how that Danny boy's doing way off in…where the hell are you, anyway?"

Daniel gritted his teeth. Patience was not his greatest virtue. There were, in fact, a fair number of people who would say he had no virtue, great or otherwise. Talent was another matter entirely—his innate gift. But even that was questionable now.

"I'm in New York."

"New York, huh? Is it raining there?"

Daniel glanced distractedly toward his apartment's south window and was awarded with an unobstructed view of Central Park. When Melissa moved out nine months ago, she'd taken the curtains with her. He realized with a touch of irritation that he missed the drapes more than he missed her. His therapist—*ex*-therapist—would strongly advise that he ponder the meaning of such a revelation. But he didn't want to ponder, for he doubted it would reflect favorably on his character. Just now, few things did. Sleep deprivation was not a pretty thing. Writer's block was butt-ugly. "No. It's not raining here."

"Too bad. Dad used to say them spring rains was good as pig shit for the fields. But Willy thought—"

"Listen, Cecil, I need to ask you something."

"Yeah?" The old man didn't sound thrilled to have his soliloquy cut short, but Uncle Cecil had always been the rambling kind and it seemed his advancing years had done little to shorten his dialogue.

"The old house. Is it still for sale?"

The line was quiet for a moment, as if Cecil had abruptly dropped the receiver in favor of a rousing game of checkers. "Willy's house? In town?"

Of course his house in town. It was the only house he had owned. That fact had been a matter of contention between Daniel's parents for the entirety of their marriage, or at least until she had left.

It was a strange thing for a boy to wake up one bright Tuesday morning and find that his mother was gone—that his world had changed irrevocably and permanently. Rather like learning the world was not really round, but as square as a cube.

For years it had surprised him that his father didn't sell the house and move into the country. William MacCormick was a farmer to the very marrow of his bones. But father and son had remained living in the ancient two-story at the edge of town. In retrospect, Daniel realized William had been waiting for her to return. But Daniel had always known better. She would never come back.

"Yes. His house in town. Is it still for sale?"

"Has been for going on two years now. Ever since Willy died. Real estate ain't exactly jumping off the map here, 'specially since the plant closed down. Then with the lousy grain prices and all, can't hardly make a dime t' sell your soul. So I'm letting—''

"Yeah. Well, listen," Daniel said, cutting him off in the middle of another windy sentence. "I've got to go, but I'll talk to you soon."

He hung up before another word was spoken, then sat staring in dull surprise at the receiver. So it was true. He was certifiably insane. There could be no other explanation for his present plans.

1

THE DOORBELL RANG. Oscar released his usual feral growl. Two spirited squeals echoed the noise. The sound carried clearly through the open, connecting door from the garage into the kitchen.

In the living room/office, the telephone rang.

Jessica Sorenson ran the baby bottle under the tap, then rapidly wiped her hands.

The doorbell rang a second time.

"Come in," she yelled, screwing on the nipple.

Oscar growled again.

"You want something?" Gnat asked, sticking his head through the doorway from the garage. His hair, nondescript in color, but memorable for its unique, unintentional style, stuck out from his head like the spikes on a porcupine's back.

"Can you get the phone?" Jessie yelled.

There were a couple of barks, joined by a few indistinguishable squawks.

"Huh?"

"Get the phone," she shouted, and hurried toward the door. It had already been one humdinger of a day. Wasn't it just like Mrs. Conrad to make it more hectic? She'd breezed in unannounced every Monday and Wednesday evening for the past six months. Murphy's Law insisted that she take this precise and harried moment to stand on formality.

"I'll get the phone," Gnat yelled, and to Jessie's eternal gratitude and not unwarranted surprise, he only tripped once as he trotted through to the office.

The doorbell rang again, followed by persistent knocking. Jessie turned the knob, bottle in hand, only to find that the door was locked, and a good thing it was, she remembered. Xena had become as much of an escape artist as Pearl, and the last thing Jessie needed was a menagerie of flower-starved animals attacking Loman's azaleas again.

She turned the lock, but a scraping noise momentarily distracted her. Leaning backward, she craned her neck past the edge of the door and hoped Gnat hadn't forgotten to close a cage. He was a good kid, and smart as a firecracker, but his attention span hadn't yet grown to the astounding proportions of his feet.

Seeing no sign of trouble, she opened the door and turned her gaze back to the porch. "Sorry, Mrs. Con—" she began, but stopped in midsentence and felt her brows fly into her hairline.

Standing between Grams's potted citronella was a man, and a rather disreputable-looking man at that. His hair was black and combed straight back, showing a high, pale forehead, sharp cheekbones, and two days' worth of dark stubble against his jaw. He was thin, dressed all in black, and his eyes were hidden behind sunglasses.

The shades alone made her nervous. She could have guessed his intentions much better without them. Eyes always told the story, in people just like in animals. If she could get a glimpse of his eyes, she could judge whether to welcome him in or bounce the baby bottle off his head and make a dash for it. But she supposed she was being paranoid—a remnant of her college days spent in the big city of Ames.

"Can I help you?" she asked, slowly wiping the remainder of the water from the outside of the bottle.

The dark brows pulled low above the wire rims. "What are *you* doing here? I thought the house was still for sale."

She forced herself not to back away. But there was something in his voice that grated against her peace of mind. "It is, but—"

"Then what the hell's going on?"

Jessica straightened her back with some effort. She hadn't busted her butt for the last ten years only to be frightened by the likes of Satan's messenger here.

"Who are you?" she asked, willing her tone to be firm. "What do you want?"

"What do *I* want?" He whipped the sunglasses from his face and glared at her. His eyes were a deep sable color and as intense as his expression, but the whites were streaked with tiny veins of red. "I want to know what the hell you're doing in my house, Sorenson."

She froze at the sound of her name. Fear and some other indefinable emotion skittered up her spine as memories crashed like cymbals inside her head. "MacCormick?" The name escaped her lips on a breath of air, but even as she said it, she was certain she was wrong. Danny MacCormick hadn't made an appearance in Oakes for more than a decade, and judging from every scathing word he'd ever said about their town, he was unlikely to do so now.

"What the devil are you doing here?" he asked.

"Danny MacCormick?"

"Good God, Sorenson!" he said irritably. "Who did you think I was?"

"I don't know," she said and laughed, both with relief and nervousness. He looked nothing like the Danny who had been her classmate for twelve years. Gone was the boy with the rounded shoulders, the cropped, sun-faded hair, the horn-rim glasses. In his place was this man—a rough, jaded etching of the boy she'd known. True, Danny had always been sharp-edged and sharp-witted, with an opinion on everything from the foolishness of pairing socks to the corroding souls of modern man. Even so, under it all there had been the shadow of tenderness in him. But this man...

"What happened to small-town hospitality?" he asked, glancing moodily down the elm-lined street. "You going to let me in or just stand there like the town idiot?"

The question snapped her back to reality. But whether it was the reality of the present or the fractious reality of their past was difficult to say. "You look terrible," she said, feeling no need to be any more congenial than he was. "Why are you here?"

"Not for your assessment of my personal appearance," he assured her, and took a step forward as if to come inside.

"Who are *you?*" Gnat asked, appearing with proprietary thoughtfulness beside her elbow.

Danny didn't answer, but met the boy's gaze with his own.

"You okay, Jess?" Gnat asked, concern in his tone as he kept his gaze glued to the man on the porch.

"Sure." She and Danny had never been friends. More like fanged adversaries, instead. Still, he had never scared her. "I'm fine. Gnat, this is—"

"An old friend of Jessie's," Danny said with flat finality.

Gnat was silent for a moment, then, "I'm Nathan," he said, "but people call me Gnat. Like the insect."

"Very Iowan."

Gnat scowled. "Yeah," he said. His tone did nothing to hide his distrust, but Jessie couldn't blame him; he had always been a good judge of character. "You want me to stick around, Jess?"

"I... No," she said, shaking herself from her stupor. "I need you to pick up those pellets, remember?"

"Yeah, but..." Gnat swept his gaze suspiciously over MacCormick's lean, dark-garbed form. Black wasn't considered a color in Iowa. Gnat's shirt was sunflower yellow with red and purple poppies emblazoned across his narrow chest. Now *those* were colors. "You sure?"

"Feed store closes at six," she reminded him.

"Okay." He pressed slowly past MacCormick and down the stairs, giving her one last glance before stepping into his father's aging Buick and pulling away from the curb.

"Your son?" MacCormick asked.

She stared in surprise. "Who?"

"Mosquito."

She thought for an instant, then, "Gnat? Of course not. Jeez, MacCormick! You're as weird as ever. Whatever happened to your investigative skills? I thought you were some hotshot reporter or something. He called me *Jess*."

MacCormick shrugged, reminding her with that one simple motion that he had, for as long as she'd known him, called his own father William. He'd always been a strange duck in a small pond.

"Just the baby, then?"

"What?"

He nodded toward the forgotten bottle in her hand. "Is it just you and the baby, or was the father dull enough to hang around, too?"

She scowled. Maybe she'd lost her edge since her high-school debating days, but she was just about ready to dredge up a scathing rejoinder when she felt the rough scrape of wool against her bare leg and heard an unmistakable bleat of hunger.

"No father," she said and, squatting down, thrust the nipple into the lamb's mouth. "It's just me and baby. The daddy left us for a ewe." She gritted a smile in his direction. "You can't trust those platinum blondes."

He didn't laugh, but narrowed his eyes and pressed past her. "What are you trying to pull, Sorenson?" Pushing the door open, he stepped inside and scanned the interior—the arched windows framed by passionflower vines, the jumble of potted herbs, the exotic flowers, aloe, horseradish, and…Xena, standing on her hind feet to gaze out the window. MacCormick was silent for a moment, as if there were too many questions begging to be asked, then, "Why is there a weasel in my living room?"

"She's not— Your living room!" she said and forced a laugh. "It's not your living room, MacCormick. It's Cecil's."

"Not for long."

Jessica felt herself go pale. From the next room, a pig grunted. "What are you talking about?"

"He's selling the house."

"He wouldn't do that," she said, but she was barely able to force out the denial. "We have an agreement."

"An agreement? That says what?" He turned on her with the speed of a black adder. "That you can turn my parents' house into a barnyard?"

"Listen, MacCormick. This has nothing to do with you."

"This has *everything* to do with me." He swept his gaze downward, over the worn flannel shirt that had long ago surrendered its sleeves to the unusual spring heat. Over her cropped and frayed denim shorts. Over her legs, tanned but scathed by a hundred minor mishaps, and onto the lamb that vigorously wagged its tail near her bare feet. "I want you and your stinky menagerie out of this house."

The slam of a pickup door made her jump. The lamb slurped noisily at the bottle, indicating it was already dry. Jessica shot to her feet, bringing the sticky bottle with her as she sped across the porch and down the steps toward him. "Cecil. You're not selling it, are you?"

"Selling what?" he asked, surprise in his gruff tone as he stumbled to a halt.

"The house." She tightened her grip on the bottle and tried to steady her nerves. "You're not selling the house."

She felt MacCormick's presence before she heard his voice. "You said it was for sale."

Cecil lifted his gaze and stared. She watched his faded blue eyes go round. "Danny? Danny boy. Is that you?"

"You said it was for sale," he repeated, more forcefully now.

"You look like you been run over by a cattle truck, boy. What happened to you?"

"I found a buyer for the house," MacCormick said.

"For Willy's house?"

"You can't sell it, Cecil," Jessie said. "I just—"

"Of course he's going to sell it!" MacCormick snapped. "You don't have any more sense than when you were a kid."

"And you don't have—"

"He giving you trouble?"

Jessie jumped. "Grams!" she gasped, turning wildly toward her grandmother. For a woman in her eighties, she had a knack for moving with spooky stealth, and the fact that she had one hand hidden behind her back did nothing to ease Jessie's panic. "I thought you were giving the boys their hemlock baths."

"I saw him pulling up," Grams said, nodding tersely toward Cecil. "And a good thing, too, or he'd cheat you blind. Just like he did me."

"I never cheated you out of nothing!" Cecil denied, his ruddy face already as bright as a radish.

"Horsefeathers!" Grams spat.

"Horsefeathers yourself! I ain't done nothing wrong. The mare was mine to begin with!"

"She was mine, and you danged well know it."

"That's not what the judge said."

"Well, that's what I say, and I got collaboration!" Grams said and yanked a pistol from behind her back.

Daniel swore and jerked violently backward.

"Grams!"

"Put that away before you blow your fool head off!" Cecil yelled, his voice raspy.

"Ain't *my* head I'm plannin' to blow!" she countered, and raised the pistol chest-high.

"Grams!" Jessie pushed the barrel toward the sky. "You can't shoot Cecil!"

"Wanna bet?"

"He's letting us live in his house!"

"Don't want to live in his blasted house. I've seen sieves that was more airtight."

Cecil reddened even more, veins popping out like flooded rivulets in his neck. "You don't like it, you can sure enough—"

"No! We love the house. Really. We're thrilled to be here. Aren't we, Grams?" Jessie looked frantically toward her grandmother for affirmation, but it was a foolish gesture. Her grandmother would rather ride through town buck naked than bend her stiff spine for the likes of a MacCormick.

"*I'm* grateful," Jessie rambled, trying to fill the silent void as she turned frantically back toward Cecil. "Really."

"I know you are, honey," he grumbled, softening his scowl as he turned to her. "But—"

"But it doesn't matter," MacCormick said, eyeing the pistol for a moment before turning back to Jessica. "Because he's selling the house."

"I am?" Cecil asked.

"You are?" Jessie breathed.

"The heck you are!" Grandma rasped, swinging her weapon toward the old man again. "You says my girl could live here till she could afford her own place, and you ain't going back on your word again."

"I never said I was. Put that thing away!" Cecil ordered.

"Why should I?"

"Cuz if you shoot me, they're gonna haul your sorry carcass off to jail. Then I'll come and take them geldings you're so proud—"

"You wouldn't come back nowhere, cuz you'd be six feet under, and I'd—"

"I'll pay rent," Jessie interrupted breathlessly.

"You don't need to pay no rent!" Grams huffed.

"She doesn't pay?" Daniel asked, incredulous. What was going on here? True, he'd never wanted the house—had gladly given the deed over to Cecil. But that was before his muse, faithless tramp that she was, had abandoned him to the desert wasteland of mediocrity.

"It's not like I haven't offered to pay," Jessica said, her tone defensive.

"Don't you worry about it," Cecil soothed.

"She'd damned well better worry about it!" Daniel's head throbbed like an African war drum, threatening to drown out every other sound. "Because—" Damn! Because why? The last thing he wanted was to voice his problems out loud. Especially here, in the armpit of America, where he'd sworn never to return. "Because the buyer's coming in tomorrow."

"Tomorrow!" Jessie's voice echoed two others.

"That's right," Daniel said into the abrupt silence. "Get the papers together, Cecil. I'll see they're signed tonight."

"Tonight! I can't do that, Danny. Like I tried to explain on the phone, I'm letting the girl—"

"The house is for sale, right?"

"Yeah, but—"

"Then sell it." Fatigue and frustration were driving through him with the force of an early morning jackhammer. "Sorenson's brighter than she looks. She can find somewhere else to live."

"Where?"

"I don't give a damn. Just get her the hell out of my house."

"Your house?" Cecil squinted at him.

"I mean...*your* house."

Jessica was staring at him with those same sky-bright eyes that used to make his stomach twist in knots and his tongue dry up like sun-cured hay—a hard blow to a boy who survived on the belief that he was not a misfit through any fault of his own but because of his own stellar intellect.

"Who do you know that's so hepped up about buying this house all of a sudden?" she asked.

"That's none of your business," Daniel told her. "If I were you, I'd worry about—"

"Well, it's sure as the devil *my* business!" Cecil said, turning his scowl on Daniel. "I'm not having any drug-running commies in my house."

"Drug-running commies?" What the hell century was it here anyway?

"And none of them...funny fellas either. That might fly where you've been living, but it ain't—"

"There won't be any *fellows*, funny or otherwise," Daniel assured him.

"Who is it, then?"

Daniel deepened his scowl, still hoping intimidation would work where logic failed. "Don't worry about who it is," he insisted, struggling to sound nonchalant. "I'll vouch for them."

"Them?" Cecil canted his head and narrowed his eyes

to crinkled slits. The veins in his neck had shrunk down to tributary size. "How many thems?"

Daniel's mind tumbled with roiling frustration and building panic. Four months ago he could have fictionalized the whole scenario, right down to the buyer's hat size. But that was when the gift had still been his. When words were his friends and he knew with every fiber in his being that the step from award-winning journalist to bestselling novelist would be no harder than a child's game of hopscotch. "Three," he said, picking a random number out of the air.

"Three! Men or women?"

Daniel hesitated, already freezing up like a jammed keyboard. Dammit! He should have said "one". "Women."

"Three women!" Cecil's face strongly resembled a beached mackerel's when he scowled. "They ain't gay or—"

"*One* woman," Daniel corrected hastily. "One woman...and her two daughters."

"Little girls?" Cecil's voice softened. "How old are they? And where's their daddy? I don't care what you young radicals say. A woman still needs a man to look after her when she's—"

Daniel swore with feeling, frustration spewing through him like rancid bile. "It's me!"

Three pairs of eyebrows rose. Three pairs of eyes stared in stunned disbelief.

"You're the father?" Cecil rasped.

"No!" Daniel swept splayed fingers through his hair and exhaled between clenched teeth. "I'm the one who's buying the house."

2

"YOU'RE MOVING BACK to Oakes?" Jessie made no attempt to keep the disbelief from her voice.

"I'm no more thrilled than you are," he growled.

"Then why are you—"

"It doesn't matter why!" MacCormick said, leaning into her face. "I just am. So I want you and your four-legged friends out of my house."

"It ain't your house." Cecil's voice was low. "You didn't want nothing to do with it."

"Well, I do now. How much do you want for it?"

Cecil's eyes narrow. Normally, he was as gentle as a lambkin, but it was best not to get him riled. Grams somehow managed to prove that on a regular basis. "Four hundred thousand."

"Four hundred—!" MacCormick sputtered. "That's insane. No one in his right mind would pay—"

"I'll buy it," Jessie rasped, but inside her head Miss Fritz, her elementary school teacher, scolded.

Don't be silly, girl. You can barely afford birdseed. If you acquire any more bills, you'll be fighting the goldfinch for your supper.

"I said not to worry on it," Cecil told her, apparently not hearing the voice that had chastised Jessie down the straight and narrow for the past decade and a half. "The truth is this here, Danny. The girl needs the house for a time, so—"

"I damn well need it more!"

"What for?"

"None of your business what for! Is it for sale or isn't it?"

"No!" The old man's chin came up another half inch, pulling the creases out of his scrawny neck. "It ain't."

McCormick pivoted away with a hissed curse, but in a moment he turned back, his dark eyes narrowed. "I bet there's some kind of ordinance against having those animals in the house. Is Joe Patton still Chief of Police?"

"An ordinance!" Cecil rasped.

"Joe's a friend," Jessie said. "He doesn't care about the animals."

"I bet he doesn't," MacCormick said, derision plain on his sharp-edged features. "But someone will. City hall maybe?"

Fear curled in Jessie's gut.

"I'm 'shamed of you, Danny," Cecil said, straightening slowly to his unimpressive height. "Picking on a sweet little thing like our Jessie."

MacCormick snorted. "Sweet little thing, my ass."

"Hey!" Cecil stabbed a gnarled finger at Daniel's chest and pulled his bushy eyebrows low. "I won't have you talking that way around the girls."

"It looks like I'll be talking to city hall."

"It won't get you the house, anyhow. Not—"

"What about the attic?" Grams said, her coarse voice breaking easily into the fray.

"What?" the two men said.

Grams shrugged her sharp, plaid-covered shoulders. "He could live up in the attic. The Bartles finished it when they was renting the place."

Jessie only stared, her heart paralyzed in her chest. She didn't want this man living in her attic. Not now, not ever.

"Thanks anyway," Danny said, his tone easily conveying his decided lack of appreciation. "But I guarantee I won't be living in an attic in Nowhere, Iowa."

"Then you'd best hike on back to wherever it was you come from," Cecil said.

"God—"

"You watch your mouth, boy!"

MacCormick ground his teeth, turned halfway around,

then jerked back. "All right, I'll rent the attic." He glared at Jessica in the fading light. "But only if you promise to keep this quiet."

"Keep what quiet?" Jessie rasped, still reeling from Grams's shocking mutiny.

"This!" He stabbed a finger at the moss that swelled up from the jagged cracks in the sidewalk. "My presence here."

Cecil snorted. "Like anyone would care if—"

"We won't tell no one," Grams promised. "Fact, if anyone asks, we'll say you're our house guest. We'll call you...Elston Rolands. I always liked the name Elston."

Cecil stared. Danny stared. Neither spoke. Perhaps they were in shock, but Jessie had long ago become accustomed to Grams' impulsive ways.

Still, it made this situation no more acceptable. Men were good and fine at a distance, but she had no intention on getting too close to one. She'd tried that before. "If you've come here to rest..." She paused, noticing, not for the first time, MacCormick's gaunt appearance. "I'm afraid you'll be disappointed." He could stand to gain fifteen pounds. Still, his shoulders were substantial, his arms sculpted, like an underweight James Bond. She'd never liked James Bond. "I mean, Oakes isn't the peaceful little community you remember."

MacCormick stared at her in silence for a moment, as if assessing whether she was joking. "I'll take my chances," he said finally.

"Too danged big for his britches," Cecil grumbled.

"Ain't he, though?" Grams chuckled as she shifted her bright, devilish eyes from Cecil to his nephew. "Just like a MacCormick. You go on in, Danny boy," she said, casually motioning toward the porch with her pistol. "You're welcome in our house."

Cecil snorted and reddened but said nothing as Jessie forced her muscles to relax a smidgen. She hadn't lost the house, and as for dealing with MacCormick—well, he wouldn't stay long. She was sure of it. After all, if there was anything she really had a knack for, it was getting rid of men.

Grams chuckled again and Jessica shifted her gaze suspiciously in that direction. Edna Sorenson could be as dramatic as a silent movie starlet when the mood struck her, but she was not overly fond of company, which meant her sole purpose in this entire charade was to tick off Cecil. Perhaps she thought that if MacCormick's very presence irritated his uncle, the guy couldn't be all bad. It could very well be, Jessie deduced as her eyes skimmed Danny's dark-garbed form, that Grams was entirely wrong.

"Need any help with your stuff?" Edna asked.

"No. I didn't bring much." MacCormick nodded toward his car. Jessie wasn't sure of the make. If it didn't have four legs and a heartbeat she was pretty much clueless, but she was quite certain the vehicle was even older than her Silverado, and Silver was well past the age of consent. "I'm going to pick up a few things before I unpack."

"Be back for supper?" Grams asked, and although Jessie was focused on Danny's response, she couldn't help but notice either Grams's trilling happiness or Cecil's lowering scowl.

"No," MacCormick said. Then, seeming to find his manners with some difficulty, he added, "Thanks," and turned away.

"Don't you worry about sheets or nothing," Grams warbled. "We'll make up the bed for you."

Cecil snorted, Grams all but giggled, and MacCormick, his fund of good manners apparently depleted, stepped into his car and drove away.

DANIEL AWOKE with a raspy groan. His throat felt dry, his head hurt, and strangely, very strangely really, his toes felt wet.

He slitted one eye open and—

"What!" He jerked his foot under the covers at the same instant that a furry creature dropped to all fours and streaked out the door he knew he'd closed the night before.

Daniel exhaled sharply and dropped his head back onto the pillow. He was still in hell. For a while he'd forgotten. For a couple of rare hours of undisturbed sleep, he had thought he was back in his apartment in New York—still writing, still successful, still focused. But no. Writer's block had brought him here, and writer's block held him in a stranglehold.

Turning his face into the pillow, he tried to pretend it was all a dream, and for one blissful second, it almost worked. Until he heard the barking. It was as high-pitched as a fire siren and just as brain-cracking. He pulled the pillow over his head, but it did no good, for even through the thick material he could hear a lamb join the cacophony. It was the clanging slam of a metal door that finally broke the camel's proverbial back.

Sweeping the blankets aside, Daniel swung his feet to the floor, grabbed his cigarettes from the nightstand, and stormed down the stairs. They creaked an ancient complaint beneath his weight. From the tiny third-story bathroom, his hairy nemesis quit splashing water out of the toilet to follow him on pattering paws.

Daniel glanced irritably behind him and headed toward the kitchen. But as he passed the open door to what had once been his mother's music room, he stopped abruptly. Jessica Sorenson was bending away from him. Encased in faded, wear-softened denim, her bottom was as round as a valentine, and below that her legs ran down for an eternity to finally end in leather work boots.

It took him several seconds to realize he was staring, several more to realize she wasn't simply posing there for his satisfaction. She was, in fact, pushing a dog's bowl into a stainless-steel cage at the same moment she was bottle feeding a lamb in the cage below.

He never knew if he made a noise or if it was the furry beast's clicking progress across the linoleum that made her turn.

"Oh. You're awake," she said. As if that was a surprise. As if one was likely to sleep late on Noah's Ark, he thought.

Still, he couldn't help but notice the incredible width of her azure eyes. "I didn't figure you for a morning person." She paused a second, her gaze skimming momentarily from his face to his black, crumpled T-shirt and back up. "I hope you slept well," she said, her voice suspiciously sweet.

Daniel scowled at her sugary tone and decided her eyes weren't azure at all. They were blue. Just blue. And a rather ordinary shade, at that.

"You look kind of…" She shrugged. The lamb slurped, the dog gobbled. "Tired." What, he wondered, had she been planning to say? Not that he cared.

"Tired?" He ran splayed fingers through his hair and glanced at the creature that had followed him downstairs. It gazed up at him with huge, seal-like eyes. It was bigger than a button, smaller than a breadbox. What the hell was it? "Why would I be tired? It was already five-thirty before that—muskrat?—started drooling on my foot."

"Muskrats," she said, tugging the nipple from the lamb's mouth, and urging him back into the cage, "have scaly tails. Xena doesn't."

"Xena?"

She nodded toward the creature of undetermined species. "She was really tiny when Ted found her. Nearly starved. We wanted to make her feel…" She lowered her voice slightly as if to make certain not to offend the thing, whatever it was. "…formidable."

It was five-thirty in the morning. Daniel had gotten something less than four hours' sleep, and he was listening to the ramblings of a certifiable lunatic.

"But now I'm thinking, maybe I should have named her Hope," she said as she made her way into the kitchen.

He followed in a haze.

"Their numbers are drastically decreasing. Shrinking habitat and all that, I suppose. Pastor Tony has a video on it," she said as she opened the fridge and extracted a bag. The contents, he soon learned, smelled like rotten tuna and looked only slightly less appetizing.

Daniel scowled at the animal. What the hell was it, he

wondered, but felt disinclined to ask. Yet another revelation his ex-therapist would probably advise pondering. "Aren't they supposed to sleep until Groundhog Day or something?"

She shot him an arched brow glance. "Groundhogs are much fatter. Although she does seem to be gaining weight. I'm hoping she's pregnant. But maybe it's just the diet. Too many fish she doesn't have to catch herself." Ah, it *was* fish in the bag. "But she goes up and down the stairs a dozen times a day and—"

"Listen!" he said, snapping himself out of the ridiculous dialogue and forcing himself to forget the fact that she had legs like Daisy Duke, not thin but…well, the word *perfect*…

No, not perfect. She wasn't his type. He liked sleek women. Aloof women. Melissa had been a runway model—his type exactly. Of course, she'd walked out on him some months ago, and he'd failed to miss her, but still that didn't mean that they hadn't been compatible. "Listen, Sorenson," he said, lowering his voice. "I didn't drive a thousand miles to live in a damn zoo. So either you shut these—"

From the street, a bomb exploded. He jumped. Snipers! Rebels! Freedom fighters—

"Jeez, MacCormick, you're as jumpy as an alley cat. You should get more sleep," Jessica said and, shoving the fishy bag into the refrigerator, hurried to peer out the kitchen window. "Ohhh, shoot."

Daniel closed his eyes and reminded himself that he wasn't in Iran or Northern Ireland or Afghanistan. He was in Iowa. Oakes, to be exact. Few places could be safer—*more boring,* he corrected. "Shoot?" His heart slowed slightly in his chest, making him think he might survive the shock. "Anyone I know?"

"Bill's here already."

Bill. Just Bill. And whoever Bill was, he probably wasn't the kind who toted a submachine gun and enough explosives to blow Iowa clear off the map. Yet another reason Daniel had decided to write a novel instead of continuing as a journalist. Maybe he was getting old, but he found he'd grown rather tired of the possibility of being blown into dust by some passing guerrilla no older than his shoe.

"And Jeremy still hasn't shown up yet," she added.

"Lazy bastard," Daniel said, steering his thoughts back into line.

"Maybe you could—" she began, then paused, her gaze stopping on him as if he were sliced pastrami set aside for her inspection. It was obvious by her expression that he didn't stack up—too dry, maybe. "Never mind," she said and, settling the baby bottle beside the ceramic sink, hurried to wash her hands.

"Maybe I could what?"

"I was going to ask you to help me unload hay." She paused again. "Sorry. I forgot."

"Forgot what?"

"That you...couldn't help me."

Of course he couldn't help her. He wasn't here to do menial labor in the backwoods of nowhere. He was here to write a bestseller and get his ass back to New York. But... "Why?" he asked.

"Well..." She cleared her throat and motioned vaguely at his chest. "You know."

"No I don't know. Maybe you can explain," he began, glaring at her, but the doorbell rang at that precise instant, and she scurried off, seeming more than happy to do so.

Daniel glanced distractedly down at his chest and arms. Okay, so maybe he was a little pale. And, yes, he could afford to gain a few pounds, but it wasn't as if he was on his last gasping breath.

"Good morning." Sorenson's voice sounded cheery from the front hall. Daniel hated cheery.

"Morning, Jess."

"Thanks for bringing it by so fast."

"No problem." *Of course,* Daniel thought. What else was there to do at five-thirty in the morning? "I'm just sorry I can't help you unload it."

"Really?"

"No," said Bill and laughed.

Sorenson joined in, her laughter light and irritatingly genuine. Daniel gritted his teeth.

A cat the size of Wyoming wandered past, his cocky tail bent near the top. Daniel watched him go with some amazement. What or who would a cat have to eat to get that fat?

"Well, listen, I gotta get going," Bill said. "Just park the truck anywhere when you're done, and I'll come get it when I get a chance."

The obligatory goodbyes were said and the door closed.

Sorenson turned back into the kitchen and jumped. "Oh! You're still here?"

He raised his brows. "And you were expecting me to be where?"

She scowled, motioning nervously toward his chest again. "You'd better get back to bed before..." Her voice fizzled out.

"Before what?"

She stared at him, her turquoise eyes wide and innocent. "It's just...if something happens...if you fall or something...I can't afford a lawsuit."

Daniel let the room go silent. "Fall?"

"I don't want you passing out or anything."

"Passing out!" As if he was some weak-kneed debutante—and her eyes definitely weren't azure or even the least bit fascinating, really. "What the hell are you talking about, Sorenson?"

She fidgeted with a pair of leather gloves she'd snagged from a basket in the mudroom, assumed a sorrowful expression, and glanced up through her lashes. They were thick, autumn-gold, and as long as an Afghanistani camel's. Now there was an image to keep in mind during his torturous sojourn here. Unfortunately, she smelled considerably better than any camel he'd ever ridden, and when she smiled...

"How long have you been like this?" she asked.

He concentrated on the camel idea and intensified his scowl. There had been times when nothing more than his glare had held off half a dozen men with rifles. Unfortunately, he feared Jessica Sorenson wasn't as shy as the average third-world guerrilla.

"I'm sorry. It's none of my business," she said and reached for the doorknob.

"How long have I been like what?" he asked, glowering at her back.

"Nothing. Sorry." She opened the door and stepped through. There was little he could do but follow. "You probably don't want to talk about it."

"Talk about what?"

"Please forget I said anything." She was, suddenly, the poster girl for contrition. "Your health is your own business," she said, then trotted down the stairs and hurried through the backyard.

Daniel gritted his teeth, trying to let her go. She was definitely a camel—irritating, stubborn, unattractive. He noticed suddenly that the backyard was not a backyard at all, but a sort of natural habitat, haphazardly strewn with low-growing wildflowers and leafy clover. Bees droned near a cluster of pink blossoms and birds squabbled and pecked at a half dozen feeders. Daniel snapped his attention back to their conversation with an effort. "What the hell are you talking about?" he asked, and strode after her. "What do you think? That I've come here to die or something?"

"No…" She threw a sideways glance at him, her eyes wide. "Of course not."

He swore with verve. "That's it, isn't it? You think I came crawling back to Iowa to curl up and croak."

"I just…" She'd reached a gate set in a split-rail fence and fiddled with the chain for a moment, as if checking to make sure it was secure. Then, taking a right turn, she strode rapidly alongside the irregular timbers. Two gargantuan gray horses followed on the far side of the fence, trying to reach her with their noses as they headed toward a faint gravel path along the edge of the small acreage. "I just have one question, and I think… Well, considering our living arrangements, I think I have a right to know."

He snapped his gaze from the uninvited horses back to her.

"Is it HIV?"

He said nothing, simply stared.

"I mean," she hurried on. "Not that I'd hold it against you or anything, but with your lifestyle…"

He canted his head, waiting for her to continue, but she did not. Not for several seconds, then, "Don't get me wrong. I'm not prejudiced. It's a man's…well, I mean…" She scanned his chest again, as if it were sadly lacking and not particularly gender-specific. "It's a *person's* choice."

They'd come to the end of the fence, where faint tire tracks led down toward the twisting path of the Skunk River at the edge of Cecil's five acres.

"Let me get this straight, Sorenson," Daniel said, his words carefully measured. "You think I'm gay?"

"It's nothing to be ashamed of," she assured him rapidly. An ancient, round-fendered truck was piled high with hay and parked in front of a low building. Vines twisted up the barn's tan, corrugated-steel walls. Jessica stopped beside the truck to pull on her gloves. "Normally I'd say it's nobody's business but your own, MacCormick. But, I mean…well, obviously you're not…" That skittering glance down his body again, as if he were clothed in a pale-pink tutu, toe shoes and all. "You shouldn't be ashamed of what you are. After all—"

"Sorenson." He stepped up close and growled her name into her face. "You're right. It is no one's business but my own, and I don't give a damn what you think, but just for the record…" He glared at her, frustration coiled tight inside him. "I am not gay, I've never been infected with anything more serious than plantar warts and I have not come here to die."

Her ridiculously pink lips parted in surprise, her sapphire eyes… No, not sapphire. "Then why—" she began, but stopped herself.

"Why…what?"

She cleared her throat. "Nothing. I'm sorry to stress you. It wasn't my intent."

"Oh yes. It was."

"No." She looked surprised and impossibly offended, as if it wasn't her number-one objective to see him scamper back to New York. As if she wasn't doing her damnedest to see him gone. "I've no intention of overtaxing you."

He would have loved to shake her until her teeth rattled, but if Cecil or Bill or Gnat, or any other drooling male whom he hadn't yet met, saw him, they might very well run him out of town on a rail. Did they still run people out of town on rails here? Or was tarring and feathering more in vogue?

"I'll stack the hay," he growled.

"What?"

"You heard me," he said, turning away.

"But you can't—"

"Can't what?" he asked, swinging his gaze back toward her.

She cleared her throat. "Well, if you're sure." Her tone was dubious.

He considered swearing again, but it hardly seemed worth the effort. If journalism had taught him anything, it was to hate redundancies. So he turned away, burying his frustration in movement as he yanked open a wide sliding door and strode into the steel building.

"Well, good morning." Jessie's grandmother stood there, a gleaming bucket of frothy milk in one hand. "You sleep all right?"

"Fine," he said and looked past her. Four stalls were built in the narrow interior. Two were empty, the third was occupied by a pair of nanny goats, and the fourth by a trio of head-butting kids.

"If you're looking for cows, there ain't none. Goat's milk," she added, lifting the bucket waist-high. "Makes the fountain of youth look like a scummy pond. I'll fix you some pancakes with it sometime. But right now I gotta feed the boys their wheat germ. Jess, make sure you tell him about Pearl's talents," she said and exited with her jerky, long stride, her bony shoulders listing beneath the weight of the bucket.

Daniel watched her go. "Boys?" he asked, without turning around.

"The geldings," Jessica explained.

"Talents?"

"Pearl's an escape artist. Gotta keep the gate chained."

"Uh huh. Wheat germ?"

"It's a long story."

"Hell is forever," he muttered.

"What?"

"I've got time."

She shrugged as she slid the door open to its metal stop. "A few years ago Grams was diagnosed with lupus. The doctors…" She paused, clearing her throat and not looking at him. "They couldn't do much more for her. So we went to a naturalist."

We, Daniel thought. Is that why she was here? Still in Oakes, Iowa.

"Anyway…" She was striding back toward the truck. He followed her hips. They weren't narrow hips, but were curvaceous and full, making her waist appear impossibly tiny and her shoulders look capable. In short, she was not a delicate woman. Except for her neck. It looked elegantly long behind her bobbing ponytail. She was, he deduced, a woman of strange contradictions. "We've learned a lot about medicinal herbs since then."

Thus the living room full of plants, he surmised.

"Is that why she moved to town? Because of the lupus?"

Near a dwindled stack of hay bales a smattering of speckled chickens pecked in the dirt.

"We lost the farm after Grams got sick, so Cecil said we could live here."

Why? "He build the barn, too?"

"Yeah. He said he needed somewhere to keep a horse or two sometimes," she said and climbed up the slatted side of the truck.

What a load of hooey, Daniel thought. Cecil had acres of land on which to keep horses. Daniel knew the last thing Cecil needed was this paltry plot on the river, but tempered his question with admirable restraint. "Why couldn't he keep them at his farm?"

"I don't know. Grams was in pretty bad shape at the time. I didn't give it much thought. Then when we lost the home place... We were just lucky to have somewhere to live. But to have a place to keep the horses too—it was a godsend." She gazed through the barn to the team of huge gray Percherons. "Your uncle's a doll."

"Cecil?" Daniel asked and speared her with a sharp gaze.

She shrugged. "Not all MacCormicks are mean-spirited."

He snorted and jerked his head toward the barn. "You want these stacked with the others?"

"That's awfully hard work. You don't—"

He glared her into silence.

She cleared her throat. "Well, all right. But you'd better at least wear gloves or—"

"Don't press me, Sorenson!" he said and yanked the first bale down from the truck. He carried it inside.

JESSIE WATCHED HIM settle the bale near the others. Why had he returned? What did he hope to accomplish, and when would he leave? Everything had been going so well. Everything was just the way she liked it, with no fickle man to distract her. So why did MacCormick have to show up now? Not that he distracted her, but no matter how hard she would have liked to believe otherwise, or make *him* believe she believed otherwise, he was anything but frail. True, he was somewhat underweight, but every ounce of him was muscle or bone, and true to his word, he could still stack bales— on their edges so the twine wouldn't rot, just the way it was supposed to be done. He worked with a kind of easy nonchalance, but then, perhaps he was only so conscientious because he was trying to impress her.

She paused in her task of tossing down the bales and almost laughed aloud at the thought. Danny MacCormick was not the type to try to impress anyone, especially some-one like her. She was hardly *his* type. Maybe he wanted to wring her neck, but he didn't want to impress her, and that was fine by her. She hadn't spent the morning slamming cage doors in an attempt to encourage him to stay, she thought. Doing her best to think about something else, she threw herself back into her work.

An hour or so later, their task was complete and they walked side by side toward the house. A meadowlark sang from a post, the air smelled of spring flowers, and a light mist was just beginning to caress Jessie's face as she stripped the gloves from her hands. A companionable silence had fallen between them, but she didn't want a companion, at least not the two-legged one of the male gender.

"So, you missed it, huh?" she asked, canting a look up at him.

"What?"

She shrugged and glanced about, not entirely certain if she was just trying to irritate him, or if she truly wanted an answer. "This. Iowa."

He snorted. "You know, Sorenson, there's treatment for your kind of dementia."

"Funny. So if you didn't come here to die, and you didn't miss it, what brings you back?"

He was silent for a moment, then placed a hand over his heart as if reciting some deep truth. "There is nothing so good for a man's soul as a man's roots."

It was her turn to snort. "I'd rosin up my bow, Mac-Cormick," she said, ascending the back steps of the ancient two-story. "But I don't like to play without the rest of the orchestra."

"If you don't like the answers, don't ask the questions," he said and reaching past her, opened the door. She noticed two things. He was in the habit of opening doors for women, and he winced.

"What's wrong?"

"Nothing," he said and ushered her into the mudroom.

"It's your hands, isn't it?"

"No."

"Let me see them."

He scowled at her. The expression was reasonably intimidating, but when you've spent the past ten years wrestling everything from irritated bulls to fractious guard dogs, you tended to form a new perspective on intimidating. "Mind your own damn business," he said, but she reached for his wrist and turned his arm to examine his left palm.

Three broken blisters glared up at her. She raised her gaze slowly, then reached for his other hand. It was slightly worse than the first. "Tell, me, MacCormick, have you always been this stubborn?"

"Have you always been this—" he began and paused. Their gazes locked. His skin felt warm beneath her fingers. Quiet settled around them.

"What?" she asked, and her voice was softer than she'd meant it to be.

He took a breath and turned his attention to his hand with a sharp scowl. "Have you always been this pushy?"

What had he really been going to say? Not that she cared. But his eyes had been so intense, so entrancing.

Against her palm, his hand felt broad and capable. He was not, she reminded herself, a small man. In fact, he stood a good five inches taller than she. In high school he'd been almost chubby. Not anymore. What had happened to him? Not that she cared. But sometimes he looked like a lost puppy, and she'd always had a weakness for—*What am I thinking?* Hadn't she learned her lesson with Brian? He'd looked lost sometimes, too, and maybe that's why she'd been attracted to him. Then again, maybe it was his money or his good looks, or the way he could make her feel like a princess.

"Brian," Miss Fritz said, *"was a horse's behind."*

"Enjoying yourself?" MacCormick asked.

Jessica dropped his hand as if it were a hot branding iron.

"You'd better not let that get infected," she said and stepped around the corner, reaching for the closest cupboard. Yanking open a door, she pulled out a plastic tube of antibiotic lotion. "Here. Wash them and put on this. I'll get bandages."

"They're fine."

"Wash them," she insisted and turned on the faucet in the spotless ceramic sink. But he only stared at her. "Now," she said and, reaching for his nearest hand, thrust it under the tap.

He washed without further prompting while she rummaged through the cupboards for bandages.

"Dry them thoroughly," she ordered, glancing over her shoulder, "then apply the ointment."

"You always this bossy, Sorenson? Because if you are, I think I know why you're not married."

Her heart did a little twist in her chest, but she kept her tone sassy. "Matchmaker on the side, are you, MacCormick?"

"I prefer the term 'marriage broker,'" he said.

She glanced up, almost duped for an instant.

He shrugged. "Times are tough. Always good to do a little moonlighting."

"Uh-huh." She was going to have to sharpen her wits. "Give me your hand."

He did so and she stretched the bandage quickly across his open wound. His skin felt warm and though she didn't meet his eyes she could feel his gaze on her face.

"So how about you? You married?" Not that she cared, but he'd started it. And she did have a right to know. After all, he was living in her house. Well, kind of her house.

"So you're not curious about me and François anymore?" he asked. His tone had an odd, feminine lilt to it.

Jessie looked quickly at him and saw, there in the depths of his dark eyes, the gleam of laughter. She shrugged, trying to look casual. "Sure. Tell me about François."

"He's got a marvy little villa in Venice, with statuettes of hunky Greek gods and—"

"Oh, please!" She dropped his hand in favor of the other one. "I had a right to know if you were…contagious. Not that I…I mean it's not like I'm going to…" *Help.*

He watched her, brows slightly raised. "Going to what?"

She pursed her lips and fumbled with the second bandage. "You know exactly what."

"You're not planning on seducing me? Is that what you were trying to say?"

She tried to appear as nonchalant as he, but the warmth from his hand was seeping through to her soul. "Exactly."

He was silent for a moment, then ventured, "So if you're not interested in seduction, what do you do for excitement?"

She scowled at her handiwork. It was a simple adhesive bandage, but somehow she'd managed to get wrinkles in it and tear part of the perforated strip. "I didn't say I wasn't interested in...that." What kind of insane conversation was this? "Just that I wasn't interested in *you*."

"Oh. So who *do* you seduce?"

She tried hopelessly to smooth out the wrinkles.

"Is it Bill?"

"Bill's wife wouldn't approve," she said, not looking at him. "And his five kids would be decidedly unhappy."

"Five," he said, and nodded in mock approval. "Impressive."

"A good number for a litter. A bit much for a family. Overpopulation, and all that."

"Are you sure? I can imagine you with a bunch of kids."

She glanced up to glare down his grin, but for a moment there was none, just an unspoken question.

The sound of the doorbell made her jump, then clear her throat once again. "Just...be careful with your hands for a couple of days," she said, and hurried gratefully toward the door.

Jeremy Bitz stood on the front porch, shuffling his feet and looking pitifully apologetic. "Sorry I'm late," he said, flipping his head toward the empty truck.

"Uh-huh." She smiled while trying to get her bearings, but her head felt strangely light. "I've heard that before."

He chuckled in a baritone that still surprised her; it seemed like only yesterday that his voice had been higher than hers. "You know it's true," he said. "Gotta get in shape for the football season. I'm tight end this year. It's either bales or weights and I get paid for bales. 'Sides…'' He grinned. "Dad'd have a cow if he knew I let you down."

"Tell your dad I highly discourage having cows. Very painful," she said. He laughed, and she felt a little better, breathing easier. "Don't worry about it, Jeremy. We did fine."

"You didn't have to do it alone?"

"No. D…a friend helped me."

"Oh. Okay. Well, sorry again," he said.

"No problem." But maybe it was. If Jeremy had been there, MacCormick wouldn't have helped her, and the last thing she wanted was to be grateful to him. Not that she should feel grateful, of course. After all, it was his own inflated male ego that had made him do it. But still…

"You'll call me next time?" Jeremy asked.

"Count on it."

She closed the door with a wan smile. But something was wrong. Something…

Smoke!

She swung toward the kitchen with the speed of light, searching for Grams and her forbidden Camels, but only Daniel stood facing her, his narrow hips propped against the edge of the counter, his fingers scissored around a cigarette.

"No!" she rasped, and flew across the floor, to snatch the thing from his lips.

3

DANIEL STARED at her in silent amazement, knowing without a doubt that not a single emotion showed in his expression. His poker face had stood him in good stead on assignment many times, but he had no idea whether or not his outward calm would have any effect on her. After all, she had just snatched the cigarette from his lips like a striking tigress, and only moments after caressing his hand with that kitten-soft touch of hers. From kitten to tigress in fifteen seconds. Scary. Good thing he wasn't a cat person.

"Let me guess," he said, his tone carefully devoid of emotion. "You don't approve of smoking."

"It's because of…" She paused, glanced toward the doorway, then down at the sleek brown animal just slinking through the pet door. "Xena," she said.

What had she been about to say? And had the looming football hero really left, or was he still on the porch hoping to impress her with his budding muscles? Not that Daniel cared, because even if Jessica Sorenson had been his type, even if she didn't live in this dead-end middle of nowhere, even if she didn't have a half dozen mouth-breathing men of every imaginable age drooling over her at any given moment, she was obviously demented and it would do him no good to get her agitated. But what the hell *was* that animal?

"I can't smoke because of…the mink?" he asked, glancing at the creature as it slunk into the room.

"Mink are darker," Jessica said, distastefully snuffing out the cigarette in the sink.

"Uh-huh. And Xena is a…"

"Allergic," she said.

"What?"

She had already turned away and was rummaging rapidly around in the fridge. It was a position reminiscent of early that morning and for one insane second Daniel was tempted to smooth his palm over the faded curve of her jeans. It was only good old-fashioned male instinct, of course. Although New York didn't have a shortage of single women, he hadn't exactly been swimming in female companionship, and suddenly he felt the dearth with a tightening in his groin.

"What?" she echoed.

He scowled and jerked his gaze from her derriere. She was not his type. Try as he might, he'd never been attracted to psychotics. "How do you know Xena is allergic?"

"She rubs her eyes, sneezes. The usual symptoms," Jessie said, and plunked a head of cabbage onto a wooden cutting board. At the same instant, a cupboard sprang open and something large and furry fell out. It hit the floor with as much finesse as a soggy pillow, then sat up groggily and shook its head.

Daniel stared in dull amazement.

"Oscar," Jessie said, as if that in itself was a complete explanation and proceeded to chop the cabbage to bits with enthusiastic zeal.

"Uh-huh." Daniel couldn't help but notice that it was not yet eight o'clock in the morning and she was dicing vegetables. She had, in fact, just added carrots to the growing pile. "What are you doing?"

"Feeding Oreo."

It dawned on him quite suddenly that the good citizens of Oakes had a problem with inbreeding. It wasn't surprising, really. He should have realized it before. After all, such genetic compaction was bound to cause problems sooner or later.

And voilà—Jessica Sorenson.

"Do you want some breakfast?" she asked.

"I have a rule; no cooked cabbage until after lunch."

"How about raw?" she asked, spearing a chunk on the end of her mammoth butcher knife.

An idea struck him like a blow. That's how his protagonist murders her lover! With a butcher knife. She's cooking him a special dinner, maybe humming to herself because she's finally found someone she can trust, someone she can love. But the boyfriend doesn't show. Then when he walks in, she smells another woman's perfume, and in a fit of rage she…

But wait. No. Too common.

"MacCormick?"

"What?" he asked, rousing himself from his reverie.

"About breakfast," she said, implying that she'd already stated her question and wasn't thrilled about doing so again. "Do you want something more conventional since you're abstaining from cabbage? I mean, not that I owe you or anything. But it *is* raining outside."

The logic escaped him. Or perhaps it was just another fine example of that inbreeding problem. "And?"

She motioned toward the drizzly window with the gigantic knife. "The hay would have gotten wet. Not that I asked for your help. But—do you want some breakfast?"

"Does your grandmother know you play with knives?" he asked.

She raised her brows and whacked a carrot in half. "She encourages it."

"Um. And your psychologist?"

She grinned and thwacked another carrot. "Do you want breakfast or not?"

The knife rather mesmerized him. Maybe it did have merit as a murder weapon if he twisted the plot a bit and—

"MacCormick!"

'No," he said. "Thank you."

"So world-famous journalists don't need sustenance like the rest of us common mortals."

"No." He reminded himself that she'd always had a sharp tongue. It was simply that the country-girl curves and the ballerina neck had distracted him. "Couple of sips of blood morning and night and I'm good for the day."

"Really?"

"Sure," he said and reached with deliberate nonchalance

for his cigarettes again. But when he glanced down he realized his breast pocket was empty. He scowled, looked up and jerked spasmodically. "What the hell's that?" he rasped, staring at the plastic bag that drooped from Jessica's fingers.

"Blood," she said, closing the refrigerator with her foot. "I like to keep some around for visiting journalists."

"Thanks, anyway." He caught his breath and just barely managed to sound urbane, but if the truth be told, he had never particularly cared for the sight of blood, bagged or otherwise.

"Wrong type?" she asked, and stashed it back in the fridge.

"So, Sorenson," he said, feeling a little better with the stuff hidden from view, "I don't remember the average Iowan keeping blood in her fridge. This something new?"

Scooping up the veggies, she dropped the lot of them into the nearby blender and punched a button. "Hemolidic anemia," she said over the whir.

"What?"

"Ed Peterson's basset hound needs a transfusion."

He stared at her for what seemed like a lifetime. But no further explanation was forthcoming. What a surprise. "And?" he said finally.

She glanced up, uncertainty shadowing her face. "I'm a vet."

He canted his head. "What war?"

"Not a..." She scowled at him as if he were a couple of vegetables short of a full patch. "I'm a veterinarian."

"You're kidding."

"Why did you think I had cages in the music room?"

"I assumed you were insane. Naturally."

She raised a brow at him, whisked a pan from beneath the ancient oven and set it on a burner. In a minute eggs were sizzling in the skillet, but she had already returned to her veggies. Tilting the blender pitcher over a bowl procured from a nearby cupboard, she dumped out the sloppy mess, then hurried to the fridge. In a moment she had returned with a small carton.

"Yogurt?" she asked, tipping the paperboard container toward him.

He shook his head. She shrugged and spooned the contents atop the vegetables.

Daniel grimaced. "Why?" he asked.

"The dalmatian," she said, tilting her head toward the unseen cages. "He's got bronzing syndrome."

"Uh-huh."

"Skin condition. He gets acne if he eats dog food," she said, but accompanied the words by emptying a bag of the same into another bowl. Retrieving both dishes, she raised her brows and showed him the contents. "Sure you don't want any?"

"Maybe later. After I've sampled Oakes's undoubtedly fine cuisine."

She shrugged, then disappeared into the next room. In a moment she had returned, flipped four slices of bacon into the hot skillet and replaced the lid.

"Let me guess," he said, glancing at the mystery animal as it peeked through the swinging pet door on the back entrance. "For the prairie dog?"

"Prairie dog?" she said, her tone heavy with disbelief.

He shrugged. "I'm running out of options."

"Prairie dogs are lighter in color." Jessica glanced at the creature that stood on its hind tiptoes by the cupboard. "Are you hungry again?" she asked, then reached for the bag of dog food and snatched up a few nuggets, which she handed to the snuffling animal. It took the offering in its clawed front feet and dropped to all fours. "And they're herbivores."

Daniel watched Xena devour her second breakfast. "Of course."

"You sure you don't want some?"

"Dog food?"

"Bacon and eggs."

"They're for human consumption?"

"Of course. I'd never feed this to my patients. Too high in fat."

"Uh-huh." He pushed himself away from the edge of the

counter, ready to refuse. After all, the last thing he wanted to do was make her think he owed her something. But the bacon did smell good. "I guess I could have a little."

"All right. Grab yourself some dishes and sit down."

He moved toward the cupboards above his head and found the plates just where his mother had always kept them. A sliver of yesterday sliced through him. He paused as memories washed the morning—real breakfasts, warm cookies, late-night hugs after—

"Get me some dishes, too, will you?"

Taking another plate from the shelf, he slammed the door on the memories.

"Orange juice or milk?"

"Doesn't matter."

"Tea? We've got chamomile and dandelion."

"No." He sat down. "Thank you." The floor squeaked beneath his chair. The sound seemed utterly familiar, as if he had never left home. As if he hadn't learned long ago to look out for himself and let others do the same. As if he had spent every day of his life in this house. But he hadn't. He no longer belonged here. Never had, really. He wasn't some backwater redneck, grunting expletives and mowing lawns. He was an intellect. A success. An award-winning writer who lived for the thrill of the next story.

Stomach growling, he plowed into his breakfast, though he barely tasted it.

"So where have you been living for the past ten years?"

"New York, mostly." But despite everything—the foreign lands he'd seen, the dignitaries he'd interviewed, this still felt most familiar. It seemed as if he could almost catch his mother's scent. In a forgotten little town of dowdy women who smelled of dish soap and ammonia, she had worn Chanel every day that he knew her. When he was nine he had scraped up all his coins and bought her a bottle for Mother's Day. It had been one of the few times he'd ever seen her cry, but he wondered now if there had been a thousand bottles more that he'd never known about. If there had ever been any since she'd left him.

"MacCormick?"

"Near Central Park!"

She stared at him, her eyes bright as the sun, and he realized suddenly that the subject had changed without him noticing.

He cleared his throat, feeling sheepish and gawky, as if the past thirteen years had never been. As if he had never gotten over his crush on the sassy, earthy girl who sat before him. "What did you say?"

She was silent for a moment. "I'm sorry about your mother."

Something clenched up hard in his gut. How did she know what he was thinking about, and if she could see through him that easily, how the hell—

"She was so pretty," Jessie continued. "And nice. I remember when Mom was sick—"

"Listen—" He slid his chair abruptly back from the table. "I'd love to discuss old times, but I've got to get to work."

For one aching moment he wondered if he'd wounded her. But he didn't care. Couldn't afford to.

"Work?" she asked softly.

Morning glories! Her eyes were the exact color of his mother's cherished morning glories. "Unpacking," he said, stabbing himself back to reality.

"Oh."

He turned away.

"MacCormick?"

"Yeah?" He glanced at her, though his mind warned him not to.

Her eyes were huge and solemn, swallowing the heart-shaped perfection of her golden face. His stomach turned over, dreading her words. He didn't need her pity. Hardly that.

"Thanks for the help," she said and, rising from the table, turned her back on him.

BY NOON Daniel had his detestable car unpacked. By one o'clock his computer was set up in front of the narrow rectangle of window that looked out toward the river and by four he had written three stellar pages. Elated and exhausted, he fell into bed fully dressed. He woke sometime after seven, reached for his cigarettes and remembered the abhorrent house rules.

The elation he'd felt earlier had dulled to a sort of disbelieving panic. Stumbling to his computer, he poked it into life and read the fresh pages. Yes. They were good. His muse was back. *He* was back, he almost screamed, but by nine o'clock frustration had settled in with a vengeance. He'd written five pages and deleted six.

Desperate to get away, he stomped down the stairs.

"If we're very careful of the dosage, I think he's got a good chance," Jessie was saying.

"And I'd have to give the shots myself?" The old voice was thin and reedy.

"Oh, it's nothing," Grams said. "Our Jess is a genius. She'll show you just how to do it, Betty."

"I'm just worried…"

Daniel didn't stop to hear more. He needed to get away, needed solitude, needed a cigarette.

TWO HOURS LATER, after all of the above, he fell into bed. But his sleep was fitful at best, nonexistent at worst. Sometime after 4:00 a.m., he sat up on the narrow, saggy mattress. Scratchy-eyed and aching, he creaked to his computer and tried to dredge up the muse.

The plot, nurtured for so long, bloomed slowly in his mind. Alysha Linden was young, smart and pretty in a tired sort of way. She was also destined for failure. Born in Newark to a single mother, she found all the odds against her—the wrong place, the wrong friends, the wrong choices….

Setting his mind on the mood, he settled onto the rickety folding chair he'd scrounged from a closet and began to type.

DAWN ARRIVED as slowly as his thoughts. Below him, the house began to awaken. A lamb bleated, something snorted, and though he told himself it was too apropos to be possible, he could have sworn he heard a rooster crow.

Directly below him, he heard the back door open, and then, without meaning to, he watched Jessica step into the yard. She was leaning back on the leash of a yellow Lab that had its ears pinned up with what looked like a chip clip. Despite his strange ear style, however, the dog wagged his thick tail and danced an ecstatic little jig as he led her onto the flower-strewn grass. Her hair, caught in a bouncing ponytail at the back of her skull, was almost the identical shade of gold as the Lab's. With the window open ever so slightly, Daniel could hear the bees singing in a patch of wildflowers and near an oversized bird feeder made of bark, a blue jay scolded a squirrel. But above the soft morning sounds, he could hear the quiet murmur of her voice. It lilted up through the sun-dappled air, capturing his attention, and he realized suddenly that he was straining to hear—

Alysha! Her forlorn fictional image yanked him back to the business at hand. Alysha was all he was interested in. Snatching his gaze from the golden duo, Daniel forced his mind back to his plot. He was here to write his novel. Nothing more. Nothing less. He was here to detail the struggles of Alysha Linden's doomed existence.

Taking a deep breath, Daniel settled more firmly into his chair and glared at the monitor.

Alysha. Dejected and alone, she struggles to find a way to break out of the path set before her. But...

In the yard, Jessica took a few more steps forward. She was wearing cutoffs again, he noticed as she bent to release the Lab—faded cutoffs with a few tendrils of fraying denim at the edges, that showed a breathtaking length of firm thigh. Her shirt, a sleeveless chambray of the same wear-softened vintage, was tucked snugly into her waistband, making her look like the poster girl for some country catalog. But when she turned just so, the sun sparkled on her dew-dappled toe-nails and he saw that they were painted a vivid violet hue, and that each nail was adorned with a tiny spark of gold.

He scowled. Contrasts. Every time he thought he had a

handle on her, he inadvertently discovered another jagged facet. Faded denim with gold toenail decoration in the shape of... He leaned forward. What *was* the shape? he wondered, but just then she glanced toward the house.

Daniel jerked back in his chair. It whined irritably under his weight.

Focus! Alysha! *Alysha—perpetually searching for happiness, only to be cheated by life time and again. Alysha, who—*

The Labrador barked wildly, and when Daniel glanced up, he saw that the dog was running in tight circles and leaping joyously toward the sky.

"Are you ready? Are you ready?" Jessica's voice seeped through the narrow slice of open air beneath the old single-pane window.

"Go get it." The Frisbee spun from her hand. The dog tore after in ecstatic pursuit. He returned it in seconds, his ears still bobbed in the same ridiculous style, and she laughed as she threw it again.

The noise trilled up to him like the sparkling sound of hope. Sunlight, just breaking from behind a bank of frothy clouds, gleamed like happiness upon her hair, and when she turned slightly, he could see her smile, that dimpled, impish grin that had kept him tossing on his bed as a boy.

She threw the Frisbee again. Her shirt stretched lovingly across her full breasts and her arms, smoothly muscled and golden brown, looked as graceful as a breeze-bent willow.

It seemed suddenly that she hadn't changed at all in the past thirteen years. That while he was being stretched thin and bitter by the passing of time, she had remained the same, a golden sliver of—

Damn! What the hell was wrong with him? He snapped back in his chair. It clanked in misery.

Misery! Not a bad title. Appropriate. To the point. Decisive. But...no. King had already used it. *Hopeless?* No. Too...obvious. *Tears.*

He scowled at the blinking cursor, arrowed it to the top of

the first page and typed in the winning title. *Tears.* A damn fine title, and very appropriate.

Alysha would shed a lot of tears in this urban twist on *Of Mice and Men.* Yes, there would be struggles and hopes, but in the end there would be tears.

The dog barked wildly. Daniel lifted his gaze. The Frisbee had disappeared.

"Can't you get it?"

The dog barked again, leaping like an insane jack-in-the-box for its toy.

Jessica's grandmother appeared, her waist, as always, cinched tight into slightly oversized jeans. She wore a long-sleeved, long-outdated western shirt. Daniel heard her raspy voice, answered by her granddaughter's laughter, and then Jessica was trotting across the lawn to retrieve the Frisbee from inside the horses' water tank.

He watched her bend and felt something coil in his gut. It wasn't that she was anything special. It was just that... Well, it was probably nicotine withdrawal. After all, it was a well-known fact that nicotine inhibited sexual arousal. With the reduction of the drug, his libido was increasing. That was all. But he had to ignore the distractions of his fickle hormones. All he wanted was a chance to concentrate, to write.

She spoke to the Lab. *Yes, shut the mutt up,* he thought, but when she bent to stroke the dog, he noticed that her shirt dipped languidly away from her torso, revealing for an instant the soft mounds of her breasts captured in a bright satiny bra that matched the hue of her toenails to perfection. Daniel's breath stopped in his throat. He leaned forward, caught like a trout on a hook, and in that instant Jessica lifted her gaze to his window.

He snapped back out of sight, heart hammering in his chest. The chair groaned a rusty protest, and he swore in unison. How the hell was he supposed to work when she looked so... When her laughter... When he had no decent chair?

That was the problem. He couldn't work because the damned chair was distracting him!

4

THERE WERE NO furniture stores in Oakes. In fact, the nearest one was a fifty-minute drive to the west, and once Daniel
had arrived there it took him an ungodly amount of time to
select an office chair. By the time he'd accomplished that
stupendous feat, he'd decided he needed a better desk than
the one he'd been wor...been *trying* to work on.

Watching the salesman struggle to squeeze his new pur-
chases into the dreaded Monte Carlo's trunk, Daniel realized
the episode might have been humorous if he'd been in the
mood for comedy. As it was, he swore with silent enthusiasm, longed hungrily for his Benz, then crammed his aching
body back behind the wheel.

Vaguely hungry, he stopped at a restaurant called the
Greasy Spoon only to find that the establishment was devoutly conscientious about delivering on its promise. Forty-
five minutes later, nauseous and somehow hungrier than
he'd been when he'd first stepped into the café, he turned
back toward the Animal House, as he'd dubbed it.

By this time his head ached for a cigarette, but upon a
patted examination of his breast pocket, he found once again
that it was deplorably empty.

The convenience store he stopped at proved to be anything but, and since he was loath to use his credit card, lest
someone discover his true identity, he was forced to pay
cash, a commodity decidedly lacking since his purchase of
the furniture. Perhaps he should have planned his trip more
carefully, but how does one pack for a journey into hell?

Finding an ATM machine in Oakes was about as simple
as nailing one's head to the moon—a strange analogy, now

that he thought about it. But finally he purchased his drug of choice and retreated hastily to his antiquated car. The first drag of the cigarette tasted like heaven, the second even better, and by the time he was wending his way down elm-shadowed Elm Street, his head buzzed pleasantly and he'd almost relaxed.

Everything was fine, he told himself. All he had to do was hole up for a few weeks and write his novel. The pinnacle of his life was upon him. No more waiting, no more delays, no more distractions…

An image of Jessica's heart-shaped bottom flashed through his mind, but he dismissed it with disciplined speed. He was Daniel MacCormick, for God's sake. He'd been able to ignore everything from mortar fire to threatening Serbs to get his story. Surely he could manage one ponytailed girl and her yapping menagerie.

Feeling better, Daniel turned his bucket of rust into the driveway. Wrestling the boxed chair out of the trunk, he staggered up the sidewalk where mossy grasses grew like living jade in the jagged cracks.

The journey up the narrow, uneven steps to the attic was interesting, but it was the assembly that proved his undoing some three hours later.

"Holy stars!" Grandma Sorenson tilted past his doorjamb to gaze in open-mouthed amazement at the jumble of anonymous pieces and parts spread across the shaggy, outdated carpet. "What an ungodly mess! You need some help?"

Daniel stifled a swear word and thought longingly of his cigarettes. They were so close, only barred from him by one cigarette-snatching lunatic. And the condition was probably hereditary, he thought, scowling at the old woman. "No. Thanks," he said. "I'm doing all right."

"You sure?" Grams took a long-strided step past the doorjamb. "You've got an unholy number of pieces there."

Didn't he just, he thought irritably, fiddling with a knob-bish piece that could have been anything from a drawer pull to the cranium of some visiting extraterrestrial.

A writer! That's what he was. If he'd wanted to be a

carpenter, he'd have bought stock in those droopy pants with the loopy things on the thighs.

"You been at this a while?"

Daniel glanced up from his position on the floor. His whole damn body hurt from stacking bales, he hadn't had a cigarette in three hours and twenty-seven minutes, not that he was counting, and he no longer cared if he won the Mr. Congeniality award. "Does the term 'dawn of time' mean anything to you?"

The old woman stared at him for a prolonged moment, then threw back her head and barked a rusty laugh. "Come on, get up."

"What?"

"Supper's ready. Cooked it myself."

"I don't—"

"You want to insult a frail old lady?" she asked, and gave him a jaundiced glare.

Okay, he'd give her *old*. She'd seen seventy a hell of a lot of years ago, he was sure of that. The shirt she wore was large and old-fashioned, and the belt that cinched her jeans and drooped wearily over one bony hip looked like it might very well have been called into service during World War I.

But frail? She was as lean as a whip and if he didn't miss his guess, she was just about as sharp.

"Get down there," she said and jerked her head toward the stairs.

He knew an order when he heard one, and though he momentarily considered refusing, he found he had to squelch a wild feeling of glee as he escaped the pile of office debris.

The kitchen smelled like... Well, he admitted, tightening a grip on his enthusiasm, it smelled a hell of a lot better than the Greasy Spoon.

"Could you get the milk, Grams?" Jessica asked as she bent over the stove.

Daniel glanced toward the stairs, saw that the old woman hadn't followed him down, and went to the fridge himself.

"Here," he said, nudging Jessie's elbow with the carton.

"Oh!" She started slightly. "Grams, your voice got... higher."

He tilted his head in concession to her anemic wit. "You must have had a good day, Sorenson. You're more complimentary than usual."

She nodded as she lifted a sauce-covered index finger to her lips. He watched its progress with a scowl. "Distocia in one of Olsen's ewes. But we delivered twin lambs. They're doing good."

"Really? Who's the father? Anyone I know?"

She slanted a look at him, one brow slightly raised. "I hope Max didn't disturb you this morning."

Daniel cocked a hip against the counter. "Entertaining a lover, were you?"

She stared at him wide-eyed as a fine blush shaded her cheeks. One point for the journalist.

"I meant the dog."

"Ah," he said, and held her gaze a moment longer before glancing languidly toward the stairs. Grams must be washing up. "Disappointing in bed, was he?"

She glared at him, but the effect was ruined by the blush. Or maybe it was just magically lightened. "The yellow Lab," she countered. "I hope he didn't wake you."

"No, you don't."

She hesitated a moment, not shifting her own attention aside. "Mr. MacCormick," she said dryly as she replaced the cover on the peas and bore the pot to the table. "It's not nice to judge others by your own sorry disposition."

"Why not?" He watched her bend over the table. The shorts were gone now, replaced by a pair of serviceable jeans. But it made little difference. He'd already seen her legs, and could now, he realized, imagine every sun-kissed inch of them.

"Because it's unfair to the rest of the world."

"You two ain't arguing, are you?" Grams snapped from the bottom of the stairs.

"No," Jessie said.

"No, ma'am," Daniel agreed. *Ma'am?* Where the hell had that word been hiding for the past decade? And why did it reappear now?

"Good," the old woman said, retrieving a wooden spoon from a crock full of similar utensils and waving it at him. "Cuz it ticks Cecil off something terrible that you're here, and I plan to enjoy that as long as possible."

Daniel settled into a chair and watched Grams take the seat across from him. The room went silent for a moment, then, "He stole my baby," she said. The words lay in the room like a dead skunk.

"I beg your pardon," Daniel said, noticing with awe that Grams looked like she was damned near tears.

"Stole her right out from under my nose," she murmured.

Jessica dished up a healthy portion of scalloped potatoes and passed them on to Daniel. "Cecil and Grams have had an ongoing battle ever since Baby's birth, five years ago," she explained.

The scalloped potatoes were creamy and delicious with more fat grams than Melissa could have counted, much less eaten on her model's diet. As for Daniel, his taste buds did a little dance of joy.

"I *never* trusted him, though," Grams said, taking a bite of her own meal. "Knew from the first that he was the spawn of Satan."

"Now, Grams," Jessie soothed, as though she'd done so a hundred times. "You know perfectly well you had a soft spot for him before the war."

"He stole my baby!" she snapped.

Jessica glanced at Daniel. "Baby was the product of Mr. Pat and Frenchy."

"Ah," Daniel said, as if he had some inkling of what they were talking about.

Jessica took a dinner roll from the basket and passed it on. "Your uncle owned Mr. Pat. Grams owned Frenchy. They were supposed to mate the horses twice. Cecil would get the first foal, Baby. Grams would get the second. But

Frenchy ruptured her stomach during her second pregnancy." She lifted the roll as if in explanation. "There never was a second foal."

"That first one shoulda been mine," Grams said. "The whole thing was my idea. I offered him a good fair price for Baby, too. But would he take it?"

Apparently not, Daniel thought, tasting the peas. How long had it been since he'd tasted vegetables? He could almost remember now why he used to eat them, before becoming a hopeless junk-food addict.

"No, he wouldn't take it," Grams said.

Daniel had guessed as much. Still, it seemed a rather anemic reason to be battling five years later. But there you had it. If the Hatfields and the McCoys could do it, so could the MacCormicks and the Sorensons.

"Blast it all!" Grams grumbled and, dropping her own roll onto her plate, rose to her feet. "The old coot's gone and put me off my feed again."

Jessica glanced up. "Where are you going?"

Grams sent one long look at Daniel and pushed her chair back. "To clean my gun."

The room went absolutely quiet except for the old woman's footfalls across the floor. Daniel poised his fork over his plate and watched her stride purposefully across the wide expanse of kitchen linoleum and up the carpeted steps.

"Should I lock my door?" he asked.

"Definitely not," Jessica answered, smirking across the table at him.

He gave her a pained smile in return. "Officer Patton might not care about the animals," he said, watching Oscar waddle into the kitchen. "But first-degree murder might be considered a little more serious, even in Oakes."

"Joe's a friend."

"Uh-huh. Even so—"

Down the hall, the door opened.

"Yoo-hoo." The face that peeked around the corner was as round as a cherry and reminded him immediately of a

Disney character. The fairy from *Sleeping Beauty*. What was her name? Flora? "I'm here."

Jessica turned nonplussed toward the hallway. "Aerobics early tonight, Mrs. Conrad?"

The elderly woman's body matched her head perfectly. Round. "No. No. But Rosy was getting lonely."

"Is she feeling better?"

"Oh my, yes. The Pepto-Bismol did wonders."

"Good."

"Come on in, Rosy. Come on in and tell Doctor Jess how you're feeling," she said and tugged on the leash that disappeared around the corner.

A pig waddled in—not a potbellied pig or anything so exotic. Just a pig—pink and fat and, well...rosy.

Daniel wished he could be surprised.

"Doesn't she look fine?" Mrs. Conrad preened.

"She certainly does," Jessica agreed, then turned toward Daniel. "Very handsome. Doesn't she look handsome?"

He gave her a dry glance, considered telling her he only liked his pig with eggs, decided against it, and said, "Delectable."

"Oh, you've got company," said...Merriweather? Was that the fairy's name?

"Yes. Mrs. Conrad, this is..." Jessica paused for a fraction of a second and grinned as if she found something amusing. "Elston Rolands."

"Elston. What an interesting name, and don't you make a lovely couple."

Daniel snapped his gaze from Jessie to the old woman, but found that his brows couldn't go any higher.

"Oh, no." Jessica laughed. "We're not dating," she said, and laughed again, sounding a little hysterical.

It wasn't, he thought, that damn funny.

"Not dating?"

"No."

"Oh. What a shame."

No response from either of them.

"Well, I must away," twittered Mrs. Conrad. "You'll take care of my Rosy?"

"Certainly," Jessica said, taking Rosy's leash in hand. In a second the plump little bundle of energy was gone.

Daniel stared at the door for an instant. "The psych ward must be pretty much empty these days," he said.

"Mrs. Conrad is very nice," Jessie countered. "In fact, she's kind of a one-woman humane society."

"So she takes in animals and finds homes for them?"

"Well…" Jessica hedged as Rosy snuffled up a pair of fallen peas. "She takes animals in. She has a little more trouble with the finding-homes part."

"What?" He attempted to give her a facetious expression of shock. "Your beloved Oakians haven't opened their homes to Rosy's unfortunate brothers and sisters?"

"It's not that. She just can't bear to give them away. Except Oscar," she said as the feline lumbered past. "Elmer Lampstead found him in his corncrib and brought him to Mrs. Conrad. But he was a bit much for her. Kept bothering her mice."

"Elmer or Oscar?"

She gave him a peeved look. "Oscar. Consequently, he's been here ever since."

"Remind me to thank her myself," he said, scowling at the cat as it began scratching at his jeans. "What's he doing?"

"That's sweet," she said as the gargantuan fur ball wrapped his legs around one of Daniel's. "I think he likes you. But wait. You said you weren't gay, right?"

Daniel swore and jerked his leg away. But the animal was as strong as a bear. Clawing his hind feet into the denim, he began chewing lazily on Daniel's knee.

Daniel half rose, but Jessica was already leaning forward with a laugh.

"Oscar!" she scolded, gently slapping the top of his head. "You're scaring Mr. Rolands."

Chagrined, Oscar dropped from Daniel's leg and retreated

stiff-tailed, to stare up at the cupboard he'd fallen from earlier.

"Scared?" Daniel watched Jessie in burgeoning irritation. Not that he cared what she thought. But... "Did I ever tell you about my work in the Irish Republic?"

She laughed. "I don't believe you have. Very brave, were you?"

"Heroic, even."

"How nice for you."

"I thought you'd be impressed," he said and fiddled with his empty cup. "Got any coffee?"

She jerked her head toward him as if startled. "Coffee's bad for you."

He almost laughed. "You've just consumed enough fat to float a battalion. And you're worried about coffee?"

"Grams and I gave up caffeine years ago."

"Ah. And you don't want to be tempted."

"It's no temptation. I'll make coffee if you like."

"No. I just thought I smelled some the other morning. Strange, I would expect to be delusional about cigarettes, not coffee."

"Must be—" she began, but the door burst open again and a trio of feed bags staggered past on wobbly legs.

"Whe du y wun these?"

Daniel stared. "I think it's for you, Sorenson," he said.

"Huh?" said the bags.

"In the kennel. I thought you were working at Casey's tonight," Jessica said, apparently addressing the bags.

"I jus' got finiffed."

"You could have waited until morning."

"No probm," muttered the bags and teetered on, but they had not yet disappeared from sight when they began to slip sideways. The legs staggered, the sacks tilted, and a muffled wail echoed through the house.

Daniel leapt to his feet, but Oscar had returned. Daniel stumbled, nearly spilling to the floor, and Jessica, quick as light, sprinted across the linoleum to grab the sliding bags of feed.

There was a moment of uncertainty as Gnat struggled and Jessica prodded, but finally the bags were stacked amidst the others beside the cages.

"Thanks," Gnat huffed. "I just wanted to make sure you didn't run out of seed before morning."

"You're working too hard, Gnat," Jessie said.

"I thought I saw a pair of bluebirds this morning."

As far as Daniel could tell their conversations were entirely unrelated, but the two seemed to understand each other.

"Did you?"

"Yeah. You got them coming back. And the orioles, too."

"Because you keep bringing the feed."

Gnat smiled shyly, showing slanted incisors and unmistakable infatuation as he shuffled his oversized feet. "Well, I'd better get at it. I'll clean the cages and stuff first, then spend some time with...who did you spay this morning?"

"Romper."

"Yeah."

"You could do it tomorrow," she suggested.

"I'm helping Pete spray beans first thing in the morning."

She shook her head. "All work and no play stunts Jack's growth."

Gnat grinned. "Dad says it's about time. I'm two inches taller than he is already."

"How's he doing?"

He shrugged as he tore open a fifty-pound bag and shoved a scoop inside. "He got a job over in Fairfield, but it's just temporary."

Jessie watched, her expression wistful. "Well, maybe they'll take him on permanently when word gets out that he's the father of a future world-famous surgeon."

"Yeah," Gnat said, his tone self-effacing, but he grinned finally and seemed to relax a little.

"Here," Jessie said, retrieving a bucket near the door. "You go on home. I'll do this."

"No." Gnat pulled the scoop aside, gazing down at Jessica like an oversized basset hound. "I want to do it. Really."

"You sure?"

"Yeah." And when he was done with that, he could try a little walking on water for her, Daniel thought, but he couldn't quite manage the proper disparaging attitude. That was probably what a home-cooked meal did to a man. Took away that killer instinct.

"Well, I'll leave you to it, then." Jessie turned back toward the kitchen, leash in hand, and jumped as she nearly ran into Daniel. "Oh!" she said.

He scowled. Rosy snorted. Where the hell did she think he was going to be this time?

"You need help with the dishes?"

"No. No." She took a steadying breath. "You'd better get some rest."

His scowl deepened. She was doing it again. Acting as if he was about to keel over like a parched daylily. It was rather disconcerting. Not to mention a bit wearing on his masculine pride. He automatically began pulling his cigarettes out of his breast pocket.

It took him a moment to realize her gaze was pinned to his chest.

He scowled. "I'll just…smoke this outside."

She scowled. "I…um…would rather you didn't."

"What?"

"It's…Gnat," she said and tilted her head toward the kennel. "He's young."

"I wasn't planning to shove his head in the toilet until he joined me."

"Whatever, you're a role model."

"He does seem attached to me. I thought I saw him glance my way once. But I was wrong. He was still staring at you," Daniel said. But no matter how sarcastic he managed to sound, she still stared disapprovingly at the cigarettes. With a mental sigh, he slid the package back into his pocket.

She dropped her gaze, her lashes long as jungle fronds against her cheeks. "Thank you."

God, she was fresh-faced. "No problem." He hated fresh faces. Give him an old gnarled mug anytime. "I enjoy nicotine withdrawal."

The corner of a smile tilted her mouth, and for a moment Daniel forgot to breathe. "Funny you haven't quit before, then."

"Oh, I have," he said. "But it's so much fun." He shrugged. "I had to start again just for a repeat performance."

"The perfect opportunity, then."

"Couldn't be better."

"So you're going to quit?"

"What?"

"You're going to quit smoking?"

Hell no, he thought, but she looked so hopeful. "Sure. Why not?"

"I always thought it was harder than that."

"Not for me."

She smiled. His heart did a little double knot in his chest, and his breath jammed. "Promise?"

"Sure."

They stood inches apart, staring at each other for a moment. Then she said, "Well, I'll let you get to sleep," and turned away.

Sleep? Doubtful, Daniel thought, but made his way up the stairs, recapping the day as he went.

Yep, this had been a red-letter day. He'd failed at writing, been attacked by a horny cat, outmaneuvered by a pony-tailed Pollyanna, and subsequently sent to bed without a smoke.

Things couldn't get much worse, he thought, but as he turned the corner to his bedroom, he stopped in the doorway and changed his mind.

Grandma Sorenson had single-handedly assembled his office furniture.

5

"JOSY SEEN YOU SMOKING!"

Mama's face was pinched and disapproving. Moral in-dignation seeped from her like… Like what, Daniel wor-ried. *Like smoke from a factory.* No. *Like stink from the garbage.* No. *Like pus from a wound.* Damn! Think! He had to think…and delete.

Moral indignation seeped from her. Period!

"I wasn't smoking," Alysha said.

"You're a liar. Just like your father."

Pain tightened like a noose around Alysha's throat. "I'm not like him." Her words were a bleak whisper of despair, like a chilling wind through clapboard siding. Not bad.

She couldn't bear to look up, couldn't bear to see the disgust on her mother's face, to know that she—

Laughter spilled up through the floor grate like un-shaded sunlight, crashing again into Daniel's thoughts. He gritted his teeth against the unwanted merriment and slapped a hand to his shirt pocket. The cigarettes were still there—out of habit. He gritted his teeth harder.

"Just had to share…with…" From the first floor, the deep voice stuttered unrelated words, then dropped into silence.

Bill. Daniel knew it was Bill. Just "come by to collect his check, if it isn't too much trouble."

Jessica laughed again. "I'll make sure Grams…"

Bits of broken dialogue drifted up to him like lazy clouds. "How…she…"

"…hard. You know…"

Silence. Finally, blessed silence.

Daniel set his fingers to the keyboard again.

Alysha's soul felt dead.

"No one understands..." Bill's voice. "...better... when Abby threatened...leave me."

What? Daniel's attention snapped irritably to the floor grate.

"...still hard..." Jessica said.

What was hard?

"If there's anything..."

The voices were quieter now, barely audible. Daniel leaned sideways. The new chair creaked. What? What was going on? Why the secret mutterings?

"...an addi..."

Addi...what? Daniel leaned precariously sideways from his chair, holding his breath and waiting for the next word.

"...all right," Jessica said. "Grams...tough as—"

A rap sounded at the door. Daniel jerked his head up, nearly squawking like a startled chicken as his chair slammed its rollers back onto the uneven carpet.

"How's that furniture working out?" The door was already open, and Grams's gray head was stuck inside the room.

Daniel searched frantically for some kind of words, some kind of expletive, some kind of explanation, then realized suddenly that he didn't have to explain anything to her. He was Daniel MacCormick. At least he used to be.

"The furniture's fine," he said.

"Good. Glad to hear it." She was quiet for a moment, then continued. "I was a farmer all my life, you know. That's why I could get them things together. You been...well...you been doing whatever you do in the city. I suppose you haven't had much time to make things."

"No."

"I gotta keep busy," she said and, dipping her gaze to

his chest, licked her parchment lips. "Idle hands is hands of the devil, you know."

Dear God! Was she propositioning him? "Listen," he said, his tone carefully gruff. "I appreciate you assembling my furniture, but just now I need some privacy." It was the voice he used to make cub reporters run back into their little dens for the winter, that made sources spill their guts, that even made seasoned editors think twice before questioning his methods.

Grams laughed. "Privacy, my foot!" she said, snapping her gaze from his chest. "If you was any more private, you'd be growing mushrooms behind your ears."

It required phenomenal control to keep his jaw from dropping.

"Come on down and have some breakfast," she said, as if they were bosom buddies.

He lowered his brows. "I don't want any breakfast," he growled, and wondered vaguely if he sounded more like an award-winning reporter or a petulant boy.

"You lose any more weight, them pants is gonna fall right off you." She grinned. "Not that you're likely to have anything I haven't seen before. Still..." She winked. "Don't want your Uncle Cecil thinking we're taking advantage of you."

They were all insane. "Listen. I'm trying to get some work done here."

It was the wrong thing to say.

"Yeah?" She was inside his room in a heartbeat. Amazing how fast the old girl could move if she wanted to. "What you working on?"

With one frantic movement, Daniel poked the monitor into blackness. "Mrs. Sorenson!" He feared his ace reporter's voice had lost a bit of edge, but he refused to believe he heard a squeak in it as he swiveled his chair back toward her. "Listen! I know you think—"

"Bet a couple of cigarettes would do you a world a good about now, huh?" she said, then scowled. "'Course my granddaughter would chew you in half if she saw you smoking." She sighed. "So—you might just as well come down and have some breakfast."

Certifiable! "I don't want any breakfast!" he growled again, leaning out of his chair.

The old woman's eyes widened. Daniel held his breath. Dammit! He'd pushed too hard. He couldn't afford to lose this pathetic little room in this pathetic little house in this pathetic little town. Not now, when he'd almost found his muse, he thought, and frantically tried to remember how to apologize.

It was then that Grams laughed.

"Oh, yeah. You got it bad. It's eating you alive," she said and winked. "Well, when you can't stand it no more, you come on over to my room."

Was she propositioning him? He tried to force out a question, but the paralyzing fear that she might answer kept him silent.

"First door on the left," she said, and, turning on a worn boot heel, exited the room.

It took him fifteen minutes to focus enough to turn the monitor back on, thirty to delve back into the story, and two hours to admit defeat.

Tiny smatterings of conversation drifted up through the floor grate again, snagging his attention. The stairs creaked, making him jump every time in anticipation of another demented visitor. He needed a cigarette more than he needed air, and every second the cursor blinked at him like a damned Cyclops.

Jerking to his feet, Daniel sent the wheeled chair careening groggily over the shag carpet, and paced. It was then that he smelled the coffee. He stopped in his tracks, sniffing the air like a wolf on a scent.

True, he wanted nothing from this house of lunatics. But giving up smoking and coffee in one fell swoop— well, when all was said and done, he'd rather donate a testicle to science.

The ancient stairs creaked beneath his weight as the scent led him downward.

From the music room, metal clinked against glass. Gnat chuckled. Jessica laughed.

He passed the doorway, drawn hopelessly toward the kitchen.

Coffee. He found a mug and poured himself a cup just as a cupboard burst open and a huge blob of fur torpedoed to the floor.

Oscar hit the linoleum with a splat, then sat up with a moody sigh.

"Huh," Daniel said as the earthy aroma of coffee curled seductively into his nostrils. He took a sip, closed his eyes ecstatically and succumbed entirely.

Half the cup gone, and feeling marginally better, he refilled it, then wandered back toward the stairs. But if he reached the upper floor, it would be difficult to find inventive ways to avoid working. Even talking to the natives seemed preferable for a moment, so he stepped into the doorway of what had once been the music room.

"You found the coffee," Jessie said.

"Yeah," he agreed, and, since the caffeine had improved his mood, added, "thanks, I—" But at that moment Gnat moved aside, granting Daniel an unobstructed view of the stainless-steel table that stood between them.

A large yellow dog lay on its back on that table. Its tongue was lolling out, but that was hardly the protruding body part that snagged Daniel's attention.

Jessica glanced up, rubber-gloved hands poised over the neat incision. "No problem. I drink chamomile tea myself, but since you're giving up smoking, I thought coffee might be a good idea."

Daniel swallowed, cleared his throat and resolutely ignored the surgery site. "Uh-huh."

She shrugged. "Ever seen a neuter performed?"

Dear God, there was something rather disconcerting about seeing his ponytailed little nemesis removing testicles, even if it was on a dog. He'd only been joking about donating his own to science. "No. Can't say I have."

"Blood doesn't bother you, does it?"

Define bother. "I thought I told you about my time in Ireland."

She grinned, then, "Tighten up on that testicle, will you, Gnat? Great. Could you bring over that bottle, MacCormick, long as you're here?"

"Bottle?"

"With the gauze. There on the shelf."

"Oh. Sure." He retrieved said bottle while glancing about in an attempt to avoid looking at the incision, or the exposed testicle, or the dog in general for that matter.

"Thanks. Open it, will you?" she asked, holding her rubber-gloved hands high.

He did so, and then she was back in action again.

Daniel told himself to leave. His novel was waiting. It was why he'd come here. But he remained where he was, staring in fascination at the dog.

"This Max?" he asked finally.

"Yeah. How'd you know?"

"Recognized the ear thing," he said, nodding toward the odd, red clip that lay on a nearby counter.

"Oh, Grams's ear-saver."

"Uh-huh," he said, trying halfheartedly to make it sound as though he had some idea what she was talking about.

She grinned. "Labs are prone to ear infections, because of the floppy ears. No air getting into the canal. So Grams invented a device to improve air flow. Helps cure the infections."

"Don't you have drugs for that?"

"Sure," she said. "But why use drugs when you can achieve the same effect for less money?"

"Because it's your business?" he guessed wildly.

She gave him a look. "My business is keeping animals healthy."

"Ah," he said and let the silence fall around them. This, then, was the very essence of Jessica Sorenson—a medical doctor who avoided medicine, Daisy Mae with showgirl toenails, a dedicated overeater who avoided caffeine like the plague. A woman of a thousand contradictions, but who was she really?

He had thought, at times, that she hadn't changed at all in the past decade, but he'd been undiscerning. If he was careful, he could see the differences—a shadow of caution born of ages and...and what? Hardships? Where she had once seemed naive in her optimistic view of the world, she now seemed...resolute—as if she could mold the world into what she wanted it to be. But was it naiveté or determination? Either way, she had somehow maintained her look of fresh-faced innocence. Not a smudge of makeup lined her eyes or colored her lips, and yet there wasn't a model in New York who wouldn't covet—

"Nolveson, please."

The sound of her voice jerked him back to the present. When not a soul moved, he wondered, a bit frantically, if she'd been addressing him. But in an instant, she lifted her gaze to her assistant.

"Gnat?"

"What?" The boy snapped to attention, a blush already rushing over his lean cheeks.

"I need the Nolveson."

"Oh." He knocked over two bottles and a small box as he fumbled for the spray. "Sorry."

She laughed as she turned her gaze back down to her patient. "What were *you* daydreaming about?"

"Nothing!" Gnat said, and Daniel almost snorted.

The poor sap, he thought as he left the surgery and hurried up the stairs. He pitied the guy pathetic enough to be mooning over Jessica Sorenson.

THE HOURS DRONED ON. The words did not.

Daniel slammed back his chair and paced again. From his newly assembled desk, the computer stared at him. The blank screen laughed. The cursor winked.

Damn it! How was he supposed to be creative when that damned cursor kept blinking?

Storming repeatedly across the room, he glared at the wall, the window, the bed. It used to be so natural, so simple. He could write while curled in a chair or lounging in bed or...

That was it! There was too much pressure. In his youth he had simply jotted his thoughts down in a spiral notebook, then eventually typed them onto plain twenty-pound on an ancient Smith-Corona.

All he needed was a notebook...and an old Smith-Corona.

PURCHASING A CARTON of spiral notebooks was simple. Locating a still functioning Smith-Corona was not. But finally he managed it.

Eight hours, an almost decent meal, and two hundred dollars later, he returned to the Animal House in the dark. Parking his dilapidated car out front, he retrieved his box of notebooks and hiked up the porch stairs. The front door was open, leaving only the screen to guard the inhabitants from the night. But judging by Oakes's sleepy main street, all was perfectly safe.

Light streamed across him in a golden slant as he wrestled the door open and stepped inside.

"Oh." Jessica turned toward him with a nervous laugh. "It's you."

Daniel glanced at her, then hurried his gaze to the man who stood not far away. He was in his mid-thirties, handsome in a mild sort of way, with a receding hairline and a sensitive face. Daniel instantly hated him.

"So, Jessica, this must be your new boarder," he guessed.

And who the hell are you? Daniel wondered. Not that he cared.

"Yes. Yes he is. Elston, I'd like you to meet Reverend Tony. He and his wife just moved here from Minneapolis a few months ago. He's an avid bird-watcher."

"And fond of other creatures of the woods as well."

"Reverend?" Daniel said, not trying to extend a hand as he focused on that one word.

"Yes." He had a melodic voice. A pastoral voice. "I'm the associate pastor at Vision of Glory."

"Oh," Daniel said, disavowing the sense of relief that washed through him.

Silence sloshed through the room.

"So, Mr. Rolands, will you be staying long in Oakes?"

"Not too long," Daniel said and, finding he was fresh out of social amenities, shuffled from foot to foot. The box was getting heavy, and why the hell was he standing around, anyway? It wasn't as if he cared if there was another man in the house. That kind of behavior was for rottweilers and husbands, not for an award-winning journalist who could buy and sell this faded little town if he wanted. So giving the pastor a brief nod, he fumbled his way up the stairs to deposit the oversized box on his bed.

The kitchen was still silent as he trekked through, only to return moments later with his typewriter.

"...should be going," the pastor was saying now and Daniel couldn't help but agree.

"Thanks for stopping by."

"My pleasure," the pastor said, then, "Do you need any help carrying your stuff upstairs?" he asked, turning his attention toward Daniel.

"This is the last trip."

"All right. Well, it was nice meeting you, Mr. Rolands."

"Uh-huh." *So go away,* Daniel thought, but he could think of no reason to remain and finally carried the typewriter up the stairs. In his room, Daniel flipped on the light with his elbow, set his precious cargo safely on the bed beside the notebooks, then hurried to his desk. A thrill of satisfaction shivered up his spine as he unplugged the computer. This was it—exactly what he needed to finish his novel. Nothing would stand in the way now. He was destined for—

"Your...wife doesn't...." Jessica's voice drifted up in hushed fragments.

"...suspect anything...mustn't...break her heart. But I can't..."

"I know...quiet...but...hard..." There was a moment of prolonged silence, then "Good night."

Daniel sat in brain-numbed silence.

Jessica Sorenson...and a Lutheran pastor!

6

DANIEL STRODE across his matted carpet once again. He'd somehow managed to sleep for a few hours during the night and had risen only to pace again.

Alysha! Troubled. Afraid. What choices would she make now? Would she crumble under her mother's harsh disapproval and become a shell of the woman she should be, or would she run away in search of freedom and acceptance only to find heartbreak and misery on the—

"Damn!" Daniel swore out loud. Sorenson and a pastor? A pastor! And not just that, but a *married* pastor. Not that he cared. At all! Why would he care? But she was so bright and— He didn't care! He was here to write a book and nothing else. But—Sorenson with a *pastor?*

He wished he hadn't heard the conversation. To another, the snatches of dialogue might have seemed innocent enough, but not to him. He was an investigative reporter, honed to learn volumes from a single spoken word, and those words—

He swore again and jerked his mind back to the matter at hand.

Alysha! Confused, needy, crushed by her mother and—

And that was another thing! Jessica's grandmother. Had the old woman made a pass at him? It seemed impossible. But...damn! "Come to my room when you can't stand it any more?" That was a hard thing to misinterpret. Still—

Daniel's thoughts crashed to a halt.

Addiction! That was the word he'd been unable to understand. That was what Bill and Jess had been talking about. Grams was fighting an addiction and Bill... Bill had the same problem. Bill, who had left a thriving practice in Chicago. Why, but because of devastating problems, something neither his wife nor his employer could tolerate. Why, but to leave a sordid past behind? Drugs were the obvious answer. His wife had threatened to leave him, so he had packed up his diplomas and left behind the environment that was too tempting—had come to Oakes for healing. Oakes, where he probably had neither the means nor the opportunity to obtain drugs. Oakes, where everything was everybody else's business. Where he would be safe from himself.

But had he been successful in his goal or—

Maybe Grandma Sorenson was supplying him!

Maybe she was a drug runner. That was it—the plants! They seemed innocent enough, but so did poppies—Poppies! Opium! And if she had opium, who was to say she didn't have heroin and—

Damn! Daniel slammed a lid on his wild thoughts. He was losing his mind. Going over the deep end with the proverbial millstone tied around his neck.

Dropping onto the end of his bed, Daniel closed his eyes and plopped his head into his palms. Yes, he was losing his mind, but who could blame him? He was stuck here in the barren wastes of the Midwest with an unfaithful muse and—

Humming! He lifted his head slightly. Was he hearing humming again? he wondered. But it didn't matter. Nothing mattered but his book. For all he knew maybe Grandma Sorenson was the deadliest drug runner in three counties. Maybe Jessica was having an affair with the Pope. He didn't know and he didn't care. He was here to write, to chronicle Alysha's tragic life. To mesmerize the American public with his tragic prose and—

It was humming! Dammit, he couldn't work with humming! Slamming the door open, Daniel stormed down the stairs.

"MacCormick!" Sorenson said, as if shocked once again to see him.

He stared. She had a neck like a prima donna and fairylike

feet, but it was her mouth that captured him today. It was carnation-pink and... No, not carnation exactly. Salmon, maybe. But anyway, it was bowed and wide and mobile. Laughter was its best friend, honesty its companion. She couldn't be an adulteress. She was—

Damn him!

"What's that humming?" he growled.

"Humming? Oh." Shuffling a box of syringes and some indefinable hose whose purpose he refused to contemplate, she nodded toward the surgery. "It's Gnat."

He lowered his brows. "The Oakes all-boy humming quartet? They can't afford instruments?"

She gave him a look. "Listen, MacCormick, I'd love to stand here and trade insults, but I gotta go," she said and, shuffling her paraphernalia again, headed for the door. "Horse with colic. Don't think it's necessary to say goodbye if you feel an aching need to head back to L.A."

"New York," he corrected and glared at her, but she was already exiting. The screen banged shut and there seemed little purpose in glowering at the door, so he strode into the surgery room. Sure enough, Gnat was sitting cross-legged in front of a cage, humming tunelessly as he petted Max with long, even strokes. The huge dog lay on its side, ears pinned up again, tongue lolling happily.

"Hummmmm," Gnat said.

For a moment, Daniel considered telling him to shut the hell up, but the boy probably wasn't to blame. Perhaps insanity was contagious and he'd caught it from the rest of the loons in this house. But then perhaps it was simply genetic and—

Of course, Gnat was probably related to the Sorensons in some way, inbreeding being what it was in—

Daniel caught his breath. That was it! All this time he'd been planning to set his book in a major city. But he'd been wrong. Alysha didn't live in Chicago or New York or Detroit. She lived in Iowa, in Oakes, Iowa. And she herself was the product of incest, but...perhaps she didn't know it.

Without another thought—without a backward glance—
Daniel rushed up the stairs to his bedroom.

THREE HOURS LATER, he felt as if he'd been trying to pull
his brains out through his ears. He knew exactly what he
had to do, exactly what he had to write. But the words,
bound inside him like wedding rice in a sparrow, refused to
come.

By midmorning, he took to pacing. By noon, his head
throbbed like a Ugandan war drum. By evening, his guts
were knotted and his back ached and barely a single page
had been written.

Somewhere in the house the phone rang. He snarled, ran
clawed fingers through his hair and continued along his
caged path. The house fell quiet again. His nerves cranked
tighter.

A knock sounded at his door. He jumped at the sound,
growling as he did so.

"What?"

"MacCormick?" Jessica called. Her tone sounded worried, but he didn't care, certainly not enough to open the
door.

"Go away."

"Listen, I've got a problem."

He snorted at the ridiculousness of the obvious, but said
nothing as he paced again.

"Danny?" She rapped twice. "Can I come in for a minute?"

"No."

But she was already opening the door.

He turned with a snarl. "Ever heard of privacy?" he
snarled. "Ever—" but she interrupted him.

"What happened to *you?*"

He glared at her. Why the hell did she always look so
damn bright-eyed. He hated bright eyes. "I'm working."

"Working? In purgatory? What's wrong."

"Nothing's wrong!" he snapped.

"Then why—never mind," she said, raising a hand impatiently. "Listen, I've got a problem."

"Yeah," he agreed, and offered no more.

"Gnat—"

"Is the product of incest, thus his limited mental capacity and—"

"Limited? He got fourteen hundred on his SATs. He's a natural-born doctor, but even with scholarships, he can't afford—" She shook her head and stumbled to a halt. "Listen, Gnat's working at Casey's. Grams is playing bingo with Betty. Even—"

"Good for you," he said, and, reaching out, grabbed her arms suddenly. "Now's your time to escape, Sorenson. When no one's around to stop you."

Her lips—were they orchid-colored? No. They parted slightly as she pulled her arms from his grasp. "What on earth is wrong with you?" she demanded.

Daniel ground his teeth and drew a deep breath. Yes, he knew this little town's ugly secrets, but apparently she wasn't prepared to admit them yet. What could he do but play along?

"What the hell do you want, Sorenson?"

She eyed him with raised brows, as if rethinking her reasons for being there, but finally she voiced her request. "I need your help."

He paused a second, waiting for her to continue. She didn't. "With—" he began, but the musical ring of the doorbell interrupted him.

Jessica snapped her head up with a slight inhalation. "There she is now. Come on. We've got to hurry."

"We?" he asked, but she had grabbed his arm and was dragging him toward the stairs.

"Yes." Her voice was low. "But you have to be calm. Act like everything's fine."

"Everything what?"

"Greta's already nervous."

"Who the hell is Greta?"

"The owner."

"Of—"

"Shh," she hushed and, dropping his arm, pulled the door smoothly open. "Come on in."

Daniel could only assume it was Greta, carrying a cardboard box, who hurried past the potted plants into the hallway. She was a plain woman, about age forty, overweight and nondescript, except for her eyes, which had the soulful draw of something between a basset hound and an angel.

"How's she doing?" Jessica asked.

"Nothing's happening." The woman's voice was little more than a whisper, her pale mouth pursed.

"When did you notice she was in labor?" Jessie asked, leading the way into the surgery room.

Greta set the box on the gleaming steel table and reached inside. "I just got home from work. I didn't know when to..." She cleared her throat and stared inside the box. "I didn't know when to expect the puppies."

"Well, let's get her out of there."

In a moment the dog was on the table. At least, Daniel *thought* it was a dog. It more closely resembled a mop that had mated with a soccer ball. It was tricolored, shaggy as a musk-ox and round as a globe.

It stood panting in the middle of the table, its legs shaking as it twisted its neck around to lick Jessica's wrist.

"Can you..." Greta's voice faded. "You can help her?"

"We're going to try."

"I mean..." Greta's gaze flicked to Daniel and back to Jessie. "I know she's just a stray." She swallowed hard. "Worthless really," she said, but when she reached out to smooth her hand over the dog's ears, her hand was shaking. "About your fee—I'm afraid I won't be able to pay you everything at once, but—"

"We'll worry about that later," Jessie said. It was not, Daniel thought, any kind of way for a sane entrepreneur to conduct business. But then, Jessica Sorenson was anything but sane. "Hold her for a second, will you? I'm going to give her something to help her relax."

Little mop dog didn't seem to notice as the needle slipped

into her hindquarter. Greta cuddled her against her bosom as Jessica did a quick exam.

"What do you think?" Greta's voice shook.

"I'm afraid things are stopped up pretty tight. It looks like we'll have to do a cesarean."

"Oh." Greta swallowed again. "Do you want....I mean, should I stay and help?"

"No." Jessica shook her head. "Thank you. We can handle it."

Greta shifted her basset-hound gaze to Daniel.

"Try not to worry," Jessica said. "Waif's tougher than she looks and...Mr. Rolands is an excellent assistant."

What?

Greta skittered her gaze to Daniel's, but he was too stunned either to glower or think up an appropriate swear word.

"Okay. I'll..." Greta cleared her throat. "I'll go, then." She turned away, then turned back and slipped her fingers over the dog's head again. "You be good for Doctor Jess, Waif. I'll...be back for you as soon as I can."

The door finally closed behind her.

Daniel scowled at Jessica.

"Watch her," she said.

"Watch her do what?"

"I have to get the anesthetic. Just make sure she doesn't jump off the table."

"I hate to intrude upon your delusions," he said, turning toward her even as he placed a hand on the dog's back. "But I am not, nor have I ever been, a veterinary assistant."

"Here." She had returned with a glass bottle and a clipper, which was plugged into the nearby wall. "Hold her up against your body. Right hand around her nose. Left behind her elbow."

"Elbow?"

"Don't be obtuse. There." She pressed the little round mop against his chest. He could feel the warmth of her hand even through his shirt. "Hold her snug now. She's a sweet little thing, but she's nervous. She might bite."

"Bite?"

She glanced up. "You're not nervous, are you?"

He scowled. If he remembered correctly, he didn't like being bitten. But there was something about looking like a weenie in her eyes that made him cringe inwardly. "I spent two weeks at San Quentin."

"As prisoner or reporter?"

"Reporter disguised as a prisoner."

She raised her brows. "How do I always manage to forget how macho you are?" she asked, and, lifting the dog's left paw, shaved a patch off the forearm. In an instant she had slipped a needle into a vein and in little more than another second or two the dog went limp in Daniel's arms.

He gazed down at the little mop with a sliver of surprise. "Are you telling me you have some idea what you're doing, Sorenson?"

"Of course I know what I'm doing. Lay her on her side."

"Listen, I don't have time for this. I have to—"

"I think you've done enough pacing for one lifetime, MacCormick."

His gut tightened. "What makes you think I've been pacing?"

She snorted. "You've worn a path halfway through the underflooring. If you don't quit, Grams'll find you in the basement with her oregano. Lift that leg."

"This one?" he asked, raising the left hind.

"Yeah. A little higher. I've got to shave her."

He scowled at the gargantuan belly, stretched tight and pink beneath the clippers. "She could make quite a convincing ad for birth control," he said.

"Yeah, well, when you can convince dogs to watch television you let me know."

"I meant—"

"Hand me that bottle."

"This?"

"Next one. There. Spray down the incision site."

Incision site! He didn't like the sound of that.

"Listen, Sorenson…" he began, but she interrupted again.

"For once you're going to have to think of somebody but yourself, MacCormick. Waif needs you. Greta needs you." She paused. "*I* need you." Lifting her face, she stared at him with somber intensity. "It doesn't make me happy, either. But there it is."

The room went absolutely silent. Try as he might, he couldn't seem to pull his gaze from her eyes.

"All right," he said finally.

"All right." She sounded relieved and breathless.

The rest of the preparations went by quickly. Waif was strapped down on her back. A tray filled with pink liquid and silver instruments was wheeled in. The little dog was draped with a towel and…

"Are you ready?" Jessica asked, glancing up at him, scalpel poised.

His stomach twisted. "You ever done this before, Sorenson?"

"I saw it performed on a pig once."

"Damn," he said, and she laughed.

For the next few moments he was too preoccupied with wondering if she was joking to notice the incision—until he saw the white line that followed the scalpel's course—the white line that slowly turned to red.

She glanced up. "You're not going to faint, are you?"

"Didn't I tell you about—"

"San Quentin?" she said and smiled, but from then on it was all business. Instruments were requested and found. Organs popped into and out of view. There was a final incision, and then a dark, slimy blob was fished from inside the dog's bloated body.

Jessica pulled it into the bright light of the room. It squeaked and squirmed in her gloved hand.

"Heating pad," she said.

"What?" He pulled his gaze from the wiggling blob with an effort. It was, he was certain, at least half the size of the mother.

"The heating pad," she said, nodding toward a cupboard. "Plug it in and grab another towel."

He did as ordered. In a matter of minutes, four puppies wiggled and grunted inside a nest made of heating pad and towels.

The suturing took some time. Daniel dabbed and fetched until finally Waif was turned onto her side and given another injection.

"To wake her up," Jessica said.

Daniel stared at the neat row of sutures. "She may prefer to sleep for a while—maybe a month."

"No time," Jessie said. "She's a mother now."

"Definitely a birth-control incentive."

"At least a good argument for abstaining from copulating with dogs twice your size."

He stifled a chuckle as he stared at her. "You're never going to fool people with those angelic looks if you say things like that."

She glanced up, grinning slightly. "I'm surprised at you, MacCormick. Still haven't learned not to judge people by appearances?"

"You didn't fool me for a minute."

"Oh," she said, and laughed as she continued her work.

In a moment Waif was lifting her head and in another couple of seconds she was lapping a pink tongue over the closest of her dark, squirming pups and thwapping her feathery tail against the heating pad.

Jessica set the boxed family on the floor and turned off the surgery light. The room settled into dim hominess as they stared at the new family.

Neither spoke for some time. Waif's tail wapped again as she nuzzled a pup toward her milk supply.

Silence. Then, "All right, I admit it," Daniel said.

"Admit what?" She raised her gaze. Morning-glory-blue. Definitely. But her mouth was still a mystery.

"You really *are* a vet."

She laughed. "You thought I was lying?"

"I thought you were deluded." He shrugged. "But I may have misjudged you."

"Well…" She lowered her eyes, fiddling with a towel that was wrapped around the pups. "I thought you were an ogre. But I may have misjudged you, too."

7

NOW WOULD PROBABLY BE the perfect time to make his way up to his room, Daniel thought. After all, when a woman started to suspect he was human it seemed a fairly strong cue to exit immediately. But...

Well, the room seemed very serene. Soothing, somehow. And Jessie... Well, there were no words for Jessie, no words for a woman who defied definition at every turn.

"You saying I've been grumpy?" he asked.

Carefully placing used surgical instruments next to the sink, she sprayed down the table and wiped off the top. "Grumpy?" she asked, slanting a quizzical look toward him. "No. Intolerable? Yes." After tossing the soiled towels into a nearby bin, she settled onto the carpet to watch the new family.

Daniel glanced down and debated leaving, but there was comfort in this room, quiet. No ghosts of failing muses or hopeless loss of talent. Even the memories of his mother seemed softened, and in a moment he too had settled on the carpet facing the box.

Silence drifted comfortably between them.

From the kitchen, something bumped noisily, startling him, but Jessie remained calm.

"Oscar?" he asked and she nodded. "Has it ever occurred to you that this is an odd place?"

"Odd?" She shook her head. "No."

"Why did you stay here, Sorenson? I have this strange and decidedly disconcerting feeling that you could be successful anywhere."

She blinked at him. "Is that a compliment?"

He winced. "God, I hope not."

Her laughter rang like the nostalgic sound of church bells in the room. He didn't like church bells, he reminded himself vaguely.

"Why here?" he asked again.

"Small towns…" She shrugged. "There's a beauty to them, but they're fading so fast, losing so much. I like to think I have a purpose here. Or maybe it's just home."

He longed to ridicule those words, but regardless of the years that had passed, the abandonment he'd known here, he couldn't quite deny that this place did have an indefinable feeling of rightness. It seemed almost as if he had never left, but had, instead, spent every day of his life in this quiet little corner of nowhere.

"And you?" she said.

"What?"

"It's no mystery why I'm here. But you—" She paused for a moment as she lifted a quizzical shoulder and reached over the box to stroke the little dog's head. "Why did you come back?"

He stared at her. It wasn't right that she had changed so little from their youth, that she had kept her wistful optimism.

"Are you ill?" she asked.

"Back to that again?"

"I'm sorry," she said. "It's just…" She paused. "You haven't been home for so long. Not even for your father's funeral."

The silence was biting.

"And you're wondering why?" he asked finally.

"No." She shook her head. "I know why."

"Really?"

"Your mother left you." Her voice was very soft, and she didn't meet his eyes. "The memories were too painful for you to come back."

His gut had cramped up tight, but when she lifted her gaze to his, he felt his tension slowly dissipate.

"Am I right?" she asked.

He shrugged. "I was going to say I was too busy."

She smiled gently. The expression pressed a crescent dimple into her left cheek. "I didn't think you were the kind to take the easy way out, MacCormick."

"You'd be surprised."

"I doubt it."

"That good a judge of people, are you?"

She glanced at the pups, a faraway look in her eyes. "He was really proud of you."

He said nothing. Couldn't.

"Your dad," she continued. "I heard him talking at the coffee shop once. About you. How talented you are."

"When was that?"

"I don't know. Seven, eight years ago?"

"After Mom's death. Maybe after he finally knew she was gone for good—" He stopped himself, remembering some discipline.

"What?"

He warned himself not to go on. Not to let down his guard, not for anyone, certainly not for her. But the warning seemed strangely dim somehow.

"Maybe when he knew she wouldn't come back he could think of something else."

"Something like you?"

Quiet settled in.

"Do I sound as whiny as I think I do?"

"No." She smiled again. His tension loosened a little more. "You've got a right to hurt, MacCormick."

"I don't hurt," he said, knee-jerk reaction kicking in with a vengeance.

"Sometimes it helps to open up a tiny crack."

He stared at her. "I don't do that, either."

"I noticed."

Daniel drew a deep breath and settled onto an elbow as he lay down on his side. "So what about you, Sorenson? Your memories can't all be that rosy."

She shrugged. "More good than bad," she said. "I like

the people. I like the place. I guess that's why I'm still here. But I never thought you'd come back.''

"Miss me?" he asked, his tone carefully light.

"I've been a long time without a sparring partner."

What? No laughter? No frantic denial? For a moment he forgot how to breathe, much less talk, but he forced something out. "Gnat not much at debating?"

"Gnat's empathetic and bright and intuitive, but sometimes he has trouble concentrating when—"

"When you're in the universe?"

She raised her brows at him as if silently analyzing his words. He winced. He rarely appeared in a favorable light under analysis.

"I'm his mentor," she said finally. "A mother figure, sort of."

"Uh-huh."

Apparently the sarcasm was obvious, because surprise showed sharply on her too young features.

He shrugged. "If Mosquito thinks of you as a mother, Saddam Hussein is my favorite aunt."

She tilted her head slightly. "I see the resemblance. In personality, anyway."

He tried to glare, but it was difficult. Her impish smile was hopelessly infectious. Their gazes met. Her mouth, full and sweet as blooming rosebuds, went serious. But finally she dropped her gaze back toward the box and cleared her throat.

"I'm sorry things are rough for you right now, MacCormick."

Rough? He would have said it out loud, but it seemed, suddenly, quite hard to speak.

"I know I've been…well…less than hospitable. I didn't mean to add to your troubles. It's just that…" She sighed. "It's been hard…you know…with Grams and school bills and…well, it seemed like things were just coming together for us when you showed up. I was afraid…" She shrugged. "I was afraid Cecil would throw me to the wolves when his wildly successful nephew returned. But I guess he—"

"Has a hard time concentrating when you're in the universe?" He hadn't really intended on saying that again, because it sounded disturbingly like an admission of her charm, but when she smiled, it seemed suddenly quite worth the risk.

"He's been a dear. Helped us a lot," she said. "I'd like to…help you in return."

He found to his surprise that he was holding his breath. Why the hell would he do that?

"Help me?" he managed, and marveled at how amazingly soft her throat looked. With her flaxen mane lying in waves against it, it seemed almost unnatural. How would it feel to kiss her there?

"I know things aren't going so well for you right now."

How many times had he fantasized about kissing her when he was a kid? Oh yeah, she'd irked him, but…damn, the soft, endless meadow of that neck.

"Things will get better."

"Will they?" he asked and thought for a moment that being this near her warmth might be as good as it got.

"Sure," she said, and pushed herself to her feet with typical briskness. She glanced down at him. "Want some tea?"

"Might keep me awake."

"It's caffeine-free."

"Then it might put me to sleep. Postpone my pacing," he said and she laughed and thrust out her hand.

He slid his palm against hers. His heart rate picked up a notch and inside him a jaded soul laughed at his childish breathlessness. Her fingers felt somehow fragile and strong at the same time. The feel of them sent a spark of sensation coursing up his arm as he rose to his feet. For a moment they stood so close he could smell the fragrance of her skin. Not perfume. Not even soap, but the deep, true scent that was all her own. Like sunlight and laughter and—

Damn! What the hell was wrong with him? he wondered. He tried to force himself to pull his hand from hers. In a moment he succeeded.

She turned toward the kitchen. From her shoulders, her torso narrowed dramatically toward her waist, and her hips were generously rounded, encased as they were in faded denim. How would it feel to slip his palm down that feminine curve?

Putting water on the stove, she stretched up on her toes to open a top cupboard. He watched her lift her arm, watched her muscles flex with graceful ease, watched her stretch her prima-donna neck to peer onto a shelf.

Damn, it was hot in here. He didn't remember Iowa being this hot. But then, he was accustomed to air-conditioning. That must be the problem. Or perhaps it was how her breasts pressed intimately against the wear-softened cotton of her blouse.

"Lemon or peppermint?"

Daniel snapped his mind back to reality. "What?"

"Lemon or peppermint tea?"

"Oh. Doesn't matter."

She nodded, glancing down as she retrieved a pair of mugs. "I've read some of your articles."

There was something fascinating about the way she prepared the tea. An efficient gracefulness of movement, poetry, really. No tea bags for her. Her tea came from squat glass jars and was soon enclosed in small metal tea balls that dangled inside the mugs.

"The one about the child labor practices in Thailand." She paused, then glanced at him. "It reminded me of you. Sensitive. How you used to talk."

He stared. "Me?"

"Well, tough on the outside, you know. But deep down..." She shrugged. "Kind."

The little kid inside fidgeted nervously, the man spoke. "You must be thinking of someone else. I'm just a hardass reporter looking out for number one."

"I don't think so."

He should deny it again, but damned if the man could manage to overwhelm the little boy's shyness.

"I didn't always agree with you, but..."

"But what?"

She filled the mugs from the kettle. "I liked the way you talked."

And he liked the way she smiled. Like hope and laughter and a thousand happy thoughts. He reached for the cup. Their fingers brushed. Heat coursed like lightning through his system. Awareness built like a flood in his veins. She drew her hand slowly away and fiddled with her own cup.

The kitchen seemed as quiet as the dawn of time.

"Why *did* you come back?" she asked.

Daniel curled his fingers around his mug and reminded himself to breathe. Suddenly, with her so tantalizingly close, it was hard to remember why he'd returned. Hard to remember anything. Just hard.

She remained silent, watching him, and it seemed he could see eternity in her morning-glory eyes.

"It doesn't matter," she said finally and turned briskly away. "You did the right thing."

"Did I?"

"Yeah." She smiled over her shoulder. "Yeah. Everything will seem clear to you soon. You look better already."

"I'm not sure if I should be insulted or flattered."

She laughed. "Well, my theory is, if you have a choice you might as well be flattered. It'll make you happier. But I just mean—Oakes is good for your soul. Pretty soon you'll find your way."

They stood very close. It almost seemed that he could feel the very pulse of her being. "Am I lost, Sorenson?"

"Yes." She said the word simply. "I think you are."

"Then who will find me?" He couldn't help but step a little bit closer.

"Do you want to be found?"

"I didn't think so. Now I'm not sure," he said and, against his better judgment, brushed his fingers against her cheek, that precise spot where her dimple so often winked.

A thousand odd sensations rushed through him. It was only a touch, only an innocent brush of skin against skin, and yet...

He heard her sharp intake of breath and shushed hormones that were far too vociferous for his jaded soul.

"I, um, I want to thank you. I mean…for your help." She fluttered a hand toward the surgery room. "With Waif. And I was wondering if you might want to make it permanent." The final words rushed out, then slowed. "I mean…for a while."

Permanent. With Jessica.

"You're so gentle…with animals, I mean, and I thought…"

He brushed his fingers over her soft lobe, then up the tight curl of her ear. Her eyelids fluttered for a moment, but she caught her breath and continued.

"I thought maybe if I let you stay here for free and—"

"Stay with you…" He breathed the words and slid his hand past her ear to skim his fingers beneath the kitten-softness of her hair. "Here? For free?"

"Yes," she said, but her voice was so tremblingly breathy, that for a moment he couldn't remember what his question was. For a moment it almost seemed that he had asked for something far more intimate. After all, he would be a fool not to. "I couldn't pay you much, of course."

Her skin felt as warm as sunshine against his fingers and when he kissed the corner of her mouth, he felt her tremble. Or maybe it was him.

"But it would be…" She paused, breathing hard. "An honest living."

He kissed her bottom lip. It was full and succulent and hopelessly inviting.

"Hard work, of course."

Hard! Yes, he was that, he thought, and pressed his hand down the back of her neck, pulling her closer. Her head fell back slightly, exposing the long sweep of her throat. He kissed her there, just beneath her jaw.

"But you wouldn't…" Her words stopped. Her eyes fell closed, her mouth slightly open. "Go hungry."

But he was hungry, ravenous, starving for the taste of her. Still he moved slowly, skimming down her throat to the tiny dell between her collarbones. It was the perfect place to kiss her.

He felt her body dip slightly and wrapped his arm about her waist, supporting her.

"MacCormick," she breathed.

"I want to make love to you." He knew he should resist, think, resist. But instead he pulled her tight against his body and kissed her lips. Passion seared him, burning on contact.

For a moment she remained still in his arms, but in an instant she was kissing him back.

His fingers trembled against the buttons on her blouse. He didn't know how they had gotten there, but it seemed quite fortuitous that they had. And just as fortuitously, her fingers were on his buttons, scrambling to set them free of their holes.

No time to question or reason or think. Just to feel her skin against his, to taste the intoxicating sweetness of her lips, to—

The door banged open down the hall.

"Jess!"

Jessica's kiss turned to a gasp against his mouth. "Gnat!" she rasped and jerked away from Daniel, stumbling backward, fumbling with her two undone buttons. But he just stood there, shirt open to his waist, thinking with rather disoriented clarity that she had incredibly fast fingers. But not fast enough, not for him and his crazed, adolescent hormones.

"I'm sorry...I just..." She was breathing hard and fast, her eyes as big as stars, her raspberry lips... Raspberry! That was it! And they were parted. "Gnat's here."

He managed a nod, though he wasn't entirely sure what it signified. Especially since, against his will and his best intentions, he leaned forward to kiss her again.

For the briefest moment their lips met, and then she snatched herself away, licking her lips as she did so. "MacCormick..." Her voice was raspy.

He stepped closer, his heart racing like a runaway train. "What?"

"I've gotta..." She motioned vaguely over her shoulder, pointing rather haphazardly in the general direction of the refrigerator. "I've gotta go."

He nodded again. He didn't know how he managed it, because all he could think of was that her lips were as lush as a whispered promise. "Then you'll come up?" he said.

"What?" The word was no more than a breath.

"Afterward..." He skimmed his thumb across her lips. They quivered beneath his touch. "You'll come up?"

"I don't..."

He couldn't resist her. She was too tempting, too succulent, too close. He kissed her, because there was nothing else he could do.

"Yes," she said, and just as Gnat started pattering down the hall, Daniel pulled himself away and forced himself up the stairs.

BY THE TIME Jessie had fumbled her top buttons shut, Gnat appeared, and by the time he was ready to exit, Greta arrived.

"Fate," said Miss Fritz, *"is the friend of fools and miscreants."*

"What does that mean?" Jessie asked, but her self-appointed conscience only raised her nose and looked pointedly down it.

"Try not to worry too much, Greta," Jessica said and glanced once more toward the steps. It had been nearly an hour since MacCormick's exit. An hour, and sanity still hadn't returned in full. But she was trying. Struggling to remember that this was her life—animals, medicine, small-town people. This is what she had worked so hard for. She had no time for anything else. Especially not for a sharp-edged man with big-city ways. "Waif's strong, and the puppies look healthy," she continued. "Just don't let her tear out her stitches. Keep the babies warm and make sure they're nursing."

"They don't need any other food?"

"Not for a few weeks at least."

"And Waif?" Greta hadn't stopped stroking the little dog since her arrival. "Does she need anything special?"

"Some breeders recommend a can of chicken-noodle soup after labor."

"Soup?"

Jessica gratefully went into detail. The dozens of questions not only kept her mind busy; they kept Fritz wonderfully silent. But finally Greta stepped onto the porch, box of dogs in hand. Jessie followed her out, carrying the bag of ointments and pills she'd prescribed.

"Remember to keep them warm," she said, pulling Greta's car door open.

"I will."

"And check their umbilical cords. Make sure Waif's not chewing on them."

"I'll remember," Greta said and, settling the box carefully on the front seat, hurried around to the far side.

"Use up all those pills."

"Two, twice a day." Greta drew a deep breath. "Thank you. So much."

"You're welcome," Jessica said and realized with something like panic that she was out of directions. There was nothing she could do now but wave goodbye.

Greta's car started with a rattle. The lights popped on, spreading a glow across the street as she pulled away from the curb.

Dimness spilled around Jessie. Across the street, Loman's shepherd barked once. Jessica stood absolutely still, wrung her hands and let out a deep breath. It sounded shaky.

MacCormick was waiting for her upstairs. MacCormick! So that was it, then. She was insane.

What had she been thinking, she wondered frantically. But in a second, she corrected herself. The question was, what had she been thinking *with?* Her hormones or her head?

Chewing her lip, Jessica glanced guiltily toward the house, realized he might be watching her even now from a dark window of the upper floor, and hurried down Elm Street.

From the river, frogs sang and something splashed. It was a peaceful scene, but her mind was churning.

What in the world was wrong with her? She'd offered Daniel MacCormick a job. MacCormick! She hated MacCormick. Didn't she? And free rent? She needed that rent money. And no way—no way!—did she want him hanging around, anyway. The last thing she needed was a man around to confuse things. She'd been doing her best to get rid of him, to go on with her life.

Then he'd kissed her and... Her knees felt rubbery at the memory. How stupid could she be? She shouldn't have let him kiss her. And she shouldn't have kissed him back. And as for trying to rip off his shirt...well, that was a definite no-no. He'd probably think she was desperate or—

"A tart?" Miss Fritz supplied.

"No, not a tart!" Jessie snapped.

But he probably didn't know she hadn't been kissed in— she thought for a moment—seventeen months and two days.

The memory of his lips against hers coursed through her. She shivered slightly in the warm night air.

What an idiot she had been. She didn't want to encourage him to stay. Hardly. But... Ragged, old memories seared her. She wrung her hands and strode down Ash Street.

Maybe kissing him was the best possible way to get rid of him. Barring sex, of course. Sex was surefire.

It had certainly worked like a charm on Brian.

And after all those years of "saving herself." Thinking it would be more special that way. When in truth, Brian hadn't cared enough about either her or her virginity to go the distance.

But maybe MacCormick—

MacCormick? She almost laughed out loud. She was losing her mind. That was the only explanation.

DANIEL PACED the length of his bedroom for the hundredth time. He'd had time to think, to cool off, to shove his hormones back into whatever dark hole they'd crawled out of, and now he knew the truth. He was insane. Certifiable. Possibly dangerous.

What the hell was wrong with him? Kissing Sorenson! He hated Sorenson. He hated this town. He hated this house and this dusty road and this— He glanced out the window. In the backyard, the moon cast a pearlescent glow over the sleepy pair of huge, dappled horses. Through the open window, he could hear the peaceful song of the frogs, and down the river something splashed.

Where was Jessica? He had to talk to her. Set things straight. Tell her the truth, that he'd come to his senses.

His hormones had gotten out of control. That was all. He had no interest in her. She was too old-fashioned and foolishly optimistic.

But when she smiled…

She wasn't his type, he reminded himself harshly. Absolutely not. After all, she was so enmeshed in this silly small town that there was no way he could have any interest in her.

Still, her skin had felt as soft as…

"Damn!" he growled and paced again.

She'd offered him a job. Him! Daniel MacCormick! Pulitzer Prize winner. A two-bit work-for-pay job as a damned veterinary assistant. It was ludicrous. No, damned insane was what it was.

But her throat was so soft, her smile so entrancing, and when he'd seen her slim, competent hands consoling that worthless little pile of fur…

Not that he'd considered her offer even for an instant. He'd have to be as insane as she was. And though his mental stability was a little questionable just now, he wasn't that crazy.

Work with her! Spend hours a day in her company! Listen to her stories, watch her move, touch her hand now and then. And maybe when the moment was right, when the lights were low, when they were alone, he would kiss her, would feel that overpowering—

Insane!

The whole idea was insane! And...and he was going to tell her so right now. Storming to the door, Daniel yanked it open and stepped into the hall just as Jessica did the same.

"Oh!"

It almost seemed that he felt her exhalation of surprise rather than heard it, and in that instant his brain kicked out of gear and his hormones revved.

"MacCormick." Her eyes looked incredibly wide in her heart-shaped face. "I just—"

And her hair. Sun-kissed, kitten-soft, as touchable as...

"I...I've been thinking about my...proposition."

Proposition? What proposition? Had she been trying to seduce him, and if so, why did she still have so many clothes on?

"About my asking you to work for me."

Oh, yeah. That proposition, he thought vaguely, and noticed that he could see her pulse beat in that tiny dell in her throat. Dammit, that was sexy.

"You'd make an excellent assistant. I'm sure you would. But us working together..."

He watched her lips move and somewhere, on a subconscious level, heard her words. Working together, living together, touching... Yes.

"It just wouldn't work out."

She was so fresh, so pretty, so...

"What?" he asked, belatedly coming to his senses.

"I'm sure you understand." She wrung her hands. "The idea was ludicrous, really."

"Ludicrous?" He took a step toward her.

She took a step back and winced. "Well, sure. I mean, you're not an animal person, you're a...a..."

"A what?"

"Well, I don't know, a...reporter."

"So you think I couldn't do the job?"

"I never said that."

"But that's what you think. You think I'm some hard-ass reporter who doesn't care about anything but himself."

"That's what you told me."

"Well, yeah!" he sputtered. "But when did you start listening?"

"I...listen," she said, her tone exasperated. "It just wouldn't work out. That's all. I just...the truth is, I can't afford to pay you. I'm barely making it as it is and...I mean...it's not like I couldn't *live* without the rent money, but—"

"The rent money!" The truth of the situation exploded in his mind like a nuclear bomb. Why the hell hadn't he realized it before? Because he'd been too distracted, that's why. Distracted by her lips, and her smile, and her eyes, and that damnable pulse in her throat. Just like every other male in Oakes. Just like Mosquito and Bill and Pastor What's-his-face and... "Cecil!" he said suddenly.

"What?" she asked.

"I'm paying the rent to Cecil, not to you."

He watched her swallow, watched her blink, watched her wince as if the horrible truth was finally out.

"Why the hell..." He kept his words slow and steady now. "Why do you get the rent money when he owns the house?"

Her shrug was weak, pathetic, backed against the wall. "He just...I just..." she began, then squared her capable shoulders and pursed her ridiculously bright lips. "I told you he was generous."

"Huh!" Daniel tilted back his head and barked a laugh. "If Cecil MacCormick is generous, I'm the damned patron saint of strays and horny alley cats!"

"Well, you're sure not a saint."

"And neither are you, huh?"

"What's that's supposed to mean?"

Cecil. Uncle Cecil. Cantankerous. Selfish. Tightfisted. And yet he was passing up the opportunity to sell this house so that this lush, little convoluted loon could continue to live here—rent-free. No, worse than rent-free. She was getting Daniel's rent. And the old man had built the barn. To stable his horses, he'd said. But that was a lie if ever he'd heard one. Cecil had five hundred acres of land on his own place to keep his animals. No. He'd built the barn for her, given the house to her, given the rent money to her. Why?

Daniel stared, his journalist's instincts buzzing. Her bright eyes, her touchable skin, her succulent lips. There could only be one reason why a wizened old coot like Cecil MacCormick would do a young woman such a kindness. Only one reason.

For a moment rage flared inside him. The thought of the old man touching her made him sick, made him nauseous, made him insanely jealou—

No. Not jealous. Of course not jealous. After all, this was perfect, really. Perfect for Alysha. *A product of incest. And now being propositioned by...her uncle? Her pastor?*

That was it! Sorenson would be Alysha's model. Sorenson was prettier, maybe. But they shared the same sordid little secrets. But then, that's what would make it work. The very incredibility of it. All he had to do was learn the truth. And what better way than to do so firsthand?

"I'll take the job," he said.

"What?" Her face had lost all color.

"The job," he repeated. "Looks like I'm your man."

8

"MACCORMICK!"

The Serbs! Daniel jerked upright, his eyes staring and his heart beating like a bongo.

Where was he? Kashmir? Nigeria? Bratislava?

"MacCormick!" The door popped open. The light, glaring in painful intensity, flashed on. "Let's go."

"Go?" He tried to growl the word. It sounded decidedly more like a dying croak.

"Yeah. Cap Fisher called. He's got a heifer with a prolapsed uterus."

"Huh?"

"Just hurry up. We don't have much time," she said and closed the door behind her.

Daniel turned his gaze toward the window. Outside, the night was as dark as ink.

She was insane, he deduced, and lay back down, but in the back of his mind the great American novel called to him.

He'd come here for a reason. Not simply to find his muse, as he had thought, but to get in touch with Alysha. And voilà, here in Oakes, Iowa, he had found her prototype. All he had to do was follow Jessica around, take notes, learn her ugly secrets, and reveal them all in his bestselling novel.

Yes, eventually, it would all be worth the price.

BEYOND THE SILVERADO'S windshield, the world was nightmarishly black, but at least Daniel had finally come to his senses. With his hormones firmly packed away, he now remembered that he wasn't attracted to her in the least. It was just a momentary lapse of sanity.

Sitting in the passenger seat, he hunched his shoulders. This damned place was just like the Sahara. Hotter than hell during the day and cold as sin at night. He wished he'd brought a jacket. Wished he wasn't too proud to wrap up in the Navajo blanket that covered the bench seat. Wished he'd never come here. Wished she wouldn't look so damn chipper.

He hated chipper.

"What the hell's a prolapsed uterus?" he grumbled.

"You don't want to know," she answered as she fiddled with the heater. No discernible warmth was forthcoming.

"Afraid I'd faint?" he asked.

"You might."

He snorted. "Then why'd you proposition me?"

"What?" She snapped her gaze to his.

He felt immediately better for her wide-eyed stare. "Why'd you propose that I work for you?"

"Oh." She shifted her gaze restlessly back to the road. "I felt sorry for you."

"Sorry. For me."

Her eyes again, trained directly on him. "That's right."

He forced a laugh. "Well, you're entertaining, Sorenson. I'll say that for you."

"Yeah, well…" She turned the pickup into a driveway, pulled up to a fence and shifted into park. The engine died with an audible groan. "You ain't seen nothing yet."

She was right, and it was strange, because Daniel had thought he'd seen everything. But the cow, lying contentedly on her side, chewing her cud, while all the while a bloody mass protruded from her backside…now *that* he'd never seen.

"Jesus!" he said.

"Yeah," she muttered, handing him a tray of generic paraphernalia. "It always helps to pray."

He didn't know if it was a joke.

"Morning, Jess," said an old fellow who stood next to

the cow. He was short and shriveled and didn't look much more concerned than the cow about her shocking condition.

"Morning, Cap."

"Sorry to get you out of bed at this hour. But Doc Barker was outta town."

Jessica smiled. "This *is* my job,"

"I know, but…" He shook his head. His cap, Daniel noticed, was neon orange and emblazoned with the word "Cap" as if he might forget what to call it—or himself. "It's just that I…" He shuffled his rubber-booted feet. "Seems like just yesterday you was in diapers."

She laughed. "I've been potty-trained for a couple years now," she said and, after removing her jacket, systematically rolled up the sleeves on her denim shirt. "How long's she been like this?"

He shook his head again, looking sorrowful. The light was dim inside the barn, and the straw beneath their feet was less than sanitized. "Don't know exactly. Went to my grandson's ball game in Fairfield. When I come back, I found her like this. But the calf's dry." He nodded toward a smaller version of the cow that lay curled near its mother's chest. "So I 'spect it's been a few hours. Sure wish Doc was around."

If she took offense at that, her expression didn't show it. "Big calf," she said.

"Ain't it a beauty." The regret in his face lessened a little.

"Sure is. Bull calf?"

"Yep. And I'm thinkin' he might be a keeper."

She laughed as she slid a needle into the rubber stopper of an inverted glass bottle and glanced around at the rest of the cud-chewing beasts that grunted and groaned in the narrow confines. "You build your herd back up to a hundred or so head and Martha might leave you."

"She won't leave me," Cap said. "I'm too damn sexy."

He laughed. She laughed.

Daniel gritted his teeth. "You going to do something

about that?'' he asked. He was not at all surprised to learn
that he was not a morning person.

"Right now," she said. "Do you have a stanchion to put
her in, Cap?"

"Nope. My cows is like puppies. Don't need no stanchion. But we can probably shag her into that pen over
there. Tie her in the corner."

"Okay. Get her up, MacCormick."

He stared at her.

"And don't get her riled," she added, "Cuz you'll have
to support her while I get that back in."

"YOU OKAY?" Jessica asked. If he just looked at her eyes,
he could almost believe her caring tone was sincere, Daniel
thought. But there was something in her voice—a hint of
laughter—that readily reminded him she was the devil's
child, regardless of her angelic looks.

"Sure," he said, doing his best to sound convincing.
"I'm fine. Why wouldn't I be?" He flexed his left arm and
wondered when his legs would stop shaking. "She was only
a cow. How heavy can she be?"

She laughed. He hated laughter. "Sorry. But she had to
stay on her feet."

"Then maybe you shouldn't have given her a damn gallon of sedative."

"Ten c.c.'s," she said, then scowled thoughtfully at the
road. It was still dark, but growing a bit lighter in the east—
perhaps. "Maybe I should use eight c.c.'s next time."

He swore.

"So…" She sounded cheerful again. His arms felt like
they'd been put through a wringer washer. "What do you
think of being a vet assistant so far?"

He thought he might strangle her, slowly, so he could
enjoy—

A crackle from the citizens band radio interrupted his
thoughts. "Jess?"

Reaching for the dash, she picked up the speaker and
pressed a button. "Grams! Is Goldy all right?"

"Yeah, she's fine. We'll send her home with Betty this afternoon, huh?"

"If her blood sugar's still on track. So far everything looks good."

"Thank goodness. Poor Betty don't need any more troubles. She thinks you're the best thing since sunshine, you know."

Jessie smiled. "You didn't have to get out of bed just to tell me that."

"Don't be a smart alec. We got a call from Stanton's."

"Oh, no."

"Yep. One of their Morgans is colicking."

Another press of the button. "Mare or stallion?"

"Stallion."

"Is it too much to hope that he's halter broke at least?"

"Probably. You know Lenny. Do you want me to come and help out?"

"No thanks, Grams. That's okay. You go back to bed." Then turning her beatific smile on Daniel, Jessie said, "I've got MacCormick here to help me. He's an ace with rank young stallions."

EVERY MUSCLE ACHED. Every bone creaked. Every tendon quivered. He was exhausted. He stank, and he would commit a major felony in Asia for one whiff of a crushed cigarette butt. And it was only his first day on the job.

Daniel dragged himself laboriously up the stairs toward his bedroom. He wasn't going to let her beat him. He'd listened to every word spoken, and he had collected data. Data that needed to be written down, mulled over, interpreted.

Staggering into his room, he glanced toward the bed. No, he couldn't collapse yet. First, he'd take a shower, then he'd write down his notes, but he used to write notes in bed all the time. In fact, it was important to relax, to start his creative juices flowing again. Perhaps sitting in bed with a notebook was exactly what he needed. Just like when he was a kid.

Sure, that's what he'd do, he thought and, snagging a notebook from the box near his desk, he groaned onto the bed.

It was his last conscious thought until morning.

"JEEZ, MACCORMICK, you sleep like a rock."

He woke with a painful jolt to gaze up Jessica Sorenson's slightly pug nose.

"What the hell are you doing in my room?"

"I was worried you might be dead. Thought I'd better come in and find out."

"And?" He shifted one leg and realized rather belatedly that he hadn't changed clothes from yesterday. They felt almost as stiff as his muscles, and he had no desire to consider what had stiffened them.

"What?" she said.

"Have you decided yet whether I'm dead or not?"

"Oh, you're alive. You just smell dead. You hungry?"

He tried to say no, but he couldn't force out the lie, not with his stomach knotted up like a pretzel. "I guess I could eat."

"Come on down," she said and turned away. But in a second she placed a hand on the doorjamb and twisted back toward him. "Take a shower first."

"Is that an order?"

"Yeah," she said, raising fair brows at him. "It is."

He arrived in the kitchen fifteen minutes later, hair still wet, feet bare.

Jessica sat at the table, reading a circular, her back to him.

"That coffee?" he grumbled, spying her cup.

She jumped, nearly sloshing the brew over the side of the cup. "No! I mean…" She shifted her gaze toward the coffeemaker. "Yes. I just…thought I'd taste it. Make sure I made it right."

He raised his brows as he reached for a mug. "You a caffeine addict, Sorenson?"

"No. Of course not. I just—" she began, but he couldn't help but laugh at her expression of guilt, and she jerked up from her chair and dumped her coffee in the sink. "The cages need cleaning, stalls need mucking out, and Bill's bringing hay by," she said, and, turning on her heel, marched out of sight.

An hour later, Daniel removed the soggy liners from the bottom of a cage and ruefully remembered that there was a time in his life when he'd written newspapers, not lined cages with them. But he'd been sent to purgatory, and until he could prove himself as a novelist, it looked as if he'd be assigned to manual labor. In fact, by the sound of the schedule, today would be as hectic as yesterday.

"Gotta hurry with that," Jessie said.

Daniel glanced up, ready with a comeback, but the words never came, because Jessie stood in the doorway. And yet it hardly looked like her. Gone were the distressed jeans, the sleeveless shirt. In their place was a gauzy floral-print skirt that swirled about her bare legs like river water. A silky lavender blouse was tucked into the waistband and on one slim wrist she wore a trio of silver bracelets. Even her eyes had changed, outlined as they were with a light tracing of sable pencil, while her mouth, though no brighter in hue, was lacquered with a glossy something.

Daniel stared. She looked in that instant as if she had stepped off the pages of a fashion magazine, and for a moment he couldn't find a single word. Damn, but it was easier to hate her when he wasn't looking at her.

The silence stretched into forever. She cleared her throat and fidgeted.

"Bill should be bringing that hay by in an hour or so." He still stared.

"It's not too much for you, is it? I mean..." She motioned nervously with a sun-golden hand. "It's only a couple of hundred bales, but if you need help—"

"No," he said, and was quite surprised, actually, that he could force out that single word. Even his toenails hurt, and damn her for standing there looking so fresh and bright and beautiful. Not that she was his type. But then, why shouldn't she look stunning, he thought, trying his damnedest to make himself feel better. While he'd been hoisting up six hundred pounds of cow and wrestling a horny stallion into a half nelson, she'd spent her time playing the gentle doctor. "I'll be fine."

She said nothing.

"Where are you going?" he asked. He'd tried to contain the question, but fatigue, it seemed, had taken a toll on his usual astounding discipline. "Just so we can get a hold of you if there are any emergencies."

She cleared her throat and raised her chin slightly. A sign of guilt? "I've got a meeting. Grams will keep an eye on the surgeries for me, and Doc Barker's back, so any urgent calls can be referred to him. But—"

"A meeting with who?" Not that he cared, but she looked so softly feminine, with every silky scrap of fabric shimmering over her smooth lines of flesh. He hated smooth lines of flesh.

"It's a…veterinary convention."

"Oh?" he said and leaned with concentrated casualness against the nearest cage. Once again he mourned his inability to smoke. He would look so damn cool if he were blowing smoke rings. Not that he gave a damn where she was planning to go. But she wasn't likely to dress like this for a room full of stodgy professors. Unless he'd been right about her and Uncle Cecil all along. Maybe she was the type to give favors—

He didn't care. He didn't. But below the fluttering hem of the skirt, he noticed a delicate bracelet encircling her sun-kissed ankle, and through the open toes of her strappy, high heeled sandals, golden stars winked from her lavender nails.

He gritted his teeth as he moved resolutely on to the next cage. "So…" Work would have to be a poor substitute for the coolness of a cigarette. "Who are you trying to impress, Sorenson?"

"What?"

He motioned vaguely toward her, carefully disregarding the broiling feelings in his chest. "What happened to the shirt with the hacked-off sleeves?"

"Oh." She glanced down at herself as if embarrassed. "This is a professional meeting."

"Uh-huh. An old lover going to be there?"

With one sidelong glance he noticed the rise of a blush on her cheeks. Anger roiled in his belly and he gritted his teeth beneath a careful smile.

"Someone you met at vet school?"

For a moment he thought she might answer, but then she said, "Just make sure you get that work done," and turned rapidly away.

HE FINISHED THE CAGES, scrubbed down the garage floor, cleaned the stalls, and finally, when Bill arrived with the hay, unloaded and stacked the bales. It was hot, itchy work, and he hadn't dealt with more than twenty bales before he'd removed his shirt and realized that he had, once again, neglected to wear gloves. But what the hell! The pain kept him from thinking about Jes—smoking!

There was really no reason he shouldn't smoke. She wasn't even there to care, but he'd told her he'd quit and if he failed she might think...

He didn't care what she thought, he reminded himself, and threw himself into his work. Finally, exhausted, sweaty, and stiff as a board, he stumbled his way into the house and up to the shower. The warm water felt like heaven against his skin. He bowed his head under the spray, letting it soothe him.

"Danny!"

The bathroom door popped open.

He swore and jumped at the same time, scrambling for the towel that hung over the glass shower door even as Grams appeared through the fog.

"Criminy sakes, I thought you was dead in there," Grams said, peering through the steam. "You okay?"

"Of course I'm okay!"

"Well, jeez, you don't have to get all huffy. I was just worrying, is all," she said and turned away.

His hand drooped in front of his body.

"Oh, and—" she peered about as he jerked the towel back up "—supper's ready. Come on down. It ain't black-tie, but you might want to slip on some pants," she said and chuckled as she left.

THEY HAD THE kind of meal Iowa was famous for. Pork chops, mashed potatoes, corn.

Daniel barely noticed. Not that he was concerned about Sorenson. He cleared his throat and stared across the table at the old woman, who offered him seconds. "Does she have these meetings often?"

"Who?" She looked startled that he had spoken.

"Your granddaughter!" he snapped, then gritted his teeth and took a deep breath.

The old woman stared, chuckled, then after turning away without a word, she strode up the stairs. He watched her go with mild surprise, but in a matter of moments she thumped a short glass bottle and small bag of dried herbs down beside his plate.

Surprise turned to bewilderment. "What's that?"

"Rosemary oil for aches and pains. Wish I had bunch-berry too, but I ain't found any yet. Bunchberry is an elixir for sore muscles."

He opened his mouth to deny the aches, but she gave him a scathing look and continued on with a nod at the dried herbs. "That's Indian pipe and…some other stuff for the smoking."

"You smoke it?"

"No, y'don't smoke it," she said, peeved at his foolishness. "It's to help you *quit* smoking. I used it and now I don't crave them cigarettes at all. Hardly…" She licked her parched lips and stared at his shirt pocket. "Where *are* your cigarettes?"

Something niggled in his mind. "You smoked?"

"Yeah, I smoked." She shuffled her feet. "They in your bedroom?"

"When did you quit?"

"'Bout four years ago. Doctor insisted, so I come up with

a cure. Works, too, but I have to keep it locked up in my room else that fat Oscar gets into it. Must be the catnip." She fidgeted, gripping her thumb between her fingers as if it were a cigarette. "Them smokes in your car?"

The pieces fell together with a clank in his mind. "That's why you asked me to your room."

"Sure, I—" she began, but stopped abruptly, her forehead wrinkling like a shar pei's when she raised her brows. "What were you thinking? That I was after you?"

"Of course not. I—" he began, but her bark of laughter interrupted his hasty denial.

"You're a MacCormick, all right," she said, still chuckling as she reached for another pot. "And you MacCormicks ain't short on self-esteem. No. Never was. I remember when I first saw your uncle, all dressed up in his navy uniform and standing so straight. Just like a statue and I thought he was the cat's pajamas, but then he come back and married—" She stopped abruptly and glanced at him as if surprised to find him at her table. "Yeah, you're a MacCormick all right. I see it in your eyes. But you been good for my Jess, just the same. Helped her loosen up a little."

He remained in silent shock.

"I only wish..." she began, but turned stiffly away, letting the sentence hang in the air.

"What?" he asked.

"Nothing," she said, already running water in the sink.

He stared at her stiff back. "You want me to tell Jessie you've been trying to find my cigarettes?"

She turned a glare on him, but there was a sparkle of something in her crafty old eyes. "You done with that?" she asked, already reaching for his plate. "I only wish Jess hadn't gone to Ames," she said. "She's found enough trouble in that place already."

"Trouble?" He tried to recall how a normal, caring person might react to that news. His memory creaked with effort. "Nothing serious, I hope."

"Not if you don't call being left at the altar too serious. Blasted pretty boy."

Jessica Sorenson? Left standing at the altar? he thought, awe-struck. But apparently his stint in Iowa hadn't affected the newspaper man in him too much, because at least he was able to keep his mouth shut and wait a few seconds before his next question. "When was that?"

"Before the baby was born."

Baby? His eyes all but popped out of his head. Jessica had a baby? he wondered frantically, but before he could voice another question, the doorbell rang.

Grams made her stiff but efficient way across the floor and pulled open the door.

"Well, good evening, Reverend."

"Hello, Edna. How are you feeling on this fine summer night?"

"Pretty fair…"

The conversation rambled on, but Daniel wasn't listening to the meandering words. Jessie had a baby?

"Nettie put up some strawberry preserves," the pastor was saying. "Asked me to bring them by. Is Jessica around?"

Whose baby? When? His thoughts roiled like storm clouds.

The sound of the door closing started him from his reverie. He stood with a jolt.

"So…" He nursed his raspberry tea, though he'd entirely forgotten about it. "The pastor seems like a decent fellow, huh?" Daniel said.

"Pastor Tony? Yeah, he's all right. Thinks the world of my Jess."

Was it *his* baby? His stomach clenched, but he kept his voice steady. "Guess she's pretty well-liked here in Oakes."

Grams said nothing, just continued washing dishes.

"Bill, Gnat, the pastor. Even Cecil seems to think the world of her, and…" Daniel forced a laugh and strove for camaraderie. "God knows my uncle isn't the most charitable man in the world."

Nothing.

Damn! If it was Cecil's baby, he'd kill the old— He didn't care. Didn't! It was just research. "I mean, the old bastard's as tightfisted as a—"

"Things ain't always what they seem to be," Grams said abruptly.

"What?"

"Time for bed," said the old woman, and, turning on a worn heel, trudged up the stairs and out of sight.

"No," ALYSHA WHISPERED. *"It can't be. I can't be pregnant."*

But the truth was as unchangeable as the earth's very core—

Jessica? A baby? *It couldn't be. Could it?* Daniel thought and ground his teeth as he stared at the opposite wall.

Of course it could be. Isn't that just why he was here? To dig up the dirt, to discover the truth, to—

Where the hell was she? With the pretty boy Grams had mentioned? And was the pretty boy the father of Jessie's baby?

Swinging his feet off the bed, Daniel paced across the room. From his window, he could see that Pearl was worrying the gate chain again. Feeling confined? Like Jessica?

Did she feel trapped? Was that why she had left today? And if so, what was she doing right now and who the hell was she doing it with?

He stopped abruptly as the sound of a car pierced his concentration. Straining his ears, he thought he heard it pull to a stop, thought he heard the engine die. Was that her? Had she returned? Turning quickly, he headed toward the door and stopped short.

What was wrong with him? He didn't care if she came home now or at dawn. He didn't care, he thought, but he was pacing again.

Was that the door? He wasn't sure. He didn't care.

Alysha. What about Alysha—*trying to escape the*

*bonds of small-town insignificance. Trying to spread her
wings—*

Was that it? Was Jessica trying to escape? And if so,
who would she escape with?

If he went into the bathroom, he'd be able to see the
street by the front door. See if she was home. Not that
he cared. But he was really thirsty, and one couldn't be
too careful about dehydration.

He was in the bathroom in an instant. By craning his
head just a little, and leaning to the left, and bending
over the toilet stool just so, he could see the driveway.

Sure enough, a car was parked there. Not Jessie's Silverado, but a car, and in the dim light, he thought he
could just see two heads tilted toward each other. His
stomach rose, his heart dropped, and he stumbled rapidly
backward. Striking his shin on the toilet seat, he cursed
with malevolent feeling and hobbled back to his room.

His book must be calling him, he thought, but his book
was disgustingly silent. He was tired, exhausted really,
and there was no shame in resting. He needed rest to
restore his creative energies. Maybe that was why his
muse had led him here. Not only to research and learn,
but to rejuvenate.

Flipping back his covers, Daniel glared at the sheets.

Maybe it wasn't even Jessica in the car. He couldn't
really tell in the dim light, and he didn't care, of course,
but... Damn, he was thirsty, and so he paced again, pattering into the hall and beyond to fetch another glass of
water. But there was really nothing to do while he slurped
down the fluids, and the car was just outside the window.
If he craned his neck and tilted his head, and...

Were they kissing? The plastic glass slammed into the
sink. He caught it on the rebound and settled it rapidly
next to the mirror.

He didn't care if it was Jessie. He didn't even like the
woman, he reminded himself as he paced back into his
room. Striding past the window, he barely noticed either
the chirping frogs or the horses' placid swishings.

The sheets felt cool against his legs. Sleep. That was what he needed, he thought and flipped the blankets across his body. Sleep. He forced his eyes closed and concentrated hard on relaxing.

From Jessie's office a clock chimed. He counted the strikes but refused to open his eyes. Eleven. It was eleven o'clock and she still wasn't in the house. Not that he cared.

But damn, he was thirsty.

Kicking off the covers, he stormed into the bathroom, ran himself a glass of water and yanked the curtain aside.

Two heads, still tilted together. What the hell was she doing out there? And who was she doing it with?

Water slurped over his chin as he chugged it down. Slapping the curtain back into place, he marched back into the bedroom. His stomach complained at its sloshing contents, but the night had only just begun. An hour later he was there for the fifth time, gulping down water as he glared at the car beyond the walkway.

Damn her! He'd just gotten over his insomnia, but how was he supposed to sleep when…when he was so thirsty.

His stomach groaned, and outside his window the night no longer looked peaceful.

Pearl stood by the gate, fiddling with the chain and—

Daniel's thoughts came to a screeching halt. Pearl, the great escape artist, was at the gate. And wouldn't it be terrible if he got loose?

9

JESSICA WAS a little woozy. Well, maybe a little more than a little. Okay, she was sloshed.

"It's getting late," she said. "And I've got a full day tomorrow."

Beside her, Brian sat silently watching her.

Brian! Brian Tuttle—her ex-fiancé. Proof positive that she was bombed, but even intoxication wasn't a stellar excuse. After all, how many times did a man have to leave her for her to learn her lesson? Still, he had looked so handsome and suave conversing with his fellow doctors, and well…she'd been weak and…

Inside her head Miss Fritz gave a disapproving tsk.

"Who are you trying to fool, Missy? Me or yourself?"

Jessie ignored her. It was, she found, easier to do after three vodka sours. Kind of surprising, really. "Thanks for the ride home, Brian."

"I could hardly let you drive home alone." He *was* a handsome man, the golden boy all grown up, and just as successful as everyone had expected him to be. "I remember how you get when you've been drinking," he said, and flashed his notorious smile. "It's been great talking to you." Even in the darkness she was startled by the blue of his eyes, the perfect cut of his perfect hair. He let the world go silent, then, "I've missed you, Jessica."

She felt her breath stop in her throat. He missed her? How many times had she imagined him saying that? And now that he had, she was flattered, *thrilled,* she told herself.

Miss Fritz snorted.

Jessie lowered her eyes.

"It's just because you're going through a rough time right now," she said. "But Kim'll be back and then—"

He halted her words as he leaned across the leather seat of his Corvette and slipped his hand around hers. "The truth is—" His voice was pained, intense, seeping with emotion. "I don't want her back, Jessica."

Jessie stared. She'd waited for years to hear those words. In fact, that was probably the real reason she had decided to go to the convention—in the hopes of winning him back. Yes, that was it, she concluded.

Miss Fritz turned away in disgust.

Brian's grip tightened on her hand. "She can't compare to you, Jessica. She never could."

Jessie's mind spun. She stared at their joined hands. There was a healing scab near her knuckles and one fingernail had been broken off in a jagged line while she was castrating a colt. She'd trimmed it with her bandage scissors, but not particularly well. His nails, she noticed, were perfect, cut to an exact length and buffed until glossy. "You don't mean that, Brian," she said. "You're hurt right now. That's all. Pretty soon—"

"No." He shook his head. "No. Even when things were good between Kim and me..." He paused, his gaze piercingly blue, his tone dramatically modulated. "I couldn't help but think of you." He drew her hand close to his chest. "Of how good we were together. Remember?" Pulling her hand closer still, he brushed his lips over her knuckles. "Remember how right we were together? Remember that night in Des Moines?"

Her heartbeat picked up pace. She did, in fact, remember the night in Des Moines. He was the only man she'd ever made love to, and it seemed her body had not forgotten. Not forgotten the feel of his skin against hers. Not forgotten the passion. It had been one of the best times of her life. She'd felt beautiful and needed and cherished. He kissed her wrist. Her hormones buzzed noisily.

"Of course they're buzzing," Fritz said. *"You're as drunk as a waterfront doxy."*

Jessie stiffened at the insult. *"I am not— Well, okay, I am, but is it so bad to get a little tipsy once in a blue moon? To get out? To have a handsome man fuss over me?"*

"He left you," Fritz said.

"He was young."

"He left you—when you needed someone."

"I'm just trying to have some fun."

Miss Fritz raised her chin and one brow in simultaneous disapproval. "Don't you lie to me young lady. I—"

"...the maître d'?"

Jessie snapped her attention back to Brian. "What?"

A momentary flash of irritation slashed across his face, but in an instant he smiled. "I said, do you remember the maître d'?" he repeated, and moved subtly closer, breathing on her knuckles.

"Not, um, not by name."

Brian stared into her eyes. She knew he'd always favored high drama over honesty. Men were like that, she reminded herself, and Miss Fritz laughed knowingly.

"Finally, we get to the heart of the matter."

"I bet he remembers you," Brian said. "He couldn't take his eyes off you. Just like me...tonight. When I saw you...it all came back to me."

She could feel a pulse beating in her throat. Even knowing that she couldn't trust him, she still felt his effects. See, she couldn't trust herself. Not where men were concerned. She was far better off with her nose to the grindstone, controlled, careful.

"Oh, for heaven's sake!" Miss Fritz was peeved. She never used such harsh language if she wasn't. "Just get to the point, girl."

"You're just as beautiful as that first day in chem class."

And MacCormick didn't even pretend he thought her beautiful. Jessie scowled mentally at the thought. What did MacCormick have to do with this?

"He's the reason you're here, you silly girl. To prove that men can't be trusted."

"No," Jessie argued.

"What?"

"No, I'm…" This wasn't good. It was generally best to avoid talking to Miss Fritz out loud. Otherwise people had a tendency to think her insane. "No," she repeated, scanning her mind in an attempt to remember what he'd been talking about. "I'm…not beautiful."

"Modest." His tone sounded pleased by her mistakenly demure attitude. "You always have been. I remember the first time I saw you. I was late for class, and there you were with an empty seat behind you. And I thought right then, Bri, you are one lucky dog. Remember?" His gaze bored into hers.

How long had it been since a handsome man had stared at her in adoration? She should enjoy it while she could. What would one night hurt?

"You're drunk," Fritz reminded. *"Drunk and embarrassing."*

"I asked you to a party at the Phi House." He smiled and, spreading her hand open, kissed her palm. "You were so shy."

"I wasn't…" Sensations skittered up her arm. She welcomed them, but the full shock of feeling seemed strangely lacking. "Shy."

"No." His expression was dramatically somber as he kissed her wrist, her forearm, the sensitive crease of her elbow. "You were saving yourself."

Yep, and she'd been saving herself again for the past four years. Jeez! Maybe it was time to quit saving and splurge for once.

"Don't you do anything stupid, young lady. I—"

"Be quiet! You aren't the one who's been living like a nun, holding down a job, taking care of everything. Why shouldn't I have sex if I want to? Maybe he's changed."

"Hmmph!"

"People change."

"You're drunk and he's taking advantage of you. Does it sound like he's changed?"

"*He's attracted to me. I'm attracted to him. Is that so horrible?*"

"*A peacock can be attracted to a sparrow. It doesn't mean they should make a nest.*"

"God!" Brian's anguished expletive startled her. "I was a fool, Jessica. A fool to let you go, knowing what we had. Give me another chance."

"Brian," she said, shocked nearly speechless, "you're still married."

He shook his head. "It's over. I always knew she couldn't hold a candle to you. It was just…rebound. When you insisted on returning to Oakes I was devastated. I've tried to pretend, but I can no longer deny my feelings for you, Jess." He moved closer still. Through the sheer fabric of her skirt, she could feel the heat of his erection against her thigh. "Tell me you share those feelings."

Her hormones sizzled, her brain swirled.

Brian leaned forward, his expression sober as a monk's.

"*Jessica May Sorenson!*" Fritz warned.

"*Shut up!*"

Fritz gasped.

And Brian kissed her. She sat very still, thinking, evaluating. It wasn't a bad kiss. Just not…earth-shattering, but maybe if she concentrated…

Something rattled off to her left.

"What…" she asked.

"It's nothing," Brian moaned and crushed her to him, but in that instant Loman's shepherd barked and a clatter of hooves snapped her to attention.

"The horses! They're out!" she rasped. Yanking out of his grip, she snatched her purse from the floor, and bolted for the house.

"What?" Brian asked, but she was already long gone.

Dropping her bag on the porch, she slammed the front door open.

"Grams!" she yelled and started back with a yelp when MacCormick stumbled into the hallway

"What's going on?" His dark hair was tousled, his expression grumpy, and for one prolonged moment she couldn't breathe for the thought that he looked like the living antithesis of Brian.

"The horses got out," she managed.

"Where are they?"

"Heading down Ash Street." She tore her attention from MacCormick's steady gaze and forced herself to turn away. "I'll get halters and grain. Tell Grams—"

"I heard," Grams said. She clumped rapidly down the steps in her nightgown, but took time to glare at Brian, who had appeared in the doorway beside her potted echinacea.

He smiled in return. "Mrs. Sorenson, Jessie tells me you're feeling better. I'm so glad," he said. She stared at him for a good five seconds before turning her gaze on MacCormick.

Brian's hundred-watt smile barely dimmed. "I don't think we've met," he said, turning to offer his hand to Daniel. "I'm Brian Tuttle III, and you are…"

"Going to catch some horses," MacCormick said and stepped past him to stride toward the door.

Grams's chuckle was almost inaudible, but Jessica heard it.

Brian scowled, but brightened with determination as he turned toward Jessica. "Come with me," he said and reached for her hand. "We'll follow them in my Vetmobile."

"The car'll just scare 'em," Grams said, scowling at their joined hands.

Jessica hesitated as she watched MacCormick's retreating back.

"I'm sure it'll be fine," Brian argued mildly.

Miss Fritz said nothing, but Jessie knew cold fury when she felt it.

"Thanks, Brian," she said, "but you might as well go home. We can handle this." Just like she'd handled everything else.

"I'll walk with you then and—"

"That your car the shepherd's peeing on?" MacCormick asked from the porch.

"What?" Brian dropped her hand and sprang for the door like a launched jack-in-the-box. Jessica watched him go, felt a pale twinge of regret, then turned and hurried through the back door to gather the necessities. The barn was very quiet.

"Mr. Tuttle the Third is very attached to his car."

Jessica jumped at the sound of MacCormick's voice. "I thought you were on the porch."

"I was. Did I imagine it or did his license plate say 'The Vet'?"

She scowled as she snatched up halters and a small bucket of grain. "How did the horses get out? I'm sure I chained the gate."

"Damned if I know." He shrugged, then canted his head at her. "You didn't let them out just to get rid of the Third did you?"

From the front of the house the Corvette's motor revved and retreated, and despite everything, she couldn't help but grin a little. "Don't be ridiculous."

"Is that a no?"

"Here," she said, and shoved the halters in the general direction of his chest. "Let's get the horses before we have a lawsuit on our hands."

A pickup truck pulled around the corner and stopped beside the barn. The door swung open. "Come on. Get in," Grams called.

Jessie climbed onto the bench seat with MacCormick beside her. His leg felt warm through the sheer fabric of her skirt. A spark of feeling frizzled toward the apex of her thighs and her breath labored a little.

"I thought a car would scare them," MacCormick said, his voice low.

"Not as much as Tuttle's pretty-boy face," Grams said.

"Ah," MacCormick said and Jessie found she lacked the nerve to glance his way. The truth was, Grams had never forgiven Brian for dumping her. Never had and never would. Forever was forever in her day.

They backed out of the drive, turned onto Ash Street and stopped after half a block. The sound of dogs barking alerted them to the horses' progress.

In the end, it wasn't very difficult to locate them. They had stopped in an alfalfa field on the west side of town and blinked wryly when they saw Grams pull up.

She cut the engine and stepped out of the truck alone, nightgown fluttering in the soft breeze. "Okay, you boys have had your fun," she said. "Time to go home."

For a moment Jessica thought they might bolt, but they didn't. Instead, they stood docilely as their halters were slipped over their ears, and suddenly, now that the excitement was over, the weight of the evening seemed heavy on her.

Wearily kicking off her silly shoes, she slipped out of the truck. "Why don't you and MacCormick go on home," she said. "I'll take the boys."

"In your skirt?" Grams argued and Jessie was hardly surprised. Grams rarely left her prized Percherons in another's care, but now she glanced to her right, paused a moment, and said, "Danny boy had better go with you."

Jessica stared in surprise.

"It's my hip," Grams said. "It's acting up."

"And?" Jessica said.

"And I'm in my nightgown. You want folks to see me walking round in my nightgown?" Her voice was defensive.

Jessie still stared.

"And don't I have a right to rest once in a while?"

"Sure," MacCormick said, taking Dapple's rope as he appeared from nowhere. "We'll get them safely home."

Grams glanced at him for a moment, gave the slightest hint of a grin, and trudged off toward her pickup. In a moment she was gone.

Quiet fell over the night, broken by the hushed sounds of a hundred night creatures. MacCormick stood close by. Jessie could feel his gaze on her.

"Well..." She cleared her throat and turned nervously away. "We'd better get started."

"You'll hurt your feet."

"What?" She glanced at him and felt the air leave her lungs.

For a moment he said nothing, just stared. Then he said, "You'll hurt your feet if you walk all the way in the dark. I'll give you a leg up."

"I can't ride home in a skirt when…" she began, but he had already stepped up close and she forgot how to breathe again.

"Afraid I won't be able to control myself if you show a little ankle?" he asked.

She forced a laugh. "No, I—"

"All right. Then bend your leg. I'll give you a boost up."

"Well…" It *was* a long way home, but if he helped her mount, he'd have to touch her leg and… She shut off her mind, grabbed a hank of Pearl's mane, and bent her knee.

"Ready?"

She managed a nod. His hand wrapped solidly around her ankle. Warmth permeated her system, snapping off in every direction in a tingling tide of longing. In a moment she was aboard, but his hand remained, warm as sunlight against her skin as he looked up at her.

Hormones and hopes spurted through her. True, Brian had left her, and MacCormick would, too. But he'd never lied about it. He was that honest at least. So why not kiss him? Why not…

But in that moment he pulled away, tied the lead rope to the off side of Dapple's halter and vaulted aboard as if it had been only yesterday that he'd left the farm.

They rode side by side, letting silence fall down around them in deep shadows. The geldings walked together as a team. Jessie's leg, bare to mid-thigh, brushed Daniel's, heating her already sizzling thoughts.

"He's not good enough for you."

"What?" She startled at his words.

He didn't look at her. "Tuttle the Third," he said. "He's not good enough."

Her heart was tripping along overtime as she searched frantically for something to say. "He's very rich."

From far away an owl called.

"Maybe I got the wrong impression," he said. "I thought money wasn't particularly important to you."

She considered lying, telling him it was all-important. But she'd never been an accomplished liar, and she doubted that had changed with the clever consumption of three vodka sours, so she searched frantically for another argument. "He's got a thriving practice."

No comment.

"Right in Des Moines."

"Ah, so you miss the city."

Dog doo-doo! He knew she didn't miss the city. But she could hardly tell him she was still attracted to Brian for one reason and one reason only—to remind herself how rotten men could be. To drive herself away from *him*. Dang it, Miss Fritz had been right again.

She scowled. "He's got a great car."

"And you live to drive."

"His father's an attorney."

"Could be worse." He shrugged. "Could be a politician."

"Brian Tuttle's a very attractive man. All the girls thought so."

"Ah, testimonials. Always helpful," he said in that ridiculously dry tone and she snapped.

"Okay! Maybe I'm just horny! Did you ever think of that?"

The night went absolutely silent. Even the frogs stopped singing. Jessica closed her eyes and wondered how a relatively intelligent woman could manage to say something so asinine.

"I've got no testimonials in my defense." His voice was deeper than the night around them. "But if that's all you're looking for..." He paused, letting the silence settle back in for a moment. "I would be willing..." Another pause. "*More* than willing...to help you out."

She blinked at him, found his gaze too steady for her fluttery nerves and turned away to stare between Pearl's tilted ears. "Help me out?"

Silence again, then, "I know we have nothing in common, but…" She heard him draw a heavy breath. "You're not exactly hideous, Sorenson."

She was certain the statement wasn't meant to be funny, and yet she couldn't quite stop the bubble of laughter. "Not exactly hideous? Are you trying to flatter me, Mac-Cormick?"

He scowled at her for a moment, but finally he ran his fingers through his hair with a sigh. "Damned if I know. Flattery's never been my forte."

"Y'think?" She laughed, and the tension drained away like dirty bathwater. She sat in the silence, letting her hips roll with Pearl's broad back, and enjoyed the quiet for a moment, then, "What is…your forte?"

He shrugged. "Seeing things as they are, I guess. It's what made me a good reporter."

"Yeah?" Her legs swung gently to the rhythm of Pearl's stride. "And what do you see here? Right now?" She gazed out across a rolling, moonlit lawn toward the river. *Her* river, her home, her country.

"I see that you're too good for him."

She swung her gaze rapidly back to him. The hard angles of his face were limned and shadowed by the moonlight. One dark lock of hair had fallen over his forehead, and his sable eyes were piercing.

"Thank you," she said quietly.

He scowled. "That *wasn't* flattery."

"I know. If it was flattery you would have messed it up somehow."

He chuckled. The sound was deep and friendly and she smiled as they rode through the silent streets.

It didn't take them long to get home, and Jessie felt a nip of regret as she slid from Pearl's broad back.

Turning the horses loose, she shut the gate behind them

and chained it carefully before turning toward MacCormick. "Thanks for the help."

For a moment he said nothing, then, "You're welcome."

Instead of entering through the back door, she rounded the house, remembering her purse. "I hope you didn't lose too much sleep because of me."

She realized, suddenly, that it wasn't true, that she hoped he had been awake all night. That he had stood in the little tiled bathroom and craned his neck in an effort to see what she'd been doing. But she knew better.

"No," he said. "I always get up at midnight to chase after horses. Good for the circulation."

"Really?"

"Sure."

"Then maybe you let them out on purpose."

They were very close. Side by side on the sidewalk. "Can't fool you," he said softly.

She laughed as she ascended the stairs and turned at the top. "Thanks again, MacCormick."

He nodded, but skimmed his gaze back out to the driveway where Brian's car had been. "Something happen to Silver?"

"Yeah." She sighed and slipped onto the porch swing. "She drank too much."

He raised a brow.

"Or maybe it was me. Luckily, Brian offered me a ride home."

"How fortunate."

She stared up at him in the silvery moonlight. "If I didn't know better, I'd think you didn't like him, MacCormick."

"Me? Dislike Brian Tuttle the Third? No."

"Ahh." She nodded. "So it's not a personal vendetta. It's just people in general you don't like."

He stepped toward her to grasp the chain at the opposite end of the swing. "Pretty much."

"I guess I should feel flattered that you can tolerate me, then."

"It's hard."

"Is it?"

"You bet. All that bright-eyed optimism of yours…" He faked a shiver. "Wears me out."

"Does it?"

"Yeah. And…" He glanced at her and stopped.

"And what?"

"And you're so…not hideous, as we've already discussed. It's…distracting."

She stared at him.

"What?" he asked, his tone defensive.

"I was wondering if it would kill you to give me a compliment."

"Never know."

"That's because you've never tried it."

For a moment, she saw the slanted glint of his grin. "Fishing for compliments, Sorenson?"

"I'm just wondering if it'd kill you."

He stared at her in silence for what seemed like forever, then, "Did you know I spent a month in Sweden?"

"No."

He nodded. "Two in Iceland. Nearly that in France."

She said nothing, just watched him, wondering what he was getting at.

"I've been to fourteen European countries, twenty in Africa and seven in Asia." He paused, still watching her. "But I've never met anyone who made the world a happier place just by being alive. No one except you."

The world went absolutely silent. "Jeez, MacCormick," she said, feeling suddenly that it was rather hard to force out the words. "When you decide to give a compliment, you really pull out the stops."

He shrugged, and a self-effacing grin slashed across his face. "I've been saving up," he said and in that moment she realized that he was really handsome. Not pretty-boy cute like Brian, but deep-down handsome.

"I'm…um…" She glanced down at her hands, not sure what to do with them. "I'm really flattered."

"And I was hardly even trying."

Maybe there lay the basic difference between him and Brian. "No?"

"No."

His eyes were so intense, his voice so deep that for a moment she forgot how to breathe. "What are you trying to do?"

"To resist you."

More silence.

"How's it going?" she asked, and suddenly noticed that, even in the darkness, she could see his knuckles were white from his grip on the chain.

"Going good," he said finally and blew out a breath.

"Yeah?" Her heart was doing a tricky little two-step in her chest. "You might as well have a seat here then. We could...not be attracted to each other." She shrugged. "Discuss politics or something."

"Politics. At three in the morning?"

She leaned her head against the chain, feeling slightly dizzy. "Sometimes I have trouble sleeping."

"You?" The swing creaked as he settled onto the far end.

"Sure, me. Why not?"

He shrugged. "The all-American girl."

"Is that what you think I am?"

"Ah." He grinned, but there was still intensity in his eyes. "Just what I've been waiting for. The awful details of your dark past."

"You might be surprised."

"So surprise me."

She scowled. "I don't think so. You're too eager."

"That I am," he said softly.

"MacCormick—"

"Yeah?" His tone was tight.

"Why are you here?"

Silence stretched between them. "I can't sleep either," he said.

"I mean...in Oakes."

"Does it matter?" he asked.

"Yeah."

"Why?"

She licked her lips and looked away. "Maybe I'm wondering how long you'll stay."

Seconds ticked by.

"How long did The Third stay?"

"What?" She was holding her breath.

"He was awfully territorial."

"And?"

"I thought maybe you two had some history."

"Who told you that?"

He shrugged. "I'm a reporter, Sorenson. What people don't tell me I make up."

She cleared her throat and faced forward again. She would rather he didn't know. But now that he did, and now that she was somewhat inebriated, he might as well know more. "We were engaged."

The owl called again.

"How long have you been disengaged?"

She smiled, then lowered her gaze to her hands. "How long are you staying, MacCormick?"

"How long do you want me to stay?"

"Jeez! No wonder people hate reporters."

He chuckled.

Glancing up, she felt a tingling thrill skim down her spine. "Kiss me," she said.

"What?"

She took a deep breath. "I was wondering if you would kiss me."

MacCormick remained unmoving. Was he holding his breath? But no. She was being silly. MacCormick was the essence of cool.

"Why?" His voice was very low.

She cleared her throat, trying to convince herself that the kiss wouldn't be for comparison's sake. "Just for fun."

He murmured something that sounded like a curse.

"What?"

"Nothing."

"You said something."

"It was your imagination."

She paused, then, "So, have you decided?"

"Yeah."

"Yes?"

"The answer's no."

"Why?"

He made an impatient motion with his hand. His teeth were gritted. "For reasons I haven't even thought of yet."

"But you said I didn't tempt you."

"Not exactly what I said. And in case you've forgotten, I kissed you already."

"But that was..." Her stomach felt funny. "Days ago."

"And so insignificant you already forgot?"

She stared at him and then, against any kind of good judgment she might have possessed, she scooted across the swing toward him. "Could I kiss you?" she asked.

He muttered something.

"What?"

"I said, you're nuts, Sorenson, and probably drunk."

"I think you might be right."

"Then—" he began, but in that instant, she curled her fingers into the front of his shirt and kissed him.

His chest felt taut as a drum beneath her fingers, and then, in a heartbeat, he was wrapping his arm around her back and returning the kiss.

His lips slanted across hers in a desperate flash of heat and hormones. A thousand sleepy nerve endings awoke with a jerk, firing off garbled messages all at once.

She leaned into him, wanting more, needing more. And he obliged, urging her lips open with his tongue, plunging into her mouth, sliding his palm down her back to squeeze her into him.

She slipped her hand beneath his shirt, skimming upward, feeling the lean muscles coil beneath her fingers.

In a heartbeat, she was wet and aching and impatient.

But just as suddenly, he stopped. No more kissing, no more squeezing, no more skin.

"What?" she panted.

"So how'd I compare?" he asked, his voice tight.

"Compare?" She could barely force the words past lips that felt swollen and foolish and disconnected.

"With Brian Tuttle the Third."

"Oh. It wasn't...I didn't..." She stopped, still breathing hard, with every nerve singing for more. "I'd like you to make love to me," she whispered.

"Jessica May Sorenson!"

"Oh," Jessie said, *"you're back."*

"And about to give up on you if you don't straighten up this instant."

"Ummm..." she said vaguely, then in a whisper she hoped would be too soft for her conscience to hear, "What do you think, MacCormick?"

It seemed like forever before he spoke, but finally he exhaled carefully and rose to his feet. "I don't think that would be the best idea just now, Sorenson."

"No?" She glanced up at him. The angle seemed odd, the floor of the porch tilted.

"No. But you could—"

"What?"

"Ask me later when you're not drunk and I'm thinking with my brain again," he said and turning jerkily away, stepped through the front door and out of sight.

In the ensuing silence, Miss Fritz tsked.

"Well," she said, her tone clipped, "at least one of my students has retained some moral fiber."

10

DANIEL PAUSED to lean a sweaty, gloved fist on the alfalfa bale by his hip. It was about a hundred and fifty degrees in the nonexistent shade, he'd been working continuously for a damn lifetime, and in all that while he hadn't had a single cigarette.

And worse yet, ever since the night of the horses' miraculous and mysterious escape, Jessica had gone to great lengths to make certain they didn't spend a minute alone.

He was insane. He should have taken her up on her offer for sex. But she'd been drunk and he wanted more than—

What the hell was he thinking? He didn't want anything from her! Nothing! He was here to write a book. She was just…research.

"Tell me again why I'm doing this," he said, irritably glaring down at her from the stack of bales atop the jostling hay wagon.

"I told you." A dusty black pickup truck was bouncing across the field toward them. She glanced at it for a prolonged moment, then swung her curved hook to stab another bale that trundled noisily from the ancient machine. "Larry's a friend and he hasn't fully recuperated from his back surgery yet."

"Uh-huh." He glanced at Larry, middle-aged, paunchy and congenial, comfortably ensconced in the air-conditioned cab of his John Deere. He looked pretty well recuperated to Daniel. "And?" The sun beat against his back like a ray gun. He'd already burned, peeled, burned and tanned. He hated tans. He was leaving his shirt on from now on.

"And so we're helping out until he's fully recovered."

"So all I have to do is have a little major surgery and I get out of the joy of baling?" he asked.

She gave him a slanted glance of disapproval. Maybe she meant it to look intimidating. But she only managed cute. Even in her battered cap, with alfalfa leaves stuck to the sweat on her nose, she was...

It didn't matter if she was cute! It didn't matter if her eyes were like morning gloss and her lips like raspberries. It didn't matter if she walked like a siren and looked like an angel. She wasn't an angel! Hardly that. There were all kinds of dirty secrets in her past. He had to remember that. Had to concentrate. Why, for instance, was she taking time away from her practice to spend time sweating in the sun? Why?

"So," he said, "what do you owe Larry?"

"Owe him!" She staggered for a moment, caught her balance on the shifting wagon beneath her feet and stared up at him wide-eyed.

Defensive? He watched her, his rusty journalist's instincts grinding noisily. He was back in action, but just at that instant, the wagon jolted to a stop alongside the parked pickup truck.

A woman exited the vehicle, and in her arms was a small fair-haired girl. A girl who looked exactly like Jessica Sorenson.

WHAT THE HECK was wrong with MacCormick? Jessie wondered. He'd been acting weird for the past week. Of course, weird wasn't uncommon for him. But he was always around, always helping. Like now, for instance. She hadn't asked him to accompany her on this horse call. But he was there, twitching the little mare as Jessie sutured a cut in the horse's shoulder.

"She'll be all right, won't she?" Andy's voice sounded very small from beside her elbow.

"Don't bother Jess now." His mother's voice was not so small. In fact it was rough-edged and coarse as she sponged away the blood that escaped from the wound.

"I think she'll heal up fine," Jessica said. Her back hurt from bending and her head was pounding, but it was Kathy she was worried about. She looked like she was close to breaking down. "You're going to have to be more careful, Andy."

"I will."

He sounded unusually timid, and for a boy whose nickname was Kamikaze, that was decidedly unusual. Jessie glanced at the boy. He was not quite ten years old, but already his eyes usually twinkled with a light that reminded her of his father. His late father. Poor Kathy. The twinkle was gone today.

Andy stepped closer and peered at the sutures as she straightened. His head bobbled close to hers.

"That's a pretty bad bruise you've got yourself," MacCormick said.

Andy straightened abruptly, his hand immediately covering his collar, his eyes going round. "It's all right."

"Did you have a doctor look at it?"

"It's nothin'," Andy said, and skimmed his gaze to his mother's pinched face. "I just...I fell when I was doing chores."

"Ah," MacCormick said, but his eyes were hard.

What the heck was wrong with him? Jessica wondered.

THE DAYS rolled away. Mucking out stalls, lifting dogs, stacking hay. The hours were long, the work hard, but Daniel hadn't felt this intense in a long while. He had found his story. Even as he lay in bed, it milled in his mind. He had been right all along. Oakes was not the kindly, faded town its inhabitants tried to portray, but a seething, aching Peyton Place with dark secrets hidden just below the surface.

Even Jessie, who seemed so sweet, so innocent, whose kisses...

He hauled his thoughts to a screeching halt. He wouldn't think of her kisses. He wouldn't think of how she looked first thing in the morning, with her hair still tousled and her eyes sleepy. He wouldn't think how it would feel to kiss her awake or to run his hands down her lovely curves.

No. She was his story. His ride to bestsellerdom. That was all. Nothing more.

But sometimes when she thought he didn't see, she looked so tired, so alone, and he couldn't help but wonder what it would be like to bring her breakfast in bed. To share a shower, to lather her with soap and watch the suds drip between her generous...

Was that a knock on the door? Daniel strained his hearing, and then, to his surprise, he heard soft footsteps patter across the kitchen floor. The door creaked open.

Daniel heard her murmur. Heard a male voice murmur in return.

Slipping from his bed, he tilted his ear toward the floor grate.

"...your wife...." Jessie's voice, of course.

"...visiting a parishioner...we'll have to make it quick."

And that was all. The door closed. The house went quiet.

Anger and frustration and a dozen uncharted emotions exploded in Daniel. But only one remained when they had burned to ash.

Determination. He would not care about Jessica Sorenson. Not now. Not ever. He would write his book, leave this sad little town behind, and never think of her again.

"WHERE ARE WE GOING?" Daniel settled back in the Silverado's passenger's seat just as Jessie clicked off the CB and set her foot to the accelerator.

"Mrs. Weaver's."

Her last client's pastures whizzed by his window as she careened around the corner.

"Let me guess. An emergency?" he guessed. It was a Murphy's Law thing. Seven o'clock at night on a hideously long day. Of course it was an emergency, but she said nothing. Her expression looked strained, her hands tense on the wheel.

"Sorenson?" he said.

She jerked. "What?"

"What's wrong?"

"Betty. She's a friend of Grams's." She shifted up. The gears ground, but she didn't seem to notice.

"And?"

"Her old terrier. He's diabetic."

"Uh-huh." He hadn't known dogs got diabetes, but the look on her face discouraged foolish questions.

"I thought we had it under control. But..."

She paused. A couple of miles seemed to whiz by in the span of fifteen seconds. They hit a bump in the road. Daniel's head banged against Silver's roof.

He winced. "But?"

"He's seizuring," she said and wheeled around another corner.

There seemed nothing to do but hold on, since he dared not distract her.

In minutes she pulled to a stop in front of a peeling white house in a not-too-distant town. She was out of the truck in an instant, snatching bottles from the Porta-Vet in back and running toward the front door.

She never bothered to knock.

"Where is he?" Her voice was breathless.

The old woman's voice cracked. "In the kitchen." She followed Jessica, wringing her hands. "I couldn't pick him up. I tried, but..."

"MacCormick, hold his leg."

He dropped to his knees beside the fat, spasming terrier and grasped a stiff forelimb.

Clamping a thumb over the vein, Jessie plunged a needle into the animal's leg.

The terrier arched his head sharply back.

"No." Jessie moaned the word as she depressed the syringe. "No. Goldy, no. Come on."

But the eyes were staring, the body suddenly still.

"Come on. Come on. Come on." She dropped the syringe and thrust her hand behind the elbow and began to pump frantically.

Nothing happened. The dog had gone limp. Rising to her feet, Jessie sprinted to her pickup and back. In an instant she was on her knees again and thrusting a needle directly into the animal's motionless chest.

"Goldy!" she said and pumped again, then shoved her stethoscope in her ears and listened.

Time halted and when she slipped the stethoscope back around her neck, her face was expressionless.

Behind them, the old woman sobbed softly.

Jessica rose slowly to her feet and turned to face the owner. "I'm sorry." Her voice was level, professional. "I thought we had a handle on it." She cleared her throat. "I'm sorry," she repeated. "Would you like us to..." She drew a deep breath. "I can take care of the body if you like."

"No." The old woman straightened somewhat, but her back was still bowed. "I'll keep him with me...for a while."

"You're sure?"

"Yes," Mrs. Weaver said, and turning, Jessie left the house.

Gravel crunched beneath Silver's wheels as they turned onto the road. Silence lay around them like a stifling blanket.

Daniel scowled. "Listen, Sorenson. You can't save them all."

"No." Her tone was flat, her eyes absolutely steady on the darkening road ahead.

"I'm sure you did everything you could."

"I did."

Silence again.

"He was too fat," she said finally, her voice clipped and succinct. Beside an ancient brick house, a little girl played with a tawny-colored collie. Jessie glanced at them momentarily. "I told Betty he was too fat. Those old dogs..." A half dozen Holsteins grazed beside a barbed-wire fence. She glanced at them too. "You have to be so careful with them. You can't..." She scowled, pulling her brows down over her eyes. "I told her exactly how much insulin to give him. I told her—" Her words stopped. She gritted her teeth, then slammed her palm against the steering wheel. A tiny hiccup of sound escaped through her gritted teeth. The pickup wobbled on the road.

"You're working too hard, Sorenson."

"I am not working too hard!" she yelled, glaring at him. "I am not..." A sob rasped between her teeth. Her shoulders shook.

"Pull over," he said.

"I don't need to—"

"Pull over," he said and she did, turning the pickup onto the side of the road and collapsing over the steering wheel.

Her arm hid her face from him, but nothing could hide the sobs.

Daniel sat in abject uncertainty. Jessica Sorenson—crying!

He cleared his throat. She gasped in a deep breath and refused to look at him.

"How old was he?"

She sniffled. "Thirteen."

"What's average?"

She sniffed. "Twelve, maybe."

He drew a deep breath and let the words settle into the silence. "The dog was older than sin, Sorenson. You can't expect to work miracles."

"What'll I tell Grams?" This was spoken directly into the steering wheel.

She'd told him Grams was a friend of Goldy's owner, but it hardly mattered. All that mattered was that she stop crying. That she smiled. That his heart would quit cracking at the sound of her sadness. "She'll understand."

"Betty was her...bridesmaid. Fifty-seven years ago. Grams was..." Another hiccup. "So proud when she first told her I was a vet, and now I've let her down. And Maggie's sutures may not hold and Andy'll be crushed and Kathy's had so much trouble already what with Maggie falling on him. He's got bruises all over. And..."

Daniel's mind spun to keep up. "That's what happened? The horse fell on him?"

"Of course. She tumbled. He landed underneath. Kathy's terrified he'll get hurt again, but she can't bear to take the horse away, and she can't afford my fee and I can't afford to pay Gnat enough to get him into college and Goldy died and…what am I going to tell Grams?"

"Jessie…" Daniel touched her arm. More than anything, he wanted to quell her sadness. "You're being too hard on yourself."

She shook her head and pulled in a stuttering breath between her teeth. For an instant he could see her face. It was scrunched and wet and terribly sad.

His heart ripped.

"Your grandmother is enormously proud of you, Sorenson. Everyone is."

"I can't even afford our own place to l-l-live and—"

He pulled her into his arms, and she came, laying her head on his shoulder and curling her fingers into his shirt like a small, sweet-faced child. Her hair felt indescribably soft against his cheek and her breath came in irregular gasps of pain against his chest.

Neither of them spoke. He stroked her hair, letting his fingers skim down her back. Minutes flowed slowly away until she drew a shuddering breath and straightened, clearing her throat.

"Sorry." She turned her eyes sideways, avoiding his.

For a moment he was tempted to tell her that it had been no great hardship, that, in fact, he would give up his spleen to hold her again.

"You okay?" he asked instead.

"Sure." She drew a hard breath. It only warbled a little.

He clenched his hands into fists and refused to reach for her again. But she wasn't okay and he knew it. "Mind if I…" Kiss you? Undress you? Apologize for not being good enough? Make love to you here and now? "Drive?"

She cleared her throat. "I'm okay."

But she looked shaken and troubled and so sad it hurt him to look at her. "I'd like to drive."

"All right," she said, and he stepped out of the truck and was soon behind the wheel.

She hadn't, his heart noticed, moved over much. In fact, there was very little of the blanket's Navajo design showing between them as he shifted into gear.

The wheels crunched against the gravel and then quieted on the pavement.

She sat silent and small beside him. It took all his sadly insufficient strength not to reach for her.

Miles rolled quietly away beneath Silver's threadbare tires.

"Have I said I'm sorry yet?" she asked softly.

He glanced at her. "When was the last time you ate?"

"What?"

He shrugged. "If you were a smoker, I'd offer a cigarette. But I suppose food will have to do."

"I don't think I'm fit to be seen in public," she said and wiped the back of her hand across her cheek. "No use causing a public panic."

He was one breath away from telling her she'd be beautiful even if she was thrown down the falls in a used apple barrel. "The natives must be a bunch of weenies, huh?"

The smallest corner of a grin peeked out. The broken pieces of his heart swelled painfully.

They'd reached the city limits of something that couldn't, by any thinking person, be called a city, but it had a convenience store. He pulled into the lot and parked around the corner from the door. She made no objections when he said he'd be back in a moment and soon he was behind the wheel again, grocery bag on the floor, as they wended their way down the country roads toward the river.

The sun was sinking past the tree line when he turned the key and killed the engine. It sputtered gratefully into silence.

From the high branches of a crooked box elder a blackbird warbled goodbye to the day.

"The river's bound to be preferable to most of the restaurants in the vicinity. Do you mind?" he asked.

She was silent for a moment, then, "This is...fine."

What had she planned to say? This is stupid? This is ridiculous? Don't ever touch me again, you psychotic loon?

Damn! When had he started trying to read women's minds, he wondered. But when he glanced at her, he knew the answer too clearly and hurried from the cab.

In a moment she had pulled the blanket from the seat and followed him to a place under the trees.

The sun sparkled golden-bright on the gentle ripples of the river and the slightest breath of wind ruffled the greenery as she spread the blanket on the grass. Settling onto the Navajo design, Daniel pulled groceries from the bag. Corn chips, dip, five kinds of pop, Oreo cookies, a half gallon of ice cream and paper cups.

"Health food," she said.

"Did I mention I've given up smoking?"

"You're only allowed one saintly act per month?"

"Per lifetime." He opened a can of Mountain Dew and offered it to her.

She shook her head, but he nudged her elbow.

"Come on. Live dangerously."

She sighed. "Can't."

"Afraid you'll tip the universe into chaos?"

"Something like that."

He stared at her.

"It's Miss Fritz."

He thought for a moment. "Our sixth-grade teacher?"

"Uh-huh."

"She lives in my head."

"That's unusual."

"Yeah." She sighed. "And you know how persnickety she is."

"I was her favorite."

She made a face. "I know. I hated that."

"Point is, she won't mind if you drink pop if it's with me."

"You think?" Her eyes looked painfully and ridiculously hopeful.

"I'm sure of it. Take a chance," he said, and she did, grasping the can and taking a long gulp. "What'd she say?"

Jessie was quiet for a moment, as if listening. "Nothing."

"There you go. Miss Fritz approves, and no universal destruction. Can't get better than that."

She grinned a little and shifted her attention to the river. "How'd you know about this place?"

He opened a paperboard carton. He wasn't ready to throw Jessica into shock by buying plastic that couldn't be recycled. "Used to make out here in high school," he said.

"You never even dated in high school."

"Oh yeah," he said. "It must have been in my imagination, then."

She smiled. He stared. It was funny—if he tried really hard, he could sometimes forget how entrancing her smile was. He pulled his gaze away with a concerted effort.

"You were always big on imagination, weren't you?" she asked and, unlacing her shoes, slipped them from her feet. In a moment she was shoving her socks inside and setting them in the grass.

Her toes were tiny, painted red and gold, and for one wild second, he could think of nothing but taking her foot in his hands and kissing each delicate digit.

Damn! He was sick and getting sicker.

"MacCormick?" she said.

"What?" He snapped his gaze to hers.

"You okay?"

Absolutely not. His muscles felt tight as springs and she hadn't bared anything but her feet. "Sure."

"I thought maybe someday you'd be a novelist." She shook her head. "But the journalist thing—that threw me."

"Did it?" He was starting to sweat. He could ask her to put her shoes back on. But he could imagine those explanations. *"Listen, my self-control isn't what it could be, so if you don't want me falling on you like a horny hound..."* Good God, he needed help. Needed to get out of this one-horse town. Or...he needed to make love to her, and the sooner the better, because, no matter what ugly secrets he'd learned about her, nothing seemed to matter but touching her, loving her, seeing her smile.

"Yeah. You were always so imaginative."

Oh yes, he was that. He could imagine her naked, could imagine her lips against his, could imagine her writhing in ecstasy beneath him, or on top of him or...

"MacCormick?"

"What?"

"Is something wrong?"

Yes. Something was wrong. He was mooning over her like some half-witted yokel. But...there was something about her. And he'd damn well better find an explanation for why he was staring like a sex-starved fiend. "So...you're feeling better?"

"Oh." She cleared her throat and dropped her gaze to her pop. "Yeah. I'm sorry about that scene in the truck." She winced, embarrassed. "I just—"

"Care too much?"

"No!" She glanced up, surprised. "It's not that."

"No?"

"No. I'm...tougher than nails." She made a fist. "Stoic."

"Uh-huh."

"I am. Well, usually." She paused. "Sometimes." A sigh. "I gotta work on that."

"I don't think so."

"What?"

He shouldn't have said that, but he was trapped now and could hardly turn back. "The caring..." He shrugged. "It shows. People appreciate it."

Her eyes were so bright they seemed to pull at his very soul, begging him to reach for her, to pull her into his arms to...

Get a grip, MacCormick! he ordered, and relaxed a smidgen.

"So what was it about this particular case?" he asked, searching for a way out.

"Goldy was Betty's family. She…" She cleared her throat again. "She's all alone now. I should have—"

"What?"

"What good were those eight years of college—expensive college," she added, "if I can't even save the Goldys of the world? If I can't even help Betty when she needs me."

"You did help her. You prolonged Goldy's life."

She said nothing.

"And when she gets a new dog—"

She shook her head. "She won't. Goldy was a stray. She didn't want her in the first place, won't admit she needs another. So now she's alone."

"What about Mrs. Conrad, Andy, Larry, Greta? You helped them. Isn't that good enough?"

"No." She hadn't delayed an instant.

He was silent for a second, thinking, then, "I had a therapist once," he said.

She glanced at him after a moment's pause.

"He said I was too hard on myself. Obviously he's never met you."

She smiled. "You saying I need a therapist?"

"At least," he said, and she laughed shakily.

"Why'd you see a therapist?"

He shrugged. "I was living in New York. It's the thing to do."

"Really?"

"You don't think I had emotional problems, do you?"

"At least," she said and smiled.

Maybe she *was* tougher than nails. Certainly tougher than he was. Because try as he might, he could not sit here with her and not want to reach out, to touch her skin, to pull her into his arms.

She took a sip of pop. Glancing through the trees, she sighed. "I've always loved the sound of the river. It's a type of therapy all its own."

"And cheaper than a psychiatrist."

"Is that why you came back?"

The river wound away to the south and east. An owl called and somewhere past the river's bend a woodpecker pecked.

"I needed to get away."

"From what?"

"Everything."

"A woman? Sorry." She cleared her throat. "I shouldn't have asked that."

He watched her. "No. Not a woman."

They were sitting quite close, their knees almost touching.

"You've never been married, MacCormick?"

"No."

"Never wanted to be?"

The sounds of the river burbled away. And not in the entire world was there another human being.

"Ask me again," he said.

"What?"

"Ask me again to make love to you."

11

JESSICA STARED at him. Her face felt hot and her hands cold. "I…" It was ridiculously difficult forcing out words. "I was drunk the other night…when I said that."

"You're not now."

"I shouldn't have…said the things I said. I—" she began, but in that instant, he kissed her.

His lips were firm and warm. Feelings, long stifled, tingled through her like strawberry wine. But in a moment he pulled away, his eyes steady.

"I…" She paused, trying to make some sense of her feelings. But she couldn't. Never had a kiss felt so right. "I shouldn't."

He sat very still, watching her. "Not interested?"

"No! I mean… No, that's not the reason. It's just—"

"What?"

Heartache burned through her. But it had been a long time since Brian. A very long time! And in all that time she'd not taken a single emotional risk. What good had it done? True, she hadn't been hurt again. But was that how she wanted to live? Afraid of being hurt? Just because she'd been burned once?

True, MacCormick wouldn't stay long. She knew that, but maybe that was good. After all, she already knew the results. There would be no surprises. She wasn't asking for love and neither was he. Just…just this moment. Her thoughts spun—weighing, considering. But in the end, only feelings mattered.

"Make love to me," she whispered.

He sat absolutely still for a moment, and then, ever so

slowly, he slipped his fingers beneath her chin and brushed his lips against hers. The caress was so light, so brief, so tantalizingly soft that every nerve ending buzzed to life.

His kisses slipped to the corner of her mouth. Butterfly soft, he caressed her there and then down the pulsing length of her neck. She felt his lips, warm and firm against her throat.

"May I?" His fingers were at the top button of her blouse.

The last rays of the day's sun were slanting warm and soft against her skin. Anyone might come by and see them. Anyone. But somehow it failed to matter. In fact, the risk thrilled her.

"Yes."

The button slipped open. His lips felt like heaven against her throat, her collarbones, the throbbing valley between them.

And then he moved lower, following the path between her breasts, kissing the lacy edge of her bra. She felt her blouse slip open. Felt his hand slide gently across her ribs. And then, through the taut fabric of her bra, she felt his fingers brush her nipple.

Her eyes snapped open as all her bravado drained away. "MacCormick!"

He raised his gaze to hers. It was dark with desire and deadly steady. "Maybe just this once you could call me Daniel," he said, and kissed the corner of her mouth with trembling intensity.

"Daniel." She whispered the word, feeling her heart pitch in her chest. She should never have agreed to this. Never. The feelings were too strong. Too intense, liable to throw her into chaos. She should stop him now, before she was beyond the edge of control, before she was hurt again…. "Maybe this was a bad idea."

His eyes never flinched. "I doubt it," he said, and skimmed his palm up her back. And that's all it took. One hand up her back and she was putty, arching against him with feline need, finding his mouth with her own. Kissing him with a terrible passion, while her fingers fumbled with his buttons.

His shirt fell open. She smoothed her palm over his chest. It was hard, mounded, warm. He moaned against her mouth and eased her back against the blanket as she scooped the shirt past the taut muscles of his shoulders.

The sun glistened in his hair, shone bright on the smooth, tanned muscles of his chest.

Her own shirt was gone, though she wasn't certain how that had happened. But still, she couldn't mourn its passing, for in its place were his kisses, hot and slow, trailing down her shoulder, her arm, tickling the crease of her elbow. She moaned at the hot, tingling sensations and pulled her trembling hand to her chest.

His kisses skimmed up her forearm. She trembled again. Lifting her hand, he turned it and kissed her inner wrist, her thumb, the hollow of her palm. She lay silently entranced, watching as he lowered his head to hers and kissed her yet again.

She felt breathless and energized, tense and alert as his kisses moved on, slipping lower again, over her rapidly rising breasts onto her belly. Squirming beneath his touch, she ran her fingers over a nipple and felt something curl like smoky heat through her stomach when he hissed a ragged inhalation.

But his hands only stopped for an instant. She felt her jeans being eased open, felt his hands curve over her hips, around her buttocks, squeezing gently, pulling her closer.

She pressed against his chest with hopeless abandon. But he was already moving lower, skimming off her jeans, and in their wake came the kisses, hot and relentless. She trembled beneath them.

His hands ran down the backs of her thighs. The sun caressed her, melding with the hot lick of his kisses, exposing her to all the world, but it didn't matter. Nothing mattered but the feelings.

Her panties slid lower. She felt them scrape past the edge of her mound, and he kissed her there. She moaned. The panties slid lower. His kisses followed. She writhed against him, but his movements were achingly slow as he traveled down, down, between her legs, kissing her swollen nub of feeling.

"MacCormick!" She jerked to a sitting position, heart thumping, breath coming hard.

"Daniel," he corrected, but the single word was terse, his expression tense as he leaned over her in proprietary need. "Remember?"

"Daniel," she breathed.

"What?"

"I'm..." Hot. Aching. Needy. "I'm not a patient person."

"Yes, you are." His eyes were unflinching as he skimmed his knuckles down her spine.

She shivered against him and clamped her jaws. "Well, not..." His fingers grazed her buttocks. She sucked air between her clenched teeth. "Not right now."

"What are you saying?" he asked and slid his fingertips along the length of her thigh.

She caught his gaze with hers. "I want to make love to you."

"I thought that's what we were doing."

"I mean..." she said, but then she noticed the shadow of a grin. Reaching forward, she caught him by the waistband.

His brows shot up. His breath caught on an inhalation, but she was far beyond mercy. The metal button slipped open, the zipper followed, and suddenly he was turgid and hot beneath her hand.

He groaned deep in his throat and dropped his head back a fraction of an inch, and it was the eroticism of that simple motion that almost drove her past the brink. But she held on to her control by her fingernails.

"I mean," she whispered, closing her hand around the hot length of him. "I want you inside me."

"Okay." The word was little more than a croak.

Somehow, together they managed to remove his clothing,

though it seemed a fierce battle. And finally they were together. Flesh against flesh, they lay down in the fading light.

They kissed long and slow, tension hot between them, and then he rolled over on his back, taking her along. Belly against belly, legs tangled. His erection pulsed against her skin. She shifted. Sitting up atop him, she slipped slowly, smoothly around him. He filled her like a flood. She stretched, pulling him inside with a moan of ecstasy, and heard him hiss air into his lungs. The feelings were tremblingly tense and they both halted, letting their bodies adjust, letting the prickly euphoria subside for an instant before they began to move.

She broke the immobility first, pressing her pelvis into him. He arched his head back into the blanket, tightened his hands like talons around her thighs and pushed in to the hilt. There was no more delay, no more slowness. Suddenly she was riding like the wind, throwing her head back, bucking against him, and he was pushing just as hard, reaching for euphoria with both clawed hands as he drove into her.

There was no thought, no guilt, no *should haves* or *I musts*, just this moment, this screaming, mindless moment in time. She galloped up the incline of desire, raced toward the finish and screamed over the pinnacle. In fact, as she fell, gasping and winded against his chest, she was quite certain she truly had screamed.

She could feel his heart pounding against hers, could feel the rough rasp of his breath against her hair.

"Are you…" He gasped a breath and stroked her calf. "All right?"

Sanity was returning in a slow tide but faster than her breath. "Yes. Fine."

"Do you always…scream?"

Embarrassment washed over her. She winced as she slipped onto her hip. Generally unthought of body parts ached. "Define always."

He kissed her hair. "When you make love," he murmured, still stroking. "Do you always scream?"

"I…" She tucked her chin into the crook of his neck,

hid her expression from him and cleared her throat. "I don't scream."

His chuckle was low and deep and so damn sexy she felt a gossamer shiver course over her. His hand skimmed over her buttocks and up her back, pulling the blanket up. She curved into him and let the feelings glide over her, soothing, relaxing. A thousand worries slipped slowly away, a thousand tensions sang into the distant past. And there, with her head on his shoulder, she fell asleep.

Daniel lay in the darkness, listening to the soft sounds of her breathing meld with the mysterious night sounds of nature. The deep croak of the river frogs, the whisper of a bird's late flight, the mournful call of a dove. It all sounded so natural, so inexplicably right that he was perfectly content—no, beyond content—to lie there and marvel at the wonders of the world.

Her hair felt soft against his chest, her hand lay open upon his abdomen. Her breasts were pressed like a dream against his ribs, the smooth expanse of her belly against his side, and one endless leg was bent across his own, but that mere contact was not nearly enough. He wanted her closer, nearer, around him, inside him. He wanted to hear her voice, feel her breath, watch the light dance in her eyes.

But he wanted her asleep too, just the way she was, silent, trusting, sated. His.

He tightened his fingers in the tangle of her hair as truth stabbed his stubborn consciousness.

He had to face it. He was falling in love.

SOMETIME long after midnight, Daniel whispered her name. Jessica stirred like a waking kitten in his arms. Something very akin to pain pierced his heart as she shifted away from him. "I'd better get you home."

"What?" Her voice was husky, sleepy. He stilled his hand in her hair and told himself for the hundredth time that he could not make love to her again. Not here. It had been risky in the first place. What if someone had seen them? She had a reputation to uphold. A business. But seeing the sun on her skin and the desire in her eyes had driven him far past the point of reason.

"I have to get you home," he said and forced himself to sit up.

"Oh. Oh!" She sat up, too, dragging the blanket to her neck and hiding those gorgeous, moon-kissed breasts from his sight. "What..." No more words, but even in the quiet darkness he could see her eyes widen. Was she blushing? He wished he knew. Wished he could watch the color spread over her cheeks and down her neck. Wished he could kiss every inch where the blush seeped and beyond, only quitting when he reached her gaudily painted toes.

But they'd already stayed too long. People would talk, so he fished around under the blanket, searching for clothes. He found other things. Soft things. Distracting things. Delectably enticing... She tensed as his fingers brushed them.

"Sorry," he murmured and wished he was, but in a moment he had found something that felt like a shirt. Unfortunately, it turned out to be hers and he had little choice but to hand it over. "Here."

She took it in her free hand without a word, still holding the blanket to her chest with the other as she stared at him.

"Do you need..." He managed to breathe without hyperventilating. No mean task. "Do you need help?"

She stared at him. An open invitation if ever he'd seen one. He took the shirt and draped it over her shoulder. She dutifully slipped an arm into one sleeve, then the other. The blanket slid away kindly.

Even the moon loved her breasts. It shone directly on them. He stared, unable to move for an instant, but finally he snapped himself from his trance and tugged the edges of her blouse together. His fingers brushed her nipples. His penis jerked to life, swelling instantaneously and achingly.

He managed one button. "Maybe...you'd better do it."

She did. Did her fingers shake? He hoped so. He hoped she shook all over. He hoped she felt the same frightening breathlessness, the same aching need.

And why couldn't they make love again, he thought, reaching for her.

But discipline or something like it made him draw back. He found his clothes in a few seconds, managed to get them on in a considerably longer time, and by then she was already behind the wheel, debris from their picnic stashed on the floor. They were home in a matter of minutes.

The house was quiet as he closed the door behind them. She turned partially toward him. "Well...good night."

It was almost impossible to resist touching her again, but he managed it somehow, knowing with some instinct he would have sworn he didn't have, that she needed time. Still, he couldn't quite manage to resist offering to assist her to her room.

"No. I'm fine," she said.

Letting her go was harder than he'd imagined, but he managed that too. His own room seemed silent and lonely. For just a moment he considered following her to hers, but when he lay down on his bed, there was no thought involved, just the deep, beloved sleep of satiety.

MORNING CAME too soon and not soon enough. By the time Daniel went down for breakfast, Jessie was gone, so he ate, cleaned the stalls, and found a dozen other odd jobs to fill his time.

Finally, from inside the garage, he heard the door open. Straightening abruptly, he nearly struck his head on the top of the steel cage he was cleaning.

"Hey." It was Gnat, looking no more well-groomed than usual. "You seen, Jess?"

"No." It was impossible for Daniel to keep the disappointment out of his voice, so he failed to try.

"Hmmph. I had a question for her. Do you know if she'll be home soon?"

No, he didn't.

She wasn't home soon. Not for lunch, not for dinner, not at bedtime. Daniel paced the length of his room. Where the hell was she?

A noise sounded from Elm Street. What was that? Her pickup? Hurrying to the bathroom, he peered out past the curtains, and sure enough, she was there, treading over the mossy sidewalk toward the house. Turning abruptly and remembering for once not to strike his shin on the toilet stool, he hurried from the room toward the sound of the voices.

Who was she talking to? A man?

No! Just Grams. Relief sliced through him. He paced to the edge of the steps, turned, then strode into his room, but the heating grate did him little good. He could only catch a few words. Footsteps finally sounded across the linoleum. Grams, on her way to her room.

Daniel waited until he heard her door close. Then he was down the stairs in a flash, his bare feet silent on the carpet. Jessica stood with her back to him in front of a cage, staring at a balding terrier.

"Jessie."

She jumped at the sound of her name. "Oh! Mac-Cormick."

MacCormick? His heart jerked spasmodically in his chest. What had happened to 'Daniel,' spoken in that glorious, breathy tone? "You've been gone a long time."

"Oh. Yes. I...had to check Andy's mare. Then Leland was having calving trouble..." Her voice trailed off. "It all took longer than I expected."

Silence stretched out tight between them.

"You all right?" he asked finally.

"Sure. Of course," she said and fidgeted with an IV tube that hung from a metal stand. "Why wouldn't I be?"

He drew a careful breath, calming his nerves. "About last night—"

"Last night!" The words sprinted out. "I've been... meaning to talk to you about that."

Something pitched in his stomach. "Yeah?"

"Yeah. I...I just wanted you to know that it...it didn't mean anything."

"What?" The pitch had turned to wild roiling.

"I mean… You'll be going back to New York. I know that. It was just a…" She shrugged again. "A diversion."

He gritted his teeth and tried to remain calm, but it wasn't likely to happen, not now, not with his emotions churning and his hormones ablaze just at the sight of her. Not with the memory of her in his arms fueling every fantasy he'd ever had. "You screamed," he said.

Her eyes widened and she took a half step back. "I did not! I just…"

"What?"

She drew in a shaky breath and pursed her lips. "It was…pleasant."

"Pleasant?"

"But listen, I've worked really hard getting this practice going and I can't afford to…" She made a wild motion with one arm. "Throw it all away."

"Pleasant?" he said again.

"Yes." Her voice shook slightly and he took that opportunity to step toward her.

"You screamed," he repeated.

"I always scream."

"When was the last time?"

"I…it…it was just sex. Nothing else, MacCormick. Just sex. I can have sex with anyone."

He stepped up close without meaning to. "No." The word lay flat in the dimness. "You can't."

She jerked her gaze up to his. "Is that a warning?"

Was it? He didn't know. A thousand emotions were rolling through him, a thousand out-of-control emotions. He wanted to shake her and kiss her and make her admit the truth. It wasn't just sex. It was…

A knock sounded at the door. Daniel jerked his head toward the sound.

She didn't move, but stared in silence.

The knock came again, and finally Daniel lurched away to whip the door open.

The pastor stood there, his collar still in place. "Oh, Mr.…Rolands, good evening. Is—"

"What the hell do you want?"

The pastor's brows shot toward his receding hairline. "I was wondering if Doctor Sorenson was—"

"Yes." She stepped up, nudging Daniel aside. "I'm here."

"Oh." He still looked startled. "I'm afraid I need your help again," he began, but at that second all hell broke loose in Daniel's psyche.

"Well, you can damn well get help somewhere else," he growled and took a step forward.

"Elston!" It took him a moment to realize Jessie was talking to him, was, in fact, yanking at his arm. "What's gotten into you?"

He turned slowly, his soul dark. "What's gotten into me?" he repeated, and shook his head. "The question is, what have I gotten into, and I'll tell you the answer."

"Elston!" She skimmed her eyes to the pastor and back, then grasped his arm and pulled him into the anonymity of the plant room. "Quiet."

"You weren't quiet," he murmured, memories roiling. "Remember?"

"Shh."

"Why should I?"

"It was just…" Her hand shook against his as she whispered. "A diversion. Nothing more." Her gaze was locked on his.

"Jessica?" the pastor called.

"Yes." She tore herself away. "I'm coming."

DANIEL SAT at his desk. A full forty-eight hours had passed since he'd made love…. Not love. Not love! Sex. It had only been sex, but since then everything had changed.

Thank God Sorenson had had the good sense to make him see the light. Damn! Sex was a dangerous thing. A license should be required in order to practice it, because it turned normally intelligent, self-possessed men into raving lunatics.

Yes, she was pretty, and yes, sex with her had been good.

Okay, better than good. In fact, the word earth-shattering came to mind...but damn. It was hardly worth throwing away everything he had worked for.

His novel. He skimmed the notebook stuffed with details and secrets.

Gnat's mother had married, and subsequently divorced, her third cousin. Bill's practice had netted more than $300,000 a year before his return to Iowa. Pastor Tony—

Jerking to his feet, Daniel paced the length of his room. Pastor Tony had left his last congregation in Minneapolis after only six months of service. And he could guess why. Because he was a damn—

Daniel ground his hands to fists and stopped his thoughts. Objectivity. That's what he needed here. Objectivity. Tony the pastor might be a freaking lecherous wart! But the truth was, he owed the good pastor his thanks. If it hadn't been for his intrusion some nights before, Daniel might very well have said things he'd regret. Things he couldn't take back. Things about forever and...

He paced again, feeling every nerve grind as he did so.

Good old Pastor Tony. Saved him from a huge mistake, from thinking that despite Sorenson's problems, he could have feelings for her. Deep feelings. Feelings that...

But he didn't. It was just the sex. Just...

A knock sounded at his door. He spurred his gaze toward it, every nerve torqued. "What?"

"MacCormick?" Jessie. His gut twisted up hard and fast. "What do you want?"

"I just...I need your help."

"Help?" He yanked the door open without even realizing he'd crossed the room. "Help?" Her eyes were as wide as forever as she jerked back. "Like you *help* the good pastor?"

"Well...yes."

The snarl escaped on its own. "Listen, Sorenson, maybe you don't see anything wrong with your little affairs, but—"

"Affairs!" She gasped the word.

"What?" He stepped up close enough so that his chest

almost touched her. "Are you telling me you're in love with him? That what *we* did was just…" He ground his teeth. "A diversion. But with him—"

"What are you talking about?"

"You've got a lot of gall, acting all innocent now after the other night."

Her face burned red. "It won't happen again," she vowed. "No matter how kind you are."

"What? What the hell are you talking about?"

"You! Acting like you care about me. Acting like you care about Betty and Goldy and looking so sexy when—"

"Goldy? Sexy? Acting?" He shook his head. Downstairs, the door opened and Gnat called out. She turned, but in that instant, he snagged her arm and pulled her inside his room in one impatient movement. "What—" He drew a deep breath and closed the door behind her. "I wasn't talking about what you did with me." And he wouldn't, because even thinking about it made him feel as if he might erupt into a flaming geyser of raw emotion. "I'm talking about what you did with Tony."

"Tony?" She blinked. "You mean…filming the otters?"

His mind blanked for a moment. "I've never heard it called that before."

She scowled. "We think Xena's pregnant. River otters aren't doing well in the wild, so Pastor Tony wants to surprise his wife with one of the babies, keep it safe, maybe raise more. We've been watching her, trying to figure out where she'll make her den." She lifted a video camera. "So we can film the birth, but I haven't seen her for several days."

Hmmph? "You mean you're not…" He ran abruptly out of words.

She canted her head at him. "What?"

"You're not having an affair with Tony?"

"He's my pastor."

"Yeah."

"And married."

"Yes or no."

"No!"

His heart took a little leap in his chest, but he was in too deep to quit now. "And Bill?"

"Bill!"

"Are you sleeping with Bill?'

She stared at him, wide-eyed, but in a moment she jerked toward the door.

He grabbed her arm and turned her back toward him.

"Are you on drugs?" she hissed.

"Not even nicotine. So my patience isn't what it might be. Answer the question."

"I am not having an affair with Bill."

"Cecil?"

Her jaw dropped. Air rasped in a windy gust down her throat and she stared at him in wordless amazement.

Silence dropped into the room like a live grenade. He fidgeted under her gaze, but refused to let go of her arms.

"Well?"

"You...are...insane!"

He scowled. Now that he thought about it, she might very well be correct, and perhaps his investigative skills had run amok, but it wasn't all his fault. It was nicotine deprivation and insomnia and...her. She shouldn't look so beautiful and smell so luscious and...scream. "I'm going to take that as a no."

"You can take that any way you like," she spat, and yanked her arms from his grasp. "And take that, too," she said, kicking him in the shin.

He grunted at the pain and reached for his injured leg, but she already had her hand on the doorknob, truncating his opportunity for self-pity.

"Jessica!" he said and snagged her arm again. Her fist came up. He raised a peaceable hand. "Are you..." He drew a deep breath. "Are you sure?"

She narrowed her eyes. "Wouldn't I know if I were having an affair, MacCormick?"

When she said it like that, his suspicions sounded less than logical, and she was still glaring at him. Probably for good reason. It may be that his hormones had caused him to jump to rather far-fetched conclusions. He cleared his throat. "Listen, I... It could be I owe you an apology."

She still stared.

"I haven't been myself lately."

"Oh?" She pursed her lips. "Who have you been?"

He winced. "A jerk?"

"I see the resemblance."

He didn't know if he should laugh or scowl, so he ran his hand through his hair and took a deep breath, preparing himself for the most foolish act of his lifetime. "Listen, Sorenson...I..." He couldn't force out the truth of his feelings. He had felt before, had loved before, and he'd been left alone. Intelligent people didn't ask to be hurt and abandoned. They avoided it instead—set up barriers against the pain, made themselves believe the worst. He was an intelligent person.

"What?" she asked.

"Nothing," he said and she turned away. "That night meant something to *me*," he rasped.

Was she holding her breath? "What?"

In too deep. Too deep. He knew better. His heart was beating overtime. "I've had just sex." He paused, telling himself to quit while he could, but he couldn't. "It doesn't feel like that."

"Like what?" Her voice was little more than a whisper.

Shut up. Shut up. "Like..." he began, but she was so beautiful, so tempting, so close. He couldn't help but reach for her, wrap her in his arms, pull her against him. Kiss her.

She kissed him back. Feelings as bright as fireworks flared through him. He gasped for some semblance of sense and drew slowly back, though he still kept her in his arms.

"Like that." His voice sounded guttural to his own ears. Her arms were wrapped fast and hard about his waist.

"Oh," she breathed. "What does it feel like?"

Love, his mind said, but his lips refused to form the word. "I don't know," he whispered. "I've never experienced it before."

She blinked. "So maybe we should try it again."

"For research purposes."

"For science," she murmured, and then he kissed her.

Feelings flooded him, body and soul, and he lifted her into his arms to set her gently on the bed. Their kiss only ended for an instant as he lowered himself beside her. Their clothes fell away seemingly of their own accord, and suddenly they were completely and marvelously naked, lying on their sides, their legs entangled. Her skin felt like heaven beneath his fingertips, her lips tasted like wine.

"Jessica." He breathed her name and skimmed his palm slowly down her arm. "I used to dream of this. Having you here, in my bed." He skimmed his hand lower, over her waist.

"You did?" she asked, gasping as his hand continued on its journey.

"Yeah."

Her eyes fell closed. "When?"

"Last night."

A glimpse of a smile curled her lips, but turned to a indescribably sexy hiss of pleasure as he smoothed his palm over her hip, pulling her closer.

"And the night before that." He slipped his leg between hers. She pressed against it. "And the decade before that."

"MacCormick..."

"What?" he asked, leaning closer to hear her whispered words.

"I want you...inside of me."

His throat went dry. "All right," he managed, and slipped into the tight confines of heaven.

Their lovemaking was breathless and burning, taking them ever higher until they fell asleep in each other's arms. But sometime during the night he awoke, and the feel of her so warm and soft in his arms was too powerful, too wonderful, too alluring to resist.

They made love again, slower this time, and long after she fell asleep again he stayed awake.

This changed nothing, he told himself. He was still here to write his book, to take care of business. But as she snuggled against him, his soul knew the truth.

This changed everything.

12

"It should heal up fine," Jessica said, wrapping the last bit of bandage around the old Airedale's damaged paw. "But I'm going to give you some pills and some ointment."

"Uh-huh." Old Mrs. Mueller had been distracted since the moment she'd opened the door, Jessica thought. And who could blame her? It was probably the sexual vibes flowing off MacCormick like heat rays that drew her attention. "So you're Willy MacCormick's boy, huh?" she asked, giving him a rheumy stare.

"No," Jessie said, shocked from her reverie. "He's Elston—"

"Oh, posh!" said the old woman, waving a dismissive hand. "Everybody knows he's Willy's boy, come home to recuperate."

"No—" Jessie began again, but Daniel interrupted.

"Really?" he said, his tone deep and full of laughter.

"Sure," said the old woman. "And that you've been busy sparking our Jessie here."

"He is not—" Jessie began, but Daniel's chuckle interrupted her.

"Sparking," he said, leaning toward the old woman slightly. "Is that what I'm doing, Mrs. Mueller?"

There was humor in her watery eyes. "Damn straight," she said. "And you'd better treat her good, but then…" She canted her head slightly, her thin neck looking as if it could barely support the weight. "By the expression on her face, it looks like you been doing all right."

Jessica cleared her throat. Her cheeks felt hot. But then, they had felt hot for a week, ever since she had gone to his

room, ever since they had made love all night, ever since...
"Yes. Well, thanks for your concern, Mrs. Mueller, but we
have to be going. Here are your pills. Your ointment. Twice
a day. Don't forget. See you later," she said and hustled
out the door to her waiting pickup.

Turning the key, she shifted into gear and pulled out of
the driveway, but she could feel his gaze on her. She ignored
him as long as she could.

"What?" she sputtered finally, turning toward him.

The slash of his grin was devilishly white against his tan
face. "Sparking," he said, his arm stretched across the back
of the bench seat.

"What about it?"

"I like the sound of it."

Nerve endings jumped to life. Passion sizzled through her
blood, and he hadn't even touched her yet. But that changed
in a second. She felt his hand slip across her waist, felt the
warmth of his kiss against her neck. She bent her head sideways slightly, letting the feelings wash through her. "Really, MacCormick..." she began, but she was breathing
hard. "I have another appointment—"

"In an hour," he said. In a minute, they were turning
onto a tree-lined country lane. "It's not much time, but it'll
have to do," he admitted, and after pulling her out from
behind the wheel, kissed her until she felt dizzy.

JULY CAME with heat and humidity, with sultry kisses and
long nights that were never long enough.

Although Daniel repeatedly tried to write, it was pretty
much hopeless. Oh, he had data, scribbled notes about people and places, but every time he tried to tell about his
female protagonist, his mind turned to kindly adjectives and
far-fetched superlatives until the piece sounded more like
Barbara Cartland than John Steinbeck. But somehow he
couldn't quite manage to care. Suddenly the sky was bluer
and the grass greener. Things he'd never particularly noticed
before became utterly enchanting—children's laughter, a
meadowlark's song, the glow of the midsummer moon. Life

was good. Better than good. Life was fabulous, and everyone should be as happy as he was.

"Jess!" Grams yelled from the porch. "Jess, look what I got."

Jessie didn't answer, but Daniel turned to watch Grams stride into the kitchen carrying a potted plant.

"Look at this!" she chimed, lifting the thing as if it were newly discovered treasure. "Do you know what this is?"

Daniel smiled. He did a lot of that lately. He loved to smile. "A plant?"

"Of course it's a plant, smart aleck," she chided. "It's a bunchberry. Remember I said bunchberry was the elixir for aches and pains? Well, here it is."

"Really?" he said distractedly, and took another sip of his catnip tea. "Where'd you get it?"

"That's the funny thing," she said, stroking a deep-green leaf. "I just found it on the porch."

"Huh. On the porch?"

"Yeah," she said and turned her crafty old eyes to him. "You don't know nothing 'bout this, do you?"

"Me? I wouldn't know a bunchberry from a porcupine. How—" he began, but at that moment Jessica appeared. She was dressed in rolled-up cutoffs and a lilac silk blouse that tied up at the waist. Her toenails were painted the exact same shade as her shirt, her feet were bare, and for a moment the ability to speak abandoned him completely.

"What's the fuss?" she asked, as if she didn't know what she did to his equilibrium. As if she didn't know she set the sun to rising each morning.

"Look here," Grams said. "Somebody put a bunchberry on the porch."

"Really?" Jess said. "Who?"

"I don't know," said the old woman, but her gaze sliced to Daniel again.

"Well…" He set his tea rapidly aside. "If we're going to see any of that baseball game, we'd better hurry."

"Uh-huh," Grams said, and Daniel smiled again as he

ushered Jessie past the dozens of plants and down the creaky front steps.

Oakes's Summer Daze was no earth-shattering event, but the whole town turned out and most folks glanced their way and murmured "hi" and "how-are-you" and shared little pieces of small-town life as they strolled along the shady, tree-lined sidewalks.

Across the street, Larry and his wife passed with their golden-haired daughter toddling between them. She looked, Daniel thought, like the spitting image of Jessica.

"Hey, cuz," the woman called. "Happy Summer Daze."

Jessie waved and Daniel felt his heart turn over. "Cuz?" he asked, keeping his tone carefully casual.

"Sure," she said. "Shelly's my first cousin. Didn't you know? People say their daughter looks just like me."

"Really?" His heart was singing. "I didn't notice," he said and found himself, for the first time in many years, thanking God.

As they made their way toward the baseball diamond, Daniel tried to keep his hands off Jessie, but it was impossible. So he slid his hand around hers just to feel the warmth of her flesh against his, and when they were momentarily hidden behind a copse of towering elms, he pulled her into his arms and kissed her.

"Hey, you two!"

Jessica jerked out of his embrace, her face already bright red, which only made him want to kiss her more.

"Pastor Tony," she gasped.

"Yeah." The good reverend laughed and squeezed the hand of the woman beside him. She was small and slim and home-town attractive. Beside her was a tiny girl with a dangerously sticky lollipop. "And here I thought this was a family park," Tony said.

"I'm sorry," Jessica said.

"You should be," Tony replied, slipping his arm around his wife's waist. He kissed her long and hard; she came up looking breathless and sparkly-eyed. "This is *our* spot."

Daniel raised a brow. Never in his life had he been happier to see that someone else had an attractive wife.

"You two going to watch the ball game?" Tony asked.

"I had other things in mind," Daniel said. "But now that you're here we might as well—"

"Yes, we are," Jessica said. Tugging on his hand, she waved goodbye to the reverend and dragged Daniel out into the sunlight.

The ball game, it turned out, was neither official nor taken very seriously. In fact, its players were a jumble of sizes and genders and the play involved more laughing and falling than most anything else.

Daniel found a place beneath a spreading oak where he and Jessie could gaze across the field at their leisure and now and then, when no one was looking, he could skim his fingers up her bare arm or smell the sunlit fragrance of her hair.

It took so pathetically little to make him happy lately.

"Beautiful day for this, huh?" said a fragile old voice.

"Betty." Jessica glanced up and straightened on the blanket. Tension tightened along her shoulders. Misplaced guilt, Daniel thought and gave her hand one last squeeze before releasing it. "How are you doing?"

"Oh, I'm doing all right. A little lonely, you know." She shrugged, her shoulders narrow beneath an old-fashioned polka-dot dress. "Goldy used to enjoy these outings so, you know."

Beside her, a younger version of the old woman drew her brows together. "I told Mom I'd get her a new dog before I went back to Ames if she—"

"I don't want a new dog," Betty interrupted, already shaking her head. "Found Goldy when he was barely bigger than a hop toad. Skinny as a toothpick, he was, so I gave him a helping hand, but I don't need another critter eating my food." Her ancient eyes looked unusually bright. "But anyhow…" She sniffled once and lifted her chin with determined pride. "I wanted to thank you, Jess, for what you did."

"I'm sorry I couldn't do more," she said, and it was so painfully true that even after the old woman's departure, Daniel's chest felt tight.

"Jessie." He brushed her hand with his own. "You're not running for God, are you?"

"What?" she asked, turning her gaze toward him.

"It's not your fault."

"I know, but—"

"No buts," he said and squeezed her hand. "You're only human." He let his fingers trail up the back of her arm and felt her shiver. "Aren't you?"

She said nothing, but caught his gaze with her own.

"I didn't see any wings, but maybe I didn't look close—"

"Hey, Jess," Gnat called in passing. "I'm gonna be working at the Dairy Inn. Come on by if you want a cone or something."

"Sure," she called back and Daniel snorted.

"That kid needs a hobby."

"A hobby—"

"Other than interrupting us," he said.

She laughed and he leaned forward, needing to kiss her.

"Hey, great day for a ball game, huh?"

Jessie jerked, wide-eyed, toward the newcomer. Daniel turned, a little more narrow-eyed. It was Bill, looking damnably cheerful for interrupting them.

Grinning, he nodded once at Daniel, then turned toward Jess. "I was wondering if you'd be needing any straw."

"Not for a while."

"Okay. Well, carry on," he said, and, shooing his gaggle of kids ahead of him, headed for the ball field. Jessie followed him with her eyes.

Daniel scowled. "Happily married?" he asked, insecurity creeping in.

She smiled a little. "That's why he came here."

"What?"

She nodded down the neatly mown park to where Bill was slipping an arm over his oldest son's shoulder. Well into his teens, the boy was nearly as tall as his dad, but he didn't shrug out from under his old man's arm. Instead, a husky duet of masculine laughter floated to them on the evening breeze.

"For them," she said. "He wanted to give them what he had grown up with."

Daniel said nothing. Okay, so his theories about the denizens of Oakes had been a little far-fetched, he thought, and realized she was watching him with laughter in her eyes.

"What'd you think? That the mob was after him or something?"

"No, I…" he began, but finally he cleared his throat and allowed the chuckle to escape. "So old one-toe Schleveglia isn't out to get him?"

Her laughter was like magic. "You always were too imaginative for your own good, MacCormick."

"Not true," he said. "I can imagine you…" He dropped his voice and leaned closer and she blushed.

The day was filled with laughter and teasing, touching and anecdotes and smiles until finally they made their way back home. Hand in hand, they traversed the uneven sidewalks.

"Listen," Jessie said, holding her breath. "Mourning doves. They're Grams's favorites."

He listened to the lonely wail, remembering. "They always made Mom sad."

"Really?"

He shrugged and drew in a heavy breath. "I thought so, but now I suppose it wasn't the sound that bothered her. But the realization that she was here forever, away from everything she was used to."

Silence stretched peaceably between them for a moment. Then Jessie said, "I'm sorry."

"Sorry?" He glanced down at her, feeling his soul swell.

"Sorry that she left. Sorry you had to be without her. Sorry she had to be without you. Sorry that she died before knowing how wonderfully you grew up."

His throat felt tight with tattered emotions, but the old barriers no longer seemed so appealing.

"I was mad at her for leaving," he said. "Really mad, but I think I resented him more."

"Your father?" she guessed quietly.

He sighed. "I guess I thought I should be enough. I mean, yeah, she was gone, but what about me?" He scowled. "Have I mentioned that I'm a selfish bastard?"

Her smile was wistful. "You were just a kid."

"Yeah, a selfish, moody kid, but now…" The air was summer-soft around them, the birds quieting with the close of the day, and she was, without a doubt, the most fantastic woman in the world. "I think I understand now why he couldn't get over her."

She glanced down as they ascended the stairs, and he slipped her a smile as he opened the door. Once inside, she lifted her face to his.

"I bet she's proud of how you turned out. Probably elbows all the other angels and says, 'That's my son.'"

"Is that what angels do where you're from?"

She laughed low in her throat. The sound did wicked things to his equilibrium. "Angels," she said, "don't scream."

He raised one brow. "Are you in a screaming mood, Sorenson?"

"I might be."

"Really?" he said, breathless at the thought. "Then let's—"

"Oh, Jess." Gnat appeared like a bad dream from the kennel. Jessie jerked away.

"Gnat! What are you doing here?"

"Just got done at the Dairy Inn." He skimmed his gaze from her to Daniel, but if he felt either jealousy or anger, neither showed in his face. "Sorry I'm so late."

"No problem." He loved it when she blushed. "It's just…you need a break."

He shrugged. "If I'm ever an intern, I'll be ready for the hours."

"You'll make it," she said.

He would, Daniel thought, if he was half as tenacious about becoming a doctor as he was about interrupting them.

"If I save up for a couple years," he said. "Till then, I guess I'll be hanging around here and, hey, I couldn't find Rex's leash."

"Oh..." She glanced momentarily at Daniel. "I'll help you."

"Well," Daniel said, taking his cue with as much grace as he could. Which, under the circumstances, he thought was pretty generous, considering what he wanted to do was shoo Gnat out of the house like the insect he was named after. "I guess I'll get to bed. See you tomorrow, Gnat. Good night, Sorenson."

"Good night," she said, but in her eyes there was a burning promise, and though it was difficult to leave her for even a few moments, he managed to force himself up the steps to wait for her.

"YOU'RE KIDDING!" Jessie said breathlessly into the phone. It was the end of a long day. Daniel had gone to the feed store for supplies, and she'd finally finished up the paperwork. "That's fantastic. Well, yeah, of course I'll miss you, but...wow! Sure! You go tell everyone. I'll see you later."

She hung up the phone and stared at the wall in utter amazement, but in a moment she thought she heard the front door open and close.

"MacCormick, is that you?"

There was a slight delay, then, "Yeah, it's me. I'll be down in a minute," he said, but she was already hurrying out of her office and into the hallway.

"You won't believe what just happened. Gnat called. He got a full scholarship. Complete!"

"You're kidding," MacCormick said, but he didn't turn toward her. Instead, he continued up the stairs. "That's great."

"Isn't it? And it was so weird. Anonymous. Right out of the blue—a scholarship for an Oakes High graduate with an

SAT of 1400 or higher. It's almost as if someone wanted Gnat to have the money.''

"People are funny. I suppose Gnat won't be hanging around here too much longer then, huh?"

"No. He'll start school in the—'' She let her voice peter out as she frowned at MacCormick's back. "Are you whimpering?"

"Umm. Yeah. Just a little...'' He coughed rustily. "Just a little sore throat.''

"Sore throat?'' she asked, but at that moment something furry and yellow flapped past his arm before being whipped back out of sight.

"MacCormick,'' she said, weighing her words carefully. "Why is there a tail sticking out of your elbow?''

He turned slowly and gave her a slanted grin as a yellow puddle of fur wriggled in his hands.

She raised one brow and said nothing, letting the silence speak her question.

He cleared his throat. "It's a puppy,'' he said.

"Yeah. I thought maybe.''

"It needs a home. I found it,'' he said like a small boy begging to keep a pet.

"Found it?'' She ascended the stairs to run a hand over the tiny yellow head. It slurped at her with a ridiculously long tongue and wiggled like an inchworm in his arms. "Where?''

He looked sheepish. "At the pet shop.''

Her brows rose further. "It's kind of thin.''

"I know,'' he said happily.

She scowled. "What—''

"Can you keep a secret?'' he asked.

"No.''

"All right,'' he said, glancing dramatically right and left. "I guess I'll have to take you with me, then. It's the only way to keep you quiet.''

IF IT WASN'T a full moon, it was too close to tell.

"What are we doing here?'' Jessica whispered.

"Sneaking," he whispered back, barely visible in the dark clothes he'd changed into.

She scowled in the general direction of his back. "You're insane."

"Yeah, I know," Daniel said, and bent nearly double as he tugged her along across a darkened yard. "You said Chief Patton is a friend of yours, right?"

"Well, it depends how many laws I break," she hissed. "Why are we here?"

He said nothing.

"MacCormick!" She ran straight into his back when he stopped abruptly behind a flowering bush. "What are we doing here?"

"This," he said and kissed her.

The puppy wriggled between them.

"We could have done that without the dog," she said a moment later, but her voice was soft and hopelessly dreamy.

"Then let's get rid of the mutt and go home."

"Get rid of him?"

"Yeah," he murmured and, grabbing her hand, turned away. "At Betty Weaver's house."

"Betty—" she began, but stopped on a gasp as the truth swamped her. "You're going to give her that puppy."

"Not *give*, exactly," he said, peering around a bush.

She watched him and felt her heart swell to the size of a watermelon. "MacCormick," she whispered. "I know the truth."

He turned toward her in the darkness, his expression solemn.

"You're a saint," she whispered.

"Hardly," he said and touched his fingers reverently to her cheek. "But let's lose the pup and you can try to convince me."

She nodded jerkily, certain she couldn't speak.

In the end the covert mission was not at all difficult. Daniel hid in the bushes beside the door and whined while Jessica did her best to shove the puppy into the middle of the sidewalk.

Within minutes Betty appeared. Wrapped in a pale house-coat, she creaked the door open and peered out into the yard.

"Who's there?" she called.

Daniel crouched lower and held his breath. The puppy failed to whine on cue, only perking his tufted ears and cocking his head at her voice.

For a moment, Daniel feared she would turn back in, but in a moment he heard the old woman's gasp of surprise and soon she was shambling down the walkway.

"Why! What in heaven's name are you doing out here? Oh." Her voice came closer as she bent. "Such a thin little thing. Just like Goldy. Come on in. We'll fix you something to eat—just until we figure out where you belong." The feet pattered up the stairs and into the house. Then there was nothing but the soft sound of frogs disturbing the night.

Within moments, Daniel sneaked out from behind the spi-rea and met Jessie behind the lilacs. There in Betty's moon-shadowed front yard, they kissed, and then, as they crept back across the lawn, they kissed again. It was no different in his car. And by the time they reached her house, they were desperate with longing.

The night was slow and breathtaking. They got up late, ate whole-grain pancakes with half a gallon of nutrition-free syrup and thanked the Lord for Sundays.

"No appointments," Jessie said.

"What?" Daniel glanced past a half dozen potted herbs at her.

"I don't—" she began, but a thud sounded from the kitchen, interrupting her.

Daniel scowled. "Oscar," they said in unison and he smiled as he took a sip of catnip-and-Indian-pipe tea.

"I don't have any appointments today," she said, sitting by the window in the plant room. "What do you want to do?"

He raised a brow. "Do you really have to ask?"

Her blush made him want to begin immediately. "We can't do that all day."

"I'm insulted."

"Not with Grams in the house," she explained.

"Why not?"

"She's got a shotgun."

"Worth the risk," he assured her.

She laughed. "I've got a better idea."

"I doubt it," he said, but an hour later, when she stood on the riverbank and slipped out of her shorts and T-shirt, he reconsidered. Her two-piece swimsuit was neither new nor nearly as revealing as it should have been, but when she bent into the backseat of his car to squeeze out the two inner tubes they'd put there, he appreciated its failing elastic with passionate emotion.

"I love inner-tubing," he said.

"You've never done it before."

"That's because I'm a moron," he said and helped her pluck the second fat tube from the backseat.

With Silver parked miles downstream near a shady fishing spot on a quiet bend of the river, they tied their tubes together some six feet apart and began their float down the broad breast of the Snake River. The sun glared down at them with mid-August heat. But the wending water was cool against their skin, the gentle waves dappled by the leafy maples, and the air sweet with late-summer wildflowers.

Lying back in their separate tubes, they talked of little things as they splashed their way downstream. But Jessica was too far away, and finally, unable to bear the separation any longer, Daniel slipped into the water and paddled over to her.

"See." She smiled down at him, her eyes bluer than the flawless sky above. "I told you it was wonderful."

"What was wonderful?" he asked, but he already knew the answer.

She shrugged and glanced around. "This. Oakes. Iowa. Every—"

"You," he interrupted and, pulling himself up on her tube, he kissed her. Her lips were honeysuckle-sweet, and when she slipped her hand behind his neck, there was nothing he could do but join her in her tube.

The day was perfect now. Their journey was slow and languorous, her hands were the same, warm as the sunlight against his chest, caressing, loving, arousing as she slipped them beneath his damp T-shirt.

"You know what I think?" she asked.

"Umm...that you should make wild passionate love to me?"

"Close," she murmured and kissed him. "I think you're wearing entirely too many clothes."

"Do you?" he asked, not bothering to keep the exhilaration from his tone.

"Absolutely."

"I can fix that," he said. Hastily pulling the shirt over his head, he draped it on his empty tube.

She slipped her arm around his hard waist. "That's better," she said, hooking a thumb in the waistband of his shorts. "But not quite what I had in mind."

He raised his brows. "Careful, Sorenson. I'd hate to shock any passersby."

"Would you?" she asked, and slid her hand beneath his shorts.

"Actually..." He gritted his teeth and caught his breath. "I live to shock people."

"Lucky me," she said, and pushed his shorts down his legs.

He considered himself an intelligent man; not for a moment was he foolish enough to object. In fact, bending his knees, he snagged the garment from his feet and hung it jauntily on the tube's air spout.

She was in his arms in a moment, warm, soft, delectable, and there was nothing he could do but love her. Sliding his hands down her sides, he kissed her throat, her shoulder, the high rise of her breasts even as he pressed her bikini bottoms lower. They slid soft as water off her hips and soon mated with his shorts upon the air spout.

There was no longer any barrier between them, no distance, no conflict, no hope of waiting. His lips brushed the satiny fabric that covered her nipple, and somehow the peaked nub straining against the yellow material only made it seem more erotic.

Tilting back her head, she wrapped her thighs about his waist, granting him full access, and when they could wait no longer, she welcomed him inside.

Her soft moans melded with the rustle of the waves. Their rocking movements flowed with the rhythm of the waters, until finally, sated and euphoric, they cuddled, scandalously unclothed in their floating paradise, and talked of nothing more important than riddles and rhythms and childhood memories.

Engrossed in each other, they let time and responsibility flow away with the waves until, quite suddenly and rather belatedly, Jessie pushed herself up by her elbows and gazed toward the southern bank.

Glancing up, Daniel watched a quiet fishing spot slip slowly into view. Two young boys and one tiny girl sat on the shore with their father, their lines dipped in the water as they gazed out across the river.

He waved congenially. They waved back.

It was then that Jessie snagged his arm in a clawed grip. "MacCormick!" she hissed. "My bottom's gone."

13

"No," he said, and slid his hand down her waist to the rounded curve of her hip. "It's right here. See?"

"My *bikini* bottom! It's gone."

Her sweetly rounded bottom felt as smooth as glass. "And this is a problem?" he asked.

"We're almost there!"

"There?"

"At my truck!"

He grinned, feeling a chuckle bubble up.

"Don't you laugh!"

"I wasn't even thinking of laughing," he said, and made a scouts'-honor sign, but just at that moment he saw Jessie's truck and swallowed his grin. "Well, okay. Here," he said and, dragging in his abandoned tube, snatched his shirt from its side. "Put this on."

"But—" she squeaked.

"It's that or nothing."

"But—" she began again even as he slipped into his trunks.

"You'd better start paddling."

"What?"

"Paddle toward shore or we'll have to backtrack down the road to your truck." He grinned. "I'll admit that I'd enjoy the view. But I don't intend to let you entertain all of Oakes," he said, slipping under her tube and gliding to his own.

"MacCormick!"

"Trust me," he insisted.

Finally, fresh out of options, she popped the shirt past her red face and dog-paddled jerkily toward shore.

Silty mud squished between Daniel's toes as they approached the bank. The inner tubes dropped lower, to their waists, then their hips. Jessica, Daniel noticed, dropped with hers. He smiled. First at the sight of the clinging oversized shirt, then at the fisherman, then at his little girl. She was about five years of age, with a missing front tooth, frizzled hair and a mud-streaked nose.

He loved mud-streaked noses.

"Great day for fishing," he called.

"Grand," the dad said.

"I caught a sunfish," said the girl. The boys stared.

Jessie hoisted the tube up to arms' length and headed like a wide-eyed automaton to the far side of her truck.

"A sunfish, huh?" Daniel said, pausing to talk as he fished the keys out of his shorts pocket. "Big as a whale?"

"Nah. Smaller than a whale." She lisped when she spoke and lit up when she smiled. "But bigger than a bus."

He laughed. From the far side of Silver, Jessie cleared her throat.

"Well, I gotta go. Enjoy," Daniel said and, skirting the pickup, bent to unlock the passenger door.

"All right. You're gonna have to drop the tube," he said.

"Are you out of your mind?"

He laughed aloud, noticed that the little girl was watching them and winked. "Yep, I think I might be, because I think I want a daughter."

"What?" The tube slipped away of its own accord.

He smiled, letting his gaze glide down the clinging T-shirt to her bare thighs. "I didn't mean right now," he said and opened the door for her.

She shimmied inside as he tied the tubes to Silver's Porta-Vet, and by the time he was behind the wheel and leaning over to kiss her one more time, the CB was crackling.

"I need to get rid of that thing," he said.

"I need some bottoms."

"I disagree," he said, but she was already answering the damned thing.

"What is it, Grams?" she asked, almost smiling.

"Jessie! Finally!" Grams's raspy voice was panicked. "It's Baby. She's in trouble."

Jessie's eyes went round as she spurred her gaze to Daniel. "She's in labor?"

"Yeah, but Cecil says nothing's happening, and he doesn't know how long she's been at it."

"Did you try Doc Barker?"

"He's not in. Hurry, Jess! Who knows what'll happen to the old coot if he loses Baby."

"Okay. Tell Cecil to hang on. Keep her quiet. We'll be there in a minute."

She snapped the CB onto the holder as Daniel started the engine. It only coughed once.

"Cecil's mare?" he asked.

"Two weeks early."

He was already pulling onto the curving stretch of highway. "Is that serious?"

"Can be." Her expression was absolutely sober. "'Specially if she's been in labor for a while."

"Do you have your stuff with you?"

She ticked her gaze to her Porta-Vet as if she had X-ray vision. "Anesthesia. Syringes—"

"Pants?" he interrupted her.

She gasped softly and jerked her gaze to her lap.

"Here." He was already pressing his trunks down with one hand. "Hold the wheel."

"What?"

"The wheel," he said, and when she did as ordered, he peeled the swim trunks past his hips. His erection popped into view like a floating log.

He caught her eye, then cleared his throat as she jerked her gaze back to the road.

"It's the shirt," he said, indicating her shrink-wrapped torso. "It's not as long as I thought."

She opened her mouth as if to speak, then snapped it shut as he handed over the wet garment. "Here. Put them on."

She snatched up his shorts and relinquished the wheel. "And you?"

"Are you kidding? You're wearing a wet T-shirt. I'll be lucky if Cecil doesn't have a stroke before he even notices I'm alive," he said, and yanked on the blanket beneath them. She lifted her bare bottom and slid into the shorts just as they careened around a corner and screamed up to a looming brick barn.

Cecil came running through white Dutch doors into the sunlight.

The old man was talking even before Jessie managed to jump out. "Jess. Holy Mother, I'm glad you're here. Baby's down and..." He skidded to a halt, his jaw dropping as he snapped his eyes to Daniel's blanket-wrapped hips. "What the hell happened to you?"

"I was in a hurry."

"To do what?" the old man snarled, but Jessie dragged him back to the business at hand.

"Is she still straining?"

"Sometimes, but she's tired."

"Okay. Cecil, you get straw bales, hot water—" She stopped as her gaze snapped up to the barn door. "Grams! What are you doing here?"

"Well," said the old woman, her tone sharp with defensive impatience. "I can't hardly leave him here alone, not knowing what he's doing!"

Jessie adjusted. "Grams, you grab my clippers out of the back. MacCormick, you get—" She snapped her gaze to him and halted. "Pants," she ordered and turned away.

PEOPLE RAN and fetched, carried and prayed and worked, and finally, after what seemed like an eternity, a wet, slimy foal was dragged from its dark home and up to its mother's nose.

"Is he alive?" Cecil's voice was barely more than a rasp, answered by the newborn's sneeze and a lift of its wobbly head. "It's all right. It's all right. Edna," he breathed and, grabbing her, hugged her fiercely to his chest. "It's all right."

"Oh, Cecil." Grams's voice was harsh with tears. "She's so pretty."

"Yeah. Yeah." He wiped his cheek roughly with the back of his hand and dragged his gaze from the foal to the old woman. "Just like her owner." The barn went quiet. "Baby's first baby. I want you to have her, Edna, along with my apology. I shoulda never took the mare from you."

"You want me..." Her voice was suspiciously wobbly, though she kept her chin high. "You want me to take the foal?"

"That's why I bred Baby to the best. So you wouldn't be disappointed."

She glanced breathlessly from the foal to Cecil. "But I can't...I mean... It wouldn't be right me taking her from you."

"Then come live here."

"What?" Grams asked.

"What?" Jessica croaked, glancing up from suturing the incision.

"What are your intentions?" Daniel asked, but Cecil noticed neither of them.

"Marry me, Edna," he pleaded.

"Been waiting twenty years for you to ask," she said. And with that one statement the feud was ended.

"YOU WERE AMAZING." Daniel settled his hip against the kitchen counter and watched as Jessie flipped on the kitchen light. His blanket had been replaced. His lower body was now clothed in a pair of his uncle's oversized, and consequently low-slung, work pants.

Jessie's gaze skimmed from his bare torso to his bare feet, then back to his face. The shadow of a smile played on her lips. "So were you."

"Really?" He raised a brow, feeling the tension of her

perusal sear him like a fire. "You like my barefoot vet-assistant technique?"

"I like all your techniques."

He felt his blood pressure pump up a notch. "You don't suppose they suspected anything, do you?"

She laughed as she plucked the too-large shirt from her chest. "Suspected anything? Are you kidding? Like what?"

He settled his arm around her waist and pulled her close. "Like the fact that we've been making love in the river all afternoon."

"How could they know?" she asked.

"How about the fact that you're wearing my pants?"

"They were focused on the mare."

The oversized T-shirt she'd borrowed from him dropped off her left shoulder. He kissed her there. "How about the fact that I'm in love—"

"Xena," she said.

Daniel turned in time to see a dark, sleek tail whisk around the corner at the top of the stairs. "Xena?"

"She's back!" Jessie cried and, grabbing Daniel's hand, leapt for the steps. They were at the top in a moment. Beneath their feet, the carpet was wet and in the bathroom a miniature mystery animal turned from the toilet, its little claws still moving as it perused the newcomers.

"What the hell's that?" Daniel asked.

She'd clasped her hand to her mouth. "A baby otter. Xena had babies already and I didn't even know."

"An otter!" he said, nearly clapping his forehead.

It was then that they heard the noise in the bedroom. Turning in that direction, they rushed into Daniel's room. Two more baby otters galloped past. Tiny paw prints went in every direction. Papers were scattered everywhere.

"No," Jessie scolded, restraining her laughter as the largest of the otters turned with a quizzical, twitching expression toward her. "Xena, I told you, only in the bathroom." Xena scampered from the desk and onto the floor, scattering a cloud of papers in her wake. "Oh, MacCormick," Jessie said, her lips twitching suspiciously as she scooped up a handful of soggy papers. "I'm sorry. I hope they weren't important."

Something like premonition twisted in his gut. "No. Not important. Give them to me. I'll take care of them."

But an impish twinkle lit her eyes and she raised her brows. "Not important, huh? You seem awfully eager. What are they?"

"Nothing."

"Hmm," she said, and shifted her gaze to the top page.

Daniel jerked toward her, but it was already too late. He knew the moment reality registered in her faster-than-the-speed-of-light mind. Knew the moment his life ended. For several seconds he could do nothing but watch her flip the pages, could do nothing but watch the color drain from her face.

"Jessica." He said her name slowly, quietly, as if he hoped that if he were careful he could turn back the clock just a few moments, draw back her smile. Pretend that he had never intended to use her kindly openness against her. "I can explain."

"You've been taking notes." Her voice was stunned, quiet.

He shook his head, though he wasn't sure why.

"On us. On..." Her gaze dropped to the page clutched in her hand. "On me."

"Listen, Jess, it's not what—"

"You think I've given up a baby?"

"That was before—"

"And Grams—" She pulled the top page aside to stare in shock at the one below. "On drugs?"

"That was—"

"It's a joke, right?"

He tried to say yes. It was all a joke. But her eyes were so huge, her voice so wounded.

"Why?" she whispered.

He took a step forward, wishing only to take her in his arms, to hold her until he could find the words to explain it all away, but she jerked back a pace.

"Is that why you came here? Is that why you came back? To make fun of us? To humiliate us?"

"No. Jessica. It's not like that. I just—"

"What?"

"I needed a place to write. To focus and—"

"To write what?"

He searched hopelessly for an answer.

"To write what?" she asked again. "About us?"

"No. It's…a novel. Just—"

"Then why the notes?"

His heart was cramping up. "I was blocked. Couldn't seem to—"

"So you thought you'd use us to give your muse a boost. Us. People who helped you. Your friends. Your family."

"Listen, Jessie." His head was spinning, his heart beating overtime. "Maybe it started like that. But that's not how it is now. That was before I realized how wonderful you are. Before I fell in—"

"Get out," she said softly.

"Listen to me, Jess!"

"Get out!" she said, teeth gritted. "Or I'll call Joe. I swear I will."

He saw the truth in her expression. Saw the unmistakable pain in her eyes. She would have him thrown out. And there wasn't a person in town who wouldn't stand behind her.

14

"SO YOU PULLED it off." Tom Malberg had never been particularly effusive. In fact, for Starburst's senior editor, those were strong words. "I don't mind telling you—" he took another sip of his martini "—I thought you were fried."

Daniel glanced momentarily around the posh restaurant, then shifted his gaze back to Tom. "I appreciate your vote of confidence."

"My pleasure." He shrugged, a big man with strangely small movements, then took another drink. "So where were you? Illinois?"

"Iowa."

"Elms—"

"Oakes," Daniel corrected.

He flapped his hand dismissively. "Some kind of tree west of the Hudson. Anyway, miracles do happen. Stephanie loved it, despite the changes from the proposal." He shrugged, not pretending he wasn't amazed. "Advance reading copies are hot off the press and winging their way to designated readers." He made a congratulatory movement with his glass. "You're back in business, Daniel, and back in civilization."

"Yeah." Outside, in the cool autumn air, a horn blared, answered by a half dozen others, but somewhere in a misty corner of his mind, frogs chirped against the silvery backdrop of river water.

"Time to get promotion rolling. Marketing's planning ads, but a book tour's on the docket. L.A., Seattle, Chicago..." His voice droned on.

Near the door a woman laughed. The sound was light and genuine, sparking off a thousand sun-bright memories.

"Any suggestions?"

Daniel yanked himself back to the present. He was still in New York, still with Tom Malberg.

"What?"

"Any suggestions where you'd like to go first?"

The world receded. All there was suddenly was memories. The smell of fresh fields, the sounds of nature, the feel of Jessie's hand in his.

"Yeah." The word came out of its own accord. "Yeah, I do," he said. Then he pushed his chair back and strode toward the door.

JESSICA TURNED down Mulberry and onto Ash Street. It was late and she was exhausted. She'd treated an abscessed hoof until after midnight the night before and barely had time to brush her teeth before falling into bed, but the phone rang well before dawn, calling her out for the day. That was good, of course. Business was flourishing. Grams's foal was thriving, as was Grams. Now that the feud was ended, she seemed enormously happy, while Cecil was giddy. They were planning a simple wedding for the following month, but Jessica suspected Grams would have moved out already if she hadn't been worried about Jessie.

Of course there was nothing to be concerned about. She'd adjusted to MacCormick's absence. After all, she'd never expected him to stay. He was just a fling, a way to relieve tension for a few short months. Everything was fine. She'd even warned Oakes's inhabitants about his forthcoming book, putting it as gently as possible. "It may not be flattering," she'd said. There had been a hullabaloo, as Grams had called it, but it had blown over. So why was she so depressed?

She was just tired. That was all, tired and…why was there a mob crushing the wildflowers on her front lawn?

Turning onto Elm Street, she slowed Silver and crept up to the curb. The crowd turned on cue, rushing up to her.

Gnat was in the lead, stumbling toward her, the book in his hand seeming to throw him off balance.

"Jess! I'm in here!"

"What?" She shimmied out of her truck as the crowd milled around her.

"In the book. He calls me Skeeter, but I know it's me. I'm a small-town doctor with the gift of caring."

"I'm Mavis." Millie Conrad crowded close. Rosy lifted her triple chin, trying to snuffle the book in her mistress's hand. "I'm rosy-cheeked and kindly and reminiscent of Merriweather from *Sleeping Beauty*."

"I'm Dave."

"I'm Bea," Betty said, hugging her puppy to her chest. "Arthritic hands, but a heart of gold."

"It's so…" Nettie began, but a dozen other voices broke in.

"…my favorite part."

"I cried all—"

"So beautiful…"

"You're in it too." Cecil shuffled his way through the crowd, book in hand as the others nodded agreement.

"Wh-what?" she rasped.

"In the book. *Miracles*," Cecil said and held up a paperback copy.

She shook her head. "What are you talking a—"

"Danny's book!" Gnat rasped. "We got 'em today in the mail and—" He glanced up and gasped. "It's him."

Jessie lifted her gaze in accordance with Gnat's and felt her throat close up like a stoppered bottle. He was there. Daniel MacCormick. Not a dream, but flesh and blood.

The crowd parted like the Red Sea. Silence fell around them as he crossed the lawn toward her.

She could find no words, not a single one, and her eyes hurt. She blinked, trying to think, but he was too close. And too thin. And he looked tired. She wanted to hug him and feed him and tuck him into bed.

"So…" It was the only word she came up with for a moment. "You wrote your book."

He said nothing, just stared at her.

She cleared her throat and concentrated. But she could think of nothing but how much she missed him. Even knowing that he belonged in New York, even knowing that it would never work out between them, she had missed him with aching ferocity. "I'm...happy for you. It sounds wonderful."

His eyes were steady, piercing, unflinching.

"Congratulations," she said, searching for words.

"Did you read it?"

The sound of his voice sent a smoky curl of longing through her. But she straightened her shoulders and hung tough.

"What?" The word only quivered slightly.

"I sent you a copy. Did you read it?"

"I...no...I didn't know. I haven't had a chance—"

"You're Madeline," Gnat murmured, as if raising his voice would break some kind of fragile spell.

Jessie snapped her gaze to the teenager.

"The angel," whispered Millie Conrad.

Betty Weaver hugged her puppy harder. "You save his soul."

"By giving up your immortality," Grams said.

"And marrying—"

"Him," Cecil said, nodding toward his nephew.

"Oh!" Her gaze snagged on MacCormick's.

"Save me," he said, his voice so low she could barely hear it.

"But I'm..." She couldn't breathe, dared not hope. "I'm not an angel."

"You are to me."

Her throat ached with the need to cry, but she had learned to be a realist, and she would not fail now.

"I can't leave here, MacCormick."

"I'm not asking you to."

"But you belong in New York."

"Not anymore."

"But, I—"

"I love you, Sorenson," he said. "Marry me."

She searched frantically for realism. This was a dream. Just a dream.

"Marry me," he said again.

"You have to," Mrs. Conrad whispered. "Think of the children."

"Children?" she breathed.

"Three little girls."

"With raspberry smiles and morning-glory eyes."

"The little angels."

"Living right here…"

"In Iowa."

"But…" She turned from the faces that crowded around them to Danny's. "But—"

"I'll never be good enough for you," he murmured. "But if you let me, I'll spend the rest of my life trying."

She had to be strong. Had to resist. But in his eyes she saw the deep promise of forever. "Yes," she whispered, and in her mind Miss Fritz smiled.

"It's about time," she said.

And as they kissed, the townspeople cheered.